Claimed by a Highlander

MARGARET MALLORY

CLAIMED BY A HIGHLANDER

ALL RIGHTS RESERVED

CLAIMED BY A HIGHLANDER copyright © 2016 by Margaret Mallory
Excerpt from Captured by a Laird copyright ©2014 by Margaret Mallory

Cover Design © Seductive Designs
Image: Couple © Period Images
Image: Landscape © Shutterstock/Kanuman
Image: Landscape © Shutterstock/Targn Pleiades
Image: Celtic Brooch © depositphotos/andreyuu

This is a work of fiction. Names, characters, organizations, places, events, and incidents are the products of the author's imagination or are used fictitiously. Any resemblance to actual events or persons, living or dead, is entirely coincidental.

No part of this publication may be reproduced, distributed, or transmitted in any form or by any means, or stored in a database or retrieval system, without the prior written permission of the author except in the case of brief quotations embodied in critical articles and reviews. For information, contact: margaret@margaretmallory.com.

BOOKS BY MARGARET MALLORY

THE DOUGLAS LEGACY
CAPTURED BY A LAIRD
CLAIMED BY A HIGHLANDER
KIDNAPPED BY A ROGUE (coming)

THE RETURN OF THE HIGHLANDERS
THE GUARDIAN
THE SINNER
THE WARRIOR
THE CHIEFTAIN

THE GIFT: A Highland Novella

ALL THE KING'S MEN
KNIGHT OF DESIRE
KNIGHT OF PLEASURE
KNIGHT OF PASSION

PROLOGUE

*Edinburgh, Scotland
December 1513*

Rory MacKenzie wiped the icy rain from his face and limped into yet another tavern. His injured leg was throbbing, his belly was empty, and he had no money, but these were not the worst of his problems.

He waited for his eyes to adjust to the murky light, then swept his gaze over the occupants. Damn. No one but a serving woman and some old men who had the settled look of regular customers. Hunching over to avoid banging his head on the blackened wooden beams of the low ceiling, he crossed the room. Out of habit, he chose an empty bench where he could sit with his back to the wall and watch the door. He gritted his teeth against a hot blade of pain that shot through his leg as he eased himself onto the bench, then took a couple of slow, deep breaths.

"Good evening to ye," he said, speaking in Scots to the old men, who were local merchants, judging by their soft bellies and Lowlander clothes. "I'm a MacKenzie, and I'm hoping to find some of my clansmen in the city."

"Haven't seen any lately," one of the men said around the pipe clenched between his teeth, and the others shook their heads.

Rory doubted these men could tell a MacKenzie from another Highlander, but he had already looked all over the city with no luck. He knew most of the taverns where his clansmen were likely to gather from the year he had been forced to study at the university.

What in the hell was he going to do? He had walked for days just to get as far as Edinburgh. He needed to get home to Kintail to protect his brother.

"Looks as if you've had a rough time of it, lad," the man with the pipe said.

"The English took me captive after Flodden," Rory said, his thoughts skittering back to the disastrous battle. The English had kept the highborn prisoners for ransom and killed the rest. "I escaped a few days ago."

Rory had known better than to wait for his uncle to pay for his release.

"Escaped?" One of the old men gave a low whistle. "Tell us your tale, and I'll buy ye a cup of ale."

Rory had the full attention of everyone in the tavern now, including the serving maid, a woman of impressive size with strands of greasy hair falling out of her filthy head covering.

"Add a bowl of stew," he said with a grin, "and I'll give ye a story that will curl your hair."

"Just looking at him is making my hair curl," the serving woman said to the others. She gave Rory a broad wink and a nudge when she brought his stew and ale. "I like my men young."

Rory did not bother embellishing his tale, as would be expected at home. These old merchants had never fought themselves, so they were wide-eyed at the bare truth. They cringed and made faces when he mentioned the number of lashes he received after being caught the first time he tried to escape. A whipping was a small matter, but the damned English had taken his horse and all his weapons—his claymore, axe, and several dirks.

"I need a horse and a blade to go home," he said, presenting his problem to the old men. The journey would take too long on foot, and only a fool would travel in the Highlands without a weapon, and preferably several.

"Ye can't buy those with a tale or your good looks," one of the old men said, and the others guffawed.

Rory had considered stealing a horse, but the city was on edge in the wake of Flodden, fearing an attack by the English, and armed men were everywhere. He could not take the risk of getting caught and failing to get home.

"I'm good at cards." He had done little else while held hostage. "Do ye know of a game where I'd have a chance of winning that kind of money?"

"Enough to buy a horse and a sword?" a baldheaded man with red cheeks asked in a high voice.

Everyone laughed, except for the man with the pipe, who said, "Mattie, aren't those fancy-dressed nobles having one of their games in your back room tonight?"

"Hush!" She swatted the man with a filthy rag. "They give me good money to guarantee them privacy and clean lasses, and they don't like to mix with us lowly folk."

"I'm a Highland chieftain's son, so I'm as good as any of these Lowland nobles." Better, in fact. When the woman still hesitated, Rory spread his arms out and gave her his best smile. "Come, Mattie, help a lad out."

"What woman could say nay to that pretty face?" she said. "All right, ye young devil."

Pretty face? Ach. Now he just needed something to start the game with. "If one of ye will lend me a silver coin, I'll return it doubled."

When his request was met by another round of guffaws, desperation clawed at his gut. He never should have left his brother Brian this long. When he answered the king's call to fight, Rory had not anticipated being held prisoner for two months after the battle.

He reminded himself that his half-brother was sixteen, same as he was, and should be able to take care of himself. Although Rory was six months younger than Brian, he'd always felt older. Brian was too goodhearted. He didn't see people for what they were, but as he wanted them to be. That was dangerous for any man, but especially for one who would soon take on the duties of clan chieftain.

Rory was reconsidering stealing a horse when the serving maid plopped down next to him with a heavy thump and wrapped an arm as beefy as a blacksmith's around his neck.

"I'll lend ye a bit of money for the game," she said, her sour breath in his face. With her free hand, she reached inside her bodice, pulled a silver coin from between her ample breasts, and held it up between her thumb and forefinger.

"Isn't that the coin I gave ye, Mattie?" the red-cheeked man complained.

"Believe me, lads," she said, turning to the others, "I earned it."

"Ye won't regret this," Rory said over the men's laughter. But when he tried to take the coin, she held it just out of his reach.

"Promise, on your mother's grave, that if ye can't repay me in coin"—Mattie paused and grinned at him, showing her brown and broken teeth—"you'll repay me in a manner of my choosing."

Rory's stomach clutched. In addition to her many unappealing attributes, Mattie probably was not clean of the pox, like the lasses she provided the men in the back room. But he could not shake the feeling that his brother was in trouble, so he had no choice.

"On my mother's grave." He jumped when Mattie reached behind him and squeezed his arse with her ham-sized hand. He closed his eyes briefly and thanked God that none of his clansmen were here to see it.

Ignoring the throbbing in his leg, he got up and followed Mattie behind a curtain into a dark corridor. At the far end, candlelight spilled through a partially closed door.

"Have a care, handsome. These are powerful men," Mattie whispered as they paused outside the door. Then she poked his chest. "You'll be no use to me dead."

Holding his breath against her overpowering smell, Rory leaned closer to see the men inside. There were five, all young and well-dressed, sitting around a table with cards and small piles of coins.

"Who are they?" he asked in a whisper.

"That one is the new Douglas chieftain, and the one next to him is his brother," she said, pointing a thick finger at two black-haired men, neither of which looked much over twenty. "Their father was killed with the king at Flodden, and their grandfather, old Bell the Cat, died last week, making young Archibald here the earl."

Rory had never met Archibald Douglas, but he had once caught a glimpse of the beautiful Douglas sisters riding through Edinburgh. He smiled to himself, remembering a giggling young lass with flashing blue eyes and hair as black as a moonless night.

"They say this young Douglas chieftain is 'comforting' our grieving queen," Mattie said, drawing Rory's attention back to the present. "I believe the other men at the table are Boyds and Drummonds, close kin of the Douglases."

Archibald Douglas must have heard her speak this time, for he shifted his gaze to the doorway and called out, "Who've ye brought us, Mattie?"

Rory stepped into the room with no notion of how this night would change his fate.

CHAPTER 1

March 1522
Kilspindie Castle,
Twenty miles from Edinburgh

Sybil set her sketch aside and covered her face with her freezing hands. She wished someone would come and spirit her far away, out of the queen's reach. She was furious with her brothers for abandoning her. After sending reassurances for months and ordering her to wait for them here at her uncle's castle, they and her uncle had escaped to France, leaving the rest of them to the queen's mercy. As if that spiteful woman had any.

A shadow fell over her. *How did James find me out here?* She had not left the warmth of her uncle's hall to sit under this tree on the frozen ground because she wanted company. Particularly his.

"I thought ye left, James," she said, still keeping her hands over her eyes. "I told ye I won't do it, so go."

When she did not hear James walk away, Sybil was tempted to kick him. Exasperated, she dropped her hands—and sucked in her breath.

A huge Highland warrior stood over her. Her heart thumped wildly as she dragged her gaze from his giant sword, the tip of which rested mere inches from her foot, to the dirks and axe tucked in his belt, and then to his broad, muscular chest. She had not yet reached his face when he spoke in a deep voice that seemed to make the ground vibrate beneath her.

"My name is MacKenzie," he said. "I've come for ye."

Come for her? Sweat prickled under her arms. The queen had found her.

"I've done nothing wrong," she said. "What are the charges against me?"

The Highlander merely grunted and held out his hand. She ignored it and forced herself to raise her gaze to his face. Despite the fierce green eyes that were locked on her like a wild cat who has found his prey, the wholly irrelevant thought that he was exceedingly handsome sprang into her head. He was young, with strong, masculine features, and she knew ladies at court who would kill to have that shade of auburn hair.

"We must go," he said, which jarred her attention back to the danger she was in.

"Do I not merit a full escort?" she asked, attempting to put on a brave front. No matter how formidable this MacKenzie was, it was odd that the queen would send a lone man to fetch her.

"'Tis easier to escape notice if we travel alone," he said.

Her jaw dropped. "Escape?"

"Aye," he said. "We must hurry, lass."

"I thought everyone had deserted us." Tears sprang to her eyes. So many had called her friend just a few weeks ago.

"Not everyone has," he said, still holding out his hand.

She was tempted to pick up her skirts and run away with this stranger, but she had learned as a young girl not to be so trusting.

"Did James send you?" she asked, narrowing her eyes at the tall Highlander.

"Who the hell is James?"

She waved off the question. "Just tell me who sent you."

"No one sent me," he said, sounding insulted. Then he dropped to one knee, and she received the full benefit of his face up close. He was dangerously handsome.

"Who are you?" Her voice came out in a whisper.

"Your husband, Rory Ian Fraser MacKenzie," he said. "I've come to claim ye."

Alas, this Highlander had not come for her after all. "A damned shame," she murmured to herself.

"That's foul language for a lady," he snapped. "And whether ye like it or no, we have a marriage contract."

Since couples sometimes did not meet until their wedding, Sybil was not shocked that the Highlander did not know his bride by sight. She was sorely tempted not to reveal that he had the wrong lass until they were miles away. But when he learned the truth, he'd probably dump her by the side of the road.

"I fear you've made a mistake," she told him.

"Most certainly," he said in a clipped tone. "But I'm obligated all the same. A MacKenzie does not go back on his word."

"That is refreshing in a man," she said. "But what I meant is that I'm not who ye think I am."

***

What in the hell was he doing here? He should have torn the marriage contract to pieces long ago. He was only, what, sixteen when he signed it? Scottish kings renounced commitments they made in their minority all the time, so why shouldn't he?

Rory's gaze drifted over the lass again. *Ach*, but she was bonny. From the moment he first spied her sitting under the tree, he had known it was her, and she had taken his breath away. But then she had covered her lovely face, and he took in the jeweled fingers, delicate slippers, and rich velvet cloak. The last thing he needed was a Lowland court creature for a wife.

No doubt the Douglas chieftain had regretted making the agreement even more than he had. Many times over the last eight years Rory had planned to make the long journey to the Douglas lands to advise Archibald that he was willing to set their agreement aside. But somehow the time had never seemed right. He had finally come to settle the matter because he needed to free himself to wed.

And now, he could not. *Damn it.* This threw off all his plans.

If only he had acted sooner. When he reached Stirling, Rory heard the news of the Douglases' fall from grace and knew he had lost his chance. He could not desert the lass now that the men of her family had been charged with treason and fled the country.

"Perhaps I can help," she said, interrupting his sour thoughts. "Who is the lass you're looking for?"

It annoyed him that his betrothed found it so difficult to believe he had come for her. Clearly, she thought him unworthy.

"My contracted bride is Lady Sybil Douglas," he said, drawing her name out, "granddaughter of the famed Douglas, Bell the Cat, and sister of the present chieftain and earl, Archibald Douglas, who is also the widowed queen's husband."

When she stared at him with wide eyes the color of violets, Rory's heart seized in his chest. Their vivid color contrasted with her midnight-black hair, ivory skin, and full red lips.

"You're even prettier than before." He never spoke without meaning to, and yet the words tumbled out of his mouth without passing through his head.

"I'm certain we've never met," she said in an arch tone.

They had not met, but he had seen her once a long time ago riding through Edinburgh with her sisters. She was not that young girl anymore. Rory tried and failed to keep his gaze from drifting to her lush breasts and the round curve of her hips. She was a woman who could fill a man's hands. The kind he liked.

"And we are not betrothed," she said. "If we were, I would have been told."

No doubt he was not the husband she expected. His boots and plaid were muddy from the long journey in the winter rains. Even without the mud, he was nothing like the Lowland courtiers she was accustomed to have fawning over her.

"Here's the marriage contract with your brother's signature." He pulled out the parchment he'd carried inside his shirt all the way from Kintail, thrust it into her hands, and tapped his finger on the sprawling signature at the bottom.

When her eyes began moving from line to line, Rory was impressed that the lass could read. Her mouth fell open as her gaze traveled down the page. *Ach*, every move the lass made was seductive. When she finished reading, she fixed those violet eyes on him again.

"I don't understand," she said. "How did ye get my brother to sign this?"

"We were gambling, and he ran out of coin."

"Gambling?" she said, her voice rising. "My brother gave me away in a card game?"

Rory shrugged. "He didn't expect to lose."

The lass opened her mouth but words seemed to fail her for a time. Finally, she said, "But he never loses."

"He did that time."

"I don't believe it. When did this happen?" she fired at him, then returned her gaze to the parchment. Her eyes flew back to him. "Eight years ago?"

"Aye," Rory said. "'Twas not long after Flodden."

"You signed a contract to marry me," she said, her voice steadily rising in volume and pitch, "and waited *eight years* to claim me?"

"Your brother said ye were too young, and I should wait a bit."

"I've been grown up for quite some time," she bit out. "In any case, I will not be your wife. This marriage contract is—"

"Look, lass, we can decide later whether we wish to abandon the agreement, so long as we haven't yet consummated the marriage..." As he said the words, his gaze fell to her breasts again, and he lost track of what he meant to say. He gave his head a shake. What was wrong with him? This was no time to let himself become distracted, but with all the blood rushing to his cock, he could not think.

"You're telling me that I'm to put my life in the hands of a complete stranger, a wild Highlander at that," she said, "and we'll sort things out later?"

"The royal guard is coming for ye," he said. "If ye wish to escape, we must leave *now*."

Sybil leaped to her feet. When Rory saw how all the color had drained from her face, he regretted his bluntness. But now that she finally appeared to understand the urgency of her situation, she made her decision quickly.

"I'll have the servants pack my trunks at once," she said. "How large is your carriage?"

"Carriage? There are no roads where we're going, lass," he said. "And we've no time to fetch your things."

"But...I can't just disappear!" Sybil, who had questioned him so coolly before, looked frantic now. "My little cousin will worry. I must tell her where I'm going."

"You'll tell no one," he said. "Someone in this household sent word to the queen that ye were here."

"That would be my uncle's vile wife," Sybil said between tight lips, then she took a deep breath. "I'll use my drawing paper to write a note so my cousin won't fret."

Rory tamped down his impatience while he scanned the hills in the direction of Edinburgh. Sybil came up behind him. By the saints, the first his wife touched him was to use his back as a damned table.

"I have been rescued," she said aloud as her quill moved across his back. "Do not worry. Will send word when I am able. Love always, S."

She folded the parchment and set a rock on top of it at the base of the tree.

"We've tarried too long," Rory said, and lifted her onto his horse.

He was going to regret this. He already did. Yet, when he swung up behind Sybil and pulled her tight against him, his heart raced.

And it had nothing to do with the twenty riders who had just crested the hill.

CHAPTER 2

The Highlander moved so quickly that Sybil found herself sitting astride his horse before she knew how she got there. She sucked in her breath when he swung up behind her.

"Hold on," he said, his breath in her ear.

An instant later, the horse bolted forward. The Highlander leaned low over her, encircling her so that every part of her was touching brawny man as they sped into a gallop.

Good heavens, she was riding off with a stranger. This was bold, even for her. Perhaps she should go back…

When she turned to look behind them, her heart went to her throat. A long line of riders was heading for the castle.

"Those are royal guards—I can see their banner," she said, peeking between the Highlander's arm and his chin. "God no, they're turning! They're following us!"

"Keep your head down, damn it," he said. "They have archers with them."

No sooner had he spoken than an arrow zipped past his arm and between the horse's ears. The Highlander curled his body around hers in a gallant effort to protect her as another arrow whizzed over their heads.

"How dare they?" she said. "The fools could hit us!"

The queen was angry, but she would not want her men to *kill* Sybil. Surely not.

She heard a *thunk*.

"*Curan*," the Highlander said in a soothing voice as he patted the horse's neck.

Sybil thought the poor beast had been struck, but when she looked for the arrow, she saw it was sticking out of the Highlander's thigh. She sighed. Her escape had been dramatic but short-lived.

Despite the blood running down his leg, the Highlander showed no sign he was aware of his injury. Instead, he continued speaking to the horse in Gaelic, urging it to gallop still faster. But surely he could not ride like that for long.

"Can't ye see you're injured?" she shouted over the wind in her face. "We can't go on."

"We're not stopping till we lose them."

The Highlander's determined tone and evident skill as a rider eased her panic. Perhaps her escape was not finished yet. They crossed the field and sailed through the air over a burn at a mad gallop. The Highlander rode as if he and his horse were one. Even before she felt him lean to the side or tighten his thighs, his horse anticipated the signal and sensed where he wanted to go.

"We're out of the range of their arrows now," he said. "Here, hold the reins."

"But—" Before she could object or ask why, he had wrapped her hands around the reins and let go. Fortunately, she was a good rider, but he did not know that.

The grass was a blur beneath them as the horse flew over the ground. From the corner of her eye, she saw the glint of a blade. The Highlander had a knife in his hand. *Heavens!*

For a moment, she feared he meant to stab her and drop her to the ground to divert the men following them. But another quick glance revealed that he was cutting a strip from the bottom of his tunic.

"I need both my hands for a wee moment," he said, "so don't fall."

Don't fall? "Ye don't intend to bandage your leg while we're galloping, do ye?"

"'Tis that or bleed to death," he said between clenched teeth as he snapped off the arrow.

While keeping his balance as if he were sitting on a rock instead of hurtling over hills and valleys on horseback, he tied the strip around his wounded thigh. Sybil's heart pounded in her ears, and she tasted blood from biting her lip.

He grunted as he pulled the knot tight. Finally, the Highlander was finished and took the reins from her. The makeshift bandage had taken only a few moments, but it had felt far longer. Sybil sagged against the stranger's chest as his arms surrounded her again.

"Ye did well, *mo rùin*," his deep voice rumbled in her ear.

He'd called her *my dear* in Gaelic, which was oddly comforting, coming from a stranger.

Despite their desperate circumstances, this Highlander was so steady, his movements so sure, that Sybil began to believe he would succeed in carrying her to safety.

She would worry later about how to escape her rescuer.

***

Rory's leg hurt like hell. Each time the horse lurched forward over the rough terrain, the point of the arrow dug farther into his leg causing a jolt of searing pain that nearly blinded him. Although he had eluded the riders chasing them for the moment, he did not dare stop long enough to remove the rest of the arrow from his leg and rebandage it. He needed distraction, and he had a burning question to put to the young woman for whom he was risking his life.

"Who's James?" Rory kept his voice even, though he wondered what the hell his pledged bride had been up to.

"Which James?" she asked.

"Which James?" Her answer did not improve his mood. He could see that if she did become his wife, he would have to mind her closely.

"There are so many of them," she said, "starting with the king."

He ground his teeth together. Naturally, he had assumed his promised bride was an inexperienced virgin. Perhaps he was wrong.

"I was referring to the James ye mentioned when I found ye under the tree," he said.

"Oh, him."

The disgust in her voice eased his concern over that particular James. But then, a woman might react that way if an affair ended badly.

"Who is he?" He stifled a curse as the horse stumbled, jarring his leg again.

"James Hamilton of Finnart, son of James Hamilton, the Earl of Arran," she said. "He paid me a visit earlier, before you came."

Rory knew the name. Though a bastard, Finnart was Arran's favored eldest son. "I thought there was bad blood between your family and the Hamiltons."

"Oh aye," she said with a humorless laugh. "The Douglases and the Hamiltons have been at each other's throats in a fight for control of the crown since the king's death at Flodden."

"So what did this Finnart want when he visited ye today?" Rory asked.

"Me."

Rory's temper ticked up a notch.

"The man won't take nay for an answer," she continued blithely. "He told me that with the men of my family banished and the threat of a long imprisonment hanging over me, I had no choice but to avail myself of his *protection*."

Rory's shoulders relaxed. He recalled her words when she mistook him for this James Finnart. *I told ye I won't do it, so go.* It was a comfort to know that his bride refused to relinquish her virtue even under such pressure.

"I left my handprint on his face," she said.

Ach, that was even better. Despite his throbbing leg and the queen's men tracking them, Rory felt almost cheerful now.

"Once he had me, James's interest wouldn't have lasted more than a month," she said. "And then where would I be?"

"Otherwise, ye would have given yourself to him?" Rory asked, his voice rising.

The lass had the gall to laugh. She turned in the saddle to look at him.

"The prospect of being beheaded for treason does tend to make a lass consider choices she wouldn't otherwise," she said, her eyes sparkling with mirth. "Such as running off with a perfect stranger."

***

"I think we've lost them," Sybil said as she turned to scan the hills behind them yet again.

"Perhaps," the Highlander said, but he continued to ride at a relentless pace.

She had not caught a glimpse of the royal guards since the Highlander turned the horse off the road and onto an overgrown footpath an hour ago. In fact, she had seen no one at all but a lad herding sheep.

She craned her neck to look ahead. Surely they must come to a village or a town soon. Once the Highlander finally stopped for food and rest, she would crawl out a window, bribe a stable lad for a horse, or whatever she had to do to make her escape. Riding off with this Highlander was the most exciting thing she had ever done, but it was time to part ways with him.

She was grateful to the Highlander for what he'd done, but not grateful enough to marry him. After thwarting her brother's attempts to marry her off for the last five years, she was not about to succumb to that wretched fate now.

She had begun to think he would never stop when he drew the horse to a halt behind a thicket of low shrubs and trees that grew beside a burn. Without a word, he lifted Sybil down, his big hands nearly meeting around her waist. She assumed he needed to relieve himself, and was glad for the chance to stretch her legs.

"The ground will be damp. Sit on this," he said, handing her a rolled-up blanket he untied from the horse. "We'll make camp here."

"*Make camp?*" she said. "Ye mean to spend the night *here*?"

"Aye, 'tis a good spot." He patted his horse. "And Curan needs to rest. I rode him hard today."

A good spot, here in the brush? There was no window to crawl out of and no stable lad to bribe. How was she to escape unnoticed from here?

How was she to escape at all?

"It will be dark soon," he said before he turned and led the horse a few yards away.

Unless she wanted to die wandering the hills alone at night, it appeared that her plan to part ways with the Highlander would have to wait until tomorrow.

Sybil had never slept outdoors in her life. She glanced around at the tall grass surrounding her and nearly laughed. When she imagined spending the night with a man, sleeping on the rough ground amidst the weeds with a stranger was not how she envisioned it.

She found a fairly flat area and spread the blanket, then sat down to observe her rescuer. This was her first opportunity to examine him closely since their chaotic flight from her uncle's castle. Even without the numerous lethal weapons strapped to his body, this Highlander would be intimidating. He was tall, powerfully built, and had a dangerous air about him.

Up until now, her fear of the queen's men had led her to disregard the threat the Highlander himself might present. She swallowed, keenly aware now that she was alone with a stranger with no ready means of escape. His men would likely be joining them soon, but that was hardly a comfort. What if he expected to do more tonight than sleep? The Highlander believed she was his to claim, and he'd gone to considerable lengths to do so.

The tension in her shoulders eased a bit as she listened to him murmur to his horse in soft, reassuring tones while he removed the saddle and bridle. He paused to rub the horse's nose and give it an affectionate pat before leaving it to graze. Nay, she had not misjudged him. Though this Highlander might attempt to seduce her—he was a man, after all—she did not believe he was the sort to force himself upon a woman.

At least, that's what she was going to tell herself. Giving into fear never did a lass any good. Worse, it was dangerous. She needed her wits about her.

She noticed he was limping as he walked toward her. He had been so stoic about his wound that she had forgotten he had been struck with an arrow.

"We should go to a village and find a healer for you," she said, thinking this would solve both their problems.

"No need." The Highlander winced as he lowered himself onto the blanket beside her.

When she saw that his leg was covered with crusted blood, she felt a surge of guilt for being the cause of his injury.

"I'd best get this arrow out now." He pulled out his dirk, then paused to look at her. "Ye may not want to watch this, lass."

Sybil had her pride too. If he could cut his own flesh, then she could watch without fainting. The Highlander wielded the blade with a rock-steady hand as he cut off the blood-soaked bandage.

She bit her lip, uncertain what to do, as he struggled to remove his trews. Though he obviously could use her assistance, undressing him might prove a risky and revealing endeavor. She did not want to do anything he might view as an invitation. When she looked up, the glint of amusement in his eyes told her he had read her thoughts.

"I don't have a great deal of experience dressing wounds"—in truth, she had none—"but I'll help if ye tell me what to do."

"If you'll grab the bottom of the leg of my trews and pull, I can manage the rest."

She gave it a tug, and her pulse jumped as she caught a glimpse of muscular bare thigh up to his hip. Once they managed to ease his trews down far enough to reveal the bloody wound, however, she could see nothing else.

Good God, how had he ridden so far with such an injury?

"'Tis not as bad as it looks," he said, and winked at her.

Sweat broke out on the Highlander's brow as he patiently worked the jagged tip of the arrow out of his torn flesh. While he showed no other sign of the pain his efforts must be causing him, Sybil's hands grew stiff from clenching them through the long and arduous process. When he finally removed the broken-off arrow and cast it aside, she took a deep, cleansing breath.

The Highlander drew a flask from inside his tunic, and she was tempted to ask him for a long drink of it.

"Ach, I hate to waste good whisky on my damned leg," he said, and uncorked the flask with even white teeth.

As he poured the whisky over the open wound, he emitted a string of colorful Gaelic phrases in quick succession. Sybil was tempted to ask him to repeat them slowly so that she could expand her vocabulary, but this was probably not the time to ask for a lesson in Gaelic cursing. Besides that, her instincts told her not to reveal that she understood Gaelic. A Douglas did not share her secrets without good reason.

The Highlander wiped his blade on the grass and began to cut a new strip from the bottom of his tunic.

"Wait," she said, touching his arm. She lifted the hem of her gown to reveal the linen shift beneath it. "See? I have more cloth to spare than you do."

Despite the fact that his wound must sting like the very devil, especially after pouring whisky on it, he stared at Sybil's calf as if he'd never seen a woman's stockinged leg before. This Highlander was far too handsome for her to believe he had not seen a good deal more of a good many women. She shook her head. *Men.*

"Give me your knife," she said, and held her hand out for it.

"Ye don't carry a dirk?"

"Why would I need one?" she said as she took the blade from him.

"To defend yourself, of course," he said. "Every lass should carry one."

"I've managed to live one and twenty years without one." She held the wicked-looking blade up and thought of the times she had been cornered by men like James Finnart. "But I will admit that a blade like this could have been useful."

"Keep that one," he said. "I have others."

When she met his gaze, the burst of heat that flashed between them drove the damp chill from her bones. *Mercy*, what was that about? She pressed her lips together and concentrated on cutting a strip of cloth for a bandage. The blade was so sharp that it sliced through her linen shift as if it were thin parchment. When the Highlander took the strip from her, their hands touched, sending another unexpected jolt of awareness through her.

By the time she recovered her senses, he was preparing to bandage his leg himself. He was already pale and sweating from the ordeal of removing the arrow. Could the man not admit he needed help?

"You've already proven you can do this on a galloping horse," she said. "Why don't you let me do it this time?"

"Aye, that would be better, for certain," he said, and leaned back on his elbow.

His ready agreement surprised her until she noticed the smile curving his lips and the devilish gleam in his eyes. Her sensible half regretted her offer, but her other half—the one that liked to play with fire—smiled back at him. Her poor mother had despaired of taming her wild side.

As she reached around his bare, muscular thigh with the strip of cloth, she was keenly aware that without his bloodied trews there was nothing but Highlander beneath his knee-length tunic. Goodness, other men's legs were like scrawny chicken legs compared to his. If she was tempted to touch more of his thigh than strictly necessary, it was not entirely her fault. It was becoming difficult to see in the growing darkness.

As she worked the cloth around his leg, she felt more than saw the unnaturally smooth skin of a long, jagged scar that ran up the side of his thigh from his knee up to his—well, she did not know how far. Curiosity was another aspect of her nature that her mother had urged her to control with little success.

"How did ye get this?" she asked, touching the scar with her fingertip.

"Ach, 'tis nothing."

"Nothing?" She raised an eyebrow.

"I was injured at Flodden."

Mention of Flodden always reminded her of her father, who was killed in the disastrous battle. Her eyes stung, and she was grateful it had grown too dark for the Highlander to see her clearly. She still missed her father.

If he had lived, everything would be different. Archie would not have taken their grandfather's place as earl and the queen's advisor. He would not have had the opportunity to seduce the queen and cause all the trouble that followed. Sybil would be safe at home with her family at Tantallon Castle, rather than sitting outdoors in the middle of nowhere at twilight with a strange Highlander.

"The English threatened to cut off my leg to save my life," the Highlander said, interrupting her thoughts.

"I'm surprised they didn't," she said. "Does the old injury still pain ye?"

"Nay." He shrugged. "Not much, anyway."

"I believe that's a lie," she said.

He gave a low chuckle that caused an odd flutter in her stomach.

"Ye must allow for a man's pride," he said. "But I will admit that the arrow didn't improve my leg any."

He kept his gaze fixed on her as he brought the flask to his mouth and took a long drink. Despite his wound, there was no mistaking the lust in his eyes, which brought her thoughts to the night ahead with a jolt.

When he grasped her arm and leaned close, Sybil's heart went to her throat.

"I didn't mean to make ye uneasy," he said, holding her gaze. "You're mine to protect. Ye needn't fear me, ever."

His pledge, spoken with that intense stare, was reassuring but not exactly calming.

"Thank you," she managed to say. "But I'm not afraid of you."

That was a slight exaggeration, though she did believe she was probably safe so long as this fierce Highlander believed he was honor-bound to protect her. But heaven help her if he learned her brothers had played him for a fool and he had risked his life for a woman who was not his betrothed.

"A burn is just over there through the brush if ye want to wash." He struggled to his feet and held out his hand.

With that wound, she should be helping him up, but he was surprisingly steady on his feet. The man was made of iron. What she really needed was a privy. She left him to find some privacy behind the bushes.

"Don't go far," he called after her. "I'll wait for ye at the burn."

She felt on edge with him out of her sight and quickly joined him at the burn. They knelt side by side to wash the blood and dirt off their hands, arms, and faces. It felt so odd to share the commonplace but intimate activity of washing with a man. She stole glances at him as he splashed water on his face and neck and watched the water stream down his muscled forearms in the last rays of sunset. When he caught her staring, she quickly finished her own washing, and they returned to the blanket.

"We'll have to make do with dried venison and oatcakes tonight," he said, as he opened a cloth bag that he had untied from the saddle earlier. "I'll hunt tomorrow."

He sounded as if he were apologizing for not being able to hunt with his injury. For heaven's sake. She could not recall ever feeling an urge to soothe a man's pride before, but the urge struck her now.

"Ye showed great foresight in bringing food along," she said with a bright smile.

He gave her a puzzled look. "It would be foolish to travel without any."

As soon as he unwrapped the oatcakes and dried meat, Sybil realized she was famished. She picked up one of the oatcakes and took a tentative bite. It was dry as dust, but she was too hungry to care.

"I'm surprised we saw no villages where we could stay the night." She still clung to the hope that she could persuade him to take her to one tonight. She was nothing if not persevering.

"I avoided the villages. We can't risk your being seen while the guards are looking for ye." He cocked an eyebrow at her. "You're the sort of lass who would be remembered."

"But how will your men know to find us here?" she asked, glancing over her shoulder into the increasing darkness. "Will they join us soon?"

"I told ye that I came alone."

Sybil inhaled dry oatcake and coughed. "I thought ye meant ye came alone to the castle but left your men waiting somewhere for ye."

He shook his head.

"Ye came all this way with no armed guard?"

He shrugged, so apparently he had.

"You're telling me ye actually *planned* to take your bride on such a long journey and through the wilds of the Highlands without a large guard to protect her?" For a moment, Sybil almost forgot that she was not the affronted bride. But this Highlander believed she was his bride, so it was an insult to her. "Why, such a journey could take days—or weeks—through dangerous lands."

The Highlander was quiet, and she sensed that, whatever his reason for coming alone, he did not wish to share it. She folded her arms and waited for an explanation.

"I was not certain I'd be returning with a bride," he finally said. "I thought your brother may have wed ye to someone else by now, despite our agreement."

"I see ye don't think much of my brother's sense of honor," she said.

He shrugged again, which was answer enough. Well, at least her rescuer was not a fool.

***

The lass had a spark in her. Though she may be a poor choice for his wife in other ways, Rory felt quite certain they would suit under the blankets. He could almost forget the searing pain in his leg as his gaze followed Sybil's ivory skin down to where her loosened bodice revealed the top of her breasts.

Even more than her physical beauty, that spark must draw men like moths to a flame.

"I'm starving," she said, and tore off a bite of the dried venison with her teeth.

Though he was hungry too, he could hardly swallow a bite while watching Sybil's red lips as she ate and talked through their meager meal.

"This venison is tasty," she said, ripping another piece off, then she peered into the bag. "Apples for dessert!"

For a lass accustomed to fine meals, she did not appear to be a finicky eater. She devoured an apple with an enthusiasm that had him imagining her other appetites. When she licked her fingers, a groan escaped his lips.

"Hmm?" She raised her eyebrows and looked up at him, then her cheerful expression faded. "Don't look at me like that."

"Like what?" he asked, though he knew damned well what she meant.

"Like ye think I'd be willing to have my wedding night lying in the dirt," she said, narrowing her eyes at him. "If ye believe that, you're quite mistaken."

"So we're only debating where, and not whether, to have a wedding night?" he asked.

"Ye told me that if I rode off with ye I could decide later if I wished to break the marriage contract," she said. "I'm holding ye to that."

"What I told ye was that *we* could decide to abandon the contract. If we don't agree, either one of us could demand that it be fulfilled." He let the word *fulfilled* roll slowly off his tongue.

"I suggest ye don't try something you're sure to regret," she said. "I do have a dirk now."

"You'd use my own dirk on me?" Rory could not help laughing. "Ach, you're a heartless woman."

"I'll not decide whether we're going to *fulfill* the marriage contract until I know ye better," she said, wagging her finger in his face. "*Far* better."

"As it happens, becoming better acquainted is exactly what I had in mind." A smile tugged at the corners of his mouth. He should not tease her, but she made it so damned easy.

"When I do marry," she said, "I'll have a proper celebration with a grand wedding feast, a gorgeous gown, and a hall full of people to witness the vows."

Rory did not laugh this time. As the daughter of a great family, she had been raised to expect such a wedding. And she should have it.

His own clan had expectations regarding his wedding as well. As he was both the son and brother of MacKenzie chieftains, Rory's marriage would call for a large clan gathering.

In fact, he suspected that plans for his wedding celebration had already begun—albeit for a different bride. There was going to be hell to pay when he arrived at Eilean Donan Castle with his Lowlander bride.

CHAPTER 3

Hector MacKenzie of Gairloch stood on the outer sea wall of Eilean Donan Castle, where he had a commanding view for miles in every direction. The castle was built on the strategic point where three lochs met: Loch Duich, Loch Alsh, and Loch Long. By controlling the waterways in the rugged land of Kintail, the MacKenzies controlled the valleys, mountains, and even the sky above. And what the MacKenzies controlled, he controlled. He was chieftain in all but name of the great Clan MacKenzie.

He watched the progress of the riders approaching the castle along Loch Duich. As they drew closer, he recognized the lead rider by his enormous size. Big Duncan of the Axe, as he was known, had served at Hector's side since their youth. He was the man Hector entrusted with tasks that required fearlessness, strength, and a lack of scruples.

He had watched for Big Duncan's return every day for a fortnight. What had taken him so long to find Hector's goddamned nephew?

His throat tightened, choking him with rage at the thought of Rory. For the ten years since his brother's death—which had not come soon enough—Hector had ruled the clan in his nephew Brian's name. He was not about to let Rory ruin that.

Each time he recalled his last conversations with Brian, he grew more furious. But Rory says... My brother disagrees with ye on that... Rory advised me...

On his own, Brian was easy to manage. Hector wondered how his brother had spawned such a trusting soul. It was as if a wolf had sired a kitten.

Rory had the wolf in him. Though he could also be a charmer, a trait he inherited from his mother, he had been fearless from birth. Other lads panicked in their first battle, but not Rory. And from the time his nephews were bairns, Rory had appointed himself Brian's protector.

Whenever Rory looked at him, Hector saw the wolf that lurked behind his eyes, ready to pounce and tear him to shreds. Well, he would pounce first.

It had always been a mystery to him why Rory, who was clearly the stronger brother, supported Brian, rather than attempt to push him aside. He could only surmise that Rory's devotion to his half-brother was a devious act. If Rory thought he could take Hector's place and rule the clan through his weaker sibling, he was mistaken.

The men of the clan, including Brian, were accustomed to following Hector. He had made sure of it. During Brian's minority, Hector had kept him under his thumb instead of training him to lead. But if Brian had the will now, he could assert his power as chieftain. Thanks to Rory, he was becoming increasingly difficult to control.

There was an obvious solution. Hector nodded to himself as a sense of certainty settled over him. The challenge would be to make certain the blame was not laid at his door.

But one way or another, Rory must die.

As the riders crossed the bridge to the castle, Hector went inside and waited for Big Duncan in the laird's chamber, which was the largest in the castle and furnished with Flemish tapestries and heavy carved furniture. He had taken the chamber for his own use after his brother died and he was named Brian's tutor. He had not given it up when Brian came of age. And why should he? He was still the man who ruled Clan MacKenzie, and everyone knew it.

Finally, the guard who stood outside the door opened it to admit Big Duncan, who looked as if he had ridden long and hard to reach the castle. The man was as ugly as he was large, and he had particular needs that Hector supplied to ensure his continued loyalty.

"What news of Rory?" Hector asked as soon as the door was closed.

"I split up the Gairloch men I took with me, and we searched everywhere," Big Duncan said. "We couldn't find him."

"Couldn't find him?" Hector drained his cup and threw it against the wall. "God damn that Rory."

"No one has seen him in weeks," Duncan said. "Not since that argument he had with Brian. Perhaps he's gone for good."

Rory had gone before, but he always returned like a bad-luck charm. He would come back to protect his brother. And when he did, Hector would be ready for him.

CHAPTER 4

"We should sleep," the Highlander said, and stretched out on the blanket beside her.

Sybil felt uneasy with him lying prone so close to her. Though he had made no advances toward her yet, he certainly had looked at her as if he'd like to. Even if she was wrong about that—which she wasn't—lying next to a man was bound to put ideas into his head. She had learned that at fourteen when she lay on her back watching the clouds with the blacksmith's son.

"I'm in a verra weakened state with my injured leg," the Highlander said, "so don't try seducing me."

She could not help smiling. She appreciated that he had read her fears and tried to calm them with a jest. All the same, she intended to wait to lie down until he was sound asleep. She clutched her knees to her chest and tucked her chin into her cloak. With nightfall, the air had grown icy cold.

"Can we not have a fire?" she whispered.

"'Tis not safe," the Highlander said. "Tomorrow we should be far enough away to risk a fire, but not now."

"I thought we lost the queen's men. Do ye think they're still following us?" she asked, peering into the black night.

"I can't say for certain that they're not," he said, his voice fading. "Go to sleep, Sybil. We must rise early, and we've a long journey ahead of us."

Their journey together would end tomorrow. Oddly, she was growing rather fond of her Highlander. Though she was safe with him for tonight, she could not continue the pretense of being his contracted bride much longer. She needed a more lasting solution to her problem.

Before long, the Highlander's steady breathing told her he had fallen asleep. She took down her hair, loosened the laces of her bodice, and gingerly lay down at the very edge of the blanket with her back to him.

Heavens, she would never sleep like this. Though she left as much space as possible between them, they were nearly touching. She could hear him breathe and feel the heat of his body.

She rolled onto her back and stared at the dark night clouds racing across the sky. What was she going to do? The tides of royal politics were bound to turn eventually. Until then, she needed a sanctuary, a place where she could wait out the queen's wrath. Where could she go?

Small animals rustled through the grass, the wind blew overhead, and a lonely owl hooted in the distance. The unfamiliar sounds of the night made her suddenly feel very much alone. She had been uprooted, taken from everyone and everything she knew. She prepared herself for a long, sleepless night.

"Sybil." The Highlander spoke her name in a low voice, heavy with sleep, and it gave her that odd, fluttery sensation in her stomach again.

"Aye?"

"Ye mustn't worry that I brought no other men with me," he said. "I promise I will keep ye safe."

She knew better than to trust a man who promised that. Had her brothers not made the same pledge? And yet a deep calm settled over her as she listened to the Highlander's steady breathing, and she drifted off to sleep.

***

Rory was roused from a deep sleep by misery and lust. The wound on his leg felt as if a blacksmith was pounding on it with a fiery axe, while Sybil's soft rump pressed against his groin ignited another kind of flame.

Still fighting sleep, he buried his face in her midnight hair. It felt like silk against his cheek and smelled of summer flowers. Instinctively, he reached for heaven, gripping her hip and pulling her against his throbbing cock. Her shrieks jarred him to full wakefulness as she scrambled away, arms and legs flailing.

Oof! Pain sparked across his vision as her heel landed squarely on his wound.

He opened his eyes to find Sybil staring down at him looking both furious and impossibly beautiful with her cheeks flushed and her hair tangled.

"What do ye think you're doing?" she demanded.

Thinking had nothing to do with it, and what he had been doing was obvious, so he did not bother answering. *By the saints*, his leg hurt. He found the half-empty flask of whisky and drank deeply to take the edge off the pain. When he set the flask down, Sybil was still glaring at him.

"You're drinking whisky before breakfast?" she said, asking another question she knew the answer to. "God help me, I've run away with a drunkard."

One drink in the morning, and he was a drunkard. Lord, was she that kind of lass? If she was, he supposed he would not have to spend too much time with her out of bed. As he took another deep swallow, his gaze caught and held on her full, perfect breasts. Her bodice had become so loose in the night that the pink tips were nearly showing.

With a huff, she sat back and drew the blanket around her shoulders. Without the view of her breasts to distract him, Rory finally took note that the sky was light. How had he slept so late? His wound must have taken a greater toll on him than he realized.

"'Tis past dawn," he said. "We must go."

They should have been gone already. He gritted his teeth against the blinding pain as he got to his feet, then began packing up.

"There's blood running down your leg," Sybil said. "We must see to your wound before we go anywhere."

"Nay. We're leaving now." He picked her up off the blanket so he could roll it up. His leg hurt like hell, and his swollen cock did not help his mood. "If ye have needs to see to, do it quickly."

"You're a stubborn man," she said.

"'Tis a good quality *in a man*," he muttered under his breath as he picked up the saddle.

He looked up in time to see her turn in a swirl of skirts and flying locks. He could not help smiling as he paused to appreciate the sight as she stomped off in the direction of the burn. His bride was going to be a trial, but he did like her spirit.

While he waited for her, he kept an eye on the hills surrounding their camp. He did not know how persistent those royal guards were. If they were not reason enough to spur him on his way, his brother was. God only knew what their uncle Hector had persuaded him to do in Rory's absence. Or done in Brian's name.

Rory regretted the fight with his brother and leaving angry. Most of all, he regretted leaving Brian alone with Hector.

What in the hell was taking Sybil so long? His patience gone, he headed for the burn.

***

As Sybil walked along the burn looking for a spot that was not slippery with mud, she began to form a plan. Somehow she must persuade the Highlander to take her to one of her sisters. Though her brothers were a bitter disappointment, her sisters would do anything for her, just as she would for them. She felt uneasy about possibly adding to their danger, but all three had powerful husbands. And what else could she do? She had no one else to turn to.

How would she convince the Highlander to take her? She could not risk telling him the truth. He did not strike her as a man who would take learning he had been duped lightly. Nay, the stakes were too high. But once she reached her safe haven, she would reveal the truth to him.

She bit her thumbnail—a bad habit. How would he take it when she finally did tell him? His pride would be hurt. If he were one of the vain peacocks at court, she might be amused at his expense. But her Highlander was nothing like them. He had come for her out of a sense of honor—though why he waited eight years she had yet to find out—and he had risked his life to rescue her. There were not many men like that in the world, at least not in hers.

It did not sit well with her to mislead him, but it was not as if the Highlander truly wished to wed her. Nay, she was an obligation, a duty that must be borne. That should not irritate her, but it did.

Giving up on finding a dry spot to wash, she pushed through the brush and knelt on a patch of moss. She rubbed at a scratch on her face and thought of all the times she had laughed and talked with the maids while soaking in the steaming tub in her bedchamber at Tantallon Castle. Would she ever have that life again?

With a sigh, she leaned over to splash water on her face—and caught her reflection. By the saints, she looked like an ill-used tavern wench! Dirt streaked her face, and her hair was a mass of tangles. When she tried to smooth the dark curls with her fingers, she pulled out bits of leaves from her hair. *Leaves.*

She looked down at herself and surveyed the rest of the damage—her torn and filthy gown, mud-covered slippers, and blood-streaked sleeves. Her disheveled appearance was a small matter and by far the least of her problems. She knew it was foolish to care, and yet losing control of this one last aspect of her life was just too much. Intent on setting herself aright, she flung her hands into the burn and scrubbed her face in water so cold it made her gasp.

***

Rory quickened his steps. It did not seem possible the lass could have wandered off and gotten lost, but she was a Lowlander. He was relieved when he found her leaning over the burn, washing her face. For a long moment, he forgot his urgency and watched her. She looked as beguiling as a wood nymph kneeling amidst the greenery with her long, dark tresses trailing into the water. He regretted having to disrupt her.

"Sybil," he said in a low voice so as not to startle her. "Are ye ready, lass?"

"My gown is a disaster." She looked up at him with wide eyes and touched the mass of unbound, glossy black hair that fell in waves over her shoulders and breasts. "Is my hair as bad?"

She looked so beautiful that he had trouble breathing.

"Ye look…fine," he managed to say. "And there's no one to see ye but me."

The look she gave him confirmed his answer had been a poor one indeed. He was usually better with women than that.

"We must go." He looked around, his sense of urgency returning with the force of a fist to the chest. "Now, Sybil."

"First let me tie a new bandage on that leg of yours." She motioned for him to sit beside her and pulled the dirk he'd given her as if she'd done it a hundred times before. The lass was a quick learner, he would give her that.

"Not now." He took her arm and pulled her to her feet. "We must put a few more miles between us and the queen's men."

"The bandage will take but a few moments," she said.

Must the lass argue? Ach, she was stubborn. "We're going *now*."

Rory barely got the words out when he heard a twig snap behind him.

CHAPTER 5

Sybil's throat went dry. The keen alertness radiating from the Highlander signaled that something was dreadfully wrong. When he put his finger to his lips and shifted his gaze to the side, she gave a slight nod to show she understood that someone was hiding in the foliage behind him.

"Ye look so lovely," the Highlander said in an easy tone, and touched her cheek.

Evidently, he did not wish to alert whoever was creeping toward them that they were aware of his presence. She wiped the fear from her face and made herself keep her gaze on the Highlander's face instead of darting glances into the brush.

"Ye must have had all the men at court following ye around like puppies," he said in the same flirtatious tone.

Despite the danger they were in, she was struck by how easily compliments flowed from his tongue when he was under pressure.

"I would have preferred puppies," she said, forcing a smile, "but the courtiers did make better dancing partners."

The Highlander laughed. Then, in a startling blur of movement, he spun around and sent his dirk flying through the air. It found its target with a sickening *thunk,* followed by a man's cry and the sound of something heavy falling into the brush.

Before she could take in what had just happened, she was grabbed from behind and hauled backward. She lost her footing, but she still had her dirk in her hand, and she flung her arm wildly, trying to stab her attacker.

Just as suddenly as he appeared, her attacker fell backward and released his hold on her. As she fell, she saw the Highlander plunge a dirk into her attacker's neck. He caught her around the waist before she landed on top of her attacker.

It all happened so quickly. Her scream was still caught in her throat when Rory hauled her against his side and covered her mouth.

"Quiet, lass," he said in her ear. "There may be others."

Others? When she nodded, he released his hand from her mouth.

"Curan is saddled," he whispered. "We're riding out of here as fast as we can."

He took her hand and led her through the brush toward their camp. When she caught sight of the second man's boot poking out beneath a bush, she drew in a sharp breath.

"Don't look," Rory said as they crept forward.

She ignored his advice and wished she had listened. The dead man was on his back with the hilt of Rory's dirk in his chest and his eyes bulging with the surprise of his last moment. When Rory jerked the blade out, Sybil started to weave on her feet before she got hold of herself. This was no time for weakness.

"These men wear the queen's colors," she said in a low voice.

The Highlander had killed two of the queen's men. If anyone learned of it, he would be in grave danger. This was all because of her—and the lie. Though it was not her lie, she had let him believe she was his to protect.

"My guess is that they split up to search for us," Rory said. "Let's hope none of the others are nearby."

At the edge of the brush, he paused to scan the rolling hills and valleys in both directions. He started to step into the open, then halted. He stood perfectly still, his gaze fixed on a point in the distance.

"Shite!" he said under his breath as a rider emerged between the hills.

Sybil's heart thudded in her chest as one rider quickly became two, then three, then a dozen.

Rory clicked his tongue, and Curan came at a trot. Under the cover of a clump of spindly alder trees, Rory lifted her onto the horse. Leading Curan by the reins, he splashed through the middle of the burn at a run for several yards before crossing to the other side.

As soon as the horse's hooves were on dry sod again, he leaped onto its back behind her, and they took off at a gallop.

***

Rory cursed himself as he crossed streams, changed directions, and rode as fast as he dared. That had been too close. After he was certain no one was on their trail, he forced himself to slow Curan to a walk to spare the horse.

Less than a day after he collected his bride, she was nearly captured before his eyes. How could he have let that happen? Sybil's long silence felt like an accusation.

"I should not have let those men get that close to ye," he said. "I'll not let it happen again."

So long as he kept his wits about him and avoided the places her enemies would expect her to go, they should not run into them again. Keeping his wits about him would be considerably easier, however, without her sweet bottom pressed against his groin and her open thighs rubbing against his.

"I'm the one who ought to apologize for bringing ye into such trouble," Sybil said.

"'Tis not your fault your brother got on the wrong side of the queen and the regent."

Archibald Douglas and the other men of Sybil's family should be flayed alive for leaving her to face the danger they created while saving their own skins.

"Ye saved me again today," she said. "I'll always be grateful."

Evidently her brothers' shameless behavior had given her low expectations of men.

"I expect we'll reach the Highlands without further trouble," he said to reassure her. Once in the Highlands, they would have to travel through lands belonging to other clans, which was never safe, but there was no reason to tell her that now.

"Ye believe we've truly lost the queen's men this time?" she asked.

"Aye."

When she leaned against his chest and dozed off, he was startled to hear himself sigh aloud. The lass did feel good in his arms. So good that a couple of hours later he was in the midst of a heated daydream when she jolted his attention with a question.

"Why did ye come for me after all this time?" she asked.

"The matter needed to be settled," he said, and that was all the explanation he was giving.

"After waiting more than eight years," she said, turning in the saddle to face him, "why did it need to be settled *now*?"

Because he had to know if he still had an obligation to her before he wed the Grant chieftain's daughter—but only a fool would tell her that. Bringing home his unexpected bride was going to cause difficulties. The clan needed the support of the Grants.

"Why now?" Sybil repeated.

Rory recalled advice he'd been given by Malcolm, the revered old warrior who had served as his grandfather's captain of the guard. Malcolm said that when it came to women, it generally saved a lot of trouble to apologize right off, whether you'd done anything meriting an apology or not.

"I should have come sooner," Rory said, and it sounded good.

"Then why didn't you?"

So much for Malcolm's wisdom about women. "I had my reasons."

"Tell me one," Sybil said.

"Are ye always so persistent?" he asked.

"Aye."

A wise man knew when to give in, so he told her, "My brother needed me."

He regretted his harsh words to Brian before he left. And the punch in the face, though his brother had deserved both.

"Your brother needed ye for *eight years*?" Sybil asked, her voice dripping with skepticism.

"Aye." Brian still needed him. No matter what his brother thought.

"Truly?" She turned again to look up at him. "Why?"

"Do ye always ask so many questions?"

"I wouldn't need to," she said, giving his arm a playful squeeze, "if ye answered the first one fully."

Ach, the lass had more charm than a sprite and more persistence than a hungry cat.

"Come, tell me." She rested her palm on his chest and leaned into him. "Please."

With her touching him like that and fixing those violet eyes on him, Rory had trouble recalling just what she wanted to know and why he did not want to tell her.

"I can see," he said, "that you're a spoiled lass who's accustomed to using her charms to get her way."

"I am," she said with a sparkle in her eyes and a smile that could melt a frozen loch.

"You're dangerous as well," he said.

"Oh, I do hope so," she said. "Now tell me all about your brother and the rest of your family. We've nothing else to do to pass the time."

Rory was not about to frighten her off by telling her the full truth about his family, and he could think of far better ways they could pass the time.

***

Odd, the effect this Highland warrior had on her. Sybil thought she would never recover from the horror of the attack this morning, and yet she felt so safe riding with his arms about her that she had fallen asleep.

And teasing him made her feel like her old self for the first time in weeks. She had lost her usual cheerful nature when her family's fortunes fell and all her friends deserted her. It felt good to smile again.

She was still grinning over his remark about her being dangerous when he lifted her onto his good leg and dropped the reins. There was a devilish glint of amusement in his eyes.

"I've been wanting to kiss ye since the first moment I saw ye," he said. "I'm going to do it now."

Sybil could not breathe, let alone form the words to object. When she moistened her lips with her tongue, she felt his heartbeat leap beneath her palm. Her gaze fixed on his mouth as he drew her to him ever so slowly.

She had expected a sweet, teasing kiss, not this explosion of passion that seared through her body at the first touch of their lips. No one had ever kissed her like this before, as if he would die if he could not have his mouth on hers. With a will of their own, her arms wound around his neck and her fingers tangled in his long, thick hair as she pulled him closer.

She was lost in the sensations and long past thought. As his kisses slowly changed from feverish to tender, she felt as if she were floating. She wanted this to go on forever.

When Rory pulled away, she stared up at him, stunned.

"That was promising," he said with a wide grin.

How could he jest after kisses like that? Apparently they had not affected him as they had her.

"I didn't say ye could kiss me," she said, trying hard to gather herself.

"Ye didn't tell me nay, either," Rory said. "And ye seemed to like it."

She did not bother arguing because they both knew she had.

"I'm looking forward to more of that." He ran his thumb over her swollen lips. "But if I'm to get ye out of the queen's reach, we must keep traveling. You'll be safe once we reach MacKenzie lands."

More of that? Heaven help her! Much as she found the notion tempting, she could not let it happen again. She had enjoyed his kisses far too much. A few of those, and a lass could forget all good sense.

As for traveling with him, 'twas fortunate indeed that she would not be doing it much longer. Now that they had lost the queen's men, it was time to set her plan in motion to find a safe haven—and escape her rescuer.

CHAPTER 6

With any luck, Sybil could reach one of her sisters before nightfall and avoid spending another night with her Highlander. Judging from those kisses, he hoped to claim his husbandly rights sooner rather than later. His injured leg, which seemed to be healing quickly, would not deter him a second night—and if he kissed her like that again, she was not sure she could trust herself to tell him nay.

Her first step to escape was to find out where she was.

"I confess that I don't know precisely where the MacKenzie lands are," she said. "Can ye tell me about our journey?"

"The MacKenzie lands are vast," Rory said. "Our journey will be long and harsh."

Well, that was not the least bit helpful. "What route will we take?"

"The least traveled."

She rolled her eyes. Before she could make another attempt, he drew the horse to a halt behind a dense holly tree. Her heart thudded in her chest as the fears she had forgotten for the last few hours came flooding back.

"Why are we stopping?" she asked, darting glances around them. Had the queen's men found them again?

"'Tis well past noon," he said. "Ye had no breakfast. I'll not see ye starve by missing your dinner too."

He wished to feed her? That was all? Sybil drew in a deep breath in an effort to calm herself. Rory lifted her off the horse and helped her to sit on a flat rock.

"You're pale," he said, looking at her as if she was a pathetic creature. "Ye need sustenance."

"I'm fine," she said. "And I'm in no danger of starving."

"I'll have it ready before ye know it."

He tucked a slingshot into his belt and disappeared into the brush. Despite herself, she felt uneasy with Rory out of sight, but in a surprisingly short time he returned with a pair of plump quail and started a fire. He really was a most resourceful man. While he cleaned and fixed the birds on sticks over the fire, she strolled over to where Curan was grazing.

She rubbed his long nose and fed him the last apple from the bag. You could tell a lot about a person by the animals he kept. This horse was well cared for and trusted his master.

"Curan likes ye," Rory said.

"How can ye tell?"

"He'd let ye know if he didn't," he said. "Curan nearly killed the last person who tried to give him an apple."

"Why would he do that?"

"The man was attempting to steal him," he said.

"He's as clever as he is handsome." Sybil leaned close to Curan's ear and whispered, "Just like your master."

As promised, Rory had the meal ready before long, and the roasted quail was delicious.

"You're a fine cook, Highlander." Sybil was surprised he knew how. Certainly no one in her family did.

"I have a name," he said, sounding a bit surly.

"Don't ye usually have others to see to your meals, *Rory*?"

"A Highlander must know how to survive alone," he said. "Anyone should."

"I may never have plucked a quail, but I've organized a grand feast of a dozen courses for three hundred guests, including royalty."

"Will ye be wanting to invite the queen to sup with us?" he asked, raising his eyebrows.

She had been enjoying the conversation, but his remark was like a cold rain dampening her spirits.

"I hope to never see that particular royal again," she said, and stared at the horizon.

"That was a poor jest," Rory said, touching her arm. "I shouldn't have mentioned the queen."

***

Rory could kick himself for upsetting her. He had not been thinking straight since he kissed her. He'd only meant that kiss to divert her from asking all those questions—and to satisfy his curiosity—but he was lost the moment their lips touched. Passion roared through him with blinding force. He had no notion how long their mouths were locked in frenzied kisses before he realized that he was actually considering lifting her skirts and taking her on the horse's back. *Jesu!* She would think he was an animal.

After that, he kissed her gently, and somehow that was just as devastating. He had an overwhelming desire to protect and care for her. And their first time should be just as she wanted—in a large bed, in a fire-lit chamber, after a wedding feast with music and dancing and toasts to their happiness.

"I know this change in your family's position must be hard on ye," he said.

"We Douglases have been in disgrace before." Sybil gave a dry, humorless laugh. "The men of my family have always been ambitious."

Rory knew some of the stories of the Douglases. When the Scottish nobles wished to depose James III, it was Sybil's grandfather who legitimized their rebellion by persuading the king's teenage son to join them. As penance for his part in the events that led to his father's murder, James IV wore a heavy chain belt under his clothes until his own untimely death at Flodden.

"The last time we Douglases fell out of favor was not as bad as this." A bittersweet smile touched her lips as she added, "Though it seemed bad enough at the time."

Her tone was light, but he could tell she used it to hide deep wounds. He would have told her she did not need to talk about this, but he sensed that she needed to.

"My brother thought he was so clever wedding the queen in secret, knowing full well the King's Council would never approve the marriage," she said. "When the council responded by removing the regency and the royal children from the queen, she fled to England, but Archie stayed and weathered the storm. After a year, he reconciled with Albany, the new regent, and was appointed to the King's Council with the other powerful magnates."

News traveled slowly to the Highlands, and Rory had not heard of her brother's first fall from power until he had regained his position.

"Regent Albany thought all was well and returned to his home in France," she said. "Of course, it all started again."

With the king still a young child, that was bound to happen. Unprincipled men would try to use the boy king's power for themselves, just as Hector took control of the clan before Brian came of age.

"Archie challenged James Hamilton, the Earl of Arran, for control of the king and council. It was a low blow when the queen sided with the Hamiltons, but I suppose she was equally infuriated when her brother Henry VIII supported Archie."

"Why did she turn against your brother?" Rory asked. "He is her husband."

"When the queen returned to Scotland hoping to regain the regency, she learned that Archie had been living with his lover in one of her castles—and even worse, he was collecting her rents for his own use." Sybil sighed and shook her head. "Now she hates my brother with as much passion as she once loved him. That should have made him cautious. God knows, I tried to tell him."

"What did he do to be charged with treason?" Rory had not stayed in Stirling long enough to learn the details. As soon as he heard that the Douglas men had fled Scotland and the queen's men were on their way to bring Sybil to the palace for questioning, he rode hard to reach her first.

"His dispute with the Hamiltons escalated until it broke out into a bloody battle on the streets of Edinburgh," she said. "The other noble families, the city merchants, and the council tolerated the usual secret deals and maneuverings of court fights, but this was too much. There were hundreds of men fighting in the streets of Edinburgh, for God's sake."

"What happened then?"

"The council sent an urgent message to Albany, begging him to return before the country descended into chaos."

"Where was the queen in all of this?" Rory asked.

"She was astute, for once, and added her voice to the call for Albany's return," Sybil said. "She was at the dock to welcome him when his ship arrived. The next we knew, she and Albany were allies, and all the blame for the street battle was laid on the Douglases."

Though Rory was a chieftain's son, he was never more aware that his bride had grown up in higher circles.

"And that's how I came to be in this fix," she said, giving him a genuine smile this time.

"By this fix, ye mean riding off with me?" he said.

"Aye," she said with an even wider smile.

He should have left it at that, but there was something—or rather someone—that still nagged at him.

"With such bad blood between your family and the Hamiltons," he said, "I'm surprised James Finnart chased after ye."

"James has been annoying me since I was twelve," she said, waving her hand as if shooing away a gnat. "At first, I believed his attention was just part of a Hamilton scheme."

"What scheme would that be?"

"To remove me from our last king's consideration," she said. "My grandfather hoped one of us Douglas lasses would attract the king's roving eye. The Hamiltons, like all the noble families, had similar hopes."

"Ye were twelve when your family did this?" How had she survived such a family?

"I was thirteen when the king died, and I thought I'd be free of Finnart then as well." She shook her head. "But he's been dogging me ever since."

"As my wife, ye can be certain he'll never trouble ye again."

"Finnart has a startling number of illegitimate children," she said. "I doubt a lass's marital status is overly important to him."

"It may not be important to him," Rory said, "but a man who disrespects *my* wife will not live long."

Sybil gave him a look he could not read, then she turned her gaze to the horizon and fell silent for a long while.

"We thought Archie's fall from grace would be like the last time," she said in a far-off voice.

"Reconciliation with Albany will not be so easy this time," he said.

"Nay, it will not," she said.

***

Rory had done Sybil a favor by reminding her of how dire her situation was. She had no more time to waste if she was to reach the safety of one of her sisters' homes before nightfall.

"We should go." Rory took her hand and helped her to her feet.

"Before we leave the Lowlands," she said, "I must see one of my sisters."

He had started to walk toward the horse, but he halted abruptly and turned to face her.

"I could be gone for months, even years," she said, speaking quickly. "I may never see any of my family again."

"The advantage we have is that the queen's men don't know who I am and therefore don't know where I'm taking ye," he said. "'Tis unwise to give up that advantage and go where your enemies expect to find ye."

"My sisters' husbands are powerful men. The queen will be hesitant to challenge them," Sybil said. "She only came after me because I'm unprotected."

"You're protected now," he said. "And that is why I won't take ye."

"Please," she said, tugging on his hand. "My sisters will worry if they don't know what's happened to me."

"Ye left a note for your cousin," Rory said. "She can tell them."

Damn, she had forgotten about that.

"My cousin is only eleven," she said. "Her mother is the one who gave me up, and she certainly won't permit Lizzie to visit any of her Douglas kin."

He folded his arms. "I'll not jeopardize your safety."

"We needn't stay long," she lied. "A brief farewell is all I ask."

She had learned to lie with ease—a necessary survival skill at court—and yet her heart beat rapidly as Rory fixed her with a hard gaze.

"Where are these sisters of yours?" His tone was unbending, but the question was a sure sign he was weakening.

"My sister Alison lives at Blackadder Castle," she said. "Her husband is the infamous David Hume."

Sybil would feel safest there. David was a powerful Border laird and the only man connected to her family that she still trusted without reservation. For a moment, her thoughts strayed to her brothers, and she had to swallow against the bitter disappointment that closed her throat.

On her list visit, Alison and David urged her to stay with them until the trouble passed. She should have listened to them. But she had been so confident that, regardless of what happened, her many friends at court would protect her. Ha! What a fool she had been.

"The Hume lands lie behind us in the wrong direction," Rory said, shaking his head. "Worse, they're far too close to Edinburgh."

Disappointment swelled in her chest, but she said, "My sister Janet lives north. She is the lady of Glamis Castle. You can take me there."

Though Sybil loved Janet dearly, Janet was the youngest Douglas sibling by several years and Sybil was not as close to her. Also, she did not know Janet's husband well. Glamis was a great lord with sufficient power to protect Sybil, but would he?

"To reach Glamis Castle, we'd have to pass between Edinburgh and Stirling—right under the noses of both the queen and the regent," Rory said. "We're not going that way. For your safety, we're taking the less-traveled route to the west, then north."

Was he trying to thwart her? She had only one sister left.

"We travel west? Well, it just so happens that my sister Margaret lives to the west," she said, propping her hand on her hip. "Will ye take me to see her, or are ye determined to refuse me?"

***

Rory did not like it one bit. Yet he could not deny that Sybil might not see her sisters for years, and he understood why she was willing to take the risk.

"Who is this sister's husband?" he asked, regretting it already.

"A distant kin," she said. "William Douglas, the 7th Baron of Drumlanrig."

"Your uncle's wife attempted to hand ye over to the queen," Rory said. "How can we trust that Drumlanrig will not to do the same?"

"He's a Douglas, and my brother is still his chieftain," she said. "He has no choice but to protect me."

Her brothers and uncle had an even greater duty, and they had thrown her to the wolves. Still, this Baron of Drumlanrig lived a healthy distance from the antics of the Scottish court, and as a Douglas, he was unlikely to risk drawing attention to himself by sending messages to the queen.

"I'll take ye, but—"

Before he could finish, Sybil jumped up and threw her arms around his neck.

"Thank you!" she said, and her face was aglow as she smiled into his eyes.

By the saints, how did anyone refuse her? He could to protect her but feared that otherwise she would always get her way. If it meant seeing her this happy and in his arms, perhaps that was all right.

Her mouth was only inches from his, tempting him to kiss her again. Her safety must come first, however, so he set her feet firmly on the ground and laid out his conditions.

"I will take ye to Drumlanrig Castle, but we shall not enter the gates until I am certain the queen's men have not arrived before us," he told her. "If I say 'tis not safe, ye shall not argue."

Sybil nodded her agreement, but he caught the shadow that briefly clouded her eyes. What was it his bonny bride was not telling him?

CHAPTER 7

"We must be getting close to Drumlanrig Castle." Sybil's pulse leaped. "I recognize this wood. I hunted here with my brothers when we visited."

Now that she was about to reach her safe haven, an unaccountable sadness weighed on her heart at the prospect of parting with her Highlander, of never seeing him again. She had barely known him two days. And yet, after what they had been through, it did not feel right that he would be gone from her life forever.

Too soon, her sister's home appeared in the distance. She was not ready to bid him goodbye.

"That's Drumlanrig, there, across the river," she said, pointing at the tower castle. "Let's walk the rest of the way."

Rory lifted her to the ground. Before he released her, he studied her with his piercing green eyes until she wondered if he had guessed her true purpose in coming to her sister's.

"You're certain ye can trust your sister's husband?" he asked.

"Of course," she said, and pasted what she feared was a too-bright smile on her face.

Despite her reassurance, Rory kept his eyes on the castle and skirted the wood where they could not easily be seen as they approached it.

"Is your sister Margaret like you?" he asked.

"Nay. Margaret is sweet and obliging," she said with a laugh. "If William Douglas of Drumlanrig were my husband, I'd have murdered him long ago."

Rory gave her a sharp sideways glance. "I thought ye trusted him."

"I dislike him, but he doesn't have the backbone to cause trouble," she said.

In dangerous times, trust no one but a Douglas. The last time she saw her brother Archie he'd had the gall to tell her that. She hoped to God she could trust this particular Douglas.

"Besides being sweet and kind, Margaret doesn't have the Douglas coloring like I do," Sybil said to turn the conversation away from her brother-in-law. "She's a tall, fair-haired beauty, like our mother was."

"I prefer a dark-haired lass with spunk." Rory gave her a wink and took her hand.

"A man admires a woman's spunk until he marries her," she said. "Then he complains that she is too lively, that she draws attention to herself, and that it's her fault every time a man looks at her."

"And how would ye know this?" he asked.

"I've seen it often enough," she said, perhaps a bit too quickly. "Both Margaret's husband and Allison's first one did their best to stomp their spirit out of them."

"I like the spark in you." Rory smiled and squeezed her hand. "I wouldn't want ye to ever lose it."

Sybil could not help returning his smile because that was sweet of him to say. Of course, he'd change his mind if she became his wife.

How she dreaded telling him that she would travel no farther with him. She hated to hurt her Highlander's pride, but it was that or marry him—a perfectly ludicrous notion.

She had grown quite fond of him, but she was realistic enough to realize that she was ill-prepared to live in a rude hovel amidst the wild heathen of the Highlands. While that life had its appeal—her gaze drifted over Rory's fine form—she would feel like a fish out of water.

Worse, Rory would come to regret being tied to a useless wife. Not that she was without skills, but the ones she had were the sort that would help her husband negotiate safely through court intrigues, not steal cattle or whatever it was that Highlanders did.

***

Rory saw no extra guards on the wall or other sign that the castle was on alert and entertaining a party of the queen's men. He and Sybil proceeded to the gate mounted, ready for a quick escape.

When the guards recognized Sybil and greeted her with respect, Rory was relieved that they did not shout and sound the alarm. Still, he noticed their exchange of nervous glances. And none of the guards offered to escort them into the hall, as if Sybil was bad news they did not wish to deliver to their laird.

If Sybil was aware of the unease her arrival caused, she did not show it. She slid to the ground without waiting for Rory to help her dismount and strode toward the keep as if ready to do battle.

An old man emerged from the stable to take Curan. When he saw Sybil, a smile spread across his weathered face.

"Lady Sybil!" he called, stopping her in her tracks. "'Tis a delight to see you."

"And you, Thomas." Sybil took the old man's hands and kissed his cheek.

"Still stirring up trouble and breaking hearts?" he asked, and gave her a broad wink. "Of course ye are."

"I've become exceedingly dull and well behaved," she said with feigned innocence.

"Not a chance of that." He turned to Rory. "I've know this lassie since she was a babe in her mother's arms. Always was my favorite."

"Is my sister here?"

"Aye." The old man's expression turned somber. "It will do Lady Margaret a world of good to see ye."

Rory gave the old man a few quick instructions regarding Curan's care, then caught up with Sybil, who was marching toward the keep again.

"Even if your sister's husband can be trusted," Rory said as he took her elbow, "ye cannot vouch for every member of this household. Ye cannot tell anyone here who I am or where we're going."

She gave him a furtive sideways glance that made him wonder again what she was not telling him, but he did not have time to dwell on that now.

As they entered the castle's hall, Rory scanned the room for danger. A finely dressed young woman sat by the hearth stitching. When she saw them, she leaped to her feet, spilling her embroidery to the floor.

"Margaret!" Sybil squealed, and she would have run across the hall to meet her sister if Rory had not kept a firm grip on her elbow.

Sybil cast him an impatient look, but he intended to remain near the door where they had a chance of escaping if need be.

Sybil's eyes shone as her sister glided toward them. "Isn't she beautiful?"

Her sister was golden-haired, willowy, and contained, in marked contrast to Sybil's black hair, voluptuous curves, and exuberant sensuality. Margaret was indeed a beauty, but she did not stir his blood like Sybil did.

***

"What a happy surprise!" Margaret said as they threw their arms around each other.

"I can feel your bones," Sybil said, leaning back to look at her sister. "Have ye been ill?"

"I'm with child," Margaret said, a smile lighting her eyes.

Sybil's throat felt tight. Margaret had lost her last babe, and she so wanted a child.

"I'm happy for ye," Sybil said, hugging her sister again.

"Who's this handsome man ye brought with ye?" Margaret whispered in her ear, then she released her and turned to Rory. "Welcome to our home, sir."

"This is Rory—" Sybil began.

"MacDonald," he said, and bowed. "Rory MacDonald."

Margaret would never be rude, but she shifted her gaze to Sybil, clearly expecting to be told more about her guest than his name.

"I was forced to leave our uncle's house in haste," Sybil said. "Rory helped me escape."

"Escape?" Margaret's hand went to her throat. "What's happened?"

"The charges of treason against our brothers and uncle have not been dropped, as we had hoped," Sybil said, attempting to break the news gently.

"God help us, they've been charged with treason?" Margaret's face went white.

"They were charged months ago." As Sybil had suspected, Margaret's husband had told her nothing of it. The hateful man treated Margaret as if she was a child. "We expected the trouble to pass, as it did the last time, but it did not."

"This is because of the battle in Edinburgh, isn't it?" Margaret shuddered. "That was a terrible day. The streets were littered with bodies."

Sybil had forgotten that Margaret had been caught in the city when the enmity between the Douglas and Hamilton factions exploded into the street fight. That was when Margaret had miscarried. Sybil took her sister's hand and squeezed it.

"What about the Hamiltons?" Margaret asked. "They were equally responsible for what happened that day."

"I expect Regent Albany chastised them in private for their role," Sybil said. "But publicly, he laid the blame squarely on the Douglases."

"But why?" Margaret's puzzled expression reminded Sybil that her sister knew little of court politics.

"'Tis the queen's influence," Sybil said.

"She's that angry with Archie?"

"Oh, aye," Sybil said with a laugh. "She utterly loathes him. Her brother, King Henry of England, only made it worse by sending letters—and then a priest—to lecture her on her duty to be a loyal wife. That was pouring salt on her wounded pride."

"I almost feel sorry for her," Margaret said.

"Sybil is in danger," Rory interrupted. "Excuse my bluntness, but can we rely on your household to keep this visit a secret?"

"Of course!" Margaret said. "Sybil will be safe here with us."

Rory darted a piercing glance at Sybil. Before she could discern why, she was distracted by a voice behind her that made her cringe.

"Well, if it isn't the scheming court beauty herself."

Her brother-in-law. Sybil barely had time to wipe the sour expression from her face before he joined them.

"Ye look well, Sybil," he said, raking his gaze over her.

His brazen assessment made her want to plant her dirk between his eyes. Though he was only two and twenty, he already had three children that Sybil knew of who were born on the wrong side of the blanket, which made Margaret suffer all the more for her childlessness.

"Congratulations," Sybil said. "Ye must be pleased to have a child on the way."

"This one will be a boy, and I'll not tolerate losing him," he said. "Praise God the two Margaret lost were only girls."

Margaret drew in a sharp breath as if she'd been slapped. As her sister blinked back tears, Sybil felt such an explosion of rage at William's callousness that she truly would have taken her dirk to him if she did not believe that would upset Margaret still more. Rory had moved away to lean against the wall in a relaxed pose, but his clenched fists told her he felt the same way she did about William.

"May this be the first of many healthy children," Sybil said, taking Margaret's hand between both of hers. "No woman will make a better mother."

And no man will make a more miserable father. She glared at William, who filled his cup from a flagon on the table and showed no concern for the anguish he caused his wife.

"If Archie thought it was safe for ye to travel, that is good news," William said, lifting his cup to Sybil in a mock toast. "I take it he's back in Regent Albany's good graces."

Before Sybil could blurt out the news, Margaret intervened.

"My dear, I've neglected to introduce our guest," Margaret said. "This is Rory MacDonald, who very kindly escorted Sybil to us."

"Archibald sent ye here with a Highlander?" William shouted at Sybil. "Have you and your brother lost all sense of propriety?"

"We did not travel alone," Rory said in hard tone that sounded as though he was dangerously affronted. "I brought a guard of twenty men. My men are camped a mile up the river."

Sybil was a trifle disconcerted to discover that Rory lied under pressure as well as she did.

"What you need," William said, wagging his finger in her face, "is a husband who will make ye behave as ye should."

Usually it took years for a man to become such a pompous ass, but William had achieved it young. For her sister's sake, Sybil bit back a reply.

"Please, William, not in front of our guest," Margaret said under her breath.

William ignored his wife and continued questioning Sybil. "Ye brought no maidservant?"

"Under the circumstances, I gave no thought at all to propriety."

"Ye never concern yourself with priority," he snapped. "What's your excuse this time?"

"My life was hanging by a thread," Sybil said. "The queen's men were shooting arrows at us."

William's eyes bulged and his arm halted midair with his cup halfway to his mouth.

"Ye haven't heard yet?" Sybil asked. "Our brothers and uncle are banished for treason and have fled to France."

She took a great satisfaction in shocking William, who spilled his wine down the front of his tunic, until she saw the distraught look on her sister's face. As usual, Margaret attempted to smooth the tension.

"What a poor hostess I am," Margaret said, and gestured for them to sit at the table. "You two must be hungry and thirsty after your journey. I'll send for refreshments at once."

"You're most gracious," Rory said with a bow, "but I must see to my horse. He was favoring a leg."

Sybil had not noticed anything wrong with Curan's leg. When she turned and caught the look on Rory's face, her heart stuttered.

He knew. Oh, God help her, he knew she was not leaving with him, that she had never intended to. Something she had said or done had given away the truth.

"We're so very grateful to ye for bringing Sybil safely to us," Margaret said. "I hope you'll stay with us for at least a few days."

"You're kind to offer, Lady Margaret, but I have a long journey ahead." He leaned over Margaret's hand and kissed it. "I must be on my way."

He was leaving so soon? Sybil's heart pounded. She was not prepared to bid him goodbye.

His tone was deceptively gentle when he spoke to Margaret. When he turned toward Sybil, his eyes were so full of anger that she sucked in her breath. He had to walk by her to reach the door. When he paused in front of her and leaned close, she had to fight not to take a step back. She could almost see sparks in his eyes.

"If ye have something to tell me before I go," he said between his teeth, "I'll be in the stable."

***

Rory paced the stable. He was seething. Did Sybil think he was a fool? Aye, she did. Because he was one. He should have guessed the reason she insisted he take her to her sister's. His promised bride never intended to travel any farther with him, never intended to fulfill their marriage contract.

The suspicion had been at the back of his mind, nagging him, but he ignored it, did not want to believe it. But when her sister thanked him for delivering her and Sybil did not say nay, she'd only come to say goodbye, he knew the truth.

Here he was, risking his life to take her to safety, and all she wanted was to leave him.

He pounded his fist against the wall, scaring the horses. Why was he so angry? He had come on this journey in the hope of being released from the marriage contract. This was what he wanted…wasn't it?

The problem was that over the last two days, he had become accustomed to the idea of Sybil as his wife. After spending every hour of that time in his company, she, on the other hand, had found him wanting. That stung.

Not that he was without doubts as to the wisdom of the match. He had plenty. Sybil was the wrong sort of wife for him. She was a Lowlander, for God's sake, and unsuited to the life she would have had with him. She had no dowry, no connections of value to him or his clan.

And yet it made no difference to him what heartache or trouble lay ahead. Now that they were parting, he realized that Sybil was the woman—the *only* woman—he wanted for his wife.

Curan snorted and stamped his foot, showing his displeasure at being ignored. Rory patted the horse's neck and rubbed his nose.

"Ach, the lass used and made a fool of me." Rory rested his forehead against Curan's. "I know, I vowed I'd never let that happen again."

This was a hard thing for a man to forgive. But as his anger cooled, he understood why Sybil had done it. After she was betrayed by her own brothers, men she had known and loved her whole life, it was no wonder that she was unwilling to entrust her fate to a man she barely knew. And how could he blame her for not wanting to be separated from the rest of her family?

Or for not wanting him.

***

Sybil left the hall as soon as she could get away and hurried to the stable. She had almost reached it when a figure stepped out of the darkness.

"Thomas!" she said, when she realized it was the old stable master. "Ye nearly frightened me to death."

"You'll need your courage if you're going in there," he said, pointing over his shoulder with his thumb. "He's calmed down, but I'd mind my step, lassie."

Sybil swallowed.

"Just approach him slow and easy," Thomas advised, "like ye would a wild horse that's stopped rearing but is still rolling his eyes and pawing at the ground."

"Thank you, Thomas," Sybil said, because he meant well.

Her heart was beating so fast that she felt lightheaded as she paused outside the stable door. She had to face Rory. She owed him that, so she stepped inside.

Her breath caught when she saw him at the far end of the stable brushing Curan in the glow of a lantern. With each sweep of his arm, the muscles of his back rippled beneath his shirt, and the light caught in glints of red and gold in his hair.

She sensed he knew she was there, but he took his time saddling Curan. When he finally turned around, she found she could not meet his gaze and fixed hers on the straw that covered the dirt floor as he crossed the stable to her.

He stood before her, waiting. Now that it was time to tell Rory that she was not going with him to be his wife because the contract was false, she could not summon the words to say it.

"Look at me," he said, lifting her chin with his finger. "I know what ye want."

What she wanted and what was the wise course were two different things. "I… I—"

"Shh, you've no need to tell me lies or make excuses," he said, touching his finger to her lips. "'Tis a simple matter. Ye want to be released from our marriage contract. Ye don't wish to be my wife."

Rory kissed her forehead, a gesture so tender that it made her eyes sting.

She reminded herself of the many reasons it would be foolish to go with him. Rory must see as many obstacles as she did. He had waited eight years to claim her for a reason.

Rory had only come for her out of a sense of obligation. Admirable as it was for a man to honor his obligations in these challenging times, he had won her at a game of cards, not chosen her because he felt a bond of affection.

The obligation he thought he had to her was a lie. It would be wrong to hold him to it.

A tear slipped down her cheek. He caught it with his finger.

"I thank ye for that wee bit of regret," he said, with a heart-breaking smile.

He accepted that she would not be his wife. She saw no point in hurting his pride further by telling him he had been duped by her brothers.

"I hope ye find a more suitable lass," she said. "One who can make ye happy."

"The prospects for that don't look bright," he said. "But I'll be content."

***

Content? That was a bald lie. He might have been content with another woman as his wife before he imagined sharing his life with this lively, raven-haired lass with the sparkle in her eyes. But not now.

He could refuse to release Sybil from their marriage contract. Instead, he would hold on to what pride he had left. He would return to his clan and take a bride who would wed him out of duty or because she needed his protection.

He could accept that sort of marriage with someone else, but not with Sybil.

God's bones, he wanted Sybil to choose him, to want him for himself, to wed him because she cared for him. Nothing less would satisfy him. How had he developed such a weakness for her in so short a time?

He knew damn well it would be a mistake to kiss her farewell. And yet his body was pulled to hers like the tide to the shore. He could not stop himself. As he leaned down, she rose on her toes to meet him.

One taste of her lips, and the word *mine* pulsed through him. Desire surged through his veins, robbing him of his reason, when she leaned into him and kissed him back. He wanted so badly to sweep her into his arms and carry her away.

He broke the kiss while he still could.

Ach, he was a fool. Knowing he was did not make leaving her any easier. He was packed and ready, so he took Curan by the reins and left the stable. He felt Sybil's eyes on his back but he did not turn around.

His heart felt heavier with each step as he crossed the dark bailey to the torch-lit gate. The guards wordlessly opened the gate for him. The wind howled as he stepped into the black night on the other side.

The heavy oak gate banged behind him with a finality that reverberated in his soul.

CHAPTER 8

"Ye seem so low," Margaret said, and squeezed Sybil's hand. "Do ye regret not going with your Highlander?"

Sybil had told her the whole story as they sat talking on the bed with their backs propped against the headboard, as they used to when they were young girls.

"How could I regret it?" Sybil forced a smile. "I hardly know him."

"I think ye do know him," Margaret said. "Though your time together did not amount to many days, I suspect ye learn more about a man when ye face danger together than ye do chatting in a crowded hall at court."

Sybil did feel as though she knew Rory's character. He was a good man. But what would he think of her if he ever learned that the marriage contract was false? Nay, she made the only decision she could.

"I saw how he looked at ye," Margaret said. "He cared for ye."

"Ye mistake lust for affection," Sybil said, rolling her eyes. "Once his lust was satisfied, I'd be a constant disappointment to him. Can ye see me living in the wilds?"

"I can see ye doing anything ye put your mind to," Margaret said.

In any case, it was too late to change her mind. Rory was anxious to return home. Without her to hold him back, he would be many miles away by now. He would soon forget her and make some lucky Highland lass his bride. Sybil's heart clenched in her chest at the thought.

"Perhaps you'll meet him again one day," Margaret said, and patted her hand.

God forbid. While Sybil wished Rory happy with all her heart, she most definitely did not wish to see him with his beaming wife on his arm.

"Margaret!"

The shout coming up the stairs jarred Sybil from her thoughts. It was William, the last person she wanted to see. Without pausing to think, she dove under the bed. She pulled her skirts out of sight just as the door scraped open.

It slammed shut and William's polished boots came toward the bed.

"Good evening, husband," Margaret said in a soft voice.

"Where are Sybil and that Highlander?"

"He left the castle, and Sybil has gone to bed," Margaret said.

"I don't want your sister here," William said. "We're already in danger because of your brother. Her presence here can only make our situation worse."

A shiver went through Sybil. What did William intend to do?

"Why did she have to come here?" William said. "'Tis bad enough that I can't rid myself of one of Archie's sisters, but I must have two of ye?"

Sybil was sorely tempted to kick William in the ankle.

"I understand your concern," Margaret said in a soothing tone. "But Sybil is my sister. Of course we must protect her."

"We must do no such thing!"

Sybil watched his boots as he stomped to the side table, and she heard the gurgle of liquid as he poured himself a cup of spirits. He must have guzzled it, for a moment later he slammed his cup down.

"I know ye can't be suggesting we turn her out, dear," Margaret said. "She has no place else to go."

"No place to go? Ha," William said. "That lass had half the men at court eating out of her hand. Let one of them take the risk of sheltering her."

"Ye know verra well that, despite Archie's efforts to persuade her, Sybil refused to accept any of them for her husband."

"None of them will take her as a wife now—but they *will* take her." William gave a harsh laugh. "James Finnart has been a fool for Sybil for years. She should have gone to him. With his father in favor with the queen and the regent, Finnart can do whatever he likes."

"She despises Finnart," Margaret said. "She would never go to him."

"Finnart would teach her to mind her tongue. Damn it, that lass is troublesome," William said. "But at least Sybil looks as if she would be a lively bed partner and a good breeder—unlike the sister I got."

William wielded his sharp tongue like a blade to pierce Margaret's heart. Sybil lay helpless under the bed with tears of rage stinging her eyes as the conversation continued its unpleasant course, with his voice loud and angry and Margaret's soft and placating.

Marriage. *God save me from it.*

As soon as William left the chamber, slamming the door behind him, Sybil crawled out from her hiding place and put her arms around her sister.

"By the saints, ye shouldn't allow him to speak to ye that way," she said.

"Ye can't blame William for being disappointed with my failure to birth a child," Margaret said. "He wants one as badly as I do."

There was no point in arguing. If blinding herself to her husband's true nature helped Margaret tolerate her miserable situation, that was probably a blessing.

"What do ye think he intends to do about me?" Sybil asked.

"William is all talk. He would never turn you out." Margaret laid her palm against Sybil's cheek and looked into her eyes. "Even if he had a mind to, I would not allow it. I'm not as weak as ye believe."

"I don't want ye to argue with him," Sybil said, knowing it would do no good. "Ye mustn't let this upset you, for the babe's sake."

"I'll speak with my husband again in the morning," Margaret said, and patted Sybil's arm. "He's sure to be in a better mood after he's had a good night's sleep and his breakfast."

While Sybil believed her sister would do anything to save her, it was abundantly clear that Margaret was powerless in her marriage. Margaret was right, however, about William being all talk. He liked to complain and criticize, but Sybil did not believe he'd have the nerve to actually throw her out.

And yet she could not shake the uneasy feeling that she had made a grave error in putting her safety in the hands of another Douglas man.

***

Hector rode through the gates of Castle Leod tired, dirty, and in need of a woman. He had ridden for days to reach Eastern Ross.

"Have the laird's chamber prepared for me at once," he ordered as he tossed his reins to one of the servants. "And send that young Maggie to me."

He had a fine tower house of his own nearby, but he stayed in Castle Leod, the traditional home of the MacKenzie chieftains, to remind people here that Hector MacKenzie of Gairloch wielded the chieftain's power. Loyalty ran deep for him in the west, where he had spent years leading battles against the MacDonalds. His support here in Eastern Ross was not as strong, so he made the journey as often as he could to shore it up.

"I believe the chieftain is using his chamber," someone said, snapping Hector's attention as he started for the keep.

"He isn't here," Hector said. "I left him at Eilean Donan Castle."

"He rode in yesterday, without his usual guard, and rode off again," the man said. "We assumed he would be back..."

Big Duncan, who was supposed to be at Eilean Donan watching over Brian, emerged from the keep. He would not have disobeyed Hector's orders without good reason. A short time later, they were ensconced in the laird's private meeting room secreted behind the hall.

"The same day you left, Brian rode out of Eilean Donan with only a handful of men. I followed them. Brian was in a hurry, traveling fast, in the same direction as you."

"How did he pass me and my men without us seeing him?"

"When he came to Loch Ness, he took the trail along the far shore through Fraser lands to avoid you."

Hector poured himself a cup of whisky from the decanter on the side table and drank it down. His worries about Rory paled in comparison to the prospect of Brian turning on him.

"He must have come here to Eastern Ross to look for Rory," Hector said. "But why now, weeks after Rory disappeared? And if Brian is not here at Castle Leod, where is he?"

"He rode straight out to Killin to see his half-sister, Agnes's daughter."

"I know whose damned daughter she is." Hector poured himself another drink.

So the girl still lived at Killin, the farm Rory inherited from his mother. Killin was a humble abode compared to the MacKenzie castles, but it had always been Agnes's favorite home. One day Hector would take it from Rory.

In truth, he had forgotten about the girl, which was a waste of a valuable asset. She had been a useless child when Hector first gained control of the clan, but she would be of marriageable age now. If she had half her mother's beauty, she would be valuable as a bride.

"According to the servant we have at Killin," Big Duncan said, "Brian told her he'd found something that proved Rory was right about everything."

"Curse him!" Hector pounded his fist on the table. *This was getting worse and worse.* "What did he find out?" *It could be any of a number of things.*

"Brian refused to tell her. Said he feared it would endanger her."

"No matter what Brian thinks he knows, he won't have the bollocks to act on it without Rory," Hector said. "I'll bring him back into the fold. I'll fetch him from Killin myself."

Hector refilled his cup again and drained it. He had not entered that house, his brother's wedding gift to Agnes, since the day she had refused him for the last time.

"He's not at Killin any longer," Big Duncan said. "He left MacKenzie lands, headed south with his cousin Farquhar Mackintosh and a guard of only a half-dozen warriors."

"Christ!"

Brian knew he would be in danger if he left MacKenzie lands. The last king held the sons of Highland chieftains in Edinburgh to ensure their fathers' loyalty. After two years, Brian and his cousin escaped, a daring act that Hector suspected Rory organized.

So long as Brian stayed on MacKenzie territory, the crown would not touch him. The MacKenzie clan was powerful, and the crown needed them to keep the ever-rebellious MacDonalds in check. Besides that, the king who issued the edict was dead, and the regent had far greater concerns now. Still, there was a warrant for Brian's arrest, so why would he tempt fate by going to Edinburgh?

What could be so important? A cold chill settled over Hector. His own support in the clan was so great that Brian could not remove him without royal backing.

Hector reached inside his shirt to rub his thumb over the talisman he wore around his neck. The leathery skin of his brother's ear served to remind him that he held the reins of the powerful MacKenzie clan, and he deserved to.

"We must get our hands on the sister and find out what she knows," he said. "Brian may have told her something that our spy failed to hear."

"He left a package of some sort with her," Duncan said. "I'll find that as well."

Hector drummed his fingers on the table. Perhaps Brian's journey to Edinburgh was an opportunity in disguise. A sign. He smiled as a plan began to form in his mind.

CHAPTER 9

Sybil sighed as she examined Margaret, who sat on the stool in front of her wearing a headdress no woman under sixty should wear. Her sister's expression in the looking glass grew uneasy as Sybil unpinned the headdress and loosened the knot in Margaret's hair.

"Though, as a married woman, ye must cover your hair," Sybil said around the pin in her mouth as she reattached the headdress farther back to show off Margaret's lovely golden hair, "there's no need to look like a nun."

When Margaret attempted to tuck the strands Sybil had just artfully loosened around her face back under the headdress, Sybil batted her hand away.

"Do ye think William will like it?" Margaret asked.

"The devil take William. Do *you* like it?"

"Ye mustn't be so hard on my husband," Margaret said. "I know he seemed unwelcoming the night ye arrived, but he never meant it. Hearing of our family's new troubles gave him a shock, that's all."

Sybil had to admit that William appeared to have reconciled himself to her presence in his household in the two days since her arrival. Of course, he still grumbled occasionally, but that was his nature.

Sybil leaned down and rested her chin on her sister's shoulder so that their images were side by side in the mirror. They were opposites. Sybil was dark-haired and rosy-cheeked, while Margaret's hair was the color of sunlight and her skin the palest ivory.

"You're the prettiest of us Douglas lasses," Sybil said.

Margaret laughed, but Sybil wondered why her sister seemed to make an effort to hide her beauty.

"'Tis wonderful to have ye here." Margaret turned on the stool and looked up at Sybil with worry creasing her brow. "But I can see that parting with your Highlander still weighs heavy on your heart."

"He was never *my* Highlander," Sybil said, and stifled a sigh.

"He could have been," Margaret said. "I've yet to see a man who could resist you."

"Ha! This one left without a backward glance." Not that Sybil blamed him. "He's gone, so there's no sense in giving him another thought."

And yet Rory was in her thoughts all the time. Fussing with her sister's headdress was just another attempt to divert herself, and it worked no better than the others. She should not miss him this much.

Sybil sniffed. How ridiculous. She was going to weep if they did not stop talking about him.

She heard the loud *creak* of the castle gate opening, and she imagined Rory riding in. Though she knew it was not possible, she raced to the window, her heart beating fast. Margaret joined her as twenty armored men on fine horses rode into the castle.

The queen has found me. Fear swept through her body and her limbs went weak before she noticed that the riders did not carry the royal banner.

She was so relieved that it took her an extra moment to recognize the banner flapping in the wind. Nay, it could not be. The lead rider dismounted and stood with his hands on his hips, scanning the castle yard as if looking for someone. She groaned aloud.

"What is James Finnart doing here?" Sybil asked.

"I've no notion," Margaret said.

"Your wretched husband must have sent for him." That explained why William had ceased threatening to throw her out.

"Why would he send for Finnart when the Hamiltons are our worst enemies?"

"I have a good guess," Sybil said, and started for the door. "I'm putting a stop to this now."

She stormed down the stairs. She was furious. That foul William hoped to ingratiate himself with the victorious Hamiltons and rid himself of a troublesome sister-in-law all at once.

Before she took two steps out of the circular stairwell, someone shoved her back inside and pressed her against the stone wall. The man who held her was none other than James Finnart himself.

Her gaze went past him to Margaret, who stood on the bottom step with her hand over her mouth.

"Release me at once," Sybil said through her teeth. "You're frightening my sister."

"She is wise to be frightened," James said, his pale gray eyes intent on hers. "You should be too."

"I'm not frightened of you." She tried to break free, but he had her arms pinned.

"You're as full of fire as ever," he said, smiling. "I've waited a long time for you, but you'll have me now."

Sybil rolled her eyes. "If I refused you before, what makes ye think I'd agree now?"

"Because ye need a powerful man to protect you," he said. "Ye need *me*."

"Ye think the wee bit of royal blood that runs in your veins makes one whit of difference to me?"

"Despite your undeniable appeal," he said, dropping his gaze to her breasts, "you'll not find another man willing to take the risk of sheltering you. The queen's fury with the Douglases is boundless."

"The queen has no cause to blame me for the acts of the men of my family." Sybil's voice faltered a bit in spite of herself.

"You're the only Douglas she can get her hands on—your brothers have fled, and your sisters have powerful husbands," he said. "The queen is a hungry cat twitching her tail, and all the other birds are out of her reach."

"Drumlanrig is a baron," she said. "He can protect me."

"William?" Finnart laughed. "To persuade him to risk his own interests for your sake, you'd need to provide him a greater incentive than devotion to your sister. And frankly, my dear, I would not trust him to uphold his end of the bargain."

That was one thing they agreed upon. William was a squirrel. At that moment, her brother-in-law appeared behind Finnart with a smirk on his face.

"Traitor!" she shouted at him.

"Sadly, that's what they're calling you, my lovely." Finnart drew his brows together, feigning concern. "I suppose they'll torture ye until ye confess."

"But I've done nothing wrong," she said, struggling again to free herself.

"We leave in the morning," Finnart said. "'Tis your decision whether ye wish to travel as my guest to my home or as a prisoner to the queen." He thrust her at William. "Lock her up."

"Ouch!" she cried out when William twisted her arm behind her back. "Let me go, you oaf!"

"'Tis time to face the facts, my dear," Finnart said, running his finger down her cheek. "I'm the only man who can protect you now."

Sybil swallowed hard. There was only one man she trusted to protect her.

And she had sent him away.

**

Sybil removed a pin from her hair and twisted and turned it in the keyhole again and again. When the lock would not budge, she kicked and pounded on the door.

"Let me out! Let me out!"

In her flight from the queen's men with Rory, she had lost the lock pick that she always carried with her, hidden in her headdress, her bodice, or the small leather pouch on her belt.

She had acquired that useful tool in exchange for a kiss with the blacksmith's son when she was fourteen, and she had made good use of it many times since. How else was she to learn Archie's schemes to marry her off except to read the letters he locked in the secret chest in his chamber? She checked her bodice again, but the lock pick was gone.

Was there no escape for her?

She slid down to the cold stone floor and sat with her back against the door. Even if she somehow managed to get out of this chamber, through the castle and out the gate with no one seeing, what good would it do her? She would die of cold and starvation wandering the hills alone, if bandits did not murder her first.

She did not, however, like her chances of surviving the queen's wrath much better.

The only sensible choice left to her was to submit to James Finnart. She brushed a tear from her cheek, annoyed at herself for giving in to self-pity. She certainly would not be the first woman to exchange her body for protection. Women were forced to make that choice all the time. What had ever made her think she could escape that fate?

Sybil's hand went to the black onyx pendant at her throat. Her mother had given each of her daughters a similar pendant, cut from a large stone that she believed held magical protective power. Sybil ran her thumb over the smooth, glossy surface. She did not believe it was magical—she was, after all, captive in a locked room—but it gave her some comfort.

As she held it and squeezed her eyes shut, Rory's face filled her mind's eye. Her reasons for not going with him had been good ones, but she wished with all her heart that she was with him now.

Wishing never did a lass any good. She sniffed and brushed a tear away. She must find her own way out of this trouble. She was strong. She could survive being Finnart's mistress. It would not be as bad as marriage because she could leave him when the political winds changed.

Though she knew she had no other choice but to accept Finnart's offer, she could not persuade herself to agree to it. Not yet.

Soon, perhaps. But not yet.

CHAPTER 10

Rory galloped through the storm with rain streaming into his eyes and a growing sense of urgency gnawing at his gut. Lightning cracked, briefly lighting the rain-drenched road before plunging him into darkness again. He would feel like a damned fool returning to Drumlanrig Castle. Yet he could not shake the feeling that Sybil was in danger and needed him.

For two days he ignored that feeling and rode away from her and Drumlanrig. He told himself that Sybil had made her choice, and it was better for both of them. But the unease that crept up his spine would not listen to reason, and he finally gave in and turned around.

How had she gotten under his skin in such a short time and when he'd done no more than kiss her? She had deceived and made a fool of him, and yet he would have taken her with him in a heartbeat.

And now he was going back for her.

It was deep in the night when Rory finally reached the castle. He dismounted and patted Curan's shoulder, which was slick with rain and sweat. Curan had a big heart. Another horse could not have done that ride for him.

He walked to the gate and hoped the guards would remember him.

"Surprised to see you back here," one of the two sleepy guards greeted him.

"My horse fell lame." Rory gave the only pretext he could think of to explain his return and get inside. If it failed to work, he would have to silence the men quickly. "Your man Thomas has a gift for healing horses, or so he told me."

"That he does," the other guard said. "But you've been gone two or three days. Why would ye ride all the way back here on a lame horse?"

"He stepped in a hole not two miles north of here. I made camp and stayed put, hoping rest alone would heal it, but he still favors that leg." Rory stroked Curan's neck. "He's a horse in a thousand. I don't want to lose him."

The guard grunted and eyed both Rory and the horse. "The laird has an important guest and won't like being disturbed."

"No need to trouble him," Rory said. "I'll just go see Thomas in the stable."

The other guard jerked his head to the side. "Go ahead, then."

Relieved he would not have to kill them, Rory returned the blade he held up his sleeve to the sheath on his belt. When he reached the stable, he woke Thomas and explained as best he could why he'd returned. He did not really understand it himself.

"'Tis pleased I am to see ye," Thomas said. "Ye have cause to fear for the lass."

"What's happened to her?" Rory said, gripping the front of the old man's shirt.

"Perhaps nothing, but the laird let those damn Hamiltons into the castle." Thomas spit on the ground. "I haven't seen Lady Sybil since they arrived. That Finnart has always had his eye on her."

"Finnart is here?" Blood pounded in Rory's head. "I'm fetching her now."

"'Tis better if ye don't show your face inside the keep," Thomas said, holding Rory's arm. "I'll find Lady Sybil and bring her here."

Rory paced between the stalls while he waited for Thomas to return with Sybil. He was making the horses nervous, so he made himself stop. Finally, he heard hurried footsteps approaching and the rustle of a gown. He rushed across the dark stable, ready to gather her in his arms. When he saw the woman's silhouette in the doorway, he came to an abrupt halt, and his spirits fell. This woman was not Sybil.

"Praise God you've come back." Lady Margaret was distraught, and she gripped his hands. "Ye must take Sybil away from here before my husband does something dreadful."

***

A flash of lightning lit the room, followed by a roll of thunder that shook the floor beneath Sybil's feet. The violent storm brewing outside echoed the turmoil inside her. As she listened to the rising wind and watched the lone candle flicker, she wondered how many hours she had until dawn, when Finnart would take her away. She guessed it was well past midnight, but the passage of time was difficult to gauge when one had nothing to do but wait.

She fought sleep, not because she expected to conjure up a means of escape, but because she knew there was none. She refused to lose her last hours of freedom to sleep.

When the latch rattled, Sybil's heart froze in her chest. But the night was still black. The guards would not come for her until dawn, and they would never be so quiet. Her sister must have slipped away from her husband's bed and come to comfort her. Sybil scrambled to her feet and put her ear to the door.

"Margaret?" she whispered.

Relief washed through her at the answering *click, click, click* of the key turning in the lock. Praise God, Margaret had the key!

Sybil stepped back as the door swung open. "Mar—"

Her sister's name died on her lips as James Finnart filled the doorway.

"I've waited far too long to wait another night for you," he said, and pulled her against his hard chest. "Sybil Douglas, you belong to me now."

CHAPTER 11

Sybil managed to grab the candlestick from the table as Finnart backed her against the wall. When she raised her arm to strike him, he lurched backward and crashed to the floor. She stood still, holding her candlestick over her head as she stared down at Finnart's body sprawled at her feet.

Slowly she looked up from his inert form and blinked at what surely was an apparition.

"Sybil." Rory stepped over Finnart's body and swept her into his arms.

"It's really you." She sagged against him and buried her face in his chest. *Praise God!* After so many others had deserted her with far less cause, she could hardly believe it.

Her Highlander had come back for her.

"We haven't much time, *mo chròi*." Rory turned to Margaret, who had hurried into the room behind him and closed the door. "Sybil will need a set of warmer clothes. We'll be traveling through the mountains."

"But how did—" Sybil began.

"We'll talk later." Rory held her face between his hands, and the intensity in his eyes silenced her. "Every moment ye remain in this castle, you're in danger."

"I keep some old winter clothes in here," Margaret said from across the room, where she knelt before an open chest. She gathered a bundle of clothes, tied them together, and gave them to Sybil. "Ye must go quickly."

"I hate leaving ye here." Sybil embraced her sister. "I'll worry about ye."

"You'll worry about *me*?" Margaret said. "You're the one traveling through the wilds to God knows where."

"Come with us." Sybil turned to Rory. "We can take her, can't we?"

When Rory nodded without hesitating, Sybil wanted to smother him in kisses.

"We'd have to steal a second horse," he said, as if that was a small matter.

"I beg ye, come with us," Sybil said, gripping her sister's hands.

"My place is with my husband. Besides," Margaret said, placing her palm on her abdomen, "I can't travel with a babe coming."

Sybil could not argue with that. Margaret had difficulty carrying a babe without riding for days, or perhaps weeks, through rough terrain.

"What about James?" Sybil nudged Finnart's boot with her toe. "He's not dead, is he?"

"Lucky for him, his death would cause us far too much trouble," Rory said, sounding as if he regretted it. He turned to Margaret. "Once your husband and Finnart learn I was here tonight, they're sure to guess that Sybil left with me. Tell them I'm a MacDonald from the Isle of Islay. That will send them a long way in the wrong direction if they attempt to follow us."

"God go with you and keep you safe." Margaret glanced over her shoulder at the door. "You'd best hurry."

"I don't know when we'll see each other again." Sybil flung her arms around her sister. They were both weeping. "I'll send word when I can."

"It will make my heart glad to know you're far away from all this with your Highlander," Margaret whispered in her ear. "I don't want ye to have a life like mine."

***

As they crept along the wall toward the outer door of the keep, Rory kept a close watch on the sleeping figures of warriors lying on benches or wrapped in cloaks on the floor of the hall. He did not like the odds here.

When he eased the door open, the wind whistled through the gap and the torches in the wall sconces flickered. Rory tensed, waiting for someone to sound the alarm. They slipped out quickly. After the door closed behind them, Rory drew in a deep breath, grateful for the cold rain and wind on his face.

Holding hands, he and Sybil hurried through the dark courtyard to the stable.

"Praise God ye found her," Thomas greeted them. "You're a good man, Highlander."

Rory was pleased that Thomas had wrapped a foul-smelling poultice around Curan's right front leg, which would lend credence to Rory's story to the guards.

"God bless you," Sybil said, and kissed Thomas on the cheek. "It's a comfort to me to know there is one loyal Douglas at Drumlanrig Castle to keep watch over my sister."

"I will," Thomas said. "Take good care of our princess, Highlander."

"How do ye plan to get me past the gate?" Sybil asked Rory. "The guards know me."

"I'm going to roll ye up in the blanket behind my saddle."

"What?"

"'Tis dark and blowing so hard the rain is coming down sideways," Rory said. "The guards won't leave the shelter of the gatehouse to take a closer look so long as they see what they expect to see—a lone man and a horse with an injured leg."

"What if they do take a closer look?"

"They won't," Rory assured her. He exchanged a glance with Thomas and touched the dirk at his belt. One way or another, he would get Sybil past the gate.

***

The voices of the guards were muffled by the blanket, and Sybil could see nothing at all. She held her breath to keep from sneezing from the strong smell of horse in her face.

Curan came to a halt, and she heard the rumble of Rory's voice but could not distinguish the words through the blanket. She thought she heard the gate creak, then the horse began to walk again, rocking her head against his side like a sack of oats. With her heart in her throat, she listened hard for the hue and cry that would erupt if her empty chamber was discovered, but she heard nothing but the wind.

Being trussed and hung over a horse's back like a goat was uncomfortable. The blood went to her head and feet, the pressure on her stomach was painful, and the motion made her nauseated. Finally, the rocking stopped.

"Let me get ye out of there," Rory said.

After the long silence, the sound of his voice was reassuring. Still blinded by the blanket, Sybil felt herself lifted up and then gently laid on the ground.

"Time to unwrap the princess." Rory slowly unrolled her from the blanket until she tumbled out and lay at his feet. He smiled down at her. "I'm going to remember this."

She forgave him for being amused at her expense because he had saved her. Again. She could forgive him almost anything now. His amusement was brief. Dawn had broken, gray and damp, and he peered through the mist as he picked up the blanket and wrapped it around her shoulders.

"We need to keep moving," he said. "Ye can sleep as we ride."

Exhausted after the long night and her ordeal, she dozed on and off while they rode for what seemed like hours. Rory stopped twice to let her stretch her legs and to rest the horse, but he did not rest himself. They ate the bread and cheese Thomas had packed for them while they rode. As the day wore on, the wind grew sharp and the landscape forbidding.

Sybil stared at the empty hills and valleys as they rode mile after mile. All her thoughts until now had been on escape, not their destination. Now she was keenly aware that she was headed into the unknown—with a man she had met only a few days before and still knew very little about. The farther they traveled from everything and everyone she knew, the more she realized that she was dependent upon Rory MacKenzie for her very survival.

For the first time, it occurred to her that she might actually end up married to him.

How had this happened? For years, she had successfully thwarted her brother's efforts to marry her off—and she had planned to continue thwarting him for a long time to come. Quite to her surprise, she did not find the idea of Rory as a husband *wholly* objectionable. He was forthright and steadfast, uncommon qualities among the men she knew. She enjoyed his company and felt closer to him than the court friends she had known for years.

And then there were those kisses. They had led to wicked thoughts of what it would be like to share a bed with her handsome Highlander.

In truth, if she ever did want a husband—which she most definitely did not—Rory would be a better choice than most.

The prospect of living the rest of her life in the wilderness amidst his wild heathen clansmen, however, sent chills up her spine.

From what she'd heard, even highborn Highlanders lived in hovels with nothing to eat all winter but soggy oatcakes.

She imagined herself trapped in a life that was so foreign to her *forever*. Nay, that could not be her fate. She had to believe that one day it would be safe for her to return to her home and her own life. Until that day came, she would have to survive whatever came.

God help her.

***

Rory stared bleary-eyed into the small campfire he'd built after they ate the trout he had caught and cooked for their supper. He was tired as hell, and his injured leg throbbed. Tilting his head back, he closed his eyes to savor the burn of the whisky down his throat. After riding through the night to retrieve Sybil from Drumlanrig and then riding hard all day, he hoped the drink would revive him for the talk he needed to have with her.

"I wouldn't mind a drink of that, if you're willing to share," Sybil said.

He poured her a cup from his flask. After taking a surprisingly long pull, she coughed and choked until her eyes watered. Rory started to reach for the cup, but she pulled it away and gulped down another long drink. This time she barely coughed at all.

He leaned back on his elbow and watched his bride as she made a determined effort to get roaring drunk. Knowing that the prospect of being bound to him for life was what drove her to drink did not sit well with him, but at least he need not worry about his wife criticizing him for taking a nip now and again.

"So tell me," she said, weaving a bit, "why did ye come back for me?"

"I was wrong to leave ye there in the first place," Rory said. "I should have known that a man who treats his wife the way William Douglas of Drumlanrig does would have no qualms about putting a kinswoman in harm's way."

"That doesn't answer it," she said. "Why are ye still willing to claim me after I…after I…"

"After ye made up your mind to set aside our marriage contract and part ways with me?"

She dropped her gaze. "I didn't mean it as an insult."

"I understand it's hard for ye to leave all ye know for an uncertain future with a stranger." This bit of wisdom had been slow to come to him. He patted his chest, where their marriage contract was tucked under his tunic for safekeeping. "I didn't destroy the contract, so we're still bound."

"I expect my dowry has been forfeited to the crown, along with my family's other properties," she said. "On that ground alone, ye could abandon any obligation ye may have to me."

"What kind of man would I be if I abandoned my bride when she most needed my protection?" Rory brushed his knuckle against her cheek. "Ye must trust that I'd never do that."

"Then I fear your Highland pride has gained you a useless bride," Sybil said, lifting her cup to him. After tossing back the contents, she held it out for more.

"I wouldn't say useless," he said, fighting a smile as he poured her a tiny measure. "Ye told me yourself you've planned twelve-course feasts for three hundred guests."

"Aye, I know who to sit next to whom," she said, slurring her words a bit, "because I also know who pretends to have power and who really does, and who is sleeping with whose wife."

"And ye can read and write," Rory pointed out. "That's impressive."

"Ahhh, those are necessary for sending and receiving secret missives," she said, waggling her eyebrows. She leaned against him, her soft warmth sending a shot of desire through him, and spoke in a loud whisper. "I was taught all the languages spoken at court and to listen for the hidden meanings and unspoken motives behind the words."

"Your family taught ye all that." Rory kept his tone light, but he thought it damned shameful the way her family tossed the lass in the snake pit of court politics to serve their interests and then failed to protect her.

"Oh, aye, I know a *great* many useless things." She took his flask and drained it, then gave him a broad wink. "But I can pick a lock with the right tool, and that's something."

Rory admired how Sybil managed to keep her sense of humor. He was, however, losing his. His bride could not drink enough to cope with having to follow through on their marriage.

Until her plans went awry at Drumlanrig, Sybil had never intended to honor their marriage contract and become his wife. She had used him, just as her family had used her. He told himself that she had only done as she had been taught. And yet it stung.

He'd be a fool to ever trust her.

Exhaustion and whisky were a poor mix, and she sank against his chest with a sigh. That talk he needed to have with her would have to wait until morning. He closed his eyes as he enfolded her in his arms and kissed her hair. Though this Lowlander lass was wrong for him in so many ways, she felt exactly right.

***

Sybil awoke with her head throbbing. She squinted up at the gray, rain-laden sky and wondered why she was sleeping outside…then everything came back in a rush. She was penniless and homeless and on her way to an uncertain life in the wild Highlands.

"How's your head this morning?" Rory gave her a reassuring smile as he sat beside her and handed her a cup. "Drink this down. It will help."

As she drank the foul-tasting mixture, she debated whether it would be rude to ask him if they would share his cottage with his cow.

"I know ye came with me because you're frightened," Rory said, taking her hand, "and ye have no one else to turn to."

Sybil lowered her gaze, embarrassed that her circumstances had sunk so low.

"I saw what ye meant about your sister's husband crushing her spirit," Rory continued. "I don't want a wife who feels caged like Margaret does."

What was he trying to tell her? Was this an excuse for leaving her? If he realized he did not want such an unsuitable wife after all, what would she do now? Though she did not relish the idea of living in a tiny cottage with a cow, she did want to live.

"On MacKenzie lands," Rory said, "I'll be able to keep ye safe."

She swallowed and closed her eyes against the flood of relief that poured through her. He did not mean to desert her after all. In a weak voice, she managed to say, "Thank you."

"I can do that without our being man and wife," Rory said.

Sybil snapped her eyes open. She should have known he would disappoint her. Men never acted selflessly.

"If not your wife, just what would I be to ye?" she said. "Your mistress?"

"Ach, that's not what I'm trying to say." Rory fixed his gaze on the horizon. "My clan will take ye in and protect ye as my guest for as long as ye need. When the winds shift at court and your brother returns from exile, I'll return ye to your home. If that's what ye wish."

Sybil was too overwhelmed to speak. Why would he do this for her?

"I don't want ye to be my wife only because ye must to be safe," he said.

She never cried, and yet tears flooded her eyes. When Rory turned and caught her wiping them away with her hands, his brows shot up.

"Did I say something wrong?" he asked.

She shook her head and choked out, "This is kind of you."

"Nay, 'tis not kindness, but selfishness." He lifted the corner of his plaid and dried her cheeks. "I flatter myself that I deserve a wife who wants me for her husband."

As she watched him through watery eyes, Sybil was tempted to tell him that she was that woman, that she wanted him for her husband. But she reminded herself that Rory felt honor-bound to protect her only because he had signed his name to a piece of parchment. She could not accept him as her husband without first telling him that it was all a lie, that he owed her nothing. She could not risk that.

"You deserve a devoted wife who loves you with all her heart," she said.

That kind of love took trust, did it not? Sybil doubted she was capable of it. Time and again, the men closest to her had put their interests before hers.

Nay, she would never let herself trust like that. Even now, despite all Rory had done for her, she was waiting for the moment when the cost of caring for her well-being became too high and he decided to sacrifice her.

When that moment came, she feared it would hurt her even more than her brothers' betrayal had. It would be a grave mistake to let herself be trapped forever in marriage to a man who could hurt her that much, time and again.

As she faced an unknown future fraught with peril, Sybil was certain of only two things. If she married Rory, she would lose her chance of ever returning home.

And she wanted to go home, to her life as it was before.

She had no notion how many months or years it would take, but her family would eventually return to power. The Douglases always did. Until then, she would do her best to adapt and survive in a harsh land among strangers.

She must also steel herself against the day that would inevitably come when Rory would fail her, and she would have no one to rely on but herself.

CHAPTER 12

You deserve a devoted wife who loves you with all her heart. How in the hell did the lass think it was a comfort to tell a man that? It was just a long way of saying nay.

"Now that we have that settled, I'd better catch us some breakfast so we can be on our way." Rory braced his hands on his thighs and got to his feet.

He'd be glad when they reached MacKenzie lands and could stop running. They had a fortnight of hard travel before they got there. That should give him time enough to change her mind about being his wife.

"Rest while ye can," he said when Sybil got up and began rolling up the blanket. "We've a long day ahead of us, and many more after that."

"I can't have your clansmen thinking of me as a useless Lowlander lady, now can I?" Sybil planted a hand on her nicely rounded hip. "Before we reach your home, I intend to learn to help ye in all the ways a Highland lass would."

"Such as?" The help he desperately needed involved unrolling that blanket—or backing her up against the nearest tree. His mouth practically watered as his gaze drifted up and down her enticing form.

"I don't know." Sybil gave an impatient wave of her hand. "Build a fire, cook."

Rory raised a skeptical eyebrow.

"Give me your flint," she said, holding out her hand. "I'll have a fire roaring by the time you're back."

"Let me show ye how."

"No need," she said. "It can't be that hard, and I've seen ye do it."

Rory admired her confidence, but making a fire from damp moss and twigs was harder than it looked. And he'd had plenty of practice. But he left her to it.

When he returned with a trout, Sybil was coughing from the smoke. Rory sighed inwardly at her pitiful attempt at a fire. The lass was as helpless as a newborn babe. He reminded himself that she had other qualities that were more valuable to him in a wife than her skill at building a fire. Besides her obvious physical appeal, the lass was witty and bright.

When she looked up, he could not help smiling at the smudges and determined expression on her face—and he was sorely tempted to kiss her. Sybil was not one to give up easily, another attribute he admired, though in her case it verged toward stubbornness.

"All right," she said. "Show me how."

She paid close attention as he shared the secrets of building a fire on a damp day.

"I was thinking about what you said earlier," Sybil said later as she watched him clean the trout, "about me having the protection of your clan without us marrying."

When he looked up, her expression was innocent, but something about the way she said it put him on his guard. Taking his time, he set the trout to cooking over the fire before saying, "Aye?"

"Well, it made me wonder," she said, "aren't your clansmen expecting ye to bring home a wife?"

"Nay." Rory could not think of a good way to explain it to her, so he left it at that.

He felt her eyes drilling into him, and he did not believe it was because she was fascinated by his skill at cooking trout.

"Ye didn't tell your clansmen the reason ye traveled all this way, did ye?" she said, resting her hand on her hip, which he was learning was not a good sign. "No one in your clan knows about the marriage contract."

Rory turned the trout over while he tried to think of an explanation that would not offend her, but nothing came to him.

"Eight long years, and ye never showed it to a soul," she said. "Why?"

***

Sybil had wondered why no one told Rory the marriage contract was signed by the wrong brother. Though Archie was the queen's husband and the king's stepfather, she had thought perhaps not everyone in that distant part of Scotland where Rory lived knew the Douglas chieftain's name. Now she realized that no one told Rory the contract was faulty because he never shared it with anyone.

That did not explain, however, why he kept a marriage contract he believed was binding a secret.

"Why?" she repeated.

"As I told ye before, I expected your brother would find a way to avoid honoring the agreement," Rory said. "I don't like looking like a fool."

"I think that when ye returned home," she said, pinning him with a look, "ye realized ye wanted a wife who would fit into your Highland clan more than ye wanted my dowry."

Rory shrugged. "It doesn't matter now."

His acknowledgment that she would make him an unsuitable wife hurt, though she had told herself as much. She recalled with grim amusement how not very long ago she had thought herself such a prize.

"What about the brother ye mentioned?" she asked. "Ye speak as if the two of ye are close. Surely ye at least told him."

"Nay," Rory said.

This struck her as odd indeed. She narrowed her eyes at him. "Are ye already married?"

"Nay," he said again, but this time she heard hesitation in his voice.

"You'd best tell me the truth." She leaned in front of him and gripped his arm so that he would look at her instead of the damned fish.

"I don't have a wife."

He met her gaze and spoke in a firm tone. All the same, she sensed there was more to this tale, and she waited for it, tapping her fingertips against her knee.

"Well, there was talk," Rory said, dragging the words out, "about a possible match with the daughter of a neighboring clan chieftain."

"I see," she snapped. "This is why ye came alone for your bride. Ye hoped to escape your obligation without anyone at home ever finding out ye nearly got caught in a disastrous marriage with no advantages at all."

"I wouldn't say *no* advantages," Rory said with a glint in his eye.

"Don't attempt to divert me with false flattery. I've known far too many charming men for ye to succeed," she said, crossing her arms. "And I understand better than most that the marriage of a chieftain's close kin is made to benefit the family and clan."

He could not deny it. As the brother of the MacKenzie chieftain, Rory was expected to make a marriage alliance that served the clan.

"This talk of a possible match is what finally brought ye to Edinburgh, isn't it?" she asked.

Rory shrugged as if this was of no importance. "I had to know if I had a prior obligation."

"And you believed that if my brother had not already dishonored the contract, he would readily agree to destroy it."

He had not come to fetch his bride but to avoid marrying her—and that was when he believed she had an enormous dowry. When he discovered that Archie was banished and she was in danger, Rory was trapped by his sense of honor to abide by the contract.

Sybil was like a rock tied around his neck at sea.

"A Highland chieftain's daughter would suit ye well," she said, annoyed with herself for being upset. "She'd be a far better choice than a Lowlander noblewoman who's lost all her wealth and powerful connections."

"Ye did not hear me say I wanted to wed the lass." Rory's eyes were fierce as he bit out the words.

"Do ye want her?" Sybil asked, her voice coming out in a whisper.

Though it should not matter that he wanted someone else, Sybil held her breath as she waited for his answer. She understood Rory's desire to wed a Highland lass who would fit easily into his way of life. That only made sense. But the thought of him desiring a *particular* Highland lass made her stomach tighten into a hard knot.

"I was prepared to wed the lass if I was free to do so because my clan needs the alliance with hers." Rory paused. "But nay, I do not want her for my wife."

Her rush of relief was brief. Rory was simply using his obligation to her to avoid an unwelcome marriage his chieftain wanted to force upon him. She could hardly blame him since she had been thwarting her brother's efforts to marry her off for years.

"Why not?" she could not help asking. "What's wrong with the lass?"

"I've no objection to her," he said. "I don't even know her."

Sybil narrowed her eyes at him. There was something more to this than Rory was telling her.

***

The Grant chieftain's daughter would be the wiser choice for Rory's bride. Though it was unjust, he was blamed for the strain in the alliance between their two clans. The proposed marriage was meant to settle the hard feelings between their families and salvage an alliance both clans needed.

But Rory would just have to think of another way to appease the Grants.

Because the only lass he wanted for his bride was Sybil.

CHAPTER 13

"The Grant and Munro clans are threats to us." Hector slammed his fist on the table. "We must strike them before they strike us."

He moved his gaze from man to man of the select group of MacKenzie warriors gathered around the high table in the great hall at Eilean Donan Castle. These were the most respected men of the clan and served as a council to Hector and the chieftain. Hector neither wanted nor needed their advice, but he had spent years cultivating their support.

Some of the men nodded their agreement, others were uneasy but silent. None openly challenged him until he came to Malcolm, an old warrior who had served as captain of the guard when Hector's father was chieftain and as a close advisor to Hector's brother.

"With respect, this is no time to break with good allies like the Grants and Munros," Malcolm said. "We should save our strength to fight the MacDonalds. They are a powerful enemy and our greatest foe."

Hector nodded, pretending to acknowledge the advice as worthy of consideration, while his fingers itched to plunge his dirk into Malcolm's heart. Rory had been whispering this same advice in Brian's ear for months. Hector needed a war to galvanize the clan behind him. The graver the danger and the more enemies they faced, the more his clansmen would realize they needed him, an experienced warrior and victor of many battles, to lead them.

"We ought to persuade the Grants and the Munros to join forces with us against the MacDonalds," Malcolm droned on, "not make them blood enemies by attacking them unprovoked."

Hector could not lay hands on the revered old warrior here in front of the others, but the old man had challenged him for the last time.

"You've served the clan well for many years," Hector said. "If ye no longer feel ye have the heart to fight, we've plenty of young MacKenzie warriors who—"

"I don't lack courage," Malcolm said.

"Good." Hector walked around the table to clamp a hand on Malcolm's shoulder. "Then I'll grant ye the honor of leading our next battle."

Hector would make sure Malcolm did not survive it. That was one obstacle removed from his path.

Unfortunately, Malcolm's objection caused rumbling among the other warriors at the table. Hector could always find a way to provoke the Munros into attacking first, and then these men around the table would be shouting for vengeance.

"Before we attack these neighboring clans who have been our allies in the past," one of the others said, "our chieftain should give the command."

"Aye, we should wait for the MacKenzie," another said. "Where is he?"

That was a question to which Hector hoped to have an answer soon. If all went as planned, there would be no shackles on his authority.

"He's gone hunting," he lied. "And of course we must wait for the MacKenzie."

He stifled a smile. They could be waiting a long, long while.

After they left, he met with a different sort of advisor. He opened the secret stairway to an old woman who had knowledge of the dark arts and a sweet granddaughter she did not want given to Big Duncan.

It never hurt for a man to hedge his bets.

***

Rory grinned as he watched the sister-in-law to the queen cooking oats for their breakfast over an open fire. She spooned the steaming porridge into two cups and handed him one.

"Not too bad," she said, frowning after she took a taste. "Better than yesterday, wouldn't ye agree?"

"'Tis perfect," he lied.

"As good as any Highland lass could make it?" she asked, tilting her head in a fetching way that he imagined she did when she flirted at court.

"Aye," he lied again, and was rewarded with a smile that shone in her eyes.

Last night when he returned from hunting with a pheasant for their supper, Sybil had a good fire going and their camp set up. She had adapted to the rough travel better than he would have imagined. From the start, she had shown herself to be determined and clever, but her desire to undertake these mundane tasks that he would have gladly done for her surprised him.

Did she do it out of pride, or was this an indication she had decided to accept becoming his wife? If she'd made up her mind, he wished to God she'd tell him. Sleeping beside her every night without touching her was torture. If she made him wait much longer for their wedding night, it just might kill him.

"Wear your extra stockings today," he told her. "We'll see snow in the mountains."

"Already have them on," she said, and gamely lifted her skirts to show him.

"A bit higher," he said. "I can't quite see them."

"You've seen all you're going to see," she said with a laugh. "Now, if you're done lazing about, shouldn't we be on our way?"

Despite the hardships, Sybil's natural cheerfulness shone through now that they had put many miles between them and her former troubles. But they were in the Highlands now. Spring had not yet come this far north, and their route would take them into increasingly rugged terrain. He worried it would be too hard on her.

"I had no notion any place could be as beautiful as this," she said, pausing to gaze at the shimmering surface of Loch Lochy and the rich green hills on the opposite shore.

When he stood beside her, she hooked her hand through his arm. Now that she was at ease with him, she touched him often without seeming to notice that she did or the effect it had on him.

"This is a bonny spot," he said. "Almost as bonny as MacKenzie lands."

"How long before we reach them?" she asked.

"A few days or more, depending on the weather," he said. "MacKenzie lands are vast, stretching from sea to sea in the shape of a giant wedge of cheese, with the wide part in the west and the narrow point in the east."

Sybil laughed and leaned against him. "To which part of the cheese are we going?"

"The west."

The route east to the MacKenzie strongholds near Inverness would be easier than the mountainous journey west, for they could travel through the Great Divide, an endless valley and chain of lochs that ran at a diagonal across the Highlands. That route, however, would take them through Grant lands and directly past Urquhart Castle, the Grant chieftain's fortress on Loch Ness. Rory intended to avoid the Grants until after he and Sybil were wed.

"We go west to Eilean Donan Castle," he said. "My brother, our chieftain, should be there."

Rory was anxious to make things right between him and Brian. And they needed to discuss how to mollify the Grants now that there would be no marriage between Rory and the Grant chieftain's daughter to heal the breach between their clans.

As Rory turned Curan westward into the mountains, an uneasy sensation passed through him. His grandmother would say someone had walked on his grave. He thought he heard a voice chanting, but there was not another soul in sight on the barren, windswept hillsides.

"What's wrong?" Sybil asked.

"Nothing at all," he said to reassure her, but he kept a sharp lookout. As a warrior, he knew better than to ignore the unease that pricked like an itch on the back of his neck. Curan was on edge too.

A lone raven flew across the sky and cawed three times. The old folk said that was an omen of death.

***

Sybil tucked her chin down against the wind whipping at her face and pressed more tightly against Rory's back as they rode. The plaid he'd wrapped around them kept most of the rain from penetrating her clothing, but the damp cold still seemed to seep into her bones. Ever since they turned westward, the journey grew harder each day.

By the time they finally stopped for the night, she could not feel her hands and feet.

"Ach, you're shaking." Rory enfolded her in his arms and rubbed her back. "I should have stopped sooner. Why did ye not tell me ye were frozen?"

"I didn't want ye to think me weak," she mumbled into his shoulder.

"You've too much pride by half," he said, and kissed her hair.

After bundling her in a blanket, he quickly set about building a fire and preparing their dinner. Sybil felt too worn out from fending off the cold to make even a feeble offer to help.

"Rain's coming tonight," he said, glancing up at the sky.

Coming? It had been drizzling all day. Rory set up a makeshift lean-to with a wool blanket that had been treated with some kind of fat to shed the rain. She crawled under it and must have dozed off, for she awoke to the delicious smell of the rabbit cooking on a spit over the fire.

"Feeling any better?" Rory asked.

"Aye."

"This is what ye need." He poured a steaming liquid into a cup, added a large measure of whisky to it from his flask, and handed it to her. "'Tis the Highland cure for whatever ails ye."

The first sip sent a welcome warmth all the way to her frozen toes. She smiled as she breathed in the steam and watched Rory over the top of the cup as he removed the rabbit from the fire. His unrelenting kindness was making it hard to protect her heart.

The rabbit was delicious, and the fire, food, and hot drink revived her. But no sooner had they finished eating than the wind picked up bringing with it a driving rain. Rory put his arm around her and pulled her farther back under the protection of the lean-to.

"We'll have to sleep verra close together to stay warm tonight," Rory said over the sound of rain pelting against the blanket overhead.

That sounded dangerous in a very appealing sort of way.

"We could get warmer still by not sleeping." His tone was light, but the desire in his eyes warmed her more than the whisky had.

"Tell me more about your family," she said quickly, and wrapped her arms around her knees. "Ye seem reluctant to speak of them, but I'll have enough to learn about living in the Highlands without ye keeping me in the dark about your family."

Rory heaved a sigh and turned to stare at the rain that was already forming puddles. "What do ye wish to know?"

"Let's begin with this brother ye fret about," she said.

"Warriors do not fret."

Sybil snorted. "Then tell me about this brother ye don't fret about."

"Brian is my half-brother, older by six months," he said. "He is the MacKenzie, the chieftain of our clan."

Older by six months. Now that was interesting, but a bit delicate to ask about just yet. "What about the rest of your family?"

"I have a younger brother and sister."

"And yet ye fret about the brother who is chieftain, not the younger ones?" That struck her as odd.

"My younger brother is a priest," he said, "and my sister is a good and quiet lass who stays at home and out of trouble."

Those two sounded dull as dirt. "Tell me more about Brian."

"His mother was a MacDonald, the daughter of the Lord of the Isles," he said. "Her marriage to my father was intended to end the strife between two great clans who were longtime enemies."

"A political alliance, then," Sybil said. "That's the basis for most marriages among the Lowland nobility."

"In the Highlands marriages between warring clans are common, despite the fact that they often have the opposite effect intended," he said. "Here, enmities run deep and can last for generations—long past anyone's memory of how they began."

"Did your father's marriage to his enemy's daughter succeed where others failed?"

"Ach, no," Rory said. "They despised each other from the start."

"Apparently they put aside their differences long enough to conceive an heir."

"Aye, they did their duty, but the marriage didn't last long," Rory said. "Soon after Brian was conceived, my father saw my mother, and that was that."

"That was that?" Sybil raised her eyebrows.

"He set his MacDonald wife aside," Rory said, "and sent her home to her father."

"*Set her aside?* He petitioned the church for a divorce?"

"Highland marriage customs are more accommodating than the church's, especially for chieftains," Rory said. "Rome is a verra long way away, and many a chief has set aside one wife to take another—or kept them both—and later asked for dispensation from the church."

Two wives at once? Sybil's mouth gaped open. These Highlanders truly were heathens.

"The Lord of the Isles, this lass's father, ignored a direct edict from the pope himself demanding that he quit cohabitating with his second wife and take back the church wife he had set aside."

"Why would he risk excommunication and everlasting hell?" While a Lowland noble might bribe a bishop to gain support for a petition, fear of the church's power led most men to respect its authority.

"The Highlands is a violent place, and a chieftain needs heirs—the more the better—and alliances that benefit his clan," he said. "'Tis common for chieftains to change wives when alliances shift or a wife cannot give him heirs."

After the depravity Sybil had seen at court, she should not be shocked. Was this not just powerful men taking mistresses and calling them wives?

"Sometimes chieftains change wives for no reason but to please themselves, as my father did," Rory said with a shrug. "Chieftains hold all authority in their clan and can do what they will."

"Then 'tis fortunate you're not a chieftain," Sybil said.

"Why is that?"

"Because if I did marry you—and I'm not saying I will—I'd murder ye for such behavior."

***

Rory smiled at her threat to murder him, for he took it as a clear sign that she was imagining her future as his wife. Despite her claim that it was fortunate he was not a chieftain, he was certain she would be far more amenable to the marriage if he was. Sybil was not raised to be the wife of a second son. Her brother had been the most powerful man in Scotland, and, as the king's stepfather, he could well be again.

But she was contracted to him, and he meant to have her.

She was wrapped in his plaid and pressed against his side like melted wax on a candlestick, which gave him hope that tonight would be the night she finally said *aye*. He was nearly blind with arousal imagining all the things they would do when the sound of her soft, regular breathing finally penetrated the vivid fantasies running through his head. He heaved a sigh. She was fast asleep.

The rain had nearly put their fire out, but there was just enough light to see her face, which was usually so lively and full of expression. In sleep, she looked serene and innocent. Awake or sleeping, she was so beautiful she took his breath away. When he gently laid her down, he felt a deep longing to make her his, to wake up every day to see her face across his pillow.

Despite his longing and a physical desire that was almost painful, he told himself it was good she had fallen asleep. Sybil was accustomed to a pampered life, and he ought not take his bride for the first time under a rough blanket on the cold, wet ground.

For this sweet lass, he would wait until they made their vows in a MacKenzie castle before his chieftain and clansmen and could spend their wedding night in a huge bed in a comfortable chamber warmed by a roaring hearth fire. Rory wanted everything to be just as it should be on the night he made Sybil his wife.

When he touched his lips to her forehead, Sybil smiled in her sleep, and his heart flipped in his chest. *Ach*, he was a lost man.

Heaven help him if Sybil decided she did not want him.

Rory did not expect sleep to come easy, but as he held Sybil in his arms and listened to the wind whip against the lean-to, he felt himself drifting toward sleep.

Caw caw caw.

He awoke abruptly in the dead of night with his palms sweating and his heart racing. During the hard days of travel through the mountains, he had forgotten about the raven's cry when they first turned westward, but the raven had come back to him in a dream.

He told himself it meant nothing. All the same, he held Sybil closer, determined to protect her from whatever evil lay ahead. He would be glad when they finally reached the safety of Eilean Donan Castle.

The wind seemed to carry an echo of his dream, and it sounded like a warning.

Caw caw caw.

CHAPTER 14

"We've crossed onto MacKenzie land," Rory said. "You'll see Eilean Donan when we crest this hill."

Eilean Donan was a rather grand and romantic name for a hovel. Sybil steeled herself for her first look at the home he spoke of with such affection and prepared herself to lie.

"The countryside is lovely." This much, at least, was the truth. The landscape was wild and magnificent, much like Rory himself.

The "hill" they were climbing was a mountain and so steep that they had dismounted to give Curan a rest. Rory climbed it as if he were strolling, but Sybil was gasping for breath long before they reached the top.

"There it is," Rory said, and she could hear the pride in his voice. "Home at last."

Sybil stopped in her tracks, mesmerized by the sight of the castle rising from the morning mist at the point where three stunning lochs met in the valley below. The long, narrow lochs cut through mountains that extended as far as the eye could see.

"'Tis the most beautiful castle I've ever seen," she said as they stood side by side looking down at it.

"Our vassal clan, the Macraes, hold this castle for us, but my brother Brian spends most of his time here," Rory said. "By tradition, the Macraes serve as our chieftain's personal guard. They're known as *the MacKenzie's chain mail*."

Though Sybil knew the MacKenzies were an important Highland clan, she had no notion that they had vassal clans, vast lands, and more than one castle.

Rory whistled a tune as they made their way down the trail. Now that they were on his homelands, he seemed to truly relax his guard for the first time since they began their journey. Sybil, however, was suddenly anxious.

"I can't meet your family like this," she said, spreading the filthy skirt of her gown. "I look like a tavern wench—one ye had your way with in the bushes all the way home."

Rory tilted his head back and laughed. "Well, I can't say I don't wish the last part was true, but ye look fine."

"I don't look fine," she said, "and this is nothing to laugh about."

"A wee bit of dirt won't matter." As he wiped a smudge from her cheek, the laughter left his eyes, and a wave of hot lust sizzled between them. "Believe me, every man in the castle will envy me the moment ye walk in."

"And none of the women will forget that I arrived looking a filthy mess," she said, forcing her thoughts back to the problem at hand. "Your brother is a chieftain. I can't meet him like this."

"As soon as we arrive, we'll get ye out of those clothes and into a hot bath," Rory said, brushing a tangle of her hair from her cheek. "And I'll have the servants find ye a fresh gown."

That sounded as if he planned to strip and bathe her himself. Though she would never allow it, she could not at the moment muster an objection.

She imagined Rory unfastening her gown and letting it slide over her skin as it fell to the floor…him kissing her neck and rubbing her temples as he washed her hair…and then sinking into oblivion as she was enveloped by the heat of the water and the sensation of his soapy hand running down her limbs.

"A bath would be…lovely," she finally managed to say, and started down the hill to the castle.

***

Rory had made light of her complaint, but the truth was it hurt his pride to see his woman in a torn gown and muddy slippers. He could hardly blame Sybil for not wanting to wed him, given how poorly he had taken care of her. Now that they had reached Eilean Donan Castle, he would see to it that she was pampered, as she deserved.

Perhaps then she could envision herself as his wife.

They remounted Curan when they reached Loch Duich in the valley. As they rode the path along the loch, he could make out the figures of the guards on the wall of the castle, which was built on a small island just offshore at the far end of the loch. At first, he and Sybil were hidden from view by the low trees and shrubs along the loch, but the guards on the wall surely saw them as they neared the bridge to the castle.

The guards should have recognized him and his horse by now and opened the gate. Had they grown lax in his absence? Rory could think of no other reason for their delay. As he turned Curan onto the bridge, he felt the guards' eyes on him.

But the gate remained closed.

***

Hector sat alone in the chieftain's private chamber to enjoy the fine meal laid out before him.

"Such a clever man," he said, lifting his cup in a toast to himself. He should have the news he'd been waiting for any day now.

He took a deep drink and swished the wine around his mouth to savor the flavor. The wine had been shipped from France at great cost, but he deserved to enjoy the fruits of his labor. Of course, it would not do to drink it in front of the men. In the hall, he drank ale like they did. It made them believe he was one of them.

He frowned as he chewed a mouthful of the peacock roasted with exotic spices, a dish that graced the tables of kings and chieftains. In truth, he liked ordinary roasted chicken better, but he ate peacock because he could.

A knock on the door disrupted his meal. He nodded to his servant, who opened the door to one of the Macrae men.

"Ye said ye wanted to know if Rory came," the guard said. "He's riding up now."

So he'd shown himself at last. "You've closed the gate to him, as I ordered?"

"Aye, but how can we deny him entry? Rory is the chieftain's bro—"

"I speak for the chieftain, and I said close the gate to him!" Hector stabbed the point of his eating knife into the table, which proved persuasive.

After the guard bounded out, Hector took his cup of wine with him to the arrow-slit window to watch the scene unfolding below at the gate.

At the sight of his nephew, a wave of hatred washed through him. Rory was so much like his father, Hector's arrogant half-brother. Rory brought no men with him, as if to tell the world he feared no one. MacKenzie warriors respected that brazen fearlessness.

And the lasses were drawn to it like moths to a flame, as evidenced by the lass on the back of Rory's horse. Even from this distance, Hector could tell she was a beauty. A memory of Rory's mother with her hair flying out behind her as she galloped her horse struck him like a hot poker in his eye.

He had seen Agnes Fraser first, had pointed her out to his brother. She was meant to be his. Instead, she chose his brother. Years later, when she humiliated him again, he made her pay for it and took what she would not give him. But it was not the same, and even in death, he could not forgive her.

The son she loved so much would suffer for the pain she caused him. He clenched his fists as he recalled the grave wrong Rory himself had done to him. Never again.

Hector's mood lifted as he watched Rory shake his fist and shout at the guards to no avail. Ha, this is only the beginning of your disappointments, nephew.

Rory was obstinate as hell, a fierce warrior, and a crafty opponent. Unlike Brian, who was weak and easy to manipulate, this nephew would be a challenge.

Hector lifted his cup to the window. Rory would test his skills, which would make crushing him all the more satisfying.

***

Rory's temper rose as the guards kept him waiting in front of the castle gate.

"I am Rory Ian MacKenzie, the son and brother of MacKenzie chieftains, as ye well know," he shouted, and shook his fist. "Open the damned gate!"

Angus Macrae, the captain of the guard at the castle, appeared on the wall.

"My apologies, Rory Ian MacKenzie," Angus called down, "but I cannot let ye inside."

"Have ye lost your wits?" Rory shouted back. "It would be foolish to challenge the MacKenzie clan."

"Aye, it would," Angus said. "'Tis not my intention."

"Then explain yourself."

"Hector of Gairloch has ordered us not to open the gates to ye."

Rory should have known Hector was behind this. "Hector is not the chieftain of the MacKenzie clan. He has no right to deny me entry to any MacKenzie castle!"

Fury burned through him. Hector had used the time of Brian's minority to establish himself in the minds of their clansmen as the only man who could lead them. When the king demanded a hostage from every Highland chieftain's family to assure their clan's good behavior, Hector had sent the young chieftain to Edinburgh when he could have easily sent another. Brian was held there for two years, giving Hector a free hand.

"Hector gave the order on the MacKenzie's behalf," the Macrae called down.

"He no longer has the right to issue orders in my brother's name," Rory shouted.

Brian had failed to put Hector in his place after he came of age, and that had been the source of all conflict between Rory and his brother. Hector was a wolf in the guise of a loyal dog. Brian, along with most of the clan, failed to see that Hector's intent was to undermine the young chieftain's authority and hold power himself at all costs.

"My brother would never agree to such an order!" Rory had to believe that. Though they had exchanged angry words, Brian knew Rory only meant the best for him.

When Macrae turned to confer with one of his men, Rory hoped he was finally recognizing the seriousness of his error.

While the Macrae commander was distracted, one of the other guards, a man Rory had fought with at Flodden, took the opportunity to draw his finger across his throat and nod toward the hills in a clear signal that Rory was in danger and should flee. Apparently, he had at least one ally among the Macraes.

Rory wanted to pound his fists against the gate and challenge the guards to try to take him. But the soft warmth of Sybil's body pressed against his back penetrated his violent thoughts and reminded him that she was in danger too.

Without hesitating another moment, he turned Curan and galloped back across the bridge.

CHAPTER 15

Sybil held on tight as they galloped at breakneck speed across the bridge and down the trail along the shore. She barely held back a shriek when Rory abruptly turned Curan and they plunged into the woods.

After a while, she realized they were following a trail, but it was so old and overgrown that the tree branches slapped at her legs. Someone would have to know about this trail to find it.

"What happened back there?" Sybil asked when Rory finally slowed the horse to a trot. "Why wouldn't they let us in the castle?"

"I don't know yet," Rory said. "But we must be well out of sight before the Macraes decide they ought to try to capture us."

Capture us?

Rory offered no more explanation. His continued silence and relentless pace sent tendrils of fear through her. After following the little-used track over hills and valleys for several miles, they came to a cottage with a sagging thatched roof.

The cottage looked exactly how she imagined the one belonging to the old hag who turned into a witch in the tales her nursemaid told them as children. Sybil sucked in her breath when a gray-haired woman hobbled out the door with the aid of a cane.

"Ye know this place?" she whispered to Rory.

"Aye," he said. "A man I can trust lives here."

Sybil hoped he was right.

"So you've come at last, Rory Ian MacKenzie," the woman chided Rory in Gaelic as they dismounted. "We've been worried sick about ye."

"'Tis good to see ye, Grizel." Rory kissed her cheek.

A man with a shock of white hair and the frame of a still-powerful warrior emerged from the cottage. He and Rory gripped forearms in greeting.

"Guma slàn dhuibh," *health to you both*, Rory said.

"Praise God you've returned," the man said. "Have ye just come from Eilean Donan?"

"Aye," Rory said. "I was refused entry."

"'Tis as I feared," the older man said. "Come inside. I've much news to tell ye."

It must be very bad news for the old couple to dispense with the customary greetings and barely spare her a glance.

"This is Sybil." Rory took her hand and drew her to his side. "We'll need to speak in English for her."

The man gave Sybil a curt nod, and his wife kept her worried gaze fixed on Rory.

"This is Malcolm, a famed MacKenzie warrior who fought at my grandfather's right hand and served on my father's council," Rory continued. "And this is his wife, Grizel, who is famed in her own right as a healer."

"Now, laddie," Grizel said, taking Rory's arm, "ye best sit down to hear this."

The doorway into the cottage was so low that even Sybil had to duck her head when she followed them inside. The cottage was surprisingly clean and cozy, considering that half of it served as a stall for their cow.

"Is this about Brian?" Rory asked as soon as he dutifully sat on the too-small stool that Grizel led him to. "Where is my brother? I thought he'd be at Eilean Donan."

Malcolm took a stool facing Rory, while his wife stirred a pot that hung over the hearth. As there was no place else to sit, Sybil perched on the edge of the bed built into the corner.

"I'll tell it to ye from the beginning, as I learned it," Malcolm said. "Brian came here, mayhaps a fortnight ago, asking where ye were. He was desperate to speak with ye."

"What did he want to tell me?"

"Wouldn't say. When I told him I'd no notion where you'd gone to, he decided to ride on to Killin," Malcolm said. "He hoped you'd either be there or that your sister Catriona would know where to find ye."

"Catriona didn't know. I didn't tell anyone," Rory said. "Did Brian say anything else?"

"Aye," Malcolm said. "After Killin, he planned to travel to Edinburgh."

"Edinburgh!" Rory ran his hands through his hair. "How did he guess that's where I'd gone?"

"Is that where ye went?" Malcolm shot a searching glance at Sybil. "Nay, Brian had no notion where you'd gone. He had his own reasons for traveling to Edinburgh."

"*O shluagh,* what was he thinking?" Rory said. "Brian knows it's dangerous for him to set foot off MacKenzie lands. How many warriors did he take as his guard?"

"Only a few of the younger men, including one of my grandsons," Malcolm said. "Your cousin Farquhar Mackintosh was with him as well."

"Ach, Farquhar has no business going to the Lowlands either. He's wanted for the same offense as Brian." Rory stood and darted glances around the small cottage like a caged animal. "I must go after my brother."

When his gaze caught Sybil's, his expression grew more troubled.

"I can't take her with me," Rory said in Gaelic to Malcolm. "The journey here was too grueling to subject her to it all again. Besides, Edinburgh is as dangerous for her as it is for Brian."

Sybil tensed. Was he going to abandon her here?

"I haven't time to take her to Killin to stay with my sister." As he glanced around Malcolm's humble cottage again, he looked as uneasy as she felt at the prospect of leaving her here. "I'll only be gone for a few weeks."

A few weeks? The thought of being separated from him made her throat close in panic. She was about to object—and reveal that she understood what he said in Gaelic—when Malcolm spoke again.

"You're needed here at home," he said, resting his hand on Rory's shoulder. "I haven't told ye the worst of it yet."

The catch in Malcolm's voice alarmed Sybil even more than his words. The older man's broad shoulders seemed to slump as if under a weight, and a deep sadness filled his eyes.

"Your brother Brian is dead."

CHAPTER 16

Rory's chest felt too tight to breathe. Claws of grief sank into his belly and tore his guts.

"Please, God, not him," he said. "Brian cannot be dead."

"He made it past Stirling, but not to Edinburgh," Malcolm said. "He was killed in the village of Torwood, near Falkirk."

"Nay, this is a lie devised by Hector." It had to be. Rory could not let himself believe it, would not believe it. Not without proof.

"I'm sorry, son," Malcolm said.

"Even if Brian and Farquhar were foolish enough to ride into the Lowlands, that doesn't mean they're dead," he protested. "Brian is probably on his way back now."

"My grandson who traveled with him rode as hard as he could to bring me the news before Hector learned of it," Malcolm said. "He was here not more than an hour before you and the lady arrived."

Rory gripped Malcolm's arm. "Your grandson saw my brother die with his own eyes?"

"Aye," Malcolm said.

Rory felt awash in guilt as he accepted the painful truth. "How did it happen?"

"The Laird of Buchanan killed him."

"What reason could he have to murder Brian?" Rory asked. "We've no quarrel with the Buchanans."

"Some years ago the king issued a proclamation allowing any man who was wanted for a crime to clear his name by bringing another criminal to justice," Malcolm said. "Buchanan had a murder warrant against him. When he met Brian and Farquhar on the road, he recognized them and recalled their escape from royal custody years before. He decided to deliver them to the crown and be relieved of his own heinous crime."

"No Highlander would stoop so low," Rory said.

"Buchanan did."

"May he burn in everlasting hell." Rory clenched his fists. He needed to punch something. "How did Buchanan find my brother in Torwood, a place Brian never should have been?"

"I'm afraid that was just bad luck," Malcolm said. "Buchanan and his men happened to be traveling north on the same road that Brian and his men were traveling south."

That coincidence struck Rory as odd. Was it just bad luck?

"My grandson says the Buchanan laird pretended friendship when they met," Malcolm said. "He and his men joined the MacKenzies at the house where they were staying for the night and shared a jug and storytelling with them until late into the evening."

The bastard had coldly calculated how to put Brian and his men at ease.

"After the MacKenzies went to bed, the Buchanans returned and surrounded the house," Malcolm continued. "They demanded that your brother and Farquhar surrender."

"Surrender? Ye said Brian was killed." Rory's throat was so tight he could barely get out the words. "What happened?"

"Brian came out of the house brandishing his claymore, and he was cut down." Malcolm swallowed. "Your cousin Farquhar surrendered after that, and Buchanan took him to Edinburgh to be imprisoned."

"Your grandson saw Brian fall, but perhaps he was only wounded." Desperation made Rory grasp at straws. "He could be imprisoned with Farquhar."

"While my grandson rode here, the others in Brian's party started for Beauly Priory with Brian's body, so that he may be buried with your father."

Rory sank down on the stool and covered his face with his hands. He could not deny the truth. His brother was gone.

"I wish to God I didn't have to tell ye this last part," Malcolm said, "but 'tis better that ye hear it from me."

When Rory looked up and saw tears glistening in the tough old warrior's eyes, he felt as if a hole had opened in the floor beneath him.

"As proof for the pardon Buchanan sought"—Malcolm paused, struggling to get the words out—"he took your brother's head to Edinburgh."

***

Sybil clutched at her skirts. She was at a loss as to what she could do or say to ease Rory's pain in the face of losing his brother to such a wretched death. His eyes were filled with horror, as if he was watching his brother die and could not stop it.

"I should have been there," he said, running his hands through his hair. "I could have prevented this. I know I could have."

In his grief, Rory kept repeating the same words, over and over.

Sybil went to stand beside him and rested her hand on his shoulder. "I'm so sorry."

"'Tis my fault he's dead," he said. "I failed him."

"You're not to blame. He was a grown man," she said, attempting to soothe him. "He made his own decisions."

"Ye don't understand." Rory turned fierce eyes on her and thumped his fist against his chest as he said, "It was *my* duty to protect him."

He got up and stormed out of the cottage. When Sybil started to follow him, Grizel held her arm in a surprisingly strong grip.

"Give the lad a bit of time," Grizel said. "He's had a bad shock."

"Trust my wife on this, lass," Malcolm said, nodding. "We've known Rory since he was a babe."

"We didn't give the lad a chance to tell us anything about you." Grizel eyed Sybil up and down. "So who are ye to our Rory?"

"I'm...I'm..." Sybil hesitated, not sure how to describe herself in a way that would explain her traveling alone with Rory.

She could see from Grizel's sour expression that the woman's opinion of her was sinking lower the longer Sybil failed to answer. Though Sybil normally could spout white lies when the situation called for it, she found herself unable to lie to this old couple who were obviously very fond of Rory.

Finally she settled on, "Rory signed a marriage contract to wed me."

That was true as far as it went. She could not very well tell them the full truth—that the contract was a fraud and Rory did not know it.

"You're Rory's bride?" Malcolm said.

Again, Sybil could not bring herself to lie outright, so she smiled and let them draw their own conclusions.

"Well then, Rory won't have to sleep with the cow tonight after all," his wife said. "The two of ye can share the loft."

"They won't be staying the night," Malcolm said. "Rory will want to be on his way to Castle Leod."

Sybil glanced over her shoulder toward the door, wondering if it was too soon to go to him. "Why does Rory blame himself for his brother's death? He wasn't even there."

"Brian was a kindhearted lad, well liked by all," Grizel said as she resumed stirring the pot that hung over the hearth fire. "But he was too trusting by half. Rory was always the strong one."

"I don't like speaking ill of the dead, but Brian never had the makings of a chieftain." Malcolm found his pipe on the table, lit it with a bit of kindling he held over the hearth fire, and sat down again. "If Rory had wanted it, I believe the clan would have chosen him over Brian when their father died, but Rory always insisted that the chieftainship rightly belonged to Brian."

"Loyal to a fault, that one." The old woman pointed her wooden spoon at Sybil. "That suited Hector. He knew he could control Brian."

"The two lads were only fifteen when their father died. Hector, as the closest adult kinsman and a man of great experience, was given the role of tutor to the young chieftain," Malcolm said around the pipe clenched between his teeth. "After Brian came of age, Hector continued to hold the reins."

"And Brian let him," his wife put in. "That's what caused the strife between the two brothers."

"Ach, Rory will have a fight on his hands now," Malcolm said.

"What fight is that?" Sybil asked, though she thought she knew.

"To take his place as the next MacKenzie chieftain." Malcolm paused to draw on his pipe. "After years of ruling in Brian's name, Hector won't let go easily."

"Rory has the better claim," Grizel said, "being both Brian's heir and his father's eldest living son."

Sybil struggled to absorb the news that Rory was about to become chieftain of a powerful Highland clan.

This changed everything.

As chieftain, Rory's marriage choice would have far greater consequences than it would as a chief's younger half-brother. His marriage must be a carefully chosen alliance for the benefit of his clan. While she was confident he would protect her as his guest, he could no longer offer her the choice of marriage. He would put his duty to his clan first, as he ought.

Rory would be grateful to her for understanding why he must destroy their marriage contract—and she would never have to hurt his pride by telling him that her brothers had made a fool of him.

"If Rory is to claim his rightful place—and keep it," Malcolm said, drawing Sybil from her own thoughts, "he must outwit a sly and ruthless opponent who has succeeded in deceiving most of the clan for years."

While there were a great many things Sybil needed to learn about surviving in the Highlands, she was well-versed in the games men played for power. She had observed them from a close vantage all her life.

She thought she left all that behind when she escaped with a wild Highland warrior. Her warrior, however, turned out to be a chieftain. Or he soon would be. After Rory had done so much for her, there was finally something she could do for him. She could help him win this power struggle with his uncle, *if he would let her.*

She had tried so hard to save her brother from the miscalculations that led to his downfall, but he would never listen to her. She shook off the bitter memory. No matter, she was determined to help Rory outwit his uncle. She would learn all she could about the players in this new game and be ready.

What he needed now, however, was the comfort of a friend, so she left the older couple and went outside. She found Rory sitting on a log overlooking the stream that ran by the cottage. She went to stand behind him.

"I'm here," she said, and draped her arms around his neck.

He clasped her hand where it rested across his chest. They remained silent for a time, watching the water ripple over the rocks in the river.

"We have to leave," Rory said. "With luck, we'll have at least a couple of days before Hector learns of Brian's death."

"Where will we go?" Sybil asked.

"To Castle Leod in Eastern Ross."

"Malcolm said that's where you'd go," Sybil said. "Why there?"

"My father built Castle Leod on the base of an ancient fort and made it the home of the MacKenzie chieftains." Rory paused. "That's where the clan will choose our next chieftain."

"Then you've decided to do it? To become the MacKenzie?"

"There's no one else who can stop Hector," he said. "A chieftain must have chieftain's blood. My younger brother is a priest, so that leaves only me and Hector."

"Are ye certain ye want this?" A sudden fear for him seized her heart. "There's always a price to be paid. My brother tried to rule all of Scotland, and now he's living in exile."

"I never wanted this," Rory said. "I admit I was frustrated with my brother at times, but I only ever wanted to help him be a better chieftain."

"All the same, you'll fight your uncle for the chieftainship?"

"Hector is attacking our neighboring clans and turning our allies against us," Rory said. "That is a dangerous path that will anger the crown and weaken our clan against our greatest enemy, the MacDonalds. I cannot let that happen."

Hector did not sound so very different from her brother Archie, who fought a bloody battle in the streets of Edinburgh to gain power and instead caused the downfall of his family and clan.

When they returned to the cottage, Malcolm and his wife were waiting outside for them.

"Ye must set aside your grief, son," Malcolm said. "The clan needs ye, and we need ye now."

"I will do my duty." Rory gripped Malcolm's shoulder. "I swear to you on the blood of my father and brother that I will defeat Hector and take my place as the MacKenzie."

"I know ye will succeed," Malcolm said. "You'll need as many clansmen at Castle Leod to support ye as we can muster. I'll send my sons and grandsons to spread the word among those we can trust."

"When the time is right, we'll need them to light the fires to call the clan to the gathering at Castle Leod," Rory said. "Meet me at Killin at…"

Sybil wanted to listen to the rest of their plan, but Malcolm's wife took her arm and pulled her inside the cottage.

"Many will say that you're a poor choice for Rory's wife, being a Lowlander," Grizel said.

Sybil already knew that too well. If the woman was going to lecture her, she wished she'd be quick.

"But I disagree," Grizel said. "Hector consorts with demons. To fight him, Rory could use a lass at his side who has the protection of the faeries."

"The faeries?" Sybil raised her eyebrows. When Grizel pointed at Sybil's throat, her hand went to the pendant her mother had given her.

"That stone holds powerful magic," Grizel said. "Never take it off."

Sybil ran her thumb over the smooth, polished surface. Malcolm's wife made her nervous.

"Your heart is burdened with lies," Grizel said, which made Sybil almost jump out of her skin. "But I believe ye mean to help our Rory."

"I do want to help him." Sybil could barely get out the words.

"Aye," the old woman said, nodding to herself. "When ye look at him, the air around ye turns a shimmering blue."

Sybil stifled the urge to make the sign of the cross for fear of insulting the older woman. Before she could ask what the blue glow meant, Grizel thrust a cloth bag that smelled of fish into her hands.

"For your supper," the older woman said. "Now, don't keep your man waiting."

"Thank you and God bless," Sybil said.

Rory was already mounted when she went outside, and he pulled her up behind him.

"We'll meet at Killin," Rory said.

"Until then, keep your sword sharp, *ceann-cinnidh*," *chieftain*, Malcolm called out and raised his fist as they rode off.

CHAPTER 17

Sybil's heart ached for Rory. Sensing he did not wish to speak, she simply rested her head against his back and held him close as they rode in silence.

When it grew too dark to ride, they made camp in the shelter of a large boulder near the winding river that ran through the valley. Sybil's frozen feet prickled as the heat from their small fire seeped through her boots while they ate the supper of smoked kippers and oatcakes that Malcolm's wife had packed for them.

Sybil drew her cloak up to her chin against the wind and watched the night clouds blowing across the moon. Rory put his arm around her and wrapped the extra blanket around them both.

The misery in his hollow eyes made her stomach hurt. Was it only this morning that he had been so happy and proud at the prospect of showing her Eilean Donan?

"I'm sorry we're living rough again tonight," he said.

"I don't mind," she said. "'Tis hardly raining and blowing at all, so I'd call this a bonny night to sleep outdoors."

Rory lifted a tendril of her hair and twirled it around his finger. "I promised ye a hot bath and servants to wait on ye."

"With so much weighing on your shoulders, ye shouldn't trouble yourself over my lack of a hot bath." She tilted her head. "Or do I smell that bad?"

Her effort to cheer him was rewarded with a brief smile, but his eyes soon clouded again. She leaned her head against his shoulder and wished she knew how to comfort him.

"I can't understand why Brian took the risk of leaving the protection of MacKenzie lands to travel to Edinburgh," Rory said. "It was not in his nature to act rashly."

"Then he must have had a good reason," Sybil said.

"I need to know what that reason was." Rory clenched his fist. "Brian died because of it."

"Didn't Malcolm say Brian went to see your sister before he left for Edinburgh?" she said. "Perhaps he told her."

"Perhaps," Rory said. "In any case, I must see Catriona and break this sad news to her. She lives at Killin, the property I inherited from my mother. It's just a few miles from Castle Leod."

"We have a plan now." Sybil brushed Rory's hair back from his forehead with her fingers. "There's nothing more ye can do tonight. Try to save your worries for tomorrow."

When Rory turned and their gazes locked, the raw need in his eyes made her breath catch. Men had wanted her before, but not like this. The strength of his hunger was a bit frightening—and all the more thrilling for it.

Before she could make her mind work and figure out what she wanted to do about it, he broke their gaze and stood.

"'Tis been a long day," he said. "Ye should get your rest."

"What about you?"

"I'm not ready to sleep."

"I don't want to sleep yet either," she said, and clasped his hand before he could walk away.

Sybil had made up her mind. She was not going to argue with herself about it anymore. Rory needed her, and tonight she wanted to be whatever he needed.

"Lie with me," she said.

"I don't know if I can sleep beside ye tonight and not touch ye like I want to," he said in a strained voice. "I need ye too much."

"I know that," she said, and flipped back the blanket for him to lie down.

His eyes flared with heat, but he remained standing over her, his stance rigid. "You're certain that ye want this? That ye want me?"

Her life was in turmoil, changing every day. She and Rory could have died today, and they could die tomorrow. No matter what the future held, she wanted this night with him.

The men at court had seen her as a prize to be won, a beauty with a large dowry and powerful family. But Rory saw her for who she really was, stripped of her dowry and jewels and position. He wanted *her*.

Even if it was only for one night, she wanted to be made love to by a man she trusted, a man who understood her. Better that she have that once in her life than not at all.

"Aye," she said. "I'm certain."

Rory dropped to his knees. Gripping his fingers in her hair, he kissed her fiercely. His mouth was hot and demanding, and his tongue thrust into her mouth in a sensual assault that sent her reeling. He kissed her with unchecked passion, holding nothing back.

Though she had not known it before, this was precisely what she wanted from him. Nay, what she needed. Throwing all caution to the wind, she wound her arms around his neck and pulled him down onto the blanket.

With a need on the edge of desperation, they tugged at each other's clothes until, at last, they were skin to skin. The sensation of his hard-muscled body against hers made her moan into his mouth. When he pressed his full erection against her, she had to break their kiss to gasp for breath.

She felt drunk on the pleasure of touching and being touched. She ran her hands over his rock-hard body, wanting to claim every inch of him for her own. Never had she expected it would feel this good.

He held on to her, fingers bruising, as if she was his anchor in their storm of passion. All the while, he covered her face and throat with endless kisses that stole away every sense of caution and made her forget where she was and even who she was.

In the far recesses of her mind, a fleeting thought tried to catch her attention. Something important she was supposed to remember. She struggled to recall what it was while his lips and tongue moved down between her breasts.

Lord above! The moist heat of his mouth was on her breast, pulling sensations all the way from her toes and emptying every thought from her head, except that she never wanted him to stop.

***

All day, Rory's grief had been a blade that cut deep and flailed him by turns with sorrow, guilt, and rage. His emotions were raw, and his need for Sybil was so intense it shook him to his soul. He wanted to lose himself in the smell of her skin, the taste of her lips, the sensation of her breasts pressed against his chest, and the silky weight of her midnight hair cascading over his arm.

Praise God Sybil had finally made up her mind to have him.

He ought to tell her how beautiful she was, that he had wanted her from the start, that he would cherish her forever. But he could not speak, could not begin to find words for the feelings raging inside him.

He splayed his fingers in her hair and covered her face with kisses—her cheeks, her eyelids, the side of her mouth, the sensitive place below her ear.

"A chisle mo chroí," *pulse of my heart,* he murmured against her skin as he ran his lips along the side of her throat.

He always knew she would be passionate in bed, but she was everything he had hoped for and more. When he suckled her breasts, her sighs and moans drove him to near madness. He squeezed his eyes shut and told himself he must slow down and be gentle this first time. But he wanted her so *much.*

"Oh, lass," he gasped as she ran her hand up his cock, "you'll kill me for certain."

Sybil's bold sensuality, like oil on an already burning fire, sent his desire into shooting flames. His bride was making it damned difficult to remember she was a virgin.

***

Sybil sensed she had driven him to the edge of control and felt a thrill of feminine power. She wanted him over the edge, to feel his passion full force and without restraint. Her own desire grew with his as she stroked her hand up and down his engorged shaft, and she swallowed when she felt the wetness on the tip.

He groaned and removed her hand, then pulled her hard against him. They rolled together, their mouths devouring each other while her hair fell in a curtain around them. Sybil was mindless, lost in deep, wet kisses, as they rolled again.

When he broke the kiss, she was on her back, and his hand was between her legs.

She was only vaguely aware of calling out to the saints and the fairies as he worked his magic with his fingers. When he began circling and flicking her nipple with his tongue as well, she thought she would go blind with pleasure.

"*Mo rùin,*" he said in a harsh whisper, "you're so hot and wet."

Then he suckled her breast, and it was too much. The tension in her body grew until she felt as if she would shatter. She bit his shoulder.

"Please!" she said, not even knowing what she wanted.

In one smooth motion, he covered her with his body. Her breath caught when she felt his shaft press between her legs. The sensation was so intense it was almost painful. And yet she wanted more.

She wrapped her arms and legs around him, needing him closer still.

"Oh, God," he said in gasps between hot, wet kisses. "I'll die if I can't have ye."

He gripped her hip, kneading, demanding, while he thrust his tongue into her mouth with a rhythm her body understood. She sank her nails into his shoulders as she kissed him back with the same fierce need.

"Are ye ready?" he asked in ragged whisper.

"Aye." Whatever he wanted, she wanted too. And she wanted it *now*.

"There's no turning back if we do this." His short, harsh breaths were warm on her face as he paused to look into her eyes. "Ye want this?"

"Aye, more than anything!" she said. "*Please*, Rory."

He made a strangled, animal-like sound and kissed her in earnest again. Through the desire fogging her mind, that niggling thought tried to surface again, but it was beyond her reach.

"Oh!" she gasped as he eased the tip of his shaft inside her. All her senses, every fiber of her being, was focused on that part of him that was just inside her.

"I'll try to be gentle," he said. "I don't want to hurt ye."

The tension inside her was unbearable. Instinctively, she lifted her hips.

"Oh my!" she cried out as he slid inside her and pushed the air from her lungs. She pulled him down into a deep kiss.

He broke the kiss, rose up on his arms, and plunged into her to the hilt. His brief attempt at gentleness was gone, thank goodness. He was all hunger and need. And an edge of something else.

"That feels…so…so…ah…ah." She lost the ability to form words as he thrust into her again and again.

Powerful sensations built inside her, and she clung to him, needing more still from him. She felt like a frayed rope pulled to the point of breaking. Her release came in pulsing, frenzied rapture. The intensity of it battered her, making her cry out as he called her name and surged inside her.

Rory rolled onto his back, taking her with him. Their breathing seemed loud against the soft night sounds. She lay depleted and utterly amazed that something so wonderful could ever happen between two people.

When she had the strength to lift her arm, she ran her hand over his chest, exploring the hard muscles with her fingertips and enjoying the sensation of the coarse hair against her palm.

"Don't ye think ye have something to explain to me?" Rory said in a flat tone that startled her.

How could he sound so cold when their bodies had just been joined in such magical passion? What on earth had she done to offend him?

"Explain what?" She felt herself flush. "Was I too loud?"

"Ye know damned well that is no what I'm asking about."

She tried to think what she could have done to upset him, but her mind was still sluggish.

"How is it, my sweet bride," he said between his teeth, "that you're not a virgin?"

The realization struck her with the force of a blow. God help her, she had forgotten to pretend. It should have been so easy. There was no white linen that would fail to show bloodstains. All she had to do was make a show of crying out in pain at the right moment.

She had lost herself to such unexpected passion that she utterly forgot to make the pretense. When he thrust inside her, she cried out in ecstasy instead of pain.

"I'm sorry," was all she could muster.

"Sorry is not nearly enough," he said. "I need an explanation."

This was exactly why she should have pretended to be a virgin. The reason for her lack of virginity was not something she wished to discuss or remember. Once it was over, she'd put what happened firmly behind her and refused to let it ruin one more day of her life.

Besides, why should her lack of virginity matter so damned much?

"'Tis not as though you're a virgin," she snapped, which she knew was a mistake even before Rory rattled off a long string of

Gaelic curses that included slanderous statements about her, her family, and the entire Douglas clan.

He leaned over her, his face hard and angry, and demanded, "Who was he?"

How could he ruin what had just happened between them? She had felt so close to him when they made love, as if their very souls had touched and become one. And now he was ranting at her. And worse, he was making her remember things that she had vowed never to think of again.

"I won't do this!" She tried to hold her hands over her ears, but he held her down by her wrists, trapping her.

"Tell me," he said, leaning down until his face was an inch from hers.

He was frightening her now, and she was having none of that.

"I was forced," she spat out, and shoved him hard. "Now get off me!"

She rolled onto her side and held herself in a ball, overwhelmed both by Rory's anger and by the memories that she had succeeded in burying for so long.

"Oh, God, Sybil." Rory rested his hand on her shoulder and his voice was thick with emotion. "Ye were raped?"

Rape was what it had felt like, though her husband had the right to do what he did to her.

She stared into the embers of their dying campfire and remembered how much her grandfather's betrayal had hurt her. She had idolized him as only a young girl can, and he had always told her she was his favorite. When she learned he had arranged the marriage to that despicable man, she was so sure she could change his mind.

He turned a deaf ear to her pleas to release her, or at least to delay the marriage until she was older. The political and material benefits to the family outweighed the certain unhappiness it would bring her, and so the marriage went forward as planned. At least it was brief.

"I will kill him," Rory said.

"Ye can't," she said. "He's already dead."

"I wish I'd been there to protect ye." Rory ran his hand up and down her arm. "And failing that, I wish I'd been the one to kill him."

"What I wish," she said, "is that ye had taken me away before it happened."

"I should have been gentle with ye," he said in an anguished voice. "I meant to be, but I wanted ye so much. And then, when I realized ye weren't a virgin... Well, I didn't understand that I still needed to be careful with ye."

"Ye didn't hurt me," she said. "Not until afterward."

***

Rory was awash in guilt. He had been an unfeeling brute, and that is what she would remember of the night he made her his wife.

"I am sorry for being such an arse."

"Ye were angry," she said in a flat tone, still with her back to him. "It doesn't matter."

"I was angry," he said, "but that's no excuse."

He'd been angry because his pride was hurt when he discovered his bride had not saved herself for their marriage. And even more than his pride, it had torn him up inside to think of another man having Sybil before him.

Or ever.

"It does matter that I hurt you." He gently rolled her onto her back so that he could look down into her face as he said it. "It matters verra much to me."

"I want to believe that," Sybil whispered.

He knew how much she hated to show any vulnerability and that it cost her to let him see the tears glistening in her eyes. He kissed her forehead.

"I don't want to disappoint ye like the men in your family," he said. "I will keep ye safe, and I'll do my best to make ye happy."

"Ye have a good heart, Highlander," she said, and rested her palm against his cheek.

At her touch, desire surged through him, but he dared not hope that she would let him make love to her again tonight.

When she gave him a soft, lingering kiss on the lips, his heart swelled with an overwhelming tenderness. His bride was more forgiving than he deserved.

"Make love to me again," she whispered. "Give me a night to remember."

This time, he savored every moment, every touch, every sigh. He would never have enough of her.

Hours later, he held his sleeping wife in his arms as he watched the dawn break in pink and gold over the green hills. *His wife*. He liked the sound of that.

The question was finally settled. Sybil had made her choice, and there was no going back. Last night they had consummated their marriage—repeatedly. He drew in a deep breath and sighed. She was good and truly his now.

The road ahead would not be easy, and the loss of his brother lay heavy on his heart. But having won Sybil's trust and commitment, he felt as if he could accomplish all the tasks that lay before him.

CHAPTER 18

Sybil snuggled closer to Rory. All she wanted was to stay right here in his arms and pretend this would not end.

"How are ye this morning?" Rory asked, and kissed her hair.

"Good." She leaned back and grinned at him. "Verra good."

She could not remember ever feeling this happy and at peace—and she refused to spoil this moment by thinking of how brief their time as lovers might be.

"No regrets?" he asked.

"None." Their lovemaking had been a revelation, from the fiery passion to the moments of unbearable tenderness. She'd never dreamed that making love could be like it was with Rory. Somehow he made her feel precious and yet utterly free at the same time.

"If you'd kept me waiting any longer," Rory said, "it might have killed me."

They both laughed, but then he went quiet.

"What's wrong?" she asked.

"I can't say I'm sorry we didn't wait." He brushed the back of his fingers against her cheek. "But I do wish it could have been like ye wanted."

"Like I wanted? Don't let this go to your head, but I can't imagine it being any better." She felt her cheeks go warm.

"Ach, lass, we'll never get up today if ye say things like that to me."

A smile curved his lips as he leaned down to kiss her. By the saints, how could she resist him? And why would she ever want to?

Sometime later, they lay side by side staring up at the midmorning sky, their bodies glistening with sweat beneath the blanket despite the nip in the air. Rory clasped her hand where it rested over his heart.

"When I said I wished last night could have been like ye wanted," he said, "I meant I wish it had been in the best bedchamber in a MacKenzie castle after we said vows before my clansmen and celebrated our marriage with a grand feast, music, and dancing."

"What?" Sybil sat up, clutching the blanket to her chest.

"Though we're already husband and wife," Rory said with an earnest expression, "I promise we'll have a marriage celebration with a fine gown for ye to wear and all the rest of it."

"But I'm not your wife." She was so startled that she blurted out the words.

"After what we've done, ye most assuredly are." A warrior's glare replaced the warmth that had been in Rory's eyes the moment before.

"But I never agreed to marry ye." She shook her head. "We said no vows."

"A marriage contract plus consummation," Rory said between clenched teeth, "makes a binding marriage."

She'd forgotten about that damned contract. What had she gotten herself into? The only way she could persuade Rory they were not married was to tell him that they had no contract in the first place.

"As for agreeing to it," Rory said as he threw the blanket off, "I believe I heard ye say *aye* more than once on our wedding night."

Sybil knew she ought to tell him the truth now, that delaying might even make it worse. Yet she simply could not bring herself to do it. Rory's stormy expression was not what held her back, though that did not help. After all they had been through and all he'd done for her, how could she tell him the contract was nothing but a jest her brothers had played on him? How could she hurt his pride by saying he had traveled hundreds of miles and risked his life to rescue a woman to whom he owed no obligation whatsoever?

Nay, she could not. Especially now, when he was grieving for his brother and carried the future of his clan on his shoulders. She must find another way out of this.

"Now that you're to be chieftain, we both know ye need a wife who'll bring the support of a strong Highland clan with her," she said. "I assumed ye would want us to destroy the contract now."

"'Tis too late for that now," he growled.

"Nay, 'tis not." Sybil rested her hand lightly on his arm. "No one else knows about the contract."

He should be relieved that she was offering him an escape from a poor marriage. Instead, he looked as if she had slapped him.

"Say ye don't think so little of me." Rory searched her face. "I'd never deceive and take advantage of ye like that."

Tears welled in her eyes because he was so damned honorable. He really did need to be more pragmatic if he was to survive as head of his clan.

"Ye offered to destroy the contract if that's what I wished," she said. "Why should I not do the same for you?"

"I offered to destroy it *before* we consummated the marriage," he said. "Like it or not, we're wed now."

"We gave in to lust." Sybil fixed her gaze on the storm clouds on the horizon because she could not bear to look at him while she spoke of what happened between them as so much less than it was. "Your clan should not suffer for our weakness."

"You and I know the truth. We are husband and wife, and I'll not deny it," Rory said. "What kind of chieftain will I make if I'm not a man of my word? I'd be no better than Hector."

Rory meant what he said now, but Sybil knew how these things went. His advisors would pressure him to make a useful alliance, and his ambitions for his clan and for himself would eventually lead him to change his mind. If he did not deny the marriage outright, then he would employ the Highland custom of setting her aside to make a more advantageous match.

This was precisely what he ought to do. And what she wanted him to do. For heaven's sake, the last thing she wished for herself was to be trapped in marriage and under a man's thumb forever.

So why did the thought of Rory taking another woman for his wife make her feel miserable and murderous?

***

We gave in to lust. Is that all Sybil thought it was?

Their lovemaking had changed everything. The moment their bodies were joined, they became legally bound as man and wife. But it was more than that. When he was inside her, Rory felt as if their very hearts and souls were bound together.

Each time he thought he understood Sybil, she confused him again.

It pained him that she had not trusted him enough to tell him she was raped. How could she believe he would blame her for that? She was accustomed to men who lied to get what they wanted and then deserted her when it served their interests, but she should know him better by now. Had he not claimed her after she lost everything?

She had been quick to forgive him for his foolish anger after their first time, and then she gave herself to him with such abandon that he believed he had finally gained her trust. Their lovemaking was nothing short of magical, a melding of two into one. Or so it had felt to him. And yet she believed he would deny what they'd done, deny that he'd made her his wife.

She had been raised in the midst of ruthless royal politics, and she was right that a different wife could bring him an alliance he desperately needed. All the same, it troubled him that she had expected him to behave so poorly—and that she had been willing to bed him regardless.

"We'd best be going." He got up and started pulling on his clothes. "I'll see to Curan."

Before he could walk away, she stood, holding the blanket about her shoulders, and brought him to a halt with the touch of her fingertips against his chest. He sucked in his breath. Though her fingers barely grazed him, they burned into his skin like hot irons.

"I didn't mean to insult you," she said, looking at him with her fathomless violet eyes, "or to suggest last night did not mean as much to me as it did. I'll hold the memory of it in my heart until the day I die."

A moment ago she had dismissed what happened between them as mere lust. Was she now just telling him what she thought he wanted to hear? Ach, he didn't know what to think.

"If the last weeks and months have taught me anything, it's that we cannot know our future." She took his face between her hands. "No matter what happens, I want ye to know, Rory Ian MacKenzie, that I treasure what is between us."

The blanket slipped off her shoulder, revealing her creamy skin, a compelling reminder that she was naked beneath the blanket, which in turn sparked vivid memories from the night before. If Rory had any resistance left, it went up in smoke when Sybil wrapped her arms around his neck and kissed him with a fierceness that sent a fiery burst of need coursing through his veins.

She gave herself to him with such warmth and enthusiasm, both then and in the days that followed, that he was sorely tempted to trust her. He wanted to believe she was as happy as she seemed to be wed to him.

And yet he could not forget her startled denial when he first called her his wife.

CHAPTER 19

Rory studied his wife of three days as she cooked the hare he'd caught for their supper. Though she filled his nights with passion and his days with easy companionship, he kept watch for signs of her earlier reluctance to accept their marriage.

When Sybil looked up and caught his gaze on her, she gave him a bright smile that warmed him from the inside out.

"I had no notion that cooking could be so satisfying," she said. "Imagining how horrified my brother Archie would be to see me makes it all the more enjoyable."

The lass seemed determined to be cheerful and adapt to whatever life handed her—even being wedded to him. Despite her efforts, he suspected his clan would not accept his Lowlander wife easily, especially when she could not speak their language.

"'Tis time I began teaching ye Gaelic," he said.

"I already know it," she said, with a wicked gleam in her eye. "Tell me, do ye call all the lasses *mo rùin*?"

"Ye wee devil," he said. "Why did ye not tell me?"

"Ye never asked," she said.

This was yet another piece of information she had not trusted him with earlier, but he took it as a good sign that she shared it so readily now.

"I confess there are some gaps in my knowledge," she said. "Ye used a number of curses I'd never heard before that I'd like ye to teach me."

"Hmmph." He held out his bowl for her to serve him a slice of the hare. "How did ye come to learn Gaelic?"

"Our last king learned it to help him win the hearts of you Highlanders," she said as she sat down beside him. "Naturally, my grandfather thought it wise that we Douglas lasses learn it as well."

"Why?" Rory asked around a mouthful of rabbit. It was only slightly burned this time, and he was hungry after another long day of travel, so it tasted delicious.

"To impress the king." Sybil gave him a conspiratorial wink. "Grandfather had high hopes that one of us would bear a royal bastard."

Rory choked on his food. The notion of Sybil's innocence being used as bait for the king incensed him. "Did your father and mother not object to this?"

"Grandfather was chieftain for fifty years, and his orders were followed." Sybil shrugged. "Besides, the other noble families did the same with their daughters."

Rory was aware that many a Highland family was pleased when a daughter bore a chieftain's child, but somehow that seemed different to him.

"My mother was deeply unhappy about it," Sybil continued, "because her sister had an affair with the king when they were young, and it ended badly."

"How badly?"

"She was murdered," Sybil said.

"Murdered?" He nearly choked again.

"Powerful nobles in both the pro-French faction and the pro-English faction feared the young, lovesick king would marry my aunt instead of making a foreign alliance," she said. "We never found out which side did it."

"*O shluagh*," Rory said, calling on the faeries for help. "After your aunt was murdered, your family was willing to put you in the same position?"

"There was no risk of the king wedding one of us, as he was already married by then to Margaret Tudor," she said in a matter-of-fact tone and licked her fingers. "However, our blood tie to the king's first love was viewed as a great advantage in the competition to become his mistress."

"Luckily ye weren't old enough to be anyone's mistress before the king died."

"My grandfather thought I was old enough," she said. "But the Douglas's hopes were really on Margaret. She's the one with fair hair like our aunt's."

Jesu.

"Though we failed to entice the king," Sybil said, "the queen knew about my grandfather's plan. She holds it against me and my sisters."

"The queen was jealous, even after the king was dead and she married your brother?"

"Archie's infidelity only made it worse." Sybil took Rory's bowl from him and washed it as she discussed the queen of Scotland. "I'd wager she's persuaded herself that all of us slept with the king."

She faced other dangers with him, but at least she was safe from the queen.

Night had fallen while they ate their supper, and he was anxious to take his bride to bed. Sybil looked lovely in the glow of the firelight, and it seemed an awfully long time since they had made love that morning...

"I want to help ye fight your uncle Hector," she said, fixing him with a dead-serious look.

"Now that ye carry a dirk," he said, "you're ready to learn to swing a sword for my cause?"

She rolled her eyes. "Not that kind of help."

He twisted a strand of her curling black hair around his finger. "What is it ye want to do for me?"

Their gazes locked and heat sizzled between them, but then she got that determined expression on her face again. It was a very fetching look.

"For better or for ill, I've lived my entire life around men vying for power," she said. "Tell me about Hector, both his good and bad qualities."

At the mention of his uncle, Rory's mood turned dark. He tossed another stick onto the fire and watched it burn.

"Hector is much admired by the men of the clan as a strong warrior," he told her. "He's a bold and charismatic leader, the sort men are willing to follow into battle. He has won many victories for our clan over the years."

"And his bad side?"

"He's a conniving master of deception whose first concern is always himself," Rory said. "The MacDonalds are our most powerful enemy. Yet Hector provokes neighboring clans, like the Munros and the Grants, who should be allies, with unwarranted attacks for no reason except to enhance his reputation as a great warrior. He endangers the clan to make himself, as the great war leader, seem indispensable."

"If your uncle is so popular with your clansmen," she said, "it will be a challenge to take your place as chieftain without alienating half your clan."

"He's been leading the clan for years now, and the men think they know him," he said. "But they don't know him like I do. The fight between us will be bloody, but I'll not let him take my place and lead our clan to ruin."

Fury burned in his belly as he imagined breaking down the barred gate at Eilean Donan.

"Surely it would be better," Sybil said, tugging at his sleeve, "to find a way to gain the chieftainship without spilling the blood of your clansmen."

"I don't see a way to avoid it," he said. "Hector will not go easily."

"How strong is his support?"

"Strong, especially in the west, where he's fought the MacDonalds for twenty years, and up in Gairloch in the northwest, where he has lands in his own right." Rory took a deep breath. The task before him was daunting.

"If he is strong, then we'll have to be quick and clever," she said in cheerful tone. "A bit of trickery may be needed as well."

"Ach, ye sound like a Highlander," he said. "In Gaelic we say, *an té nach mbíonn láidir ní folláir dó bheith glic.*" *He who is not strong must be cunning.*

"A powerful ally would be helpful." She tapped her finger against her chin, then gave him a sideways glance. "I don't suppose ye have one of those?"

Rory heaved a sigh. "I may."

"That's good news," she said. "Who is it?"

"My mother's brother is the Fraser chieftain, Lord Lovat."

"I've seen him at court," she said.

"Lovat is a powerful man in his own right," Rory said. "He's also close to Lord Huntly, the crown's deputy in the north."

"Huntly, the so-called Cock of the North? Excellent!" she said. "But why don't ye look pleased? Such powerful allies will help your cause considerably."

"I know them too well," Rory said. "If Lovat and Huntly help me, they'll think they own me."

"Then they don't know ye very well, now do they?" Sybil said with a grin.

Rory cupped her cheek. Odd how this lass could make him feel that the obstacles that stood in his way were not so great and that he could overcome any challenge with her at his side.

"I must first go to Killin and gather support among my own clan," Rory said. "But then we'll pay a visit on Lord Lovat and ask for his help."

***

Rory's willingness to listen to her and take advice made Sybil flush with pleasure—until she realized the danger the visit to Lovat would put her in.

"What if Lord Lovat recognizes me?" Her hand went to her throat. "I can't go with ye."

"Ye needn't fear the queen any longer," Rory said. "The crown needs the MacKenzies to contain the MacDonalds. No matter what the queen might wish, the regent and King's Council will not risk offending the new MacKenzie chieftain by attempting to arrest my wife."

But she was not his wife, merely his lover. And how long would she be that once he was made chieftain?

"Ach, I can see that was poor reassurance," he said, brushing his thumb across her cheek, "after I've told ye the challenges I face to become chieftain."

"Ye will succeed." She was determined that he would.

"Whether I become chieftain or no, I'll never let anyone take ye away from me." Rory held her gaze as he spoke. "I would protect ye with my last breath."

Sybil blinked back tears. Why did Rory have to go and say that? She tried her best not to think too much about her own future. She wanted to make the most of the time she had with him, not ruin it with worries about what would happen when it ended.

But her Highlander was going to break her heart for certain.

CHAPTER 20

"How long before we reach Killin?" she asked, though what she really wanted to know was how much more time she would have with him.

"We should arrive tomorrow."

Sybil sighed and rested her head against Rory's back as they rode. How she would miss this! Her former friends at court would be amazed that she could tolerate, much less enjoy, spending every hour of so many days and nights with just one person. She surprised herself.

She had persuaded herself not to ruin the present by fretting about the future. Now the future was fast approaching, and she would pay the price.

"I've decided to stop at Beauly Priory on our way," Rory said. "I expect it's too soon, but I need to find out if my brother's body has been brought there yet."

She tightened her hold around his waist to comfort him. Most of the time he hid his grief, but she knew his brother's death weighed heavy on his heart.

In late afternoon they reached a large body of water.

"This is a firth, an inlet from the sea," Rory said. "Ye can sail from Beauly at one end of it to Inverness at the other, and from Inverness, ye can sail to anywhere in the world."

Not long after, she saw a large stone building next to a river that emptied into the Firth.

"That's Beauly Priory," Rory said. "It was sacked when I was a boy. My father funded the repairs, which were made under the direction of my uncle, who was the bishop at the time. They are both buried here."

It was growing dark by the time they dismounted at the priory gate and rang the bell. When a monk appeared, Sybil expected they would be turned away until morning. But Rory's family was an important benefactor of the priory, and his name and his wish to visit his father's tomb was sufficient to gain them entry.

Without a word, the monk led them across the grounds to a side entrance to the church. When the monk left them, Rory appeared in no hurry to go inside. She and Rory stood side by side, gazing up at the angled roof, which was designed to draw the eye upward to heaven. Sybil found the tranquil strength of the building soothing and hoped Rory did too.

Finally, Rory pushed open the heavy wooden door. Inside, the church was eerily empty, lit only by flickering candles and the remaining light of the day that filtered through the intricately designed stained glass window at the far end. Rory dipped his fingers in the font of holy water next to the door, made the sign of the cross, and waited while Sybil did the same.

Like all great churches, it was built in the shape of the cross. Rory took her hand and led her down the long nave and past the monk's choir to where the two parts of the cross met. On either side, an elaborately carved tomb was set into the wall at the entrance to the transepts.

Rory paused before the tomb on the right, which had an effigy of a churchman, and made the sign of the cross again. "My uncle the bishop lies here."

The tomb on the other side, at the entrance to the north transept, had a life-sized effigy of a warrior in armor. Rory did not need to tell her whose tomb it was. When Rory dropped to his knees and rested his forehead against the engraved border of the crypt, she stepped back to give him some privacy. He murmured prayers for his father, then raised his voice.

"Dear God, why did ye take my brother and leave me?" Rory clenched his fist against the tomb. "Brian had such goodness in him."

"That he did."

Startled by the voice behind her, Sybil whirled around to find a large figure in priest's robes. He carried a lantern, but his face was hidden by his hood.

"Goodness never ensured a long life, particularly here in the Highlands," the priest said, and rested his hand on Rory's shoulder. "But Brian is sure to have a place in heaven."

Rory stood and the two men embraced.

"We lost him before he had a chance to be the chieftain we hoped he could be," the priest said. "Now it falls to you, Rory."

"How did ye know I was here?" Rory asked.

"I've been keeping watch for ye," the priest said. "I thought you'd come here once ye heard of our brother's death."

"This is my younger brother, Alexander," Rory said, turning to Sybil. "The priest of Avoch."

Alexander pushed his hood back, revealing a young and handsome face. He gave her an appraisal that was most un-priestly and a warm smile. He struck her as unsuited to his calling, but a younger son often went to the church regardless.

"Come, let's go to the tavern in the village where we can talk," Alexander said.

They left Curan grazing outside the priory wall and walked along the river to the tiny village that consisted of a handful of cottages and the tavern. Several small boats rested upside down along the bank.

The tavern had a dank, musky smell from the river and nearby firth. They sat in a dim corner, where they were served ale by the surly tavern keeper in cups that Sybil doubted were clean.

"Any more troubles with the bishop over your wife?" Rory asked once they were settled.

Sybil thought she must have heard wrong.

"No trouble at all, thanks to you," Alexander said, raising his cup.

"Ye have a wife?" Sybil blurted out.

"Aye, and two pretty babes," he said. "My wife is near her time with our third."

Rory smiled when he saw the shock on her face. "We've too few priests in the Highlands to cast a good one aside for a wee infraction."

A wee infraction? And they wondered why Lowlanders called them heathens? Sybil quit worrying about the cleanliness of the cup and took a big gulp of her ale.

"God wouldn't be so unreasonable as to expect a Highlander to be celibate," Alex said, and jabbed his elbow into his brother's side. "Especially a MacKenzie, aye?"

One of Sybil's uncles was a bishop and another an abbot, and they both had mistresses. She supposed having a wife was no worse and certainly more honest.

"Ach, the new bishop is a sour man," Alex said. "He fails to see that women are God's gift to men."

"He says lasses are the devil's tool," Rory said, giving Sybil a wink.

"He threatened to have me defrocked if I didn't put my wife and our two wee babes out." Alex put his hand on Rory's shoulder. "Until my brother here persuaded him to turn a blind eye to my marriage."

"I did nothing," Rory said. "I simply accompanied ye when ye went to discuss the matter with him."

"My big brother has quite a reputation as a warrior," Alex said. "If ye don't know it, he can look rather fierce when he puts his mind to it."

"I've seen that look," Sybil said.

"I tell ye, he frightened the piss out of my bishop," Alex said.

"I believe the sword showing beneath your robes caught the bishop's notice as well," Rory said.

Sybil downed the rest of her ale while the two men had a laugh reliving how they had terrorized the bishop.

"We must speak of serious matters now." Rory spoke in a low voice and motioned for Alex to lean closer. "Even here, Hector may have spies."

Sybil realized now that the backslapping and laughs had been for the benefit of the few other men in the tavern, who by now had drifted back to their own conversations. Alex listened intently while Rory told him what happened at Eilean Donan and what Malcolm had shared about Brian.

"The news of our brother's death reached me through church channels just two days ago," Alex said. "I'm told that the men carrying his body were injured and had to stop at a monastery to recuperate."

"Malcolm said Brian was headed to Killin before he left for Edinburgh," Rory said. "He was looking for me."

"He didn't stop to see me," Alex said, shaking his head. "And I haven't spoken with Catriona in a few weeks."

"We're on our way to Killin now," Rory said. "Hopefully Catriona knows what he was so desperate to tell me."

"I expect Brian just wanted to make peace with ye," Alex said. "He always hated to have ye cross with him."

"I regret how often that was." Rory pressed his lips together. "There had to be more to it than that for him to ride the length and breadth of MacKenzie lands looking for me."

"His reason for traveling to Edinburgh is equally mysterious," Alex said.

"Something has been nagging at me," Sybil said. "We're told that Laird Buchanan's party met your brother's party on the road near Falkirk, a place your brother was unlikely to be."

"Go on," Rory said when she hesitated.

"Well, Buchanan should not have been there either," she said. "There was a warrant for his arrest too, and yet he also left the safety of his clan's lands. Does that not strike you as an odd coincidence?"

"I've been troubled by that as well," Rory said, nodding. "How did Buchanan happen to take that risk and be in that place at the one and only time that Brian was there?"

"What do ye suspect?" Alex asked.

"Someone knew where Brian was going and arranged it with Buchanan," Rory said.

"Who would do that?" Alex said.

"Who would benefit by having your brother out of the way?" Sybil raised an eyebrow. "If Hector feared Brian would no longer give him a free hand…"

"I dislike Hector, but he shares our blood." Alex turned to Rory. "Ye truly believe Hector wanted our brother murdered?"

"I doubt he expected Brian to fight and get killed in the scuffle," Rory said. "More likely, the plan was for Brian to be captured and imprisoned in Edinburgh Castle for years."

"Then Hector could continue ruling in Brian's name," Alex said.

"Either way, Brian murdered or in prison, the outcome would be the same for Hector," Rory said. "Or so he thought."

"The clan needs you to be chieftain," Alex said, clamping a hand on Rory's shoulder. "Ye know I'll do whatever ye ask."

"Malcolm and some of the other men who were on our father's council are meeting me at Killin day after tomorrow to make our plan," Rory said. "Join us if ye can."

***

Sybil struggled to keep her spirits up as they rode the final miles to Killin. It was all happening too quickly. Rory's fight for control of the clan would leave little time for her. And once he became chieftain, she could count the days until she lost him forever.

"Ye never finished telling me how your mother came to marry your father when he already had a wife." Sybil hoped the tale from the past would take her mind off the future.

"It all began with a wedding," Rory said. "The Gordon chief, who was grandfather to the current Earl of Huntly, invited the MacKenzie and Fraser chieftains to celebrate the marriage of his daughter, and my mother accompanied her father, Lord Lovat, to the gathering."

Sybil imagined the couple sneaking off for quiet talks and stolen kisses.

"By all accounts, my parents didn't speak a word at the gathering. The Frasers and the MacKenzies were not on friendly terms at the time," Rory said. "But from the moment someone pointed out the lively Fraser lass, my father made up his mind to have her."

"Just like that?" Sybil said with a laugh. "But he was married. What could he do?"

"As soon as he returned home, he sent his MacDonald wife away."

"That seems harsh," Sybil said.

"She was as anxious to leave as he was for her to go," Rory said. "Of course, sending her back was a grave insult to the MacDonalds, but that did not sway my father."

"How long did he wait before courting your mother?"

"He set off at once with two hundred warriors to lay siege to Lord Lovat's castle."

"Good heavens!" Sybil said.

"My grandfather Lovat stood on the castle wall and demanded to know what in the hell my father intended by this unprovoked threat of force."

"What did he answer?"

"My father said he was in need of a wife, as he had just rid himself of one that did not suit him." Rory chuckled. "He demanded that Lovat give him his daughter in marriage—and do so at once. In return, he promised a bond of friendship between their clans. But if

Lovat refused, he swore he would be an enemy to Lovat and the Fraser clan to his dying day."

"By the saints!" Sybil's hand went to her chest. "What did Lovat do?"

"Now, we Highlanders appreciate a bold gesture," Rory said. "Lovat was verra fond of his daughter, but he could see that this brash young MacKenzie chieftain would make either a strong ally or a dangerous enemy."

"So he simply handed over his daughter?" She was disgusted, but not surprised.

"Lovat was inclined toward the match, but he said he'd let his daughter decide," Rory said. "He sent for her to join him on the wall."

"Since they did marry, I assume she said aye to protect her clan from attack."

"That's not the reason she gave me."

"What persuaded her, then, his fine looks?" She was only half joking. If Rory took after his father, she could understand.

"Perhaps that was part of it," Rory said with a chuckle. "But as she told the tale to me, it was what my father said to her when she stood on the wall."

Sybil gripped his elbow. "Did he threaten her?"

"He told her she had stolen his heart and that he would love her until the end of his days."

Sybil could not help but sigh. What woman would not be tempted to run off with the handsome young chieftain who would make that declaration in front of the warriors of two clans? But such bold gestures and extravagant promises bespoke of a passion that could leave as quickly as it came. Most likely he broke the poor lass's heart and took a mistress within a year.

"'Tis a lovely story," Sybil said. "Did she come to regret going with him?"

"My parents' marriage was a happy one," Rory said, but the jocular tone he used while telling the story was gone. "My mother drowned during a storm a month after my father died. Some say she slipped into the river. Others say she could not bear to live without him."

***

Rory urged Curan into a canter as they followed the familiar path home. He was anxious to finally reach Killin and speak with his sister. Yet when he heard the sound of the waterfall, he slowed Curan to a walk and turned toward the river, as he always did.

The roar of the falls grew louder as they rode on the trail through the thick brush to the river. Rory brought Curan to a halt beside the large, flat rock ledge overlooking the top of the falls, where he always stopped, and watched the rushing river tumble over the falls to the jutting black rocks twenty feet below.

"What is this place?" Sybil asked.

"Rogie Falls," he said. "This is where my mother died."

The rock ledge was slick from spray even in good weather, and it had been storming all that day. Rory imagined the trail slippery with mud, the driving rain bouncing off the rocks, and the wind pummeling his mother's cloak against her legs. It would have been easy for her to lose her footing.

And yet Rory could never quite accept that his mother had fallen. She was familiar with the path and the danger of the falls. He could think of only one reason for her to come here in the midst of a storm. Absorbed in her own pain over the loss of her husband, she chose to end her life and leave her children orphans.

At fifteen, Rory had been nearly a man, but he found it hard to forgive her for abandoning his younger brother and sister. Losing her had been hard, especially after their father's death. At least Alex and Catriona did not know what she had done. Her parting gift to them was to make her death look like an accident.

"You and your mother were close?" Sybil asked.

"I thought we were." He thought he knew her, but he never would have guessed she would abandon them.

Rory felt someone watching them and snapped his gaze across the river. The brush was too thick to see if anyone was hiding there, but it probably was his imagination. Ever since his mother's death, the falls made him feel uneasy, as if there was a hidden evil here.

"What's wrong?" Sybil asked.

"Nothing," he said, and turned Curan around. But he did not relax until the sound of the falls faded behind them.

CHAPTER 21

Two miles after the falls, Rory's spirits lifted when they crested a hill and he saw the familiar two-story stone house in the midst of green, fertile fields. He dismounted and lifted Sybil down to stand beside him.

"That's Killin," he said, pointing. "It was my father's wedding gift to my mother. She always loved it, and they came here often when they wanted to get away from the castle."

"I can see why." Sybil tucked her hand into the crook of his arm and leaned her head against his shoulder. "'Tis so peaceful here."

"My mother left it to me when she died," he said. "Though I'm not able to spend much time here, I consider it my home."

"Won't Castle Leod be your home now?"

If he succeeded in becoming chieftain it would.

"Perhaps I should grant Killin to my sister," he said. "Catriona likes a quiet life, and she has lived here since our mother moved out of Castle Leod after our father's death."

"That would be kind," Sybil said. "I'm sure it would have pleased your mother."

"Killin always reminds me of her." He kissed Sybil's hair. "I wish the two of ye could have met. She would have liked ye."

"No mother would be pleased to see her son make such a poor match," Sybil said with a laugh.

"If she had any qualms," he said, "the first grandchild would have won her over, for certain."

Sybil's hand went to her flat belly, then she looked up at him with wide eyes.

"Aye, ye could already carry our child." His heart swelled at the thought, and he leaned down to kiss the sweet spot below her ear. "If ye aren't with child soon, it will not be for lack of trying."

When they rode down the hill and he saw no one in the fields, his cheerful mood turned to unease. The farm was eerily quiet. No dog barked to warn the household of their coming, and no one moved about the yard and outbuildings.

"Wait here," he told Sybil when they reached the house and no one came out to greet them.

He dismounted and unsheathed his sword. Slowly, he opened the front door. No fire burned in the hearth, and the house was so still that his footsteps echoed as he crossed the floor.

Sweat broke out on his palms. Where was Catriona? He kept watch on the doorway to the kitchen and upstairs as he leaned down to touch the stone floor of the hearth. It was cold. Catriona had been gone for at least a couple of days.

Upstairs, he found open drawers and chests, as if someone had packed to leave in a hurry—or had come looking for something. Alarm rose in his throat, and he hurried back outside.

When Sybil saw him, she started to dismount, but he held up his hand.

"Stay put," he ordered. "I'm going to have a look around the back of the house and the outbuildings."

He heard movement and spun around brandishing his claymore. When a lad and a dog appeared around the corner of the cowshed, he took a deep breath to calm the battle fever pulsing through his body.

"Ewan Òg," Rory called to the boy.

"Good day to ye, Master Rory," the lad said. "Have ye brought mistress Catriona home?"

"Nay," Rory said. "Do ye know where she's gone?"

Ewan shook his head. "She said it was best we didn't know."

O shluagh, Rory silently called on the faeries for help. "When was this?"

"Before that big storm we had," Ewan said. "Thought I'd lost some of the sheep in it, but I found—"

"Catriona left on her own?" Rory pressed. "No one took her?"

"Aye."

"How long has she been gone?" Rory asked. "And don't tell me after the storm."

Ewan scrunched his face up. Apparently, calculating the passage of time was a difficult task for him, and Rory struggled to be patient.

"'Twas two days ago, right after we heard that the MacKenzie had been killed." The lad crossed himself. "She took off on her horse."

"Did she take any of the men with her?"

"Nay." Ewan shook his head. "She told us to take the cattle to the next farm and stay in the village, but I couldn't leave the sheep, now could I?"

Rory could strangle Catriona for going alone. He turned to glare at the horizon. Where in the hell was she? And why would she send the servants away?

His worry over his sister spilled over into anger when Sybil appeared beside him. "I told ye to stay put."

Sybil merely raised an eyebrow.

"Catriona left ye a message," Ewan said.

"A message?"

"She said that if ye came, I'm to tell ye not to worry, that she's gone somewhere safe." The lad scrunched his face up again with the effort to recite the message. "She'll come find ye at Castle Leod once she hears you've returned."

"*Somewhere safe*," Rory bit out. "What kind of message is that?"

"Ye did a fine job remembering all that," Sybil said to Ewan, then she took Rory's arm and started walking him back toward Curan. "Your sister has lived here most of her life, has she not?"

"Aye," he snapped.

"Then she would know where she would be safe," Sybil said. "Or would ye say she's prone to foolishness?"

"Not before this," he said. "She's always seemed a sensible lass. Wise beyond her years."

"Then try to have some faith in her judgment," Sybil said, patting his arm. "I doubt she's changed since ye last saw her."

"She's my responsibility," he said. "Brian is dead because I failed him. I *cannot* fail my sister as well."

"Ye didn't fail your brother."

"I did." He paused and took a deep breath. "I'm sorry to take my anger out on you."

"You're a good man to care so much for your sister," she said. "Not all brothers do."

"I wish I knew what made Catriona so afraid to be at Killin that she would send the servants away and flee," he said. "It was always safe here."

"Someone else came looking for her right after she left," Ewan piped up behind them.

Rory spun around to face him. "Who was it?"

"I didn't know him, so I stayed hidden behind the cowshed."

"That was wise." Rory rested his hand on the lad's shoulder. "Did ye get a look at him?"

"Aye. He was huge," Ewan said, rising on his toes and stretching his arm up. "And he was marked by the devil."

"Marked by the devil?" A wave of cold fear for his sister ran through Rory, but he kept his voice even. "Ye mean he was pockmarked?"

"Aye," Ewan said.

"That was Duncan of the Axe." Praise God Catriona was gone before he came. What was Hector's henchman searching for? "Has anyone else come?"

"I've kept watch on the house," Ewan said. "No one's come since him, except for you."

"I appreciate ye keeping watch, but I don't want ye here alone," Rory said, leaning down to look Ewan in the eye. "Take the sheep into the hills and stay there until the others return to the farm."

"Can we still stay here tonight?" Sybil asked. "I admit I was looking forward to sleeping in a real bed."

"Duncan did a thorough search, so I don't believe he'll come back." And Rory sure as hell was not going to be chased from his own home by one man.

Dusk, the shadowy time between day and night, had fallen. Rory scanned the fields in the valley and hills that surrounded the farm and saw nothing to worry him.

***

Whoosh. Whoosh.

Rory held his shield up to protect himself from English arrows flying at him. The smell of smoke filled his nose, and he heard the crackle and snap of flames. Good God, the English had set the field on fire.

He was back in the Battle of Flodden, but through the fog of his dream something nagged at him. There had been no fire in the battle… Curan's frantic neighs pierced the air, and Rory bolted upright, wide awake to find the bedchamber filled with smoke.

"Sybil!" Rory shook her by the shoulders, but she would not wake up.

He pulled her to the floor where the smoke was not as thick. He reached for the basin of water and drying cloth on the side table and splashed water on her face.

"Is that fire?" she asked in a weak voice.

"Aye, we must get out quickly." Praise God she was awake. He soaked the cloth in the water and pressed it to her face. "Keep this over your mouth."

Sybil attempted to rise, but she was too groggy from the smoke. He pulled his boots on, slung his sword over his shoulder, and picked her up. When he opened the chamber door, the blast of heat knocked him backward.

As he lay sprawled on his back still holding Sybil, the thatched roof overhead exploded into a fireball, dropping flames to the wooden floor. He got to his feet again.

"We'll have to jump." The smoke was growing thicker by the moment, and the heat from the floor burned the soles of his feet.

Sybil was limp in his arms as he carried her to the window. He had no time to lose. Coughing against the smoke filling his lungs, he unhooked the shutters with one hand and rammed his shoulder against them. They did not budge. He rammed them again.

God damn it, the shutters were nailed shut from the outside. Someone was trying to burn them alive.

Fury blazed inside him brighter than the flames. Coughing and hacking and blinded by tears from the smoke, he kicked at the shutters again and again and again.

With a *crack*, they finally broke. Rory grabbed Sybil's cloak from the floor and wrapped it around her for what little protection that would offer from the fall. Holding her across his chest, he flung one leg over the windowsill. Flames shot up through the floor as he pivoted on the sill and brought his other leg through.

He hoped to hell whoever was trying to kill them was not waiting below.

O shluagh, it was a long drop. With the fire scorching his back, his instincts screamed *jump, jump!* He shifted Sybil to one arm so that he could hang from the window to ease their fall.

As he reached for the windowsill with his free hand, the fire burst through the chamber door with a force that sent him flying through the night sky in a spray of sparks.

CHAPTER 22

Sybil awoke falling into a night lit by fire.

"Oof!" She landed with a hard thump, her fall cushioned by Rory's body beneath her. Rory scrambled to his feet while she remained on the ground, coughing and hacking, trying to clear her burning lungs.

Through watering eyes, she saw him, backlit by the flames, standing between her and the darkness. He was naked except for his boots and brandishing his sword as if he expected demons from hell to emerge from the darkness. When none immediately appeared to challenge him, he dropped to one knee.

"We must move *now*," he said, his eyes darting back and forth between her and the darkness. "Can ye walk?"

"Aye," she said, though she felt woozy, her eyes were streaming, and she could not stop coughing.

All at once she understood that someone had intentionally set the house on fire and that they could still be in danger. When Rory lifted her to her feet and took her hand, she held on for dear life and ran.

He helped her over a stone fence, and they crouched behind it. The entire roof of the house was ablaze now, and flames were shooting out the upstairs windows. She wiped her eyes and held her cloak over her mouth to stifle the sound of her coughing.

Rory was still for a long time, his gaze sweeping the house and the field surrounding them. "He's gone."

"Are ye certain?" she whispered.

"Aye," Rory said. "If Duncan of the Axe was here, he would have attacked us the moment we hit the ground."

***

"You're the finest horse in all of Scotland," Rory said, rubbing Curan's nose after the horse trotted out of the darkness. "Ye saved us tonight."

Rory retrieved their saddle, rolled blankets, and extra oats for Curan from the barn, and they slept in the open field.

At least Sybil slept, showing more trust than Rory deserved. He lay awake, furious with himself for putting Sybil in danger. In his pride, he'd been confident he could protect her, but he had misjudged the risk. They had survived the fire only because Duncan had also made a misjudgment by not staying to make certain they died in the fire.

He pondered Duncan's lapse as he stared at the black sky. Most people assumed Duncan was dimwitted because of his size and reputation for brute force, but Hector's henchman was clever and excruciatingly thorough in the execution of his dark deeds.

Perhaps Duncan had searched elsewhere, still not found what he was looking for, and returned to torch the house on the chance it was hidden there. If he came in the night, he might not even have realized they were there.

Whether Duncan meant to murder them or not, the fire brought home to Rory that his pursuit of the chieftainship put Sybil in danger. The one thing she needed from him after what her brothers had done was to feel safe, and he'd failed her.

Dawn was just breaking when he saw the silhouettes of a dozen Highland warriors—and one priest—riding toward them. He kissed Sybil's brow to wake her.

"*Mo Leannain,*" *my sweetheart,* he said. "Malcolm and the others are here."

After some ribbing about his state of undress, one of the men lent him some extra clothes, and Rory told them about the fire.

"Is sleamhainn leac doras an taigh mhòir," the chief's house has a slippery doorstep, one of the older men said with a nod toward the smoldering house. "So long as Hector wants to take your place, ye must watch your back."

There was a general murmur of agreement.

They moved into the barn, leaving two men outside to keep watch. Though the hour was early, someone had brought whisky to facilitate the discussion.

"Tonight the fires will be lit on hilltops all across MacKenzie lands to call the clan to the gathering at Castle Leod," Malcolm said. "My sons have seen to that, and they'll arrive over the next few days with many clansmen to support you."

"Good," Rory said, nodding his thanks.

"The clan has a week to travel to the gathering to select the new chieftain," Malcolm continued. "If we're lucky, Hector won't learn of Brian's death until he sees the fires, but I expect he already knows."

"Then he's on his way to Castle Leod to make his claim for the chieftainship." Rory lifted his cup. "But I'll be there first. I'll not have him bar the damned gates to me as he did at Eilean Donan."

The men clanked their cups together and drank.

"I know I'll have my supporters, but our clansmen are accustomed to following Hector," Rory said. "He's led the clan in my brother's name for many years."

"And deceived them even longer," Alex said.

"Hector always saw ye as a threat," one of the other men said. "The clan knows your reputation as a warrior, but Hector made damned sure ye were never allowed to lead a battle or sit on the council."

The men contemplated their whisky in silence for a time.

"If ye want your clansmen to see ye as a chieftain," Sybil said, "then ye must look and act like one."

From the way all the men turned to look at her, it was apparent they had either forgotten she was there or never expected her to speak. She took a deep breath and forged ahead.

"Rory should ride through the gates on the last day accompanied by two hundred warriors," she said, spreading her arms, "and all the people shouting his name!"

Rory laughed, and the others stared at her as if she were daft. In the long, awkward silence that followed, she thought they all had dismissed her advice.

Malcolm pulled out his pipe and chewed on the stem.

"There's something to be said for the lass's plan," he said after a long pause. "Hector goes nowhere without a guard of twenty, as if he's been chieftain all along. He sleeps in the chieftain's bedchamber and sits in the chieftain's chair too."

"Hmmph," Rory grunted. "Sitting in the chieftain's chair doesn't make a man worthy to lead."

"If ye don't believe appearances matter, consider my bishop. Dress that fool in his white and gold robes and pointy hat, and people believe he's a font of wisdom," Alex said, then grinned and added, "Not that you're a fool."

"The point is," another man said, "'tis easy for folk to see Hector as chieftain because he's played the part for years. As the lass says, ye can help your cause by doing a bit of that yourself."

She could see that this went against the grain for Rory. She reached for his hand and squeezed it. "In time, your clansmen will come to admire ye for the qualities that will make ye the great chieftain I know you'll be," she told him. "But ye only have a week. Help them see the chieftain you'll become."

"Ach, you'll give my brother a swollen head," Alex said, but he gave her a nod when Rory was not looking.

"I can't risk Hector arriving at Castle Leod before me and barring the gates."

"I'll go and hold it for ye until ye come," Malcolm said. "I trained most of the senior men at the castle. They won't take orders from Hector now that he's not giving them in Brian's name."

The men spoke at length about the men of influence in the clan that Rory ought to meet with in the coming days. Then they stood as if ready to depart but made no move to go.

"What is it ye need to say?" Rory asked.

The men all shifted their gazes to Malcolm.

"Ye can't have the lass with ye when ye travel about to meet with the men," Malcolm said. "It isn't done."

"Ye know I like Sybil, but Malcolm is right," Alex put in. "She's not only a lass, but a Lowlander as well. They won't like it."

Sybil's heart raced as panic set in at the thought of being separated from Rory. She could not let him leave her behind.

"Once you're chieftain, ye can do what ye like," Malcolm said. "But now ye must persuade the clan that you're wiser than Hector. Bringing along your mistress—and a traitor's sister at that—is not likely to persuade them."

"Sybil is more than that," Rory said through clenched teeth.

"Of course she is," Alex, the peacemaker, said. "But you've already dragged her across most of Scotland, and in winter yet. For God's sake, let the poor lass rest at Lovat's for a few days."

"I intend to do that," Rory snapped, "but only because she'll be safer there."

Sybil waited until the men mounted their horses and left before voicing her objections.

"You're not leaving me anywhere," she said. "I'm staying with you."

"The course I am embarked upon is dangerous—it nearly killed ye last night." He cupped the back of her neck and rubbed his thumb along her jaw. "You'll be safe with Lovat behind the strong walls of Fraser Castle."

"I won't feel safe with anyone but you," she said, shaking her head violently. Even people she'd known her whole life who called themselves her friends refused to help her when she was desperate. She tried to calm herself, but her chest felt too tight to breathe.

"I don't know where my sister is or if she's safe," Rory said, his tone turning angry. "I'll not let something happen to you as well."

"I won't go." She couldn't. He was sure to forget her and never return. That's what her brothers had done. "You said you'd protect me with your last breath."

"Protecting you is what I'm doing," Rory said, closing the subject like a slamming door. "I'm not arguing about this. You'll stay at Lovat's out of harm's way until I can bring ye to Castle Leod."

CHAPTER 23

Sybil drew in a deep breath as Rory led her up the steps of Fraser Castle. It was her own damned fault they were here. She was the one who had advised Rory to seek Lovat's support and to delay going to Castle Leod until he gathered his supporters.

This was a fine time for a man to finally take her advice.

Rory's decision to leave her had caught her by surprise, and she'd shown unpardonable weakness by giving in to panic. She would not do that again.

He had not deceived her yet. As she had no choice, she decided to believe he would not abandon her here.

They were escorted into the castle's great hall, where they were greeted by Lord Lovat, a tall Highlander in his forties with fading red hair, sharp green eyes, and thin lips.

"This is Lady Sybil," Rory introduced her, omitting any mention of her family name or explanation for her presence.

Lovat examined her closely down his long, narrow nose as if trying to place her, but perhaps he was merely curious as to who she was to Rory. Then again, she may not have gotten all the cinders out of her hair.

"I have news that's best discussed in private," Rory said.

Without a word, Lovat turned and led them through a hidden doorway at the back of the hall that was disguised as a panel and into a windowless room. Lovat made frequent use of this private domain, judging by the glowing brazier, which thankfully kept it warmer than the hall, the lighted lamps, and the table on which rested several parchments as well as a flagon and cups.

Lovat gestured for them to sit, poured whisky for each of them, then took the third chair and fixed his gaze on Sybil.

"I know you." It sounded like an accusation. "You're Archibald Douglas's sister."

"She's a MacDonald now," Rory said. "Lady Sybil is my wife."

Lovat's face flushed in unbecoming blotches. Ignoring his uncle's obvious displeasure, Rory proceeded to tell him about his brother's death.

"Brian had no Fraser blood in him," Lovat said. "If he had, he wouldn't have let Hector of Gairloch use him like a puppet on a string."

Sybil refrained from mentioning that Brian had the blood of the MacDonalds, who were famed for their warriors and unrelenting rebellion.

"He would have made a good chieftain in time," Rory said. "Don't speak ill of him to me."

"Ye always had a soft spot for that MacDonald spawn," Lovat said.

When Rory looked as if he wanted to punch Lovat, Sybil gave his arm a gentle squeeze to remind him this would not help his cause.

Rory told Lovat what happened at Eilean Donan.

"*Guidh mallachd air.*" *A curse on him.* Lovat downed his drink and pointed a finger at Rory. "That Hector is no fool. He always knew you were the real threat to his power."

"He's sure to challenge me for the chieftainship," Rory said.

"You have the better claim, as both Brian's heir and as your father's eldest living son," Lovat said, "while Hector's claim goes back to your grandfather."

"Hector has chieftain's blood," Rory said. "That's all that's required if the clan wants him."

"By Highland custom that is true, but the crown will only recognize you as the heir under the king's law," Lovat said, lifting his cup to Rory. "The MacKenzies would be fools to choose a man the crown won't recognize. Your clan has gained half its territory from royal grants of lands forfeited by the MacDonalds and other rebels. There will be no such grants to a chief the crown does not recognize."

"You and I know the crown's recognition is important, but it will not weigh heavily on the minds of most of my clansmen," Rory said. "What will matter is whether our powerful neighboring clan, the Frasers, will be a strong ally if I am chieftain."

"Your father should have named ye heir in the first place, rather than his son by the MacDonald woman," Lovat said. "You're my only sister's son. Of course I will support ye."

***

Sybil tossed and turned, alone in the big bed, waiting for Rory. How quickly she had become accustomed to going to sleep with his arms about her. She wrapped one of the blankets around her shoulders and went to look for him.

On her way down the circular stairwell, she saw a thin line of lamplight beneath the door to the chamber below theirs. Sybil started to tiptoe past when she heard the low rumble of Rory's voice and the high-pitched tones of Lovat's through the door.

Since they were having this conversation in Lovat's chamber rather than in the hall, she assumed they did not want to be overheard. She had been taught by her family that this was precisely the kind of conversation that was the most fruitful to listen to. On the other hand, she wanted to believe Rory would tell her anything they discussed of importance, and he surely would be offended if he knew she'd eavesdropped on his private talk with his uncle.

With a sigh, she turned to go back up the stairs—but then she heard her name. Lovat spat it out as if it was spoiled food. No woman could be expected to walk away after hearing that. She put her ear to the door.

"Lady Sybil is a beauty to be sure," Lovat said in his nasal voice, "but she's a Douglas, for God's sake."

"Aye," Rory said, "that she is."

"No matter how high and mighty her brother was," Lovat continued, "he's in exile now, and her family is branded as traitors."

"They are," Rory said in the same calm tone, which seemed to agitate his uncle further.

"Ye couldn't have made a more unfavorable match if ye tried," Lovat said. "Why not just bring a lass from an Edinburgh whorehouse home to be your wife?"

A chair scraped against the floor. A moment later, Sybil jumped as something thudded against the wall. Desperate to see what was going on inside the room, she pressed her face to the crack and peered through it with one eye.

God have mercy, Rory had his uncle by the throat against the wall.

"Sybil is my wife," Rory said. "I'll not hear ye speak another ill word about her."

"I didn't mean to insult her, for she is certainly charming and well bred," Lovat said.

With a start, she realized the two men were crossing the room. She feared she'd be caught before she could run up the stairs, but then they settled back into their chairs.

"However, there's truth in the old saying that a man's best fortune, or his worst, is his wife," Lovat continued. "A Lowland lass from a disgraced and powerless family is of no value at all."

Lovat was changing tack but not conceding. And Sybil had to agree with him. A different wife would better serve Rory's ambition to be chieftain.

"Now there you're wrong," Rory said. "She's of great value to me."

"If ye want my help, you'll listen to my advice," Lovat said. "Set her aside and take a wife whose clan will be of use to us against Hector."

"I'll listen to your advice on other matters," Rory said, "but I'll not tolerate your interference regarding my choice of wife."

"Ach, you're as stubborn as your sainted mother," Lovat said. "Do ye want to be chief of the great MacKenzie clan or no?"

"Not without her," Rory said.

"Have ye lost your wits?" Lovat said.

"I know ye don't understand this, but Sybil is the wife I need," Rory said. "And I'll make a better chieftain with her at my side."

Sybil closed her eyes and leaned her forehead against the door, overwhelmed by what Rory said about her. Men had flattered her, professing boundless devotion, but she'd always known they were empty words, just part of the game played at court. At least at this moment, Rory meant what he said to his uncle. She would hold that to her heart.

At the same time, Lovat's persistence told her she was right about the strong opposition Rory would face if he claimed her as his wife. Even Alex and Malcolm, who liked her, had told Rory she was a detriment. His supporters and advisors would urge him to take a wife who would bring a useful alliance to the clan. They would make their case again and again.

In the end, Rory would do what a great chieftain ought to do. He would set his personal desires aside and do what best served his clan.

At least he *wanted* to keep her. And that meant everything.

***

Sybil felt at loose ends after Rory left, with nothing to do except wait and fret. Rather than spend time in the hall, where she would have to talk with Lord Lovat, she wheedled parchment and a quill from Lovat's scribe and returned to her guest chamber to write letters to her sisters.

Letters she would never send and they would never receive.

The knock on the door sometime later startled her. When she looked down, she saw that instead of writing letters, she had filled the parchment with drawings of Rory. There was one of him as she first saw him, looking dangerous and handsome as he stood over her with a scowl on his face and his claymore in his hand. In another, he was rubbing Curan's nose, and she could almost hear him murmuring in Gaelic.

Knock, knock, knock. "Lady Sybil?"

When she heard Lovat's voice, she quickly flipped the parchment over and called out, "Come in."

She stifled a scream when she glanced down and saw Rory in the nude on the back of the parchment. She managed to sit on it just before Lovat opened the door.

"I brought some excellent wine that I hope you'll share with me," he said, holding up a flagon. "You and I need to have a wee talk."

A talk that required excellent wine was unlikely to be pleasant. She smiled and gestured to the only other chair in the room. "Please sit down."

"I've witnessed a few marriages between Highland men and Lowland women in my time," Lovat said as he filled their cups and handed her one. "I've yet to see a happy one."

"Really?" Sybil knew when a message was being sent. She took a sip and watched him over the rim of her cup.

"I can tell that you're stronger than most of your kind," he said. "But our Highland ways are rougher than you're accustomed to."

"Rougher than court politics?" she said. "I find that hard to believe."

Lovat laughed. "Rough in a different way. This is a harsh land and prone to violence."

His insistence that she was not suited to this life she was forced to enter was getting under Sybil's skin, but she was not about to let him see it. She propped her feet up on the stool between them and crossed her ankles. "As ye say, I'm stronger than most of *my kind*."

"I don't mean to insult ye, but to offer my assistance."

She raised an eyebrow. "And what assistance would that be?"

"If ye should decide that ye wish to return home," he said, "come to me, and I'll see that ye get there safely."

"I fear you're under the false impression that I have someplace else to go." Sybil set her cup down carefully. "I assure you, I do not."

"Don't be modest," he said. "You and I both know that a lass with your looks and wits is never without choices."

His words brought back memories of how she had been primped to be shown to the king at thirteen, propositioned countless times at court, and offered Finnart's protection when she was nearly desperate enough to take it.

"I hope you're not suggesting," she said in light tone, "that I become some man's whore."

"Mistress is a more accurate word for it. And isn't that what ye are to Rory?" he said. "For ye cannot be his wife."

"Then why are ye so worried?" She stood. "I appreciate the wine, and our talk has been informative, but now ye should leave."

"Think of Rory," he said when his hand was on the latch. "He needs a marriage alliance with a clan that has warriors to fight for him. Defeating Hector will be no easy task. And then there are the MacDonalds."

"I want Rory to succeed," she said. "I'll help him in whatever way I can."

"Then we are in accord," Lovat said. "I, too, will do whatever he needs me to do."

***

Sybil blinked to clear the black spots that danced before her eyes as she crossed the castle courtyard. She hoped a walk in the fresh air would do her good, but she still felt sluggish and lightheaded.

"Good day to ye."

Her host's appearance at her side unnerved her because she had not seen him coming. What was wrong with her?

"I see you're taking advantage of the break in the rain for a wee stroll," Lovat said. "May I join ye?"

She could hardly object as it was his courtyard, and she did not truly mind. After his initial attempt failed, he seemed to have given up on persuading her to return to the Lowlands. In the days since, Lovat had shown her nothing but courtesy.

Her vision went black for a moment. When she started to stumble, Lovat caught her arm.

"Are ye well, my dear?" he asked. "I can see that waiting for word from Rory is taking a toll on ye."

That was true. She worried constantly and missed him even more. But worry and heartache did not generally cause dizzy spells, sweaty palms, and shortness of breath.

"Come inside," he said. "I'll send to the kitchen for something to eat and drink."

"I'm not hungry."

"You're wasting away," he said, patting her arm. "Rory will be disappointed if ye lose that fine figure of yours."

If she were not feeling so weak, she might have kicked him. Instead, she gritted her teeth and concentrated on putting one foot in front of the other as they walked back toward the keep.

"I appreciate your concern," she said when they reached the hall and he offered again to send for refreshments. "But I'll just lie down and have a rest."

"Certainly, my dear."

Sweat broke out on her brow as she climbed the stairs. The wheeled steps seemed to go on forever and made her head spin so badly she had to keep one hand on the curved wall to steady herself. Once she finally made it to her chamber, she collapsed on the bed.

This was so unlike her. She was never ill. A wave of loneliness swept over her, and she suddenly missed her mother very badly. She wrapped her hand around the black stone pendant her mother had given her. Each of her sisters had a similar one cut from the same stone, which their mother claimed had magical protective powers. Whether it did or not, holding the pendant made Sybil feel closer to her mother and sisters. She drifted off to sleep with it clutched in her hand.

When she awoke, she felt somewhat better. She had slept like the dead. She sat up and saw a tray of food and a flask of wine on the side table. Her host must have asked a servant to bring it while she was asleep.

Her throat was parched, and she was starving. Because she was still a bit lightheaded, she took care as she eased herself to the edge of the bed to reach the tray.

She was so thirsty. She poured herself a cup of the watered wine, but something made her stop. While she tried to bring forward the wisp of the dream she'd had before waking, her hand went to her pendant. She stroked the smooth stone with her finger.

The dream was more of a memory, something from her mother's tale about the stone. Her mother had seen a mysterious old woman appear out of the mist. Was that it? Nay. Suddenly it came to her.

Poison.

Her mother's three sisters were poisoned. While her mother walked along the river and met the old woman who gave her the black onyx, her sisters consumed poison with their breakfast. They were dead by nightfall.

Sybil sniffed the plum wine and the honeyed pear with cinnamon. Both had sweet, strong flavors that could disguise a poison. She thought Lovat had instructed his cook to use a heavy hand with the cinnamon, an expensive spice, to flaunt Lovat's wealth. After the first evening when she remarked on how delicious the spiced pears were, Lovat had instructed that a bowl of it be brought to her at every meal.

She had thought it a kindness. And he'd meant to kill her.

CHAPTER 24

Sybil had not spent years around court intrigues to let this threat go unanswered. Lovat had gotten the better of her once. He would not succeed again. Now that she knew his scheme, she would teach him a lesson.

But first, she needed sustenance. Fueled by pure determination, she made her way down to the kitchen in the undercroft. Like all castle kitchens, it was busy with servants chopping leeks, turning spits, and scrubbing pots. When she entered, all activity stopped.

"Go on with your work," she said with a smile. "I don't mean to interrupt, but I found I'm too famished to wait for supper."

"Ye needn't have come here yourself, m'lady. I'll send someone to your chamber with whatever ye wish." The man who spoke stood at the center of a long worktable with a brace of pheasants beside him and a large cleaver in his hand. He appeared to be in charge of the kitchen.

"No need to send it up when I'm already here," she said, and pulled up a stool. "Is that venison stew I smell? I'll have some of that, if ye please."

"But—"

"I'm a bit homesick, and that smells like the stew our cook used to make," she said, turning her charm on. "When I was a wee girl, I was always sneaking down into the kitchen. I loved the smells and the bustle, and the servants spoiled me with sweet buns and such."

A middle-aged woman in a kerchief took a bowl from the open shelf, spooned a hefty scoop of the stew into it from the huge steaming pot that hung over the fire, and set the bowl on the worktable in front of Sybil.

"There ye are, dear," the woman said with a kindly smile. "And here's a nice big cup of ale to wash it down."

"Thank ye kindly," Sybil said, and dug in.

There was no chance that a bowl from the common pot would have poison in it.

"'Tis nearly time for supper," the cook said between vicious whacks on a head of cabbage with his cleaver. "Ye don't want to eat too much and spoil your appetite."

"Don't fret about me," she said. "I expect to thoroughly enjoy the meal tonight."

***

Every person has a weakness, and Lovat's was his eldest son. Alain was a cocky young man about Sybil's age. Up until now, she had avoided him as much as she could because of his unseemly fascination with her breasts.

Tonight, however, she waited in the stairwell for him.

She was playing a dangerous game, but she had to take drastic measures or she would have to worry about being poisoned by Lovat or his surrogates for as long as she lived in the Highlands—or at least until Rory set her aside.

Of course, she could take all her meals in the kitchen and tell Rory when he arrived, but he would not handle the problem with the necessary pragmatism. At worst, he would run his blade through his uncle; at best, he would refuse to accept Lovat's support. She needed to handle this on her own. The tricky part was teaching Lovat that he threatened her at his peril without jeopardizing his support for Rory.

She stayed hidden until Alain entered the hall with two of his companions and timed her own entrance to cross paths with his. Alain bowed and remained bent over her hand with his gaze fixed on her chest until he finally remembered to straighten.

"We've had great success hunting this afternoon," he said.

"I'd love to hear all about it over supper," she said, taking his arm. "Will ye sit beside me tonight?"

She felt Lovat's disapproving glare as Alain guided her to the table and took the seat next to her.

"You're not sitting in your usual seat?" Lovat asked, and gestured to the seat next to him.

"Sorry, Father, but Lady Sybil is a damned sight prettier to look at than you."

When the rest at the table laughed, his father could not object without appearing surly. Sybil gave Lovat a level look to let him know she'd planned it.

"How are ye feeling tonight, my dear?" he asked.

"*Much* better, thank you." She gave him a bright, false smile to make him wonder what she was up to.

He watched her like a hawk. Good, her host was worried now.

The meal seemed interminable with Alain leaning over her and attempting to rub his thigh against hers. Sybil drank deeply from the cup of wine she shared with him, knowing it would be safe from whichever servant was dispensing the poison for Lovat. At the end of the meal, as she expected, the cook himself brought her a small bowl of honeyed pears that smelled strongly of cinnamon.

The cook failed to notice the silent signal Lovat attempted to give him before he set the bowl in front of her. When the cook looked up and saw Lovat shaking his head, he reached for the bowl.

But Sybil was quicker. She thrust her wine cup into his open hand. "More wine, please."

"M'lady, let me take those pears back to the kitchen," he said. "I apologize, but I see that the bowl was not properly cleaned. I'll have the lass who washed it punished severely."

"Nonsense," Sybil said, gripping the bowl with both hands. "'Tis perfectly fine."

When he tried to take it from her, Alain intervened.

"Leave it," he said in a sharp tone.

Sybil toyed with the dish of pears with her spoon as she chatted with Alain. When she glanced at Lovat, there was a sheen of sweat on his brow.

"Alain," she said, raising her voice just enough for Lovat to hear, "'tis rude of me to eat these delectable pears on my own. Let me give ye a taste."

She held her spoon out. If Alain did not take his gaze from her breasts, she just might give it to him instead of spilling it at the last moment. She had been eating the poison for three days now, so one spoonful would not hurt him much.

"I'd like a taste of more than your pears," Alain said, and slurped the spoonful up before she could pull it away.

"Don't!" his father shouted a moment too late.

"Please forgive my rude remark, Lady Sybil," Alain said, misunderstanding his father's outburst.

When Alain squeezed her thigh under the table, she was tempted to feed him the whole bowl of pears, but she satisfied herself by giving him a hard pinch.

"Behave yourself," she whispered, then raised her voice. "I hope you'll sit with me at every meal until Rory returns for me."

"Of course I will," Alain said.

Sybil turned to meet his father's gaze. "Would ye like some pears as well? Or have we all had enough?"

"Quite enough." Lovat dipped his head, conceding that she had bested him. "As the lady wishes, there shall be no more."

***

The next morning, Lovat gave her a trunk of his dead wife's gowns as a peace offering.

"I hope ye know I had no intention of doing ye permanent harm," he told her over more excellent wine. "Just a bit of encouragement to leave."

"At first I did think ye meant to murder me, but the poison ye chose was too weak," she said. "While I disagree with your method, I understand you were trying to protect Rory."

"Rory has a difficult path, and I did not believe a Lowland noblewoman would be up to the tasks ahead." He raised his cup to her. "I admit I was wrong."

"I want to protect him too, so ye needn't worry that I'll tell him about this…incident," she said. "That would cause a breach between ye and serve him ill."

"Of course," he said. "You're far too clever to make that mistake."

"I do understand that Rory will need a different wife." Despite herself, her bottom lip trembled. "I'll not stand in his way when the time comes."

"I see," Lovat said. "What is your plan, my dear?"

She gave him a weak smile. "I don't have one yet."

"Don't be in a hurry to leave," he said, patting her hand. He hesitated before he spoke again. "I've done something ye ought to know."

"Besides poisoning me?"

"The day ye arrived, I sent a message to Edinburgh, to your uncle the bishop," he said. "I told him where to find ye."

The message would fall on deaf ears. None of the men in her family had troubled themselves over her plight before she escaped. And they'd all known where to find her.

When Rory rode through the gates a short time later, Sybil's heart swelled with joy, and she ran across the courtyard to meet him. He appeared tired and weighed down by troubles until he saw her. He caught her in his arms and spun her around, laughing.

"Ye came back for me." *Thank God.* She closed her eyes and buried her face in his chest.

"I told ye I would," he said.

A part of her had doubted him, despite his promise and what she'd overheard him say to Lovat. Trust was so hard after how she was deserted by her brothers and all her friends.

"You're my wife," Rory said. "I'll always come back for ye."

She felt like a thief, knowing the loyalty he gave her was based on a lie. If Rory knew she was not truly his wife, would he still return?

The final leg of their journey was far different from the rest. Sybil had her own horse, and they were accompanied by Lovat and a large number of MacKenzie warriors, with more joining them with every mile. This was much like she used to travel in her old life, but she missed riding with just her and Rory on Curan.

"Your meetings with your clansmen must have gone well," she said, turning to look at the long line of MacKenzie warriors riding behind them.

"Aye, but I missed you," he said with a wink.

She felt a warm glow of happiness. After a time, she asked, "Did ye find your sister?"

"I asked everywhere I went." Rory's jaw tightened. "No one has seen or heard a word about her."

"She said she'd come to ye at Castle Leod, so I'm sure you'll see her soon." Sybil prayed it was true, but Rory did not look convinced. "What will happen when we get to the castle?"

"I'll make my claim," Rory said, "and Hector will either swear his loyalty to me or he'll challenge me."

"What happens if he challenges you?"

"Then the men of the clan will decide between us," Rory said. "The one not chosen must swear an oath of loyalty to the new chieftain, as will every man present, or be executed."

Executed? Sybil prayed even harder that Rory would prevail.

"If Hector does challenge me," Rory continued, "it could take several days for the men of the clan to come to agreement on who should be the new chieftain."

"And if they don't agree?"

"The clan will be divided," he said, "and there will be bloodshed until one of us concedes, dies, or emerges as the victor."

Sybil prayed that it would not come to that. Her heart beat fast as she got her first view of Castle Leod. The large L-shaped tower house was built of beautiful rose-tinged stone and set on a rise amidst gently rolling hills of fertile fields and forest. It looked deceptively peaceful.

As they approached, she watched the gates, remembering what happened at Eilean Donan, and willed them to open. Suddenly, a horn sounded, loud and clear. The gates opened, and the sound of cheering reached them.

When they rode into the castle, the courtyard was filled with well-wishers shouting Rory's name. Tears stung at the back of Sybil's eyes. This boisterous welcome was better than anything she had dared hope for.

Rory waved to the crowd and dismounted, leaving her on her horse. She felt the speculative stares of three hundred MacKenzies when he took her horse's reins and led her through the crowd to the keep, pausing every few feet to grip a man's arm in greeting or slap his back. She was sure he only meant to keep her from getting lost in the crush, but he was drawing more attention to her than he ought.

When they reached the keep, Rory lifted her down from the horse, took her hand, and climbed the steps. She paused at the entrance to the castle's great hall. The hall had no windows, and though it was lit by torches, candles, and the fire in the enormous stone hearth, crossing the threshold was like traveling from day into night.

Sybil felt as if she was crossing another kind of threshold, one she could not cross back once she stepped through.

The walls of the large, cavernous room were covered with shields, axes, and various other weapons and seemed to serve as warning to anyone challenging MacKenzie power. Antlers of impressive size hung in the few spaces that did not hold weapons. More intimidating than the weapons were the scores of brawny MacKenzie warriors.

The crowd parted for Rory, creating an opening down the length of the hall to a raised platform at the far end that held a single chair. Sybil knew without being told that it was the chieftain's chair. This was Rory's moment, a day that would be remembered in songs and stories that told the history of his clan.

"I'll wait here," she told him.

"Nay. I want ye at the front with Alex where he can watch over ye," he said, then turned to his brother, who had appeared out of nowhere. "Ye know what to do."

Rory strode ahead of them through the parted MacKenzies like Moses through the Red Sea and climbed onto the raised platform. Alex gave Sybil a wink as he took her arm, then proceeded to follow Rory, stopping just short of the raised platform.

From her vantage point at the front of the crowd, she was able to see the details of the chieftain's ornately carved chair, which appeared to be very old. The arms were carved wolves with bared teeth, and the legs were wild boar with wicked tusks. An image of a stag was carved on the chair's back. On the wall above the chair, mirroring the antlers on the stag in the carving, was the most massive set of antlers she had ever seen.

"The stag's head is the symbol of the MacKenzie chieftain," Alex said in her ear.

The crowd pressed against her and grew noisy.

She looked back over her shoulder at the sunlit doorway at the opposite end of the dusky hall. Though she did not understand why, she could not shake the premonition that her life was about to change again and that nothing would ever be the same.

CHAPTER 25

Where in the bloody hell was Hector?

Rory scanned the hall again. Hector would not give up this easily. If he came and lost, Hector would have had to swear his allegiance and this fight would be over. He must have decided the risk was too great. Though he may have conceded the battle today, that did not mean Hector had given up the war. This would not be settled until Hector swore his allegiance to Rory—or one of them was dead.

But today belonged to Rory.

He stood on the dais, mindful of the legacy of the MacKenzie chieftains who had come before him, particularly his grandfather, Alexander the Upright, and his father, Brian of the Battle. Now more than ever, his people needed a man of strength and fortitude to lead them.

Rory must be that man, and he would be for them.

He raised his arms, and the noise in the hall died.

"I am Rory Ian Fraser MacKenzie," he said in a loud voice. "I am the brother, son, and grandson of MacKenzie chieftains, and their rightful heir."

Several men shouted their approval.

"I hereby claim, as my right and duty," he said, letting the words that his father and grandfather had spoken before him ring out through the hall, "my place as chieftain of the great Clan MacKenzie!"

The hall burst into thunderous applause. The crowd shouted and clapped and stamped their feet until the floors and walls shook. Rory raised his hands for quiet again.

"As your new chieftain," Rory shouted, "I demand, as is our custom from ancient times, that every man of our clan swear his oath of loyalty to me."

Every head turned toward the back of the hall to see who Rory had chosen for the honor of being first to swear the oath. Malcolm, who had fought many a battle at his grandfather's right hand, stood in the open doorway holding a claymore sword across the flat of his palms. With slow, measured steps, Malcolm crossed the hall.

When he reached the dais, he knelt and held out the blade with outstretched arms. Rory recognized it at once from the carved stag on the hilt that was worn smooth from use. He had not expected to see this sword again.

"This sword belonged to two great chieftains, your grandfather and your father," Malcolm said, speaking in a booming voice that could be heard throughout the hall. "It rightfully belongs to you now."

The sword had disappeared when his father fell in battle. The story was that it was stolen by the enemy that day, but Malcolm must have saved the sword and hidden it away.

Rory swallowed against a surge of emotion as he accepted the blade.

"Rory Ian Fraser MacKenzie, the 9th of Kintail," Malcolm called out, giving him the MacKenzie chieftain's title, "I swear before our Lord Jesus Christ and every member of my clan that I shall give you my fealty and loyalty. My sword and my life are yours to command, and may God strike me dead should I ever break my oath to you."

One after another, the men knelt before him, kissed the blade, and pledged their loyalty. Rory felt the weight of responsibility heavy on his shoulders as he accepted each man's pledge. The fate of these good men and their families depended upon his ability to lead.

Deep in his soul, he sensed that this was his destiny, the role he'd always been meant to play. He prayed to God that he would do honor to the memory of the chieftains that came before him and become the chieftain his clan needed him to be in the troubled times ahead.

***

Sybil's heart swelled with pride on Rory's behalf, and she joined in the noisemaking, raising her hands and shouting with the best of them.

Though she understood the dangers and difficulties he faced, she knew in her heart that he would make a great chieftain. He certainly looked the part, strong and commanding, as he looked out over his people from the dais.

When Rory raised his arms, signaling for silence yet again, she looked around, wondering what came next in the ceremony. She hoped there would not be a lot of long speeches.

"We will bear the challenges ahead and fight the battles we must," Rory said, "but we will share our joys as well. As to the joys…"

Rory shed his solemn expression, and his eyes flashed with good humor. It was good to see him enjoying this momentous event.

"…I know you're all wondering about the lovely lass I brought home with me," Rory continued. "As my first act as your new chieftain, I invite you all to bear witness to our marriage vows on the morrow and celebrate with three days of feasting!"

Sybil was too stunned to move. When Rory held out his hand for her to join him, she gaped at him. What had he done? With Alex pushing her from behind, she stumbled forward. Rory clasped her hand, pulled her onto the dais, and held her against his side. She looked out at the sea of shocked faces. They could not be more surprised than she was herself.

Alex and a few others began clapping. After an uncomfortable delay, others joined in. Eventually, all the MacKenzies applauded, but with noticeably less enthusiasm than before. Beneath the cheers, she heard the low rumble of objection.

The new chieftain's first act was unpopular, and Sybil feared it was also unwise. Questions whirled through her head at lightning speed. Why had Rory acted so precipitously?

And what, in heaven's name, would she do now? Rory believed the ceremony was just a formality, but she knew it would be an end to the pretense, an end to their false marriage.

If she said those vows tomorrow, she would be good and truly wed.

***

Rory tucked Sybil's hand in his elbow and began moving through the crowd of his clansmen.

"Ye should have forewarned me," Sybil said beneath the noise of the hall.

"My clansmen must see you from the start as the chieftain's wife, not my mistress, or they'll never accord ye the proper respect."

He'd been counseled against the match too many times already, and he decided to act before most of his clansmen had time to form an opinion. Now they would have no choice but to accept Sybil, and at the wedding celebration every last one of them would swear to protect her.

"This group gathered by the hearth are all well respected men in the clan," he said as he guided her toward them. "Others will be guided by their opinion."

"You're Uilleam Mòr, are ye not?" she said with a winning smile before Rory could give her the first man's name. "I remember your name from when ye took your oath."

She gave each man a heavenly smile and flattered him by remembering his name, as if he were special, when in truth she apparently had memorized nearly every one.

"How do ye do it?" Rory whispered as they moved to another group.

"Douglas training," she said, humor lighting her eyes.

"I can see that it was not just your beauty that made ye a success at court."

"And I can see that your clansmen are verra pleased with their new chieftain," she said.

"Not all of them are pleased," he said. "None of the Gairloch MacKenzies came to swear their oath, and many others stayed home as well. They're waiting to see what Hector will do."

Whatever Hector's next move was, Rory had to be ready.

***

Sybil was exhausted from the strain of greeting so many strangers, all of whom were suspicious of her and prepared to judge her harshly. She would not care so much about winning them over, except that if she fell short it would reflect poorly on Rory.

"My face hurts from smiling so much," she whispered to Rory.

"You were wonderful," Rory said.

Late that evening, while everyone else was still celebrating, Rory brought her with him to meet with Malcolm, Alex, and Lovat in the chieftain's private room behind the hall, similar to the one at Frazer Castle.

"What news do ye have of Hector?" Rory asked as soon as they had settled around the small table.

"He arrived two days ago at Fairburn Castle," Malcolm said, "in plenty of time to answer the call to the gathering, if he were so inclined."

"Fairburn is Hector's home here in Eastern Ross," Rory explained to Sybil. "'Tis only a four-mile ride from here."

"I'd say we should drag him out of Fairburn, but it would be a bloody fight," Malcolm said. "He's brought at least a couple hundred MacKenzie warriors with him from the west and northwest who are loyal to him."

"Damn him," Rory said. "By bringing those men here, he's leaving us vulnerable to an attack by the MacDonalds."

"That's not all he's doing," Alex said. "He's also spreading rumors about your birth."

"Ach, those old tales about our parents' irregular marriage will gain him nothing," Rory said. "I have chieftain's blood, and that's what matters."

"The lies are not about your legitimacy." Alex cleared his throat. "Hector claims you're not our father's son at all."

Rory slammed his fist on the table. "What exactly is he suggesting? That our mother was unfaithful?"

"He and his supporters are telling anyone who will listen that our mother was already pregnant by another man when she wed our father."

"Hector goes too far this time," Lovat said. "I'll have his head for maligning my sister."

"Our father openly claimed me," Rory said. "He even had us legitimized through the church, or so I was told."

"He always meant to," Lovat said. "It was only in that last year when his health was failing that he finally did as I'd urged years before and sought a papal bull sanctioning his marriage to my sister Agnes and declaring the three of you as legitimate."

"If the church did legitimize us," Alex said, "no one could question whether Rory has chieftain's blood without questioning the authority of the Holy Father in Rome."

"I never saw the papal bull," Lovat said, "but I believe it arrived in that chaotic time around your father's death."

"That could be what Duncan of the Axe was looking for at Killin," Rory said. "If that's where Mother kept it, it's in cinders now."

"It could take years to get a copy from Rome. Such an important document, however, which is signed by the pope himself, would have passed through our old bishop's hands and been recorded," Alex said. "I'll look for a record of it at Fortrose Cathedral."

"Do that," Rory said with nod to his brother. "Has anyone seen or heard from Catriona?"

Sybil squeezed Rory's hand under the table. She knew how much it distressed him to not know his sister's whereabouts.

"I received a message yesterday," Alex said.

"And ye waited until now to tell me?" Rory said. "Where in the hell is she?"

Alex hesitated before answering. "The message was from the new Munro chieftain."

"Why would he send a message about Catriona?" Rory asked in a low, dangerous voice.

"Apparently he has her," Alex said.

"The bastard has taken our sister!" Rory shouted.

"The tone of his missive was courteous," Alex said, raising his hands in a gesture of caution. "He assures us that Catriona is safe and well in his care."

"If the Munros have laid a hand on her, I will murder every last one of them," Rory said. "There will not be one left to mourn their dead."

Rory got to his feet and started toward the door. Sybil and Alex exchanged a look and jumped to their feet as well.

"What do ye intend to do?" Sybil asked, and clasped his arm.

"I'm going to gather the men and collect my sister."

"This may not be what ye fear it is," Alex said. "The Munro chief neither asked for a ransom nor made a threat."

"He wants something," Rory said. "Why else would he take her?"

"We should wait and find out what it is before starting a bloody war we can ill afford," Malcolm said. "The Munros have a legitimate complaint against us. I suspect their chief merely wants assurance that the raids under Hector's direction will halt."

"No matter how just his complaints may be," Rory said, "he made a grave mistake taking Catriona to get what he wants."

Alex shot Sybil another look asking for help.

"From what Alex said, this Munro chief took pains to assure your family that your sister is safe," Sybil said. "Have ye considered that launching an attack could put her in danger?"

"Damn it to hell," Rory said under his breath, and clenched his jaw.

"Sybil is right. 'Tis safer for Catriona to wait for the Munro's next move," Alex said. "Besides that, the hall is filled with people expecting your wedding on the morrow."

The wedding. Dear Lord, she had almost forgotten.

***

"They're celebrating over at Castle Leod," Big Duncan reported.

Hector poured more whisky and imagined the clamor filling the hall as Rory stood on the dais beneath the great stag head as the warriors took turns kneeling before him to take their oath. That should have been him.

That would *be him one day soon.*

The plan had been for Buchanan to deliver Brian to the crown for imprisonment, leaving Hector to continue ruling in his nephew's name without the impediment of his nephew's annoying presence. When Hector learned of Brian's death, he realized he had been thinking too small. He was meant for a greater fate.

Wielding power through another had run its course. It was his time now. Time not just to rule with the authority of the MacKenzie, but to be *the MacKenzie.*

And Rory had snatched it right out of his hands.

If he'd known Buchanan was going to kill Brian, he would have been at Castle Leod and declared himself the new chieftain before most of the clan even knew Rory had returned from wherever he'd gone.

Somehow Rory had learned of Brian's death first and outmaneuvered him. It would not happen again.

He rubbed the talisman around his neck and imagined adding Rory's ear to it. His plans for his nephew's downfall were already in motion.

"At least ye don't have to worry about Rory's sister telling tales." Duncan leaned back and picked his teeth with the point of his dirk. "Whatever Brian brought her is burned."

"Ye went too far," Hector said. "That lass was valuable to me."

Duncan was a useful weapon, but he could be hard to control. Sending him on an errand like that was like unleashing a dog that has developed a taste for killing sheep and expecting the lambs to be safe. When Catriona disappeared, Duncan did not just burn Killin to the ground. He returned every night until he saw candlelight in the upstairs window, and then he burned it.

"Any other news from Castle Leod?" Hector asked.

"Your nephew has got himself a bride," Duncan said. "Getting married tomorrow."

"Curse him!" What a clever move to gain another ally quickly. "What clan is she?"

Hector hoped the lass was not a Campbell or a Munro—and for God's sake, not a Gordon. He should have forced Rory to wed an inconsequential lass from a weak clan years ago.

"He's wedding a Lowlander," Duncan said.

"A Lowlander?" That caught Hector by surprise. "Who is she?"

"A Douglas, I hear."

"A Douglas?" Hector laughed so hard he choked on his whisky. "I thought Rory was brighter than that. Ach, I'll crush him in no time. How in God's name did he come to wed a Douglas?"

"'Tis a mystery," the Axe said. "But they say she's a rare beauty and that Rory has lost his heart to her."

"He must have, for the lass is useless, with no clan alliance, no property, and no connections." Finally some good news. "He's like his father, losing all sense over a woman."

And it would be the end of him.

"As the poor lass comes with nothing, I'll send her a wedding surprise."

Hector threw his head back and laughed again. He just wished he could be there to see it.

CHAPTER 26

Time had run out for her. The wedding was *today*.

Sybil twisted her braid, a bad habit from childhood, as she paced the floor of the bedchamber. All night long, she had debated with herself over what to do.

If she refused to go through with the marriage ceremony, after Rory had made it his first decision as chieftain, she would make him look an utter fool before his clan. Hurting his pride would be the least of it. Humiliating him when he was just establishing himself as chieftain and fending off his uncle could do irrevocable damage.

On the other hand, once she said her vows, she would be good and truly wed. The false contract would be irrelevant. These Highland chieftains may tell themselves they could disregard both the church and the king's law regarding marriage, but she had no such illusions. There could be no escape from marriage for her but death. For the rest of her life, she would live here on MacKenzie lands.

Miles of rugged mountains and wilderness separated her from her former life. Though she had already suffered the loss of her brothers and friends when they deserted her in her time of need, the prospect of that great physical divide permanently separating her from the rest of her family was painful.

Oh, what a mess she was in! The only way to avoid the marriage was to tell Rory about the false contract. He would hate her for not telling him earlier. She clenched her fists and squeezed her eyes shut. Why had she not told him sooner?

She thought she would have more time to explain about the false contract, if his advisors did not persuade him to change his mind about the marriage first. She never expected Rory to outmaneuver his advisors by making an immediate announcement of their marriage celebration. She would have admired the cleverness of his move, except that he had outmaneuvered her as well.

Sybil dropped onto the wooden chest at the foot of the bed. What should she do? Her hand went to the pendant her mother gave her, as it often did in times of stress. As she rubbed her thumb over the smooth, shiny surface, she imagined what her mother would say to her. She could almost hear her mother's voice…

You're making this far too difficult, when the question is a simple one. Do ye want this Highlander for your husband or not?

"Mother, ye know I never wanted to marry and give a man that much control over me," Sybil said. "I'm tired of serving as a pawn in the games of men."

But darling, how is your Highlander using you? What does he hope to gain?

The bare truth was that Rory had nothing to gain from the marriage now. But eight years ago it would have been advantageous to him—in truth, her wealth and position was high above what he could have expected in a wife.

"And he won me and such bright prospects in a damn card game!" It was insulting, really.

But he did not come to claim you until after you lost your wealth and position.

That was true. Rory was marrying her with no ulterior motive that she could discern. He could have deserted her when her fortunes fell, as everyone else had. When she was in trouble, he did not run. He came for her. When times were hard, he held fast.

Has this man changed your mind about marriage?

Sybil stamped her foot, as she often did when she was a willful child. "I don't know!"

When it's safe to return home to Tantallon Castle, will ye want to leave him?

Tears stung her eyes at the thought of never seeing Rory again. "Nay, I couldn't leave him."

Then you have your answer. Her mother laughed. *If he's a good man, this is not a bad thing.*

"Good heavens, I *want* to marry him," Sybil admitted for the first time. That frightened her more than anything. It gave Rory the power over her happiness, the power to disappoint her, the power to cause her untold pain.

Sybil squeezed her eyes shut as she tried to hold on to the comfort of her mother's presence. Her mother had seemed so real, but she was slipping away like a wisp of wind. Was it her mother's spirit, or was her memory of her mother so vivid that her mind could conjure up exactly what her mother would say?

If ye marry him, there ought to be honesty between ye. Before ye say those vows, tell him what you've been keeping from him.

Sybil did not know whether the voice was her mother speaking to her from the grave or her own conscience, but she understood the message well enough.

Sybil jumped at the sound of a knock on her door. This was no ghost. She tucked her pendant back inside her bodice and smoothed her gown while she gathered herself.

"Come in," she called.

Her heart skipped a beat when the door opened and Rory filled the doorway.

"How are ye settling in? Have the servants provided ye with everything ye need?"

"They've been most attentive, thank you," she said, her voice coming out unusually high.

He hovered at the door, as if torn between staying and leaving.

"We've had no time to speak alone since we arrived," she said.

"I've had much to do."

"I know, but the wedding ceremony is almost upon us." Desperation rose in her throat. "Please, we must talk."

"Of course." He closed the door and stood before it with his hands clasped behind his back. Now he definitely looked as if he would rather leave.

"I'd feel more at ease if ye sat beside me," she said.

He heaved a sigh and came to sit next to her on the bed. He must sense she had something terrible to tell him.

Unless lightning struck her down, she was going to enter into a true marriage with Rory before the day was out. She needed to set things right with him.

She needed to tell him the truth. *Now.* The tension mounted between them as she debated how to tell him. Before she could find the right words, he spoke first.

"I'm sorry if ye regret consummating our marriage and committing yourself to me," he said.

"I—"

"What's done is done," he said, holding his hand up. "But I hope the celebrations tonight will please ye."

Sybil took his hand and pressed it against her heart. "I don't regret what we did."

"Just the consequences." He pressed his lips together in a tight line.

"I confess that I wasn't sure about it before," she said. "I had dreaded marriage for so long that it was difficult for me to consider that it could be anything other than odious. But I've come to see that marriage to you will not be like that."

"The prospect of being my wife is less than odious." He tilted his head. "Ye flatter me, lass."

"What I'm trying to say is that I do want to be your wife."

"Ye mean that?" Rory examined her with piercing eyes, as if he were trying to see into her soul.

"No one could be more surprised than me," she said. "But I want this marriage."

"Don't tell me that because ye know it's what I want to hear," he said. "The one thing I cannot abide is deceit."

Sybil drew in a shaky breath and prayed he would forgive her.

"Above all, I need the truth from you." He took her hands in his and looked deep into her eyes. "There are so few people I can trust. I need to know I can trust you."

"The truth is that I never expected to have a husband who suited me, but it's as if God made ye just for me," she said. "I could not ask for a better man, and I find I want to be a good wife to you. I want to make ye happy."

She tried to summon her courage to say the rest, to tell him that they had no marriage contract, that he had every right to turn his back on her.

Before she could choke out her painful confession, Rory swept her into his arms and gave her a long, deep kiss that made her head spin. One kiss led to another and another. She dug her fingers into his shoulders, needing him so much and afraid that he would never want her like this again after he knew the truth.

His hand was on her breast and she was tugging at his shirt when they were interrupted by a knock on the door.

"Whoever it is, send them away," Rory said as he nuzzled her neck.

"M'lady," a woman called through the door, "we're here to help ye prepare for your wedding."

So soon? Nay, she needed more time!

"I know you're in there too, Rory." This time, the voice was Grizel's. "Let us in!"

"*Mo chroí*, we'll have to save this for after the wedding celebration." Warmth filled his eyes as he brushed a loose strand of hair behind her ear. "The women will have my hide if I interfere with their preparation of the bride."

"Rory, I—" Sybil should send the women away and tell Rory her secrets, but the words died on her lips. It was too late. His clan was already gathered downstairs in the hall for the celebration.

Besides, what if he did not want to marry her once he found out the truth? What would she do then? She had no place to go, no refuge. And most of all, now that she had finally figured out that Rory was the one man she wanted, she could not bear to lose him.

Nay, she could not risk telling him now.

She would wait to reveal her secrets until Rory loved her enough to forgive her.

CHAPTER 27

After giving her one more kiss, Rory opened the door, and a flood of women poured through it, led by Grizel. Two of the women carried a wooden tub between them, while several others brought in buckets of steaming water.

"We've come to wash your feet," Grizel announced.

"Wash my feet?" Sybil asked.

"'Tis a Highland wedding tradition," Rory said.

While the women with buckets filled the tub, others surrounded Sybil, plunked her down on a stool, and began removing her shoes and wool stockings.

The women laughed and made bawdy remarks to Rory as they did the same with him.

"Have you lasses opened the whisky keg early?" he asked.

"Of course we have," a plump woman with graying hair said. "'Tis no every day we have a chieftain's wedding to celebrate."

"Did ye bring a dram for the poor bride?" Sybil asked, stretching her arm out. "I'm begging ye, please."

That set them all to laughing again. Though she had made a joke of it, she was desperate for a drink to calm her nerves. The women cheered when she leaned her head back and drained the cup.

"She drinks like a Highlander," one of them said.

Sybil decided this was going well, but then she shrieked when two women grabbed her ankles and rubbed soot from the hearth all over her feet.

"I thought ye were going to *wash* them," she said.

"The ash represents the past," Grizel explained. "Now we wash it away so ye can start the marriage clean and new."

Sybil liked the idea of that very much. Could it be so simple to wash away her past, to erase the dishonesty that had brought them to this day? She hoped so.

For her wedding day, she would let herself believe it. Someone poured her another dram, and she drank it to help push aside her worries.

The women rubbed ash on Rory's feet as well. While the women scrubbed her and Rory's feet in the tub, the younger ones giggled and whispered behind hands, and the older women openly speculated about the likely duration and frequency of what would occur between the bride and groom tonight in this bedchamber.

Sybil met Rory's gaze, and the sounds of the women's voices faded. Today they would begin their marriage and a new life together. Nothing that came before should matter.

When the women finished, Rory helped her to her feet. She stood in the tub with her skirts tucked up, facing Rory and surrounded by twenty chattering women.

As they stood staring into each other's eyes, she felt overwhelmed by how she had gone from feeling despair to such hopefulness for the future. He cupped her neck and started to pull her in for a kiss.

"There will be time for that later, laird!" one of the older women shouted, and pulled on his arm. "Leave her to us now, or there will be no wedding today."

"I entrust my bride to your good hands." Rory bowed to the gathered women and winked at Sybil before he went out the door.

For the next hour, the women fussed over her, dabbing lavender scent on her wrists and throat, brushing her hair until it shone. They left the back of her hair loose and wove tiny braids on the sides that they pinned back.

They cooed as they worked. "Lucky lass, thick hair as black as midnight." "Have ye ever seen eyes that shade of violet?" "Milky skin as smooth as a babe's bottom."

The door opened and all the women, including Sybil, sucked in their breath as a tall, bony woman came in carrying a dazzling blue gown.

"'Tis blue for luck, of course. The color will be lovely with your eyes," the woman said. "The laird asked me to alter it for ye. This is the gown his mother was wed in."

"Ach, I remember that day well," Grizel said, wiping a tear. "May you have a marriage as happy as hers."

"Oh, thank you!" Sybil said. "I could not wish for a lovelier wedding gown."

"The laird's mother was a head taller," the woman who brought it in said. "I did my best, but let's see how it fits."

Sybil lifted her arms, and the seamstress dropped the voluminous skirt over her head. A collective sigh went through the women as the silk slid over her skin and fell into place.

The seamstress tugged the laces on the bodice tight, rested her hands on her hips, and leaned back to examine Sybil. "I did a fine job, if I do say so myself. A good thing, too, for the blue color would never outweigh the bad luck of a wedding gown that doesn't fit."

"I remember the laird's mother in that gown," one of the older women said. "Ach, she was a beauty, tall and fair with red-gold hair. Our chieftain had a fever for her from first sight."

It was in a man's nature to feel that way at the beginning. After Rory's fever cooled, would he regret letting desire cloud his judgment? Even if he never learned of the deception, would he come to resent being tied to a wife who brought nothing but herself to the marriage?

"One last thing for luck." Grizel stuck a small sprig of white heather in Sybil's hair. "'Tis early for it to bloom, but I found this bit growing in a corner of the castle garden where it was protected from the wind and cold."

"A sign of spring to come," Sybil said. *And hope.*

One of the women held up a looking glass.

"Oh my, I do look like a bride." Heaven help her, this really was happening.

"Aye, and a bonny bride ye are," the woman said. "But where's your smile gone, lass?"

"If you're worried about what will happen here tonight," another woman said, and patted the bed, "I'd be willing to take your place."

"Wouldn't we all?" another said, and the women laughed and refilled their cups.

"Every lass is a wee bit nervous on her wedding night." The woman who spoke this time must have imbibed more than her share, for she was slurring her words. "Another nip will help."

Sybil took the flask and let the liquid courage burn down her throat.

"No matter what everyone else says," the woman said, squeezing Sybil's shoulders, "I think our young laird made a fine choice."

Before she could drink another long gulp, the women took the flask from her and pushed her toward the door. Sybil paused in the doorway and looked over her shoulder at the women.

"You've all been very kind to me," she said. "Thank you."

Kind as they were, she wished her sisters were here. She had never imagined she would marry without a single member of her family present.

***

Rory smiled to himself as he dressed in his best saffron shirt and plaid for the ceremony. There could be no changing their course regardless, but his heart was glad that Sybil wanted to be his wife.

When he started to fasten the plaid over his shoulder with his broach, Malcolm shook his head and took it from him.

"Ye must wear this one now." Malcolm held out a familiar silver broach worked in the image of a stag's head, the symbol of the chieftain of the MacKenzies.

"Where did ye find it?" Rory narrowed his eyes at him. "This disappeared just like my father's sword did when he died."

"I put them away for safekeeping until we had a chieftain worthy of your father and grandfather's legacy."

"Ye should have given them to Brian," Rory said.

"I'd not let them fall into Hector's hands so long as I have breath in my body," Malcolm said. "And ye know damned well that's who would have them now if I hadn't protected them."

Rory hated the thought of Hector wearing the broach and sword that had been his father's most prized possessions. And Malcolm was right. Hector would have used these revered symbols of the chieftainship to help legitimize his claim.

"You were wise to hide them," Rory said. "I shall try to be worthy of them."

"I've no doubt ye will." Malcolm was quiet a long moment. "Are ye not being a bit hasty with taking Sybil as your wife before the whole clan?"

"Ye advised me to act decisively, and so I have."

"That's what I advised about claiming the chieftainship, not a wife," Malcolm said. "Ach, you're as rash about rushing this wedding as your father was about marrying your mother."

Rory grinned. "I'd say that portends well for our future."

"That's what my wife says," Malcolm said with a long-suffering sigh. "But what about the Grants? They'll not take this well. Not well at all."

Malcolm was right about the Grants. But Rory would worry about the Grants and his many other troubles another day.

Today he was celebrating.

***

When Sybil entered the hall, the room fell silent except for the intake of a hundred breaths, including his own. Rory found her beautiful in a filthy gown with her face smudged with mud and her hair in tangles, but she was utterly magnificent as a bride. The rich blue color of the gown matched her eyes, and her shining black hair was set off with his mother's jeweled silver combs.

The gown shimmered and flowed, making her look like a faery princess as she glided across the room to him. She looked at no one but him, and her smile lifted his heart. He found it hard to believe she was really his.

He took her hands and began his vows.

"I, Rory Ian Fraser MacKenzie, son of Kenneth of the Battle, the 8th of Kintail, and grandson of Alexander the Upright, the 7th of Kintail, take you, Lady Sybil Elizabeth Douglas, daughter of…"

As he recited her name and pedigree, fear flashed in Sybil's eyes at the realization that every person in the castle now knew who she was. Rory squeezed her hands to reassure her and continued his pledge.

"…to be my wife. Before God and my clan, I promise to protect and keep you and to be a faithful and loyal husband until God shall separate us by death."

Sybil seemed to pale at the reminder that she was bound to him until death, but she recited her vows to him in a clear voice.

When Rory pulled his dirk, her eyes went wide, and he realized that as a Lowlander she was not familiar with this part. He should have warned her. Praise God she did not scream, for that was just the sort of reaction those who were critical of his choice of a bride expected.

He held her gaze, willing her to trust him, as he turned her right hand over. Sybil did not even flinch as he cut across her palm, leaving a thin line of deep red blood. After drawing the blade across his own palm, he clasped his hand to hers, palm to palm.

As he wound the symbolic strip of linen around their joined hands, he recited the ancient words. He repeated them three times, the number that provided a couple's bond with magical protection.

"Our blood is joined, and we are one
Our blood is joined, and we are one
Our blood is joined, and we are one."

As he spoke the words the final time, they seemed to echo inside his head and heart. *We are one. One. ONE.*

***

The room seemed to spin and blur behind Rory as he wound the linen around their hands and repeated the chant. Sybil kept her gaze locked on his and felt as if there was no one else in the hall at this moment but the two of them. *We are one. One. ONE.*

When someone cleared his throat, she remembered that Alex stood before them in his priestly robes. The church's blessing was not required to make a marriage binding, but it did make a marriage more difficult to escape.

"I bless this union in the name of the Father, and the Son, and the Holy Spirit."

Alex dipped his thumb in the small bowl of holy water, touched it to Rory's forehead, and made the sign of the cross. She felt the cool damp of his thumb on her forehead as he did the same to her.

"May your bond never be broken," Alex said, "and may God bless you with many children."

The words had barely left Alex's mouth when Rory raised their joined hands. The hall erupted as everyone shouted, stamped their feet, and raised their fists or weapons in the air. Sybil did not think it could get any louder, but then Rory pulled her into a passionate kiss that made her knees weak and sent the MacKenzies into a frenzy.

When he released her, she felt dazed and happy. She had expected to feel weighed down by the pledge she had just made that bound her for life. Instead, she felt so light she could have floated over the crowd.

The MacKenzies did not let their unease with their laird's choice of a bride interfere with their celebration. The hall was soon noisy with talk and laughter. The whisky flowed like water as one man after another made a toast.

"*Gun cuireadh do chupa thairis le slainte agus sonas.*" *May your cup overflow with health and happiness.*

"*Slàinte, sonas agus beairtas!*" *Health, happiness and wealth!*

"*Móran làithean dhuit is sìth.*" *May you be blessed with long life and peace.*

Sybil would have had the food served before so many toasts, but this appeared to be the Highland custom. Judging by the increasingly bawdy jokes, she was not the only one feeling a bit tipsy by the time the trestle tables were set up for the wedding feast. At last, Rory led her toward the head table, a signal to everyone to find their seats.

But he halted as something across the room caught his attention. Sybil followed his gaze to a guard who was pushing his way through the crowd of revelers, heading straight for Rory.

"Laird, I apologize for disrupting the festivities," the guard said when he reached them, "but we have a score of Munro warriors approaching the gate, and they're armed to the teeth."

CHAPTER 28

"I'll come out at once," Rory told the guard. "Open the gates."

"Is that safe?" Sybil asked, trying to keep her voice calm.

"A score of men is not enough to attack a castle," Rory said, his expression hard. "They've come to negotiate my sister's release."

"Then I'll come with ye," Sybil said.

"You'll wait here inside the keep," Rory said. "I want ye out of the way should harsh words turn to drawn swords."

Rory strode off without a backward glance, evidently assuming she would follow his orders. He should know her better by now.

Sybil followed him outside and stood a few feet behind him with Alex and Malcolm. The gates opened and the Munro warriors entered the castle riding two abreast. A striking young woman with strawberry-blonde hair rode beside the leader.

"Thank God, they've brought Catriona," Alex said. "And it doesn't look as though they've harmed her."

"Rory must handle this delicately," Malcolm said in a hushed voice. "We don't need a war with the Munros."

"I agree," Alex whispered back. "But Rory looks as though he wants one."

The tall young warrior who rode at the front beside Catriona dismounted. After helping Catriona down from her horse, he kept his hold on her while the two exchanged words.

"That's their new chieftain," Malcolm said. "He's young and easily offended. Ach, this doesn't bode well."

As the Munro chieftain brought Catriona across the castle yard to them with his warriors following close behind, Sybil glanced at Rory. He was gripping the hilt of his dirk as if contemplating plunging it into the Munro chieftain's chest.

When the Munro halted in front of them, Rory grabbed Catriona by the wrist and pulled her across the narrow divide between the MacKenzies and Munros. He pushed her behind him, clearly failing to notice his sister's resistance or the look that passed between her and the young Munro chieftain.

"Rory is overly protective of Catriona," Alex said in an urgent whisper. "We must stop him from doing something he'll regret."

"We can do nothing," Malcolm said, holding Alex's arm. "It would do Rory even greater harm for you and I to show we doubt his judgment in front of the clan."

Well, that left it to her.

Sybil hurried to Rory's side and hooked her arm through his, then gave both him and the Munros a bright smile. She could almost see steam rising from Rory's skin, but her presence seemed to remind him that this was not the time nor place for a violent confrontation.

"We welcome you to Castle Leod," Sybil said, and held her hand out to the young Munro chieftain. "I'm Lady Sybil, the MacKenzie's bride."

She ignored Catriona's gasp of surprise and widened her smile. When the Munro chief bowed stiffly over her hand, she felt the tension of all the warriors around her decrease palpably—with the exception of Rory, who was clenching his jaw so tightly she expected to hear his teeth crack.

"Thank you for bringing Catriona home to us in time to celebrate our wedding," she said. "That is a great favor to me, as my own sisters cannot be here."

"It was my pleasure," the Munro said.

"Your *pleasure* to return my sister?" Rory ground out. "How dare ye say that after ye kidnapped her."

"Kidnapped?" The Munro stood taller, and fire lit his eyes. "She came to me for protection. You should take better care of your sister."

Rory made a sound like a growl and took a step forward.

"'Tis true!" Catriona said, stopping him in his tracks. "I did go to them."

Rory turned slowly to face his sister. "Ye went to the Munros?"

When she nodded, he stared at her, his eye twitching.

"It appears I have been remiss in not thanking you," Rory said in an icy tone. "I will protect my sister better in the future, as you suggest, so that she will feel no need to go to *strangers*."

Evidently the Munros had provided Rory's sister with a safe haven, not kidnapped her. Catriona's return presented an opportunity to build a friendship between the two clans. Rory, however, looked as if he'd like to murder their chieftain. The Munro's attitude did not help matters.

"I wish you and your men a safe journey home," Rory said, and gripped Catriona by the arm. "Now, if you'll excuse me, my sister and I have much to discuss."

Sybil watched in dismay as Rory dragged his sister off. She caught Catriona's distraught expression as she looked over her shoulder at the Munro chieftain.

Nay, this would not do at all. She waited until she was sure Rory was out of earshot.

"Must ye leave so soon?" she asked the Munro. "It will add to our joy if you would stay and join the celebration of our marriage."

***

"How could ye go to the Munros?" Rory shouted at his sister. "God have mercy, did ye lose your senses?"

"Of course I went to the Munros. Where else could I go?" Catriona planted her hands on her hips. "Have ye forgotten that Father pillaged and burned the lands of our other neighboring clan, the Roses?"

What had happened to Catriona? He remembered her as much more compliant.

"What about our uncle, Lord Lovat," he said. "Ye could have gone to him."

"He's a sneaky bastard," she said. "And would ye really want me to ride that far alone?"

"I don't think ye realize this could have turned out verra badly." Rory was not ready to let it go. "I don't like how that Munro looks at ye."

Catriona tilted her head. "How does he look at me?"

"Ach, you're too naïve for your own good," he said. "But don't worry, he won't trouble ye again. I'll see to that."

She opened her mouth to speak but seemed to change her mind.

"Why didn't ye go to one of our own clansmen?" he said. "I looked all over for ye. No one knew where ye were."

"After I heard about Brian's death, I was afraid." Her lower lip trembled. "I didn't know which of our clan were Hector's men."

He could not argue with her judgment on that, and he was annoyed with himself for yelling at her. He put his arms around her, which is what he should have done in the first place.

"I can see ye made what ye thought was the best choice," he said. "I'm sorry I wasn't there to protect both you and Brian."

"He came to Killin," she said. "He was angry with Hector and looking for you."

"Did he tell ye why?"

"Nay, but I'd never seen him like that," she said. "He gave me two books to keep for him. I hid them in the safe place Mother showed me in the barn."

"Books?" What use would they be? He was no closer to learning why Brian had set out for Edinburgh.

"All he told me was that if he did not return, I should hide the books and disappear until you came," Catriona said.

"I'm glad you're safe." Rory kissed her cheek. "We ought to join the others in the hall."

"Who is that lass who greeted the Munros," Catriona asked, "and why did she pretend to be your bride?"

***

Sybil took a deep breath when Rory entered the hall and saw the Munros.

"It appears they've decided to stay for our wedding feast," Rory said when he joined her. *"Ge b'e thig gun chuireadh, suidhidh e gun iarraidh."* Who comes uninvited will sit down unbidden.

"But I did invite them," Sybil confessed.

"Ye knew I wanted them gone," he said. "Why did ye interfere?"

Sybil judged that Rory was not ready to hear that his sister had formed an attachment to the handsome young Munro chieftain.

"Interfere? I was simply trying to be a good Highland wife," she said. "I thought it was a matter of honor to graciously welcome every guest, even your worst enemy."

Rory blew out his breath. "What was your real reason?"

"Ye said yourself that Hector should have tried to make the Munros allies rather than enemies," she said.

"That was before I knew their young chief was an arrogant arse."

Munro's accusation that Rory had failed to protect his sister stung because he felt it was true. Her telling him it was unjust would not change that.

"And I don't like how he looks at Catriona," Rory said.

"Your sister is a lovely lass," Sybil said. "Men will look at her."

"Hmmph."

"Worry about Munro tomorrow." She rose on her toes and kissed him.

"You're right, of course," he said, smiling down at her. "I'll not let anyone spoil our celebration."

They ate course after course, and in between courses, there was still more toasting. After the feast, the trestle tables were moved to clear the floor, and the distinctive sound of bagpipes, drum, and flute filled the hall.

"I don't know how to do your Highland dance," she objected when Rory pulled her to the middle of the floor.

"Ach, 'tis no more than hops, skips, and a few twirls," Rory said with a wink.

The music filled her ears and her feet seemed to fly to the lively beat of the drum. She had never expected to enjoy her own wedding, but she was having a grand time. When Rory twirled her, she leaned her head back and laughed with reckless joy.

But every now and then, she felt a nagging sense of guilt in the pit of her stomach for the secret she had not yet told him.

***

"I thought they would never leave us," Rory said when they were finally alone in their bedchamber.

Sybil swallowed as she watched Rory's naked backside as he crossed the room with the grace and unconscious ease of a warrior to bar the door. She let her gaze run over his broad, muscular back, narrow waist, and long legs as well. By the saints, the man was beautiful.

And he was hers now.

When Rory turned around, the heat in his eyes made her pulse jump. Her gaze traveled down his muscled chest and rippled stomach to his full erection, and it jumped again.

He looked as if he'd like to swallow her whole, so she was surprised when he sat beside her on the bed and gently took her face between his hands.

"I'm such a lucky man to have you."

"Lucky?" She gave a light laugh. "You've wed a Lowland pauper."

"I've wed a lass with the courage of a lioness, the cleverness of scholar—and most of all, a true heart. I know you'll stand beside me no matter what comes."

"I will," she whispered. "Always."

She pushed away the stab of guilt for not telling him she had not been his bride until today. This was her true wedding night with him, and she was not going to let anything ruin it.

"This is our beginning," she whispered against his lips as she leaned forward to kiss him. "Nothing else matters."

He took her in his arms and covered her with kisses—her cheeks, her eyelids, her forehead, the sensitive spot beneath her ear, the side of her throat.

"Ye smell like heaven," he said, burying his face in her hair.

She pulled him into an open-mouthed kiss and tangled her fingers in his hair. As their tongues moved together in a slow, sensuous dance, tendrils of desire spiraled low in her belly.

Without lifting his mouth from hers, he leaned her back on the bed and slid his hand up her thigh, pushing her night shift up to her hip.

"This has to come off," he said. "I need to feel ye against me, skin to skin."

Oh, aye. She lifted her hips and raised her arms as he pulled the gown over her head.

He raked his gaze over her, lighting sparks across her skin and making her nipples taut.

"God, you're beautiful," he breathed.

His eyes darkened as she ran hands down his chest. The coarse hair felt good against her palms. When she trailed her fingers down to his belly, he stilled above her. He sucked in his breath as she ran her tongue across her top lip and brushed her fingertip against the damp tip of his shaft.

"We're taking this slowly tonight." He took her hand away and gave her a wicked look as he kissed her palm. "Verra slowly."

When she pulled him down into another deep kiss, his chest felt so good against her bare breasts that she nearly purred. After a time, he broke his mouth away to run kisses along her jaw and down her throat. Her breathing grew shallow as he kissed and licked his way down the center of her chest. Her breasts felt heavy and her nipples taut with anticipation.

"Mmmm," she sighed when he covered her breasts with his big hands. Her sighs turned to moans as he rolled her nipples between his fingers and thumbs.

He ran his tongue along the underside of her breast and then circled and flicked his tongue over her nipple. Finally, he sucked on her breast, sending shards of pleasure all the way to her toes.

"I want to taste and touch every inch of ye tonight," he said.

Rory rolled her onto her stomach and drew her hair to the side to kiss her neck. She felt his warm breath in her ear as he whispered the wicked things he wanted to do to her. Teasing her, he let his shaft rub against her buttocks as he brushed his fingers along the side of her breast.

She rose up on her elbows, and he took the invitation to cup her breasts. While giving her hot, sucking kisses on her neck, he played with her nipples. Waves of desire rippled through her body and settled between her legs as an aching need.

When his shaft brushed against her again, she raised her hips.

"I want to feel ye inside me," she said.

"Ach, 'tis verra tempting, lass," he said with a smile in his voice, "but 'tis far too soon for that."

His long hair felt like feathers softly tickling her sensitive skin as he ran kisses down her back. When his lips reached her buttocks and he ran his hand up the inside of her thigh, her breathing grew shallow and tension coiled in her belly.

She sucked in her breath when his fingers slid between her legs. When he felt how wet she was for him, he groaned and nipped her bottom with his teeth.

But he made her wait, continuing downward, kissing her thigh, the back of her knees, her calf. He bent her leg, and she smiled as she felt his soft lips on the bottom of her foot. When he sucked on her toe, she never dreamed that could feel so sensuous.

Her anticipation mounted when he turned her over and started his journey back up her body. He kissed her knee and then her hip, his hair brushing along her skin. Her pulse quickened as he ran his tongue across her abdomen and trailed his fingers up the inside of her thigh. All her attention was centered on his fingertips as they circled closer and closer, inching upward.

She was ready to beg when her finally reached the sensitive juncture between her legs. *Aye.*

She fisted her hands in the bedclothes and squeezed her eyes shut as he worked his magic with his fingers. At the same time, he moved up her body with his lips and tongue until he reached her breast. He gently bit her nipple, causing a shock of pleasure that was almost painful.

Her every nerve and muscle jangled with tension. She clutched his hair in her fingers as it built and built inside her. Good heavens, what he did to her!

When she was on the very edge, he took her breast in his mouth, sucking hard. A burst of stars sparked across her vision, and she cried out his name as spasms of pleasure pulsed through her body.

But now she felt a desperate need to feel the force of his passion, to be lost in the tempest with him. She wanted their bodies joined and their hearts and souls to become one.

***

God how he loved to hear the little high-pitched sounds she made as he pleasured her, loved to feel her wet heat against his hand, loved to hold her as her body quivered and she cried out with her release. His cock was so hard he feared he would come against her side.

Before he could gather himself, Sybil pushed him onto his back and gave him a deep open-mouthed kiss that sent fire coursing through his veins. He felt drunk with passion, lost in the sensation of her soft curves pressed against him, the smell of her skin, the heat of her kisses. His hands roamed her body, seeking, stroking, caressing as they rolled on the bed.

She sucked on his tongue and rubbed her palm down the length of his cock, making him moan. *O shluagh*, he could not take much more of this sweet torture.

When she was on top of him, she rose up and guided the tip of his shaft inside her. He gasped against the rush of pleasure as she sank down, burying him to the hilt in her wet heat.

He loved to watch her above him while he held her hips and they moved together. Loved how she bit her bottom lip as she found her rhythm. Loved to watch her full breasts as her nipples grew taut. Loved to see how her lips parted and her head fell back.

He wanted to lick the sheen of sweat off her body.

She leaned over him until the tips of her breasts brushed against his chest, driving him to near madness. He pulled her down against him, and they rolled with their arms and legs entwined until she was beneath him. He swallowed her moans in passionate kisses.

He needed her in a way he'd never needed her before. Her legs were like a vise around him, as if she, too, was trying to meld into him. His blood pounded in his ears as he tried to hold back. But she egged him on, lifting her hips to meet him as he thrust inside her again and again, harder and faster.

"Aye. Aye. Aye!" she gasped as her body clenched around him, destroying his last shred of control.

He cried out her name as they fell over the edge together.

Good God! Afterward, he lay on his back gasping for air. When he could move his limbs again, he pulled her into his arms and buried his face in her hair.

When he leaned back to look into her face, she gave him a smile that radiated with happiness. He felt an overwhelming tenderness for her as he looked into her violet eyes.

He felt as though things had changed between them, as if she was his in a way she was not before.

"I'll never want another woman," he told her. "It's only you, now and forever."

"Aye," she whispered. "You belong to me, and I to you."

***

Sybil ran her fingertips over Rory's chest. Though her body felt weak and sated after their long night of lovemaking, her emotions were in turmoil. Each time they made love, she felt more and more guilty.

Secrets were a common currency at court. She had learned at her grandfather's knee that a wise person drew out other people's secrets and kept her own. She had followed his admonition without guilt for years.

Yet the deeper Rory found his way into her heart, the more it felt wrong not to reveal her secret to him.

"I'm amazed at how fate brought us together," Rory said, and kissed her forehead. "The wisest thing I ever did was gamble with your brother."

She squeezed her eyes closed and prayed to God to grant her the strength to tell him the truth.

There's something I must tell you... As she practiced the words in her head, her heart pounded like a caught rabbit that sees the cleaver in the cook's hand.

Rory propped his head on his elbow. This would be easier if he were not looking at her like that. She licked her dry lips and drew in a deep breath.

"I wanted you from the first moment I saw you," he said. "But everything about you warned me not to trust you."

Perhaps he was right not to trust her then, but he must see that he could trust her now.

"You'd spent too much time at court," he continued, "and your family is known for their lack of loyalty and their utter disregard for anyone or anything that does not serve their own interests."

Knowing that, she was surprised he hadn't left her where he found her.

"If that weren't reason enough," he said, "I could see ye were a beauty accustomed to bending men to your will, and you were desperate."

Her heart ached. She had never meant to carry the deceit this far. She'd only intended to rely on the deceit until she found a safe refuge. She had not known that her only refuge would be here with him.

"Day by day, ye broke through all the barriers I erected." A soft light warmed his eyes as he cupped her cheek with his palm. "Ye showed me a generous spirit and a loyal heart, supporting me at every turn."

Sybil choked back tears.

"When we make love," he said, "I feel as though ye show me your soul and look into mine."

Aye, it feels exactly like that.

"I need to tell ye what is in my heart, *mo leannain*," he said, brushing the tear that spilled down her cheek with his thumb. "I love you."

Mary, Mother of God, help me. She had to tell him now. Not because he would forgive her now that he loved her, but because she loved him too.

Until she told him, this lie would always be between them, corroding their bond, eating away at her heart and tainting the beauty of the love that had grown between them.

"I love you too, with all my heart," she said. "I think I have for a long time."

"I was afraid to hope." He pulled her into his arms and gave her a deep kiss. His lips were warm and soft, and she never wanted the kiss to end. And yet she forced herself to push him away and sit up.

"My love," she said in a choked voice, "there is something else I must tell you."

"What more do I need to know than that ye love me?" Rory sat up and took her face between his hands. "You've made me a happy man."

Rory's smile faded as he examined her face. The wariness that entered his eyes tested her strength, but she could not let this deceit lie between them for another day or another hour. She took his hands from her face and held them in her lap. Before she lost her courage, she forced herself to meet his eyes and tell him.

"I have a confession to make."

CHAPTER 29

"A confession?" Tension pulled Rory's shoulders tight, clenched his stomach, and made his eye twitch as he waited for Sybil to answer.

"I should have told ye this long before now," she said. "I did try to tell ye at the very first, but when ye misunderstood me…well, I let it go."

Rory had always sensed Sybil had a secret, something she was not telling him. Was he finally going to learn what it was? She licked her lips, as she always did when she was nervous.

"Come, lass, it can't be that bad," he said, though he suspected it was bad enough because Sybil was not easily rattled. "You'd best tell me and get it over with."

"Ye had no obligation to wed me and no obligation to protect me," she said, looking up at him with watery eyes. "In truth, ye had no obligation to me at all."

"We've been through this before." Was this all she was upset about? "If I had no honor, I could have used the loss of your dowry or found some other excuse to abandon ye. Ye should know me better by now than to believe I could turn my back on my contracted bride when ye were in danger."

"I was never your contracted bride." She dropped her gaze. "There was no marriage contract between us."

"We had a binding marriage contract." He had no notion what she was talking about. "Ye saw it yourself."

"I did see it," she said. "It was not a valid contract. It was a fraud."

"Now that I've told ye I love ye, ye want out of the marriage?" he said, his voice rising. "Is that why you're saying this?"

He shoved the bedclothes aside and got out of bed. He paced up and down the room, but it did not help calm the turmoil inside of him.

"Rory, I—"

The words died on her lips when he gripped her arms and leaned over her to look her in the eyes.

"If ye wished to break the contract before we bedded, I would have allowed it," he said. "But it's too damned late now."

"I don't want out of the marriage."

"What other reason could ye have to make up this tale now?" he said, flinging his arm out. "I know that is your brother's signature on the contract. I watched him sign it."

"One of my brothers did sign it," she said, her voice barely a whisper. "But it was the wrong brother."

"The wrong brother?" Rory felt numb.

Sybil tried to touch her fingertips to his cheek, but he brushed her hand away.

"It must have been my brother George who lost to ye at cards, because that was George's signature on the contract," she said. "Archie is the chieftain and head of my family. Only he had authority to make a binding contract for my marriage."

Rory stumbled backward as if he had taken a blow. The room faded as his memory took him back to that night in Edinburgh so long ago. He saw it all again as if he was sixteen years old and back in that tavern…the dim, low-beamed room…the maid with the missing teeth who grabbed his arse…the Lowlander merchants who bought him stew and ale in exchange for his tale.

He felt the pain in his leg and his desperation to return home as he followed the tavern maid down the dark hallway. Her sour smell filled his nose as she opened a door a crack to reveal the well-dressed nobles gambling in the back room.

"That one is the new Douglas chieftain, and the one next to him is his brother," she said, pointing a thick finger at two black-haired nobles who looked about the same age.

"Who have ye brought us, Rosie?"

Rory had assumed, without even realizing he did, that the brother who spoke first and had the largest pile of coins in front of him was the Douglas chieftain.

The other Douglas brother left when Rory joined the table, and Rory never gave him another thought. His attention was fixed on his goal of winning the coin he needed to purchase a horse and sword. The easy charm and wit of the Douglas who stayed to gamble fit the brash young chieftain who had seduced the queen so soon after the king's death that she still carried her dead husband's child.

Rory remembered how the candles were pools of wax, marking the hours that drifted by as they played through the night. Though he had done well, he worried that the pile of coins he had won might not be enough. Only he and the Douglas were left in the game now. Rory kept his gaze on the man across the table as he swept the coins from the last hand toward him.

"I can't leave it like this," the Douglas said. "One last round?"

Rory nodded. If he doubled the coins he'd already won, he would have enough to buy a sword and a fine horse to get him home. He pushed all he had to the center of the table.

"You've won all the money I had with me," the Douglas said. "Loan me some of it back."

Rory shook his head.

"Do ye know who I am?"

"You're the Douglas chieftain who married our widowed queen," Rory said.

"If ye know that," the Douglas said with an amused smile, "then ye know I'm good for the loan."

"What I know," Rory replied, "is that enforcing payment against a man with your connections would be difficult."

The Douglas laughed and poured them both another drink. "You're wise beyond your years."

Rory could hold his whisky, but they had been playing cards and drinking steadily since his meager supper. His head felt thick, and the whisky no longer dulled the throbbing pain in his leg.

"Come, Highlander, one more hand," the Douglas said, tilting his head.

"I would if ye had anything left to put on the table."

Though the Douglas was so wealthy he would not miss the money he'd lost, it was clear he was not accustomed to losing. Tonight, however, luck was with Rory and not the Douglas. It was a damn shame the man had run out of money.

"'Tis late," Rory said, and stood up. "Thank ye for a fine game."

"Damn. What else have I got that I could wager?" the Douglas said, patting his tunic. He looked up with a grin and raised his finger. "I know! I'll give ye one of my sisters."

Rory blinked. "You'll wager your sister?"

"Aye, in a marriage contract," the Douglas said. He turned to one of his companions, who was slumped in a chair, and shook him. "Tell him what a Douglas lass is worth."

"The dowry of one of his sisters is worth many times the coins you've won tonight," the friend said. "Ask anyone."

Rory did not want to be bound to a Lowlander lass, no matter how great her dowry. And yet he could not help recalling the time he'd seen the Douglas sisters ride by. The image of the black-haired Douglas lass with laughter in her eyes filled his head, and the question tumbled out of his mouth.

"Which sister?"

"Which one do ye want?" The Douglas's satisfied smile showed he knew he'd offered an inducement that tempted Rory.

"Sybil." One of the other girls had called her name, and it had stuck in Rory's memory like a burr. When he spoke it aloud, it felt like spiced wine on his lips.

"Ye made a good choice, since the two older ones are already wed," the Douglas said with good humor. "Not that it will matter, as you'll lose this last game."

"Ye must think me a fool." Rory was annoyed with himself for nearly agreeing. "I won't play for a promise of a marriage contract any more than I'd rely on coin ye don't have in hand. You'll wake up sober tomorrow and forget the debt."

"I'll write the contract myself right now and sign it." He pointed to one of his friends. "Give me that letter ye received today. I'll write the marriage contract on the back."

The friend produced the parchment, and the Douglas began writing with a fluid hand.

"I, Archibald Douglas, Earl of Angus, chieftain of the Douglas clan, and guardian of my sister Lady Sybil Elizabeth Douglas, do hereby enter into binding marriage contract on her behalf…"

He read the words out loud as he scrawled them across the page. Rory listened carefully as he named the properties, as well as the silver and jewels that comprised her dowry. When the Douglas was finished, he signed it with a flourish, then slid the parchment across the table.

"You sign here." He pointed as he handed Rory the quill. "Then my friends will sign as witnesses."

If Rory won, he could borrow against her dowry for the rest of what he needed to get home. And years from now when they wed, he'd be a wealthy man. He told himself those were the reasons he sat back down at the table.

"If ye win, I'll give this parchment to ye," the Douglas said. "If ye lose, I'll tear it up and take every last one of your coins."

Rory studied the man. "Why would ye make such a wager?"

"A wild Highlander would suit my sister Sybil, wouldn't ye say?" he said, turning to his friends, and they all laughed. He turned back to Rory. "But it will never happen because you'll lose. Fair warning—I always win the last hand."

Rory should have taken the money he'd already won and left. But he imagined a lass's shining black hair falling over his chest, and he signed his name, which was all he could write.

For years he had told himself that he agreed to that last, unusual wager for the wealth and powerful connections such a marriage could bring to him and his clan.

Now he saw the truth. He had done it for a chance to spend his days and nights with the bonny black-haired lass with laughter in her eyes.

He had been so damned certain that night that luck was on his side.

But luck, like the lass herself, was fickle.

CHAPTER 30

Rory felt like a caged animal as he paced the chamber. He'd been taken for a fool by Sybil's slippery, smiling brother.

"Ye knew from the very beginning when I showed ye the parchment that it was no binding contract," he ranted. "And ye knew I didn't know it was false."

He had no right to take Sybil away with him. Kidnapping a bride was not uncommon in the Highlands, but a man ought to know when he was doing it.

At least Sybil had the grace to look guilty.

"Why did ye not tell me?" he shouted. "Why?"

"Well…" Her gaze flitted away. "I didn't want to disappoint ye after you'd traveled such a long way to fetch me."

"Sybil!" He clenched his fists at his side. "The time for games is at an end."

"I had the threat of imprisonment and a charge of treason looming over me," she said. "And you were looming over me as well, just as ye are now. Before I became accustomed to that icy stare of yours, ye could be a wee bit frightening."

"Don't ye dare mock me." He'd had enough of her sarcasm.

"Ye don't understand—"

"Oh, I understand perfectly now," he said, folding his arms.

"Ye don't."

"Ye needed a man to take ye away. Who better than an ignorant Highlander?" He backed her up against the wall and leaned in close. "Ye used me."

"That wasn't—"

"Ye never intended to become my wife." He felt as if a fist was pounding against his head. "Ye went to bed with me. Why? To make me believe we were bound?"

"Nay, that wasn't the—"

"What else have ye lied to me about?"

When she looked off into the distance as if she was struggling to recall all the ways she had deceived him, he thought his head would explode. A terrible suspicion crept into his mind. God's bones, he hoped he was wrong.

"Ye lied to me about why ye weren't a virgin, didn't ye?"

Her face drained of color. *Christ,* how could she?

"Ye lied about being raped." The words tasted like ashes on his tongue.

"I never m—"

"You're every bit as deceitful as your brother," he said, pointing his finger at her. "Ye only went to bed with me after ye learned my brother died and there was a good chance I'd be made chieftain."

"That's not why I did it!" she said. "You were grieving. I wanted to comfort you."

"I know what ye wanted," he said. "Ye wanted me to believe we were bound in marriage, while you were still making up your mind about whether ye had to marry the heathen."

"In the end, I did choose to marry you," she said. "I made my pledge before your clan—"

"Aye, *after* I was made chieftain." He was so angry his vision blurred.

"I said those vows because I wanted ye for my husband."

"That was your worst deceit—ye made me believe that ye wanted *me*." He pressed his thumb to his chest as he spoke.

"I did want you," she said. "I *do* want you."

"What ye wanted was a chieftain for a husband," he said. "No second son would do for Lady Sybil Douglas, pursued and flattered by all the powerful men at court."

"I didn't want to marry a chieftain," she said. "I wanted to disappear."

"Ha! Ye didn't want to be my wife until I became the MacKenzie," he said.

"You're twisting everything!" she said, clenching her fists.

"Ach, you're a Douglas through and through." He spit on the floor. "You've no true loyalty, no heart. All that matters to ye is power and position."

"Ye said ye loved me. How can ye believe such things about me?" She gripped his arm, and what he knew were false tears filled her eyes.

"I loved the woman ye pretended to be," he said. "Ye played me for a fool, just like your brother did."

He could not be in the same room with her another moment. When he started toward the door, she clung to his arm, and he shook her off.

"Don't leave like this," she pleaded.

"Ye got what ye wanted. You're a chieftain's wife," he said from the doorway. "You'll find that cold comfort at night."

***

Rory slammed the door so hard it shook the room. His harsh words rang in Sybil's ears as her knees gave way and she sank to the floor. She felt as if she had shattered into a thousand tiny pieces, each piece sharp and brittle.

Would she ever feel whole again?

She drew her knees up, buried her face in her arms, and wept as she had not wept since she was a child. Her strength drained out of her like water through a cracked jug.

She had prided herself on always rising to every challenge. Nothing had defeated her before. Even when her brothers deserted her and left her to the queen's mercy, she had not broken. Instead, she had taken the biggest risk of her life, trusting her fate to a stranger by riding off with him.

Once again, she was alone with nowhere to go. She could not return to her former home and the life she'd left, yet how could she stay here when Rory did not want her?

Rory did not want her.

After devoting so much effort to avoid being wed to a man she did not want, she found herself bound to a man who did not want her. She would have laughed at the irony if she was not weeping so hard. She rocked herself and wept until she had no more tears left as she waited, hoping Rory would return.

But he did not come.

CHAPTER 31

Rap, rap.

Sybil did not bother lifting her head. The knock on the chamber door was too light to be Rory's. The servant was bound to go away.

Rap. Rap. Rap. This servant was persistent.

"I'm resting," Sybil called, her voice coming out as a croak.

When the door scraped open, she cursed herself for not crawling across the floor to draw the bar across it.

"Ye missed supper."

Oh, hell, it was Rory's sister. Catriona would not be dismissed as easily as a servant.

"*O shluagh!* What are ye doing on the floor in the dark?" Catriona said.

"Let me be," Sybil said.

The door shut with a click, but Catriona had not gone. Light footsteps crossed the room to the table and a lamp flared. Sybil flinched against the sudden light.

"Ach, it's freezing in here as well. Your brazier's gone out," Catriona said. "I'll take care of that as soon as we get ye up off the floor."

When Catriona knelt beside her, Sybil ignored her, hoping she would leave her to her misery.

"By the saints, what's wrong?" Catriona shook her arm. "Tell me."

"Your brother doesn't want me," Sybil said. "He regrets marrying me already."

"I don't believe that," Catriona said. "When ye stood up to him and invited the Munros to stay, I knew ye were the wife he needed. And I've no doubt you're the one he wants."

"Nay! He regrets ever seeing my face. Ever hearing my name. Ever bringing me here." Sybil shook her head as she spoke. "He regrets *everything.*"

Catriona lifted Sybil off the floor and dragged her to the low bench against the wall. After adding peat to the brazier and relighting the fire, she sat beside Sybil.

"If it's any comfort, my brother is in a dreadful state as well," Catriona said.

A sliver of hope entered Sybil's heart.

"He's not weeping, of course, but he's so foul-tempered that Alex threatened to throw him into the loch," Catriona said. "I watched the two of ye dancing last night, and ye both looked so happy. What happened?"

In halting words, Sybil told the story of her escape with Rory, the deception, and the rest, leaving out the intimate parts.

"I should have taken the secret to my grave," Sybil said. "But once I fell in love with him, I had to tell him. I just had to."

"Of course ye did," Catriona said. "I can see why Rory is upset that ye did not tell him sooner, but it makes perfect sense to me."

It made Sybil feel a wee bit better to have someone see her side of it.

"Let's get your face washed and fix your hair," Catriona said. "My mother used to say that will make ye begin to feel better."

"Mine said that too, but it won't help this time."

"Well, my mother also said that wallowing in misery never fixed a thing." Catriona leaned back and narrowed her eyes at Sybil. "Surely the two of ye can mend this breach."

"I don't know how to go about it," Sybil said. "Rory will never trust me again."

"After all ye went through to get here, ye seem like a determined and resourceful lass to me." Catriona patted Sybil's knee. "My brother is bullheaded, for certain. But you'll find a way."

Would she? Sybil had maneuvered through the politics and hidden undercurrents of court using the assets God gave her—her wits, her charm, her beauty. But what use were those in winning Rory's trust and forgiveness?

"Come, lass, where's your pride?" Catriona said with an encouraging smile. "Most of the clan believe you're just a weak Lowlander. They'll expect ye to give up at the first bump in the road. Ye want to prove them wrong, don't ye?"

"We Douglases may have our faults," Sybil said as she dried her tears, "but we are persistent."

Sybil straightened her shoulders. She would fight for Rory and her place as his wife. She had to. He might believe he could set aside their marriage, but she never could. She took a vow before God to be Rory's wife until death.

She would never let him go.

Damn it, Rory loved her. Even if he did not want to believe it anymore. She would find a way to earn his trust and win her Highlander back.

She must, for he owned her heart.

***

BANG, BANG, BANG!

Now *that* was Rory's knock. Though Sybil had been waiting for him for hours, she did not respond but remained by the window with her back to the door. When it crashed against the wall as he flung it open, she drew in a deep breath to prepare herself. Slowly, she turned around to face him.

She fought to maintain a placid expression while her heart lurched at the sight of him filling the doorway. With his icy expression, tousled hair, and angry green eyes, Rory looked as if he had swept in on the harsh northern wind like a Norse god of legend.

"Ye haven't been downstairs to the hall all day," he snapped. "Have ye forgotten we have a castle full of guests to celebrate our marriage?"

"Strange as it may seem, I don't feel much like celebrating."

When she turned her back on him again, he spun her around and glared down at her, his chest heaving. She was determined not to cower.

"I'll not have ye embarrass me like this," he said. "Half my clansmen already question my judgment for taking ye for my wife without proving them right on the first goddamn day."

"Perhaps ye should set me aside, then," she said in even tone.

"Don't tempt me." He took her arm and started walking her toward the door. "If ye don't want me to send ye back where ye came from, then you'll play the part of loyal wife in front of our guests. We both know how good ye are at pretending."

"I suggest you pretend you're not a brute for a moment and take your hands off me." She planted her feet and glared up at him until he released her arm, then she drew in a calming breath and brushed her skirts.

"Like it or no, ye will come with me," he said.

"My mother raised me to be a gracious hostess, no matter how trying the circumstances." As she spoke, she tidied the strands of hair that had fallen loose from her headdress. "So I will go charm our guests and pretend to be the *happiest* of brides."

Sybil marched down the stairs, determined to dazzle them all. She would show these MacKenzies—especially *the* MacKenzie. She was tougher than any of them knew.

And she was playing to win.

***

Rory watched Sybil move among their guests with her usual grace and beguiling charm. Though he had asked—nay, demanded—that she do precisely that, the ease with which she masked her feelings and led everyone to believe she was the happiest of brides irritated him to no end.

"Can't take your eyes off your bonny bride." An older man named Fergus elbowed him in the side and chuckled. "I had my doubts about ye taking a Lowlander for a wife. Thought she'd be haughty and cold, but Lady Sybil is a delightful lass."

"And she knows how to tell a good joke," the man on his other side said. "Want me to tell it to ye? Well, it starts with …"

Rory was wretched, and his wife was telling jokes? The group that surrounded her burst into laughter as if to prove it. In the center of them, Sybil's eyes sparkled and her cheeks were pink as she told a tale with great animation. Even more than her beauty, she had an inner glow that drew every person in the room to her.

Especially the men.

Malcolm appeared behind him and clamped a hand on his shoulder. "If ye can take your eyes off your bride for a wee bit, there are some men over by the hearth ye ought to speak with."

As the evening crawled by, Malcolm drew him from one group to another. Rory hoped he showed more patience than he felt while he listened to old men urging caution and young men arguing for an attack on Hector. They all offered simplistic platitudes, rather than useful advice.

He watched Sybil across the room as she, too, moved from group to group. Each time he glanced her way, the men surrounding her were hanging on her every word.

When he could not stand it anymore, he decided to find out what she was telling them that was so damned fascinating and pushed his way to her side.

"*A chuisle mo chroí,*" *pulse of my heart,* she greeted him. She looked so sincere when she smiled up at him that he could almost believe she meant the endearment.

Worse, he wanted to believe it, which made him angry all over again.

"I must see that another keg of ale is brought up," she said, and excused herself.

The man next to him spoke, dragging Rory's attention away from the sway of Sybil's hips as she glided away. "Your wife told us all about your plan."

What lie had Sybil told them? He should have known she would try to undermine him when she agreed so quickly to come to the hall.

"You're wise not to act rashly and attack Hector," the man said, nodding. "Better to proceed with caution."

"I agree," another man said. "If our clan is spilling each other's blood, the MacDonalds will see our division and seize upon our weakness."

"The MacDonalds are strong," a third man said. "We MacKenzies must fight as one if we are to push them back to the isles where they belong."

Rory wondered how Sybil had succeeded in persuading these recalcitrant men that his decision was sound—and even more, why she'd done it.

All evening, men filled Rory's cup to drink to his good fortune at finding such a bonny and clever wife. They could not see past her beauty and charm to her calculating and deceitful heart. She had fooled them, just as she had fooled him.

He was bleary-eyed with drink when the subject of their toasts slipped out of the hall and up the stairs. Luckily, Rory need not trust his wife to bed her.

"I'll leave ye now, lads." He stood up too quickly and had to grip the table to steady himself. "Wouldn't want to disappoint my bride."

The men laughed and slapped his back. Rory could hold his whisky better than most, but the circular stairs set his head to spinning.

When he pushed their bedchamber door open, Sybil was sitting on a stool, running a comb through her tumble of midnight hair. She looked up at him with those violet eyes and her full red lips parted, and desire tore through him like an angry storm.

God's bones, how he wanted her. When he crossed the room in three strides and pulled her to her feet, she looked up at him from under her lashes and her lips curved up at the corners. Good, she did not intend to deny him. He could take her to bed with no pretense that it meant anything more to either of them than lust. Isn't that what she had said after their first time?

Even drunk as he was, he knew he should wait until after he took her to bed to ask her what he wanted to know. The best course was to take her without a word. And yet he could not stop himself. He had to ask the question that had been burning a hole inside him ever since she confessed to her lies.

"Tell me, *wife*," he said, "how many men did ye have before me?"

Sybil slapped his face hard enough to sting.

"How many?" He held her wrist to prevent her from slapping him again.

"How dare ye ask me that?"

When her eyes filled with unshed tears, he stifled a twinge of remorse. Doubtless she could weep false tears as readily as she lied.

"Tell me," he said between clenched teeth. "Who had ye before I did?"

"Why does a man need to be first?" she said. "Was I yours?"

"Answer me, damn it," he said. "I've a right to know why my bride wasn't a virgin."

"I was not a virgin," she said, glaring up at him, "because I was married."

"Married!" Rory fell back a step. His heart could not take any more. "Jesus, Joseph, and Mary, ye have a husband?"

"I *had* a husband," she said. "We were wed a week when he died."

Sybil was widowed. He tried to take it in. Well, that would explain why she was over twenty and unmarried. He waited for her to say more, but Sybil's mouth was clamped shut.

"Is that all ye have to say about it?" he said. "Ye lied to me about being raped. For God's sake, do ye know what that lie did to me?"

He had been torn apart with rage and misery imagining how her innocence was violently stolen from her. And her tale of rape had made him feel so ashamed for not being gentle with her that first time.

"I spoke the truth when I said ye were the first man I gave myself to freely." Sybil stared past Rory's shoulder as she spoke. "My grandfather had toppled a king and ruled our clan for fifty years. I was a pawn and not permitted to refuse the marriage he arranged for me."

"An arranged marriage is no the same as rape," Rory bit out.

"To a woman, I assure you, it can feel very much the same." She brushed past him and went to stand at the window with her back to him.

"Tell me the rest of it," he demanded.

"Perhaps one day I will," she said. "You're not ready to listen now."

He heard a catch in her voice. By the saints, she could twist him in the wind if he let her. Talking had brought him no satisfaction, but he had a good idea of what would.

"'Tis late," he said, and pulled back the bedclothes. "We should go to bed."

"We're not both sleeping in this bed," she said, folding her arms. "Not after the things ye said to me."

"We're man and wife. We don't have to like each other to fook." He deliberately used the crass word for what he had foolishly thought was an act of love between them. What a fool he had been.

"You're not sleeping with me." She tugged the extra blanket off the bed and tossed it across the floor.

"I'm chieftain," he said. "I'm no sleeping on the floor."

"There's a servant's pallet under the bed. Ye can use that," she said. "But if ye prefer, ye can sleep in the hall and let all the men wonder what you've done to your new bride that she won't have you."

"Perhaps they'll think I'm the one who won't have you." He knew that was a ridiculous argument even before she rolled her eyes.

"After all my efforts to persuade your clansmen that I'm worthy to be the MacKenzie's wife and that you've made me *blissfully* happy," she said, "it would be a shame to ruin it."

"I don't find your gift for deceiving an entire hall full of people reassuring."

He pulled the pallet out from under the bed and fixed his gaze on her as he began unwinding his plaid.

She blew out the candle before he was bare-arsed. Apparently she was not as anxious to see him naked as he was to see her. He listened to the soft rustle of her removing her clothes and imagined her gown slipping off her shoulders and over her breasts… He was breathing hard long before the ropes holding the mattress creaked as she climbed into the big bed. No matter how much she had wronged him, he longed to feel her skin sliding over his, to move inside her, to hear her sighs and moans…

She was so quiet she must have fallen asleep, while he lay staring up at the ceiling with his feet hanging off the servant's pallet and his cock painfully hard.

"Have ye not tortured me enough?" he said aloud into the darkness. "After making me your husband with your lies, you've no right to deny me our marriage bed."

"After how it was between us before," she said. "I'll not have ye touching me when your heart isn't in it."

***

Sybil awoke to an empty room and fought the urge to draw the bedclothes over her head and weep. Instead, she dressed and steeled herself for a long day of pretending, for the benefit of their guests and household, that all was well between their chieftain and his new bride.

Before she had prepared herself, Rory came through the door and shut it behind him. Her heart swelled with unbridled hope.

"I apologize for my behavior last night," he said. "Though I was sorely disappointed to discover ye were untrustworthy and a liar, there was no call for me to be rude."

Sybil felt as if he had slapped her. "I know I was wrong, Rory, but ye judge me too harshly."

"I could forgive ye for deceiving me in the beginning, before ye knew me," he said. "But ye kept on lying to me. Every day for weeks ye continued to deceive me."

There was no point in arguing or trying to explain again. And the way he was speaking to her was beginning to prick her temper.

"Like it or not, we're wed now," she said. "And I'll not let ye set me aside."

"I can do nothing now without looking a fool, and ye know it," he said. "So for the time being, let's attempt to get along as best we can."

Without another word, he left her.

"Ye made vows to me, Rory Ian MacKenzie," she said, though he could no longer hear her, "and I'm holding ye to them."

CHAPTER 32

Rory's mood did not improve as the days wore on. He could avoid seeing Sybil most of the day, but he still spent his nights on the floor. He was so tired from lack of sleep that he did not notice Alex approach him in the courtyard until his brother was beside him.

"I'm surprised to see ye out of bed," Alex said, slapping him on the back. "You're still a newlywed."

"I'm also a chieftain with a great deal to accomplish." Rory was not telling his blissfully married younger brother that he had no reason to stay in bed, which was still a pallet on the damned floor.

"I see," Alex said. "Things are not well with you and that lovely wife of yours?"

"They're fine," Rory snapped. Alex was always too perceptive.

"That bad?" Alex said. "What have ye done?"

It irritated him that his brother assumed he was at fault. "I'm not prepared to discuss my wife with ye."

"I'm a priest. I could hear your confession…"

"*Alex*," he ground out. "Shouldn't ye be at home with your own wife when she's about to give birth?"

"My wife assures me all is well, but I've come to fetch Grizel to have a look at her just the same," he said. "If ye can spare him, Malcolm will come with us."

"Of course."

"While I'm here, Catriona and Grizel asked me to knock some sense into that stubborn head of yours," Alex said. "I'm sure ye can work this out with Sybil. Ye do know that with women ye have to talk?"

"I've nothing to say to her," Rory said. "And there's nothing she can say to me that will make a damned bit of difference."

"Ach, Rory." His brother's tone turned serious. "That's no way to resolve it. But if ye don't want to talk, try taking her to bed."

Sybil had made it clear that was unlikely to happen anytime soon.

"Go home," Rory said, and stomped off.

That night he lay awake again with his feet hanging off the too-small pallet and stared at the ceiling, while every fiber of his being was keenly aware of Sybil on the bed.

He could hear her breathing. He could almost feel her heartbeat.

It had been a week since their wedding night. Seven long days and longer nights. They could not go on like this much longer. At least he couldn't. Celibate and married. He'd gotten the worst of both.

His body did not care that Sybil had deceived him or that he could never trust her again. Every muscle was tense, and his cock was rock hard. He wanted her so badly his teeth ached.

She was his wife. His bride. He needed to beget an heir. They had a duty, for God's sake. Given Sybil's passionate nature, she had to give in sometime. But *how long* would it take?

Sybil sighed, and he imagined her breath on his skin. Could his cock get any harder? He'd never sleep like this. He threw off the blanket and got up.

"Rory?"

Desire drenched him at the sound of the soft voice calling his name.

"Aye?" He was afraid to hope. Tension thrummed through him as he stood waiting.

He stopped breathing when he heard her get out of bed and walk lightly across the floor to him. Then she brushed her fingertip along the side of his hip, and he thought he would explode.

"Ach, Sybil," he said. "Tell me this means you'll let me have ye."

***

Denying Rory her bed had not gained Sybil what she wanted and made them both miserable. She could only hope that by giving in to passion she could break through his barriers and force him to see her. In this battle to win back his heart, she feared he would break hers again. But she had to take the risk.

Because she simply could not bear another night without his touch.

"Sybil?" he said in a strained voice.

"Aye." She barely got out the word before he hauled her up against him and crushed his mouth against hers.

The pent-up hunger of the last week exploded between them like grease on a hot fire. Their kisses were bruising, and his hands demanding as he backed her against the wall. When he lifted her off her feet, she clasped her legs around his hips. Her heart was racing, and her chest felt too tight to breathe. When she broke her mouth away, he sucked on the side of her neck. His hands were everywhere, prodding, kneading, squeezing.

At last. At last. She wanted him so much.

"I need to taste you." He dropped to his knees and gripped her hips.

She gasped as he thrust his tongue over the sensitive nub between her legs. No slow build, no teasing caresses. He was relentless with his mouth and tongue, circling and sucking. She leaned her head back against the wall, swamped by the raw intensity of the sensations coursing through her body. When she did not think she could stand any more, he began thrusting his finger inside her while he continued his sensuous assault with his mouth and tongue.

Her release came with such force that her knees gave way. He gave her no time to recover. In one smooth motion, he rose to his feet, wrapped her legs around him, and thrust inside her. His mouth ravaged hers, and she dug her nails into his shoulders as the tension inside her quickly peaked again.

"Ah! Ah! Ah!" She came in a rolling release as Rory pounded against her and spilled his seed on a last anguished cry.

It was over so quickly.

She was breathless and her heart pounded in her ears. After climaxes that left her weak and shaking, she could not say he had failed to satisfy her.

Yet when he pulled out of her, she felt bereft. There had not been one tender moment, not one whispered endearment. It was a physical act, the satisfying of a need, and it left her feeling hollow inside.

Rory had not spoken her name. She could have been anyone.

With no warning, she burst into tears. It was the last thing she wanted to do. When she tried to hide her face, Rory held her arms away.

He looked down at her with wild, feverish eyes. "Ye wanted it as much as I did. Ye came to me. Ye said *aye*."

"I want it like it was before," she whispered, and touched his cheek. "I love you."

"That's not fair, Sybil. Lie to me about anything else, but not that." He backed away from her, shaking his head. "I can't do this. I can't."

***

Rory had been gone for days when a priest arrived at the castle leading a mule.

Sybil only knew where Rory had gone because Catriona told her he was taking her to Killin to retrieve something hidden in the barn and to get the local men started on rebuilding the house.

Sybil thought nothing of seeing the stranger in priestly robes at supper that evening. Churchmen were always welcomed and given provisions when they stopped at noble houses on their journeys. She felt too low to engage him in conversation, as she usually would.

Long after she had blown out her candles and gone to bed, there was a knock at her door. Her first thought was that something had happened to Rory, but when she flung the door open, the strange priest was there.

"I was sent to give this to you." He spoke in Lowland Scots, the language of home, which she had not heard in weeks.

She took the folded parchment he handed her. When she turned it over and recognized the seal, her hand went to her throat.

She glanced up and down the dimly lit stairwell. "You'd best come inside while I read it."

She quickly lit a candle, broke the seal, and unfolded the parchment. A second message was enclosed inside the first.

She glanced up at the messenger. "How did ye get this?"

"Your uncle is my bishop," he said. "As soon as he learned where you were, he sent me to deliver it to you."

Edinburgh
My dear niece,
Several weeks ago I received the enclosed message for you, along with a request to make the necessary arrangements. Word has just reached me that you have taken refuge at Castle Leod. The man who carries this missive will take you to Inverness to board a ship

bound for Calais. I have sacrificed precious funds to arrange your passage so that you may join your brothers in France.

The signature at the bottom was indeed her uncle's. She opened the second message that was enclosed in the first. Tears stung her eyes when she saw the familiar handwriting. While she was still angry with her brothers, she had not realized until this moment that she also missed them.

George had scrawled his note and signed it with his familiar but illegible signature—the very one that had started her on her journey with Rory.

It distressed me greatly to leave you behind. I took comfort in knowing that if you were ever truly in danger, there were always men willing to play the hero for you. But a wild Highlander? That was unexpected, but then, you always did like an adventure. I daresay you'll entertain us for hours with the tale.

You will adore Paris. I predict you'll have all the men at the French court falling at your feet within a week. We could use your help in gaining support.

With great affection from your loving brother,
G

Archie had added a line at the bottom in his elegant hand.

Gather what jewels and other valuables you can and come to Paris. – A

Fighting angry tears, she read the letter again. No apology. No expression of concern for her safety. And her escape from the queen's clutches through dangerous lands with a stranger was *an adventure*?

"Lady Sybil," the priest said, "are you ready to leave for the ship?"

She ought to go. Rory did not want her here. He and the MacKenzies would be better off if he took a different wife. But she did not want to go. Not to Paris. Not to her brothers.

Nor anywhere that Rory was not.

"Thank my uncle, but tell him I cannot leave," she said. "At least not yet."

"Are ye certain, m'lady? If ye change your mind, the ship doesn't set sail for a week." The priest asked for ink and quill, then wrote the name of the ship and the date it sailed on the bottom of her uncle's message. "Ye know how to get to Inverness?"

"Aye." She remembered Rory telling her one could sail there from Beauly. "But I won't come."

After the priest left, she put the ink and quill back in the drawer where she kept her drawings. She hesitated, then tucked the messages underneath them.

CHAPTER 33

When Sybil learned that Rory had returned while she was down in the kitchens speaking with the cook, she went looking for him. Patience was not one of her virtues, and it was past time he forgave her. She was determined to find a way to mend things between them. She had to try. Despite how much he had hurt her, she missed him terribly.

As she started past the door to an empty chamber, she heard someone moving inside and peered in. Her husband and his sister were leaning over a table staring at the pages of an open book. Both wore intense, puzzled expressions.

The pair looked up as she entered the room. When Rory's gaze locked on hers, she knew he was also remembering the last time they saw each other—both the violence of their passion and how he'd left her with the flush of pleasure still on her skin and tears in her eyes. From his worried frown, she thought perhaps she had broken through his barriers that day after all.

Or perhaps he just feared she would start weeping again. He need not worry about that. She did falter for a moment, but then she drew herself up and put on a pleasant smile.

"You two look perplexed by that book," she said. "Perhaps I can help?"

"Nay," Rory said at the same time Catriona said, "Aye."

Sybil chose the response she wanted and joined them at the table. The book looked like a ledger, with items written in neat columns. A second book was under it.

"Can ye read?" Catriona asked.

Sybil nodded. "I take it this ledger is important?"

"Don't—" Rory said.

"Our brother Brian brought these two books—ledgers, as ye call them—to me for safekeeping," Catriona said. "I'm thinking they must hold a clue as to why he was angry with Hector and rode off to Edinburgh."

"Let me take a look," Sybil said, and squeezed between them.

This was not how she envisioned winning Rory back, but she knew to take advantage of an opportunity when she saw one. As she ran her finger down the page, she forgot about her problems with Rory and became absorbed in the puzzle.

"'Tis written in Latin, probably by a scribe," she said. "This column on the left appears to be a list of names."

They were colorful Highlander names that loosely translated into Black-haired Donald, One-eyed Collum, and Handsome Ullium with two wives.

"This column on the right contains an assortment of items, mostly farm animals and grain." She read them off as she ran her finger down the column. "One pig. Two geese. Thirty pounds of oats. One chicken."

"It's the ledger of tenants' payments to the laird," Rory said, rubbing his jaw. "I wonder what Brian found amiss. He wouldn't become upset because a tenant held back a chicken."

Sybil flipped the book closed to read what was written on the front cover. "It says Eilean Donan."

"The ledger is supposed to stay at the castle," Rory said. "Brian wouldn't have taken it without good reason."

"Brian could read Latin?" Sybil asked.

"Aye," Catriona said. "He was good at numbers as well. He should have been a scholar."

"Let me study these for a while," Sybil said. "Perhaps I can figure out what is in them that upset your brother."

She pulled up a stool and opened the first page.

***

Rory watched Sybil pore over the page, feeling irritated that he needed her for this. Though he did not trust her, he could at least be certain she was not in league with Hector. When she bit her lip as she worked, his mind drifted to all the times he had kissed those lips.

But as he watched her, those tantalizing memories were replaced by the image of her the last time he saw her, leaning against the wall after their frenzied passion. It was not her tears that had haunted his days and nights since—he suspected she could turn them on and off at will—but the sadness that had shone in her eyes and weighed down her bright spirit. Now she behaved as if nothing had happened. Which was an act?

She looked up and seemed surprised to find him and Catriona still in the room.

"This could take some time," she said, making a shooing motion with her hand as she returned her attention to the page. "You two should go eat or...something."

After an hour, Rory returned, but she did not even look up. Catriona came back with him after supper and brought a platter of food, which Sybil absently munched on as she slowly flipped through the pages. She was working her way through the second ledger now.

The candles were burning low the third time he and Catriona returned. He was going to insist Sybil stop for the night when she looked up with a glint of victory in her eyes, like a warrior who knows he has won the battle.

"Ach, your uncle Hector is a wicked man," she said. "He robbed your brother blind."

Rory folded his arms and waited for Sybil to explain.

"Both these ledgers have lists of animals, bags of grain, and coin for each quarter of the year," Sybil said, then tapped the ledger on her right with her forefinger. "But the quarterly lists in this second ledger have no men's names, and the lists are short with large quantities—twenty pigs, twelve goats, and such. I had to add it all up to be certain, but the entries in the second ledger are sums of the entries in the first. So, one pig each from five tenants in the first ledger will be listed as five pigs in the second."

"You're good with figures as well as reading," Catriona said.

"My brothers' tutors thought so," Sybil said as if this were nothing and opened the second ledger. "Now I'm getting to the interesting part. This second ledger records what was done with all these pigs and fowl and bags of grain."

Rory saw how confident she was and knew she was onto something, but he still had no notion what it was.

"Some of the stores were kept at Eilean Donan to be consumed at the castle," she said.

"What else could be done with geese and oats?" Catriona asked.

"All the surplus was taken to Edinburgh and sold," Sybil said. "The coin from the sales there plus any coin originally collected from the tenants was then taken to your uncle's estate in Gairloch."

Rory sat up straight. "To Gairloch? Are ye certain?"

"Aye, 'tis clear as day once I figured out the pattern," she said. "Your uncle had an arrangement with an Edinburgh merchant who sold the goods on his behalf. Judging by how the money and goods appear to flow smoothly back and forth, my guess is that this was a well-established arrangement."

"What do ye mean by that?"

She lifted one shoulder in a feminine shrug. "This arrangement has likely gone on for years."

"What proof do ye have that the coin was taken to my uncle's own estate in Gairloch?"

This was the important part. There was nothing wrong in selling the surplus unless Hector took the money for himself.

"Let me find the clerk's notation," Sybil said, flipping through the pages again. "Ah, here it is. *I..., clerk and loyal servant to Sir Hector of Gairloch, this twenty-seventh day of February in the year of our Lord...*"

By the saints, how did she have the patience to wade through such tedious detail for hours? Even if Rory could read, he could not have kept his eyes open.

"*...did place the above recorded amount*," she continued, "*into the hands of Big Duncan of the Axe to deliver to Gairloch.*"

"That proves it," Rory said, stabbing the open ledger with his forefinger. "Duncan is Hector's most trusted man, and he took the money from the chieftain's castle at Eilean Donan to Hector's lands in Gairloch."

Hector had stolen from the chieftain, which was stealing from the clan.

"I'm going to kill Hector!" Rory clenched his fists. "When I'm done with him there won't be enough left of him to feed to the crows."

"Killing him may not be necessary," Sybil said, "when you can use this information to keep him in his place."

Rory *wanted* to kill him, but killing him might do more harm than good.

"News of his thievery will badly damage Hector's reputation in the clan," he said. "I'll announce it in the hall in the morning, and word will spread fast."

"I believe this will also help sway the regent and council to throw the crown's support behind you," Sybil said. "After all, they are all chieftains. This evidence of Hector's theft from his chieftain will weigh heavily against him."

"I can't leave MacKenzie lands to make my case to the council."

"Let Lord Lovat show them the evidence," Sybil said. "He'll know how best to present this to your advantage. As your mother's brother, he's also in a good position to persuade them that Hector's lies about your birth are false. He's sure to argue passionately for the crown to recognize you as chieftain."

Rory had to admit, at least to himself, that she was right.

"What would we do without you?" Catriona kissed Sybil's cheek and gave Rory a pointed look. "I'm leaving tomorrow to help Alex's wife with the children, so I'll bid ye goodbye now. Ye should get some rest. Ye must be exhausted."

The excitement that had animated Sybil's face faded like a cloud passing over the sun. She squeezed Catriona's hand and then left them without a word.

"Would it hurt ye to show your wife a wee bit of gratitude?" Catriona put her hands on her hips and glared up at him. "Ye wanted to know what Brian was desperate to tell you and why he rode to Edinburgh. Sybil not only found the answers ye wanted, but she also gave ye a powerful weapon to use against Hector."

"That served her own interests. She wants to keep her position as a chieftain's wife," he said, though his sister's criticism did tug at his conscience.

Catriona raised her hands as if beseeching the heavens. "How can the big brother I've always looked up to be such a fool?"

"You've no notion just what a fool she made of me," he said. "I'll not let her do it again."

"Sybil told me everything," Catriona said with a dismissive wave of her hand. "If ye ask me, her brother's trick brought ye the best luck you'll ever have."

"She used and deceived me," Rory said. "I'll never be able to trust her."

"Of course ye can," Catriona said. "Can't ye see that she loves ye?"

Was it possible, despite her deceit, that her feelings for him were true? He did not know what to think anymore.

He slept in the stables with the damned horses. In the morning, after announcing the theft in the hall and telling his men to be ready to ride to Lovat's, he decided to take the advice Alex had given him days ago. He went to talk with Sybil.

She was still in her night shift and brushing her hair when he entered their bedchamber. Her toes peeked out from under her white shift, making her look young and innocent, which she was not, but the sight somehow made him feel protective.

"When ye told me ye were married before, ye said there was more ye could tell me when I was ready to listen," he said. "I'm ready to listen now."

She was quiet for so long he did not know if she would speak.

"I was wed when I was thirteen," she said.

Ach, that was young to wed. Rory recalled his sister at thirteen. Though Sybil would have been far more sophisticated at that age than Catriona, it did not sit well with him.

"I was a young girl, happily spoiled by my parents and the servants," she said. "I thought life was a joy and I was special. My husband taught me that was a lie."

"Ye said he died after only a week." Rory folded his arms. How much could she have suffered in a week with a feeble old man on death's door? "I suppose ye had this elderly husband wrapped around your wee finger."

"He was a strong and handsome young man." Sybil fixed him with an unwavering gaze. "He was also an arrogant, unfeeling, selfish brute—both in and out of bed."

Did Sybil lie to him now? His gut told him no. Her tale had the ring of truth.

"I can understand when a man must inflict harm on an enemy to protect himself or others," she said. "But to take pleasure in being cruel and to do it simply because he can, well..."

Jesu. Rory rubbed his hands through his hair. "He hurt you?"

"After being sorely used and beaten by turns for a week," she said, "I told him that if he ever touched me again, I would kill him."

Where were the men of her family? In the Highlands, the lass's family would come with their swords drawn. And if the bride was a member of the chieftain's family, mistreating her could easily lead to a clan war.

"He laughed at my threat. Why wouldn't he? I was just a weak, young girl." Sybil turned to face him, and she had that determined look in her eyes. "But I would have killed him."

Even at thirteen, she had expected to deal with a threat to her life on her own. His heart ached for that brave young lass.

"His horse threw him and broke his neck that very day," she said. "That's how God spared me from committing the sin of murder."

Sybil was a survivor, and she did what she had to do.

Rory wished she had trusted him instead of deceiving him. He wished even more that she loved him. But if she was only trying to protect herself, he had judged harshly.

He started to reach for her hand when someone pounded on the door.

"Laird," the man called through the door, "the men are ready to ride."

"I must go now," he told her. "But we'll speak more when I return."

Rory had much to think about, and the ride to Lovat's and back would give him the time he needed.

CHAPTER 34

"How dare that weasel Hector of Gairloch call my sister a whore," Lovat said as he paced in front of a giant portrait of himself. "I'll tell the council this is an affront I'll not tolerate."

Rory was relieved Lovat was willing to go to the king's council on his behalf, though Lovat was perhaps more motivated by the insult to Fraser honor than by his desire to see Rory's claim to the chieftainship recognized by the crown.

"Of course, Hector can have no proof to support his despicable lie because there is none. No man knew my sister Agnes, before or after your father," Lovat said. "But if you could find that papal bull, that would settle the matter for good."

"If my mother had it at Killin, it was destroyed in the fire, and Alex has not been able to find the church's record," Rory said. "But I brought something else for ye to show to the council."

Rory set the ledgers from Eilean Donan on the table. As Lovat looked through them, Rory explained the thievery Sybil had uncovered.

"These will be an enormous help in swaying the regent and council against Hector. As chieftains themselves, they will judge him most harshly for stealing from his laird," Lovat said, which was exactly what Sybil had said. "Not only will I ask for a royal declaration that you are the rightful heir, but I'll also petition for an order commanding Hector to relinquish Eilean Donan into your possession and to repay all that he's stolen over the years."

"I appreciate your going to Edinburgh to speak on my behalf," Rory said as Lovat walked him out.

"Ye say it was Lady Sybil who uncovered the scheme?" Lovat said. "She's a clever lass."

"Aye." Rory waited for Lovat to harp again about Sybil being the wrong wife for him. She may have won over Alex and Catriona, but Lovat was a cynical man of the world.

"I confess I made an error in judgment about your wife," Lovat said with a smile. "She'll watch your back, that one will."

Rory thought of the times she had stepped in to support him, even when he did not know he needed the help, as with the Munro chieftain.

"Ach, what a queen she'd make," Lovat said, shaking his head. "That lass understands the fine art of negotiation and how to gracefully apply the right pressure at the right time without engendering hard feelings."

Rory was not sure he liked Lovat giving his wife extravagant compliments any more than he had appreciated him insulting her.

"Trust me," Lovat said, putting his arm around Rory's shoulders, "you'll find these useful qualities in a chieftain's wife."

"How is it that ye came to learn all this about my wife?" Rory asked.

"Let's just say the two of us reached an understanding." An amused smile played on Lovat's lips. "A remarkable woman. I wouldn't want her for an enemy."

Rory rode home as if the devil was chasing him. He had let his pride blind him. Sybil had learned to maneuver through court politics because her family required her to—and she had to in order to survive. Instead of criticizing her for it, he should appreciate the skills she gained, not the least of which were her quick and acute perceptions about the motives and true nature of others she met.

She had not set out to deceive him about the marriage contract or done it out of spite or cruelty, but because she was in fear for her life. She did not confess sooner because she had not trusted him enough to tell him. After how she had been abandoned by her friends and family, it was no wonder she was slow to trust. He was slow to trust himself, so he should have understood.

She could have kept the secret forever. Instead, when she finally did trust him, she told him the truth. And what had he done? He had shouted and berated her. Insulted and rebuffed her. Used her and made her weep.

He spurred Curan to a gallop. He needed to get home to Sybil and try to make things right.

***

Hector drank down another whisky. He was going to skin his clerk at Eilean Donan and then boil him in oil for letting those ledgers out of his hands. As both Catriona and the ledgers had arrived safely at Castle Leod, Duncan had failed to burn them with the house at Killin.

Even if Rory had the ledgers, how in the hell had he figured out the theft Hector had successfully hidden for so many years? Now half of Hector's own men were eyeing him with questions in their eyes.

He took another drink. The ledgers did not matter. His plans were set in motion. When he was done with Rory, no one in Clan MacKenzie would remember the theft.

It was long after midnight when the bishop, of all people, arrived at his door and interrupted his drinking. Hector eyed the churchman. He was a squirrelly man, physically weak and pompous.

"Good evening to ye," Hector said. "What brings ye out to see me at such a late hour?"

The bishop smoothed his robes with his long, slender hands. Christ, what man did that?

"I've found something I believe will interest you."

"A young virgin with parents desperate for coin?" Hector laughed.

"I believe you'll find what I have is far more valuable." The bishop paused. "I assume you heard of your brother's request for a papal bull declaring his marriage to Lovat's daughter valid and the children of the marriage legitimate."

The bishop had his full attention now. "What do ye know about this papal bull?"

"The request was supported by my predecessor to our cardinal, who, in turn, forwarded it to Rome."

"Did the pope act on it?"

"He most certainly did," the bishop said with a thin smile. "The Holy Father granted your brother's request in all regards."

"Goddamn it to hell." Hector slammed his fist on the table. This was the last thing he needed now. It could ruin all his plans. "Do you have it?"

Rory surely did not have it. If he did, he would have waved it from the tower of Castle Leod when he heard the lies Hector spread about not being his father's true son.

"The papal bull arrived shortly after your brother's death," the bishop said. "I delivered it personally to his widow, Lady Agnes, who destroyed it."

"Why would she do that?"

"She confided in me that she feared it would put her son Rory's life in greater jeopardy." The bishop laced his long fingers together. *"To be blunt, she believed you'd have him murdered."*

Agnes was as clever as she was beautiful. Hector gulped down the rest of his whisky to dull the old, familiar pain. She should have been his. If she had been, her sons would have been his and they would not have been at cross-purposes.

"She said she would destroy it, and she begged me never to disclose that the petition was ever granted."

"How much did ye make her pay for your secrecy?" Hector asked.

"The emerald ring was a generous gift to the church," the bishop said, admiring the glinting stone on his pinky. *"That could not, of course, dissuade me from performing my duty to keep meticulous records for the church."*

The bishop was finally getting to the point of his visit.

"'Tis not every day we receive a document from the Holy Father himself," the bishop said. *"Only the original document had the pope's leaden seal, but I made a copy for our records."*

"So you've come to ask what I'll pay ye to destroy these records."

When the bishop gave him a smug smile, Hector took hold of the front of his robes and backed him into the wall.

"If ye believe I'd murder Rory, who is my own flesh and blood," Hector said, *"what makes ye think I won't slice the throat of a churchman who threatens me?"*

"I'm not threatening you," the bishop said in a calm voice. *"I'm offering a service you need. After the unfortunate news about the theft at Eilean Donan, the value is even greater than before. Tsk, tsk. Such a shame about those ledgers."*

"Once I'm chieftain," Hector said, *"I'll donate a grand sum to the church for ye to use as ye see fit."*

"I'd prefer something now."

Hector laughed. The bishop had ice in his veins and was driven by greed and ambition. They could no doubt work together. When he tossed a bag of coin on the table, the bishop nodded in agreement and pulled a rolled sheaf of parchment from his sleeve.

"You're certain this is the only evidence this bull was issued?" Hector asked.

"There will be a record in Rome, but it could take years to obtain confirmation from the Holy See."

Hector held the copy of the papal bull over the candle and watched it burn until there was nothing left but a few black cinders on the table. That was one less obstacle.

"There's something else I'll need ye to do for me," Hector told the bishop. "I'll get word to ye."

"I find being of service most rewarding," the bishop said, and took his leave.

"Fetch the old woman," Hector shouted to the guard who stood outside his door. Thinking she might need encouragement, he added, "And bring her granddaughter up from the dungeon."

When the time came, the old woman would say and do exactly what he told her to.

***

"There are visitors riding up to the gate, Lady Sybil," the guard told her. "The MacKenzie is not back yet."

"Who are they?"

"Members of the Grant clan, including their chieftain and"—he paused and cleared his throat—"his family."

"The Grants are friends of Clan MacKenzie, are they not?"

"'Tis hard to say," he said, scratching his neck. "They used to be."

The Highland custom of showing hospitality to all guests, friend or foe, was practically sacred, so she wondered why he was so uneasy.

"Thank you," she said. "I'll come out to the courtyard to greet them."

"I'd best ride out to meet the laird," he said. "He's expected soon, and he'll want to know the Grants are here."

After tidying a loose curl that had escaped and brushing her gown with her palms, Sybil hurried outside. She was waiting at the top of the steps to the keep when the gate creaked open to admit a large party of riders. The gray-haired warrior who led them was the Grant chief, judging by his air of authority and the jeweled pin that fastened his plaid on his shoulder.

On either side of the chief rode two men who shared his strong features and hard expressions. They were an intimidating trio, and behind them rode thirty Highland warriors armed with claymores, axes, and dirks. Sybil put on a bright smile and started down the steps.

The Grant chief dismounted, and at his signal, all his men did the same. When the chief started up the steps, she came halfway down to meet him.

"*Mìle fàilte oirbh,*" *a thousand welcomes*, she said.

Her greeting—in fact, her very presence—seemed to sour the Grant chief's already cheerless expression.

"Who are you?" he demanded.

Sybil was startled by his rudeness. She straightened to her full height, which still left her a head shorter than the Grant chieftain.

"I am the wife of the MacKenzie," she said.

His brows shot up. After a long moment of stunned silence, he seemed to recall his manners and gave her a stiff bow. "I apologize for my discourtesy. I'd not heard that Rory had taken a wife."

"I understand your surprise," she said, though she was puzzled by how strongly he reacted to the news. "Our marriage is quite recent."

"Aye, it would be," he said. "Let me introduce my sons."

The Grant chief motioned to the two warriors who looked like younger versions of himself, with their straight, dark hair, piercing gray eyes, muscular builds, and wicked-looking weapons. As his sons stepped forward to join him, several MacKenzie warriors moved to either side of Sybil, ready to draw their weapons. She gave them a warning glance and a slight shake of her head, but they remained at her side.

When the first of Grant's sons swept her a deep bow as his father introduced him, she sensed the tension of her guards ease a fraction. The other brother followed suit. Sybil was distracted by the sound of thundering hooves approaching the gate and failed to catch his name.

"And this is my grandson," the Grant chieftain said, stretching out his arm in the direction of the Grant warriors.

Sybil looked past them to see Rory and several of his men galloping through the gate.

"Come, lad," Grant said, drawing her attention back to her guests.

Sybil caught a glimpse of a young boy with copper curls emerging from the Grant warriors, but quickly shifted her gaze back to Rory, who leaped off his horse, dropped the reins without waiting for the stable boy, and started running toward them. Everything about him signaled urgency. But why? Did he not trust her to greet their guests properly?

Remembering her manners, she smiled as the chieftain's grandson, a boy of eight or nine, came forward. Her smile faltered as she found herself looking into familiar green eyes.

"This is Kenneth Grant MacKenzie." The Grant chief raised his voice so that it carried throughout the courtyard. "He is your husband's son and heir."

The ground seemed to shift under her, and a small, high-pitched gasp escaped her throat. Sybil felt as if she was falling backward into a black, bottomless chasm as her gaze traveled over the child's face. He had Rory's dimple in his chin and the same wide, expressive mouth.

And still, her mind could not accept what the Grant chieftain said as true. Nay, Rory would not have kept something—rather, someone—so important a secret from her.

"Sybil—"

She raised her gaze from the boy to Rory, who had come to a halt behind him. The truth was written in the guilt on her husband's face. She understood now why the guard had hurried to fetch Rory, why the other MacKenzie guards were so uneasy about her meeting their guests, and why Rory had raced back to the castle.

The Grant chieftain had told her the truth. This boy was Rory's son.

She felt as if an iron clamp was tightening around her chest and struggled to draw breath. How could Rory have hidden the boy's existence from her? She knew instinctively that every MacKenzie and every Grant here knew what Rory had failed to tell her, his wife.

She felt the sting of tears at the back of her eyes as she and Rory locked gazes over the boy's head. It was bad enough that her husband had mistrusted and disrespected her—and that everyone knew it. She would not humiliate herself further by letting them see how very much the insult wounded her.

For once, she was grateful for the years she spent navigating her way through the slings and arrows of court life. She needed the lessons of every single day of it to maintain her composure. These Highlanders saw that Rory had made a fool of his ignorant Lowlander wife.

She refused to let them see that he had also ripped out her heart.

CHAPTER 35

Rory's labored breaths filled his ears like an echo of the accusation he saw in Sybil's eyes. As soon as he heard that the Grants had come to the castle, he turned his horse homeward at a gallop, in the hope that he could speak to her first.

But the time to tell her was long since passed.

One look into his wife's face, and Rory understood the depths of the error he had made. She only let it show for a moment before a mask of calm shuttered her expression, but the naked pain he saw in that moment pierced his heart like a hot blade in the center of his chest.

Now, the slight tremor of her fingers against the skirt of her gown was all that betrayed the storm of emotions she was hiding. God in heaven, would she ever forgive him?

Grant cleared his throat with growl, reminding Rory that he faced not one, but two disasters.

"Kenneth has reached his eighth birthday, the age at which tradition dictates a child should leave his mother's clan for his father's." Grant clamped a hand on his grandson's shoulder. "Your son should be raised as a MacKenzie."

Rory could strangle Grant for forcing the issue now. His timing had nothing to do with tradition and everything to do with Rory's unexpected rise to clan chieftain.

"Ye shouldn't have brought the lad," Rory hissed in a low voice.

Tension flowed among Rory, Grant and Sybil like a surging river on the verge of breaching its banks and drowning them all.

"Nonsense, *mo chroí*," Sybil said with a smile on her lips and daggers in her eyes. "I would not have wanted to wait a moment longer to meet your son."

"He's no—" Rory started to say but bit his tongue. This was not the time or place, in front of the boy.

Sybil looked down at the lad then, and showed once again just how remarkable she was. Genuine warmth filled her eyes, and she took the lad's hand and leaned down to speak to him.

"I can see you're a wee bit worried by all of this, but ye needn't be," she said in a soft voice Rory had to strain to hear. "Ye see, I've left the comfort of my home and family to come live with these MacKenzies too, so I think you and I are going to become the very best of friends."

While he and Grant postured, Sybil showed her generosity of spirit by recognizing the lad's fears. She had as much pride as any of them and more reason to feel affronted. And yet, out of kindness, she welcomed the child into her home and family as if his arrival was a gift she had long hoped for. Rory loved her even more for it, and he knew he did not deserve her.

"What do ye say, Kenneth," she said, "shall we be friends and mind each other's backs among these wild MacKenzies?"

After studying her face, the lad gave her a solemn nod.

"I'd wager that a growing young man like you must be hungry after your long ride."

The lad nodded, more vigorously this time. Sybil straightened and bestowed her smile on the rest of the Grants—but definitely not on Rory.

"Again, welcome to our home," she told them. "We'd be honored if you would join us for dinner."

The lad held tightly to Sybil's hand as she led them up the steps of the keep. Just before the guard opened the door and she swept inside, she gave Rory a look over her shoulder that could have frozen a loch.

***

It was a wonder Rory did not get frostbite sitting between Grant and Sybil. And Grant was the warmer of the two. While Sybil engaged in a lively conversation with everyone else at the table, each attempt he made to converse with her was met with a *hmmph* or nothing at all. She refused to even look at him.

He wished he could take her upstairs at once and explain everything to her, but relations with the Grants were already at the breaking point without insulting them by leaving the table.

Sybil was all charm and smiles to their uninvited guests, especially Grant's grandson, whom she had seated on her other side. Placing the lad in an honored position above his uncles at the high table, as if he were Rory's heir, was *not* helpful. Rory could not move the lad to a more appropriate seat without creating still more trouble with the Grant chieftain, and she damn well knew it.

"You've never been to Castle Leod before?" he heard her ask.

The lad, who had stuffed a large piece of roasted pork in his mouth, shook his head.

"But surely ye must have spent some time with your father?" she said. "Was it at one of the other MacKenzie castles or perhaps at your grandfather's?"

"Nay," the lad said around the food in his cheek. When he noticed Rory was watching him, his cheeks turned pink and his gaze dropped to the table.

Though Sybil's face was turned away from him, Rory could feel her indignation. She was judging him, though she knew nothing of the circumstances.

He had his reasons for not seeing the lad. Good reasons. But he should have told her long before now.

The moment the meal was finished, Sybil stood to leave.

"It was a delight to meet you all, especially Kenneth." Sybil squeezed the lad's shoulder, and the two beamed at each other. "Now I'm sure you men have matters ye wish to discuss."

"We most certainly do," Grant said, his eyes burning holes into Rory.

Without sparing Rory a glance, she left the table. He watched her straight back as she walked toward the stairs.

The outside doors to the hall banged open, jolting his attention as a young woman burst inside. Her hair was loose and tangled, and her eyes red from weeping.

"Why have ye taken wee Kenneth, Father?" she cried out.

Rory dropped his head onto his arms on the table.

Jesu! This was Grant's daughter, the lass he was supposed to marry.

***

Sybil stood frozen, transfixed by the young woman's startling appearance. She looked like a distraught Viking princess, tall and striking and uncontrolled. The violence of her emotions was evident in her red-rimmed eyes, dirt-smudged face, and unruly tangle of blond hair.

"Why are ye here, Daughter," the Grant chieftain ground out, "and not at home where ye ought to be?"

"As soon as I found out ye took him," she said between gasps for breath, "I had to come."

"By all that is holy," Grant shouted, "tell me, Flora Grant, that ye did not ride all the way here by yourself?"

"I did," his daughter said.

From the state she was in, she had ridden hard to get here.

"Ye bring shame upon me and our clan." Her father's face was growing dangerously purple. "Wait for me outside in the courtyard."

"I must know why ye brought Kenneth here," the lass persisted, clenching her hands. "I'll not let ye leave him here with no one to protect him."

God help her, was this Kenneth's mother? And Rory's lover? Sybil felt faint.

There was talk of a marriage between me and a chieftain's daughter. The pieces fell together, like blocks of stone. No wonder Grant was angry upon learning that Sybil was Rory's wife. This lass was the chieftain's daughter that Rory was meant to marry.

The woman he *would* have married, if he'd known his marriage contract with Sybil was false.

Sybil had managed to keep her composure through the shock of learning he'd kept the existence of his son and heir from her. But this was too much. And yet she remained at the bottom of the stairs, unable to leave until she heard the rest.

"Why would the lad need protection in the MacKenzie castle?" Rory's voice was low and dangerous, and his eye twitched. "Are ye suggesting I would harm a bairn?"

"Ye don't want him," the lass said, "or ye would have claimed him."

"I haven't claimed him," Rory said between clenched teeth, "because I don't believe he's mine."

How could Rory say that to the mother of his child? And in front of the child, for God's sake. Sybil's gaze caught on Kenneth. The poor boy was struggling against one of his uncles, who was preventing him from running to his mother.

"How dare ye insult my dead daughter!" the Grant chieftain roared.

Dead daughter? Sybil had no time to absorb this information.

Swords were about to be drawn. Sybil had to stop this before blood was spilled.

***

Too late, Rory realized that he'd let his temper get away from him and gravely offended his guest. He needed to make amends with the Grants and keep them as allies, not cross swords with their chieftain.

"Stop this at once!" Sybil shouted, drawing everyone's attention. "Can't ye see you're frightening young Kenneth? And if there's to be a fight, it will *not* be inside my hall."

Before they recovered from their shock at her bold words, she crossed the hall to the high table and pointed at Grant's son, who was holding the lad.

"Release him, please," she told the uncle, and he complied.

She took the lad's hand and led him to Grant's daughter, who threw her arms around him. The only sound in the room was the lass's weeping, while the men who had been on the verge of fighting all stared at the three of them.

When the lass finally released the boy, Sybil said something to her. The two women then whispered back and forth, nodding. Then, to Rory's amazement, Grant's daughter embraced Sybil like a long-lost sister.

Sybil's face was drawn as she again approached the high table, where he and the Grant men were all still gaping.

"I'm sure the MacKenzie regrets any offense he may have caused," she said to the Grants. "Now if you'll forgive me, I really must retire."

After a torturous and fruitless discussion with Grant over the boy, Rory climbed the stairs with more trepidation than he ever felt going into battle. He had given Sybil a couple of hours to calm down, so perhaps she had gotten over her anger by now.

After drawing a deep breath, he pushed the door. It did not budge. He put his shoulder to it. She must feel uneasy with outsiders in the castle, for she had barred the door.

"Sybil, it's me," he called. "Open up."

He put his ear to the door and heard a rustle of movement inside. His relief when he heard her slide the bar back did not last long.

Before he could reach for the latch, she flung the door open and stood glaring up at him.

"Sybil, I—"

"Not here in the doorway," she hissed. "I'll not be further humiliated by having your feeble excuses overheard by curious servants who are no doubt listening at the bottom of the stairs."

Clearly, she was not over her anger yet. He was tempted to turn around and give her another hour or two. The hard glint in her eyes suggested that would be another error, so he stepped inside.

She shut the door with more force than needed and spun around to face him. "Ye have a son and heir, and ye didn't tell me. How could ye keep something so important from me?"

"You didn't tell me you'd been married—that ye had a husband when ye were supposed to be my contracted bride."

"I had a dead husband, not a living son," she said. "For the last fortnight you've made me suffer for not telling ye the marriage contract was false. And all the while ye were keeping this from me!"

"'Tis not the same."

"Aye, 'tis not! The marriage contract was my brother's deceitful act, not mine," she said. "Ye could have found out the truth any time ye wanted in the last eight years by showing it to someone or coming to claim me."

"But you knew the truth, and ye didn't tell me."

"I didn't tell because my life was at risk!" she said. "What reason could you have for not telling me about your son?"

"'Tis no simple matter."

"Everyone knew about him but me," she said, flinging her arms out. "Your clan, the Grants, probably half the Highlands!"

Rory could not deny it.

"It hasn't been easy for me to be accepted by your clan when every one of them was against me from the start," she said. "I've tried so hard!"

Oh, Jesu, her eyes were filling with tears. He felt like shite.

"Now you've made it nigh on impossible for me by showing your clansmen that ye neither trust nor respect me," she said. "How am I to overcome that?"

"Ye already have." He tried to take her hands, but she pulled them away. "They saw how well ye handled our guests and the…situation with the lad."

"The *situation*?" She swiped angrily at a tear that slid down her cheek. "Ye still haven't told me why ye kept this from me."

***

"I don't believe the lad is mine."

"Ha!" Sybil could not believe Rory would lie to her now. "Will ye tell me next that ye never bedded the lad's mother?"

Rory heaved a sigh. "I wasn't the only one who did."

"Don't insult her as well as me." His answer made her so furious she wanted to throw something at him. "Do ye count us all as fools? The lad looks exactly like you."

"He—"

"Get out!" she shouted.

Sybil had to make him go before the tears welling in her eyes spilled down her face. Once she started weeping, she feared she would never stop.

She tried to shove him out the door, but it was like pushing on a boulder. She dropped her arms and turned her face away from him. If she looked at him, into the face of the man she had recklessly given her heart to, she would lose control.

"Please, Rory," she choked out, "just go."

"I didn't mean to hurt ye," he said before the door clicked shut behind him.

She heard each footstep as he walked away, then she collapsed on the bed and wept for the lost dream she should never have believed in.

Suddenly, she remembered the priest and the message from her uncle. She did not have to stay here. There was a ship waiting for her at Inverness.

With shaking hands, she changed into warm clothes for her journey.

CHAPTER 36

Rory's back ached from sleeping on a bench. Before the other men sleeping in the hall awoke, Rory rose silently and again climbed the stairs to their bedchamber. He prayed that after a night's rest, Sybil would be less angry. With his heart in his throat, he rapped lightly on the door. Sybil did not answer.

He did not want to wake her, but he longed just to see her, to watch her in her sleep.

When he eased the door open, the room was empty, the bed not slept in. He stepped inside and turned slowly. Her shoes, which she usually left beside the bed, were gone, as was her cloak from the peg by the door.

His heart stopped in his chest. She'd left him.

God help him, was she out there alone? It was not safe for her to leave the castle. Sybil did not know these lands, had no kin or friends to give her help or protection. Yet she had wanted to be away from him so badly that she had gone anyway.

He ran down the steps, crossed the hall filled with snoring MacKenzies and Grants, and hurried to the stables.

"Have ye seen my wife?" he asked the stable lad.

"The lady asked me to saddle a horse for her," the lad said. "She said you'd follow her soon and that it was a game ye were playing."

A game? "When was this?"

"Too early for riding, if ye ask me," he said. "Sky held no more than a hint of dawn."

Rory saddled and mounted Curan and headed to the gate, where he learned she'd used the same ruse to persuade the guards to open the gate. Ach, that lass could persuade a river to flow upstream if she set her mind to it.

"Lady Sybil told us she was not going far, and that the laird"—the guard paused and waggled his eyebrows—"would know where to find her."

Rory closed his eyes. Without actually saying so, Sybil had managed to convince the guards that he and his bride were meeting for an outdoor tryst. If he found her quickly, no one would be the wiser.

"That wife of yours had such a fetching way about her when she said, *Don't spoil our fun.*" The older guard tilted his head and batted his eyelashes in a ridiculous imitation. "Ach, brought back sweet memories from when the wife and I were newlyweds."

Christ above. "How long ago did she leave?"

"The sky was glowing pink with the coming dawn," the older guard said.

The guard was a damned poet. Rory clenched his jaw to keep from shouting.

"In truth, we didn't expect ye to keep her waiting."

"How long has it been?" Rory asked.

"An hour, perhaps more," the other guard said.

Rory stifled a curse. Sybil was a skilled rider, and she had a good lead on him.

"Keep our secret," Rory said, and winked. "Not a word of this to anyone."

He spurred his horse and galloped out the gate. *Please, God, keep her safe until I find her.* Wherever she was and however far she'd gone, he would find her. He had no notion how he would persuade her to come back with him once he did, but one way or another, he would bring her home.

Now that he had driven her away, he knew in his heart the only truth that mattered.

Sybil belonged with him.

When Rory came to the river, the trail split in opposite directions. Ignoring the branch that followed the river inland, he turned Curan east toward the sea, where Sybil could seek a boat to carry her away.

He had ridden no more than a half-mile from the castle when he saw her sitting on a rock by the river with her back to him and her horse grazing nearby. She appeared in no hurry.

Since she did not look as if she had taken a fall and injured herself, Rory dismounted and approached her quietly through the tall grass. He did not want to spook her. Sweat glistened on the horse's back. She had ridden him hard and farther from the castle, but something had made her turn around. He hoped it was him.

When she looked over her shoulder and saw him, she did not seem surprised. He sat down beside her, careful not to touch her. He felt as if she had a protective layer around her that he should not attempt to breach, at least not yet.

"I was five miles down the trail," she said, staring at the river. "Ye would never have caught me."

He did not argue the point, though he most definitely would have found her and brought her home.

"I'm grateful ye decided to turn around."

"I didn't do it for you," she said. "I did it for the boy."

The boy? It took him a long moment to realize she meant the Grant lad.

"I remembered my promise that I would be his friend and mind his back among you MacKenzies," she said. "So I couldn't leave yet."

Yet. The word hit him like a punch in the gut. The fact that she had no place she could go was no comfort.

"Let me explain," he said.

"'Tis a bit late for that, don't ye think?" she said. "I believe I understand all I need to know."

"Ye don't."

"Ye have a son, ye refused to wed his mother," she said, ticking her points off with her fingers, "and now that the poor lass is dead, her family expected ye to make things right through a marriage to her sister."

"It sounds far worse than it is," he said. "There's more to the story, if you'll only listen."

"Oh, aye, there's more," she said. "I forgot to add that all the while ye were seducing innocent young lasses, ye believed ye were bound to wed me!"

Now she was being ridiculous, but he had the sense to bite his tongue. No man was expected to abstain before the marriage contract was consummated.

"Whether ye listen or no," he said, "I'm going to tell ye what happened."

"I can't stop ye."

"A few months before we fought at Flodden and I was taken prisoner, my father hosted a gathering of Highland chieftains," Rory began his tale. "Grant brought his family, including his eldest daughter. I didn't know at the time that Hector had an eye for the lass and had asked my father to negotiate a marriage between them during the gathering."

Sybil folded her arms and turned her face away. Still, he knew she was listening.

"The lass was seventeen, beautiful and headstrong. As best I can guess, thinking about it afterward, she met Hector and decided to thwart the marriage plan."

***

"She wished to wed you instead of Hector?" Sybil's curiosity got the better of her, and the question slipped out.

"She didn't wish to wed me," he said. "She only wanted to use me to ruin the marriage arrangement with Hector."

"What do ye mean by that?"

"Even as a bairn, I knew Hector had a deep grudge against me, but he kept it well hidden from everyone else while my father was alive," he said. "Grant's daughter was an astute and determined lass, and I believe she saw it."

Despite herself, the thought of Rory as a child being the focus of his uncle's hatred tugged at her heart. She would not, however, let sympathy for the boy he once was excuse how he had hurt and humiliated her.

"So she forced ye against your will, did she?" Sybil said, letting her voice drip with sarcasm.

"I was fifteen and not likely to say nay when a lass that beautiful told me to meet her in a storage room in the undercroft. I thought she meant for us to steal a few kisses," Rory said. "I won't say I was blameless, but when things moved quickly beyond kisses, my wits lagged behind."

Sybil narrowed her eyes at him. "But it wasn't just the one time ye met her, was it?"

Rory gave her a how-in-the-hell-did-you-know look and heaved a sigh. "Every time the lass crooked her finger, I went to meet her."

Of course he did. "I take it her plan to avoid marrying Hector succeeded."

"She told Hector she'd given her virginity to me," Rory said. "That was a lie, but all Hector needed to hear was that I'd had her first."

"What I don't understand," she said, "is why your fathers didn't force you and the lass to wed."

"She said that if I told anyone we'd been together, she'd deny it," Rory said. "She told me she would never have me for a husband. Though I was not keen on marrying her either, the lass was so adamantly against it that she slashed my pride."

"But Hector must have told."

"Nay," Rory said, shaking his head. "It would have shamed him to have everyone know that the lass he wished to wed had gone to bed with me. He and I knew, and that was bad enough. It was one more reason for him to hate me."

"And you told no one either?"

"That would have ruined the lass's reputation," he said. "I assumed she planned to pretend to be a virgin when she did wed."

"If no one told, then what broke off the marriage negotiations?"

"Hector didn't say it was me, but he advised the two chieftains that the lass had been with other men," Rory said. "The chieftains gave out the story that the pair was unsuited, which was true so far as it went. I thought that was the end of it.

"Three months later, I left with the MacKenzie warriors to fight the English. As ye know, I was injured in the Battle of Flodden and held prisoner. Sometime after I returned, I heard that Grant's daughter was with child and refused to name the father. There were whispers that the lass said she had been with too many men to remember."

"Do ye believe that?"

"I did at the time," Rory said. "I was too inexperienced to see the anger beneath her laughter and flirtation. Now I suspect there was a man she wanted to marry but could not. Perhaps he was someone her father did not deem important enough for a chieftain's daughter."

"If she refused to name you, how does her family know you're the father?" Sybil asked.

"They don't *know* I am," Rory said. "She died of a fever a few months ago. The Grant chieftain claims she confessed on her deathbed that the child is mine."

"Ye did bed her." *Every time she crooked her finger.*

"Aye, and if she had told me the child was mine, I would have accepted it as my duty to claim the lad whether I believed her or no," he said. "But years later, when her family attempts to dupe me by concocting this story of her deathbed confession? Nay. I cannot accept that."

Sybil did not speak another word on the ride back to the castle or as they walked from the stable to the keep. She ignored the curious looks as they crossed the hall and continued up the stairs to their chamber in silence. He shut the door and still she did not speak.

"Now that I've explained it all," he said, "do ye understand why I didn't tell you?"

"I do," she said. "Ye didn't trust me. Ye still don't. And ye used me to avoid marrying Grant's other daughter."

"I didn't want to marry her, but that is not why I came for you."

"You berated me and broke my heart because of what I didn't tell you," she said. "All the while, you were keeping all this from me—the boy, the marriage negotiations, the would-be bride."

He felt like shite for hurting her. He reached for her, but she slapped his hands away.

"I should have told you," he said.

"Aye, ye should have, instead of making a fool of me in front of the entire clan."

"We each had our secrets. I promise I'll not keep things from ye again. From here forward, I want us to be honest with each other."

"All right, then, I'll be honest." She planted her hand on her hip and poked his chest. "I believe that boy is your son. And you've no cause to deny him because his mother wouldn't have ye."

CHAPTER 37

Sybil took a deep breath and knocked on the door to the guest chamber. The servants had told her that Flora Grant had not left the chamber since her dramatic arrival yesterday. So long as Sybil remained here as the chieftain's wife and lady of the castle, she would not shirk her duties. As painful as the situation was for her, she ought to ease her guest's discomfort if she could.

"I told ye before," Flora called out in response to Sybil's repeated knock, "I don't need anything."

When Sybil opened the door, Flora jumped to her feet. Her hair and clothes were as disheveled as when she arrived, but now her high color was gone and her eyes were red and puffy.

"I'm sorry," Flora said, looking flustered. "I thought ye were a maidservant."

"I'm sorry to disturb ye, but I want to speak with ye," Sybil said. When the lass looked wildly about her as if searching for an escape, Sybil added, "If it's any comfort, I'm uneasy about this as well, but we must talk for young Kenneth's sake."

Flora nodded and sat on the edge of the lone bench with her back straight as a board. Sybil sat beside her and smoothed her skirts.

"Ye do understand," Sybil said, "that as the MacKenzie chieftain's only son and heir, Kenneth must be raised here with his father and clan?"

Flora's bottom lip trembled. "Aye. My father is set on it."

"I imagine you've been like a mother to Kenneth since your sister died. The bond ye have with him will always be special." Sybil laid her hand over Flora's. "I want ye to know that you're welcome to visit him as often as ye like."

Flora burst into tears and wept so hard her shoulders shook. Sybil patted her back and gave Flora her handkerchief.

"Do ye mean it?" Flora asked in a voice muffled by her hands covering her face.

"I do," Sybil said. "I want what's best for the lad, just as you do."

Flora startled Sybil by throwing her arms around her. The lass's hair was such a wild mess that Sybil had to lift her chin to breathe.

"I was afraid I'd lose him forever," Flora blubbered.

Sybil was exhausted by all the emotions of the last day, but she had one more thing she needed to say. Gently she eased Flora to sit up on her own.

"I understand that you expected to become Rory's wife—and ye would be if not for me." Sybil swallowed and forced herself to go on. "I am sorry for the pain and embarrassment I've caused ye."

"Ye can rest easy on that account," Flora said, waving the damp handkerchief. "While Rory MacKenzie is a verra fine looking man, I never had my heart set on him. In truth, I'm furious with him for refusing to claim Kenneth and even angrier with my father for forcing my nephew on a man who doesn't want him."

"Ye did appear to be a *wee* bit upset when ye arrived."

"A wee bit?" Flora said. "Ach, I must have been a sight!"

"I'm afraid ye were," Sybil said, fighting a smile.

When Flora threw her head back and laughed, Sybil joined her. It felt good to share a laugh with another woman after so many days of tension and misery.

"I'm in no hurry at all to wed anyone," Flora said. "I would have married the MacKenzie so that I could be here to protect my nephew, but I can see now that you'll do that for me."

"Rory would never harm Kenneth, nor any child."

"Hmmph." Flora gave her a skeptical sideways glance.

"For as long as I'm here, I'll look out for him," Sybil said.

"I know ye will," Flora said, gripping Sybil's arm. "Ye may look and act like a princess, but underneath, you're a fighter like me."

"I'm sure your family is worried about ye," Sybil said. "'Tis time ye came down to the hall."

"I'm too embarrassed after the scene I made."

"Sometimes a lass has to make a scene," Sybil said. "In my family, I'm rather famous for them."

"But I'm such a mess," Flora said, looking down at herself. "My father will chastise me for weeks for coming to the table looking like this."

"I've already sent for a bath and a clean gown." Sybil stood to leave. "I'll return to help fix your hair, and then we'll go downstairs together."

When Flora embraced her once more, Sybil squeezed her eyes shut against a sudden wave of longing for her sisters. Though no one could replace them, she was glad to have made a friend.

The warm glow she felt was but a brief respite from despair, and it drained out of her like water through a sieve the moment she closed the door behind her.

***

Rory's hall was crowded with Grants, which soured his mood. Why were they still here? He despised being pushed and had no intention of giving them what they wanted.

Ignoring the glares directed his way, he poured himself a whisky and kept watch on the arched entrance to the stairwell that led to the upper floors. He had not seen Sybil since they returned to the castle and she slammed the bedchamber door in his face.

At least she had not left him, but he'd lost her heart. And he had no idea how to win her back.

He swallowed hard when Sybil swept into the hall leading Grant's daughter by the hand. What was Sybil up to now? Their guest had undergone a remarkable transformation from a raging demon to a respectable lass, but Rory kept his eyes on Sybil.

When Grant charged toward them, apparently intent on ranting at his daughter for her earlier behavior, Sybil took his arm and drew him aside. Rory started across the hall to protect his wife, but she caught his eye and shook her head. She and Grant proceeded to have what appeared to be an intense conversation. What in the hell did she have to say to him?

As soon as Grant left her side to speak with his sons, Rory joined her.

"How did ye get that madwoman to calm down?" he whispered, glancing at the Grant lass.

"She's not mad," Sybil said. "She was upset, and understandably so."

"That lass was screaming like a banshee yesterday," he said. "How did ye manage to calm her down?"

"I assured her that ye would not harm the lad."

"Ach! As if that needed to be said."

"It did," she said. "And I can't say she was persuaded."

Rory was offended. He was also very grateful he didn't have to marry the Grant lass. Now if he could only get rid of his guests, he could try to make amends to his wife.

"I don't suppose that stubborn old man told ye he's giving up and going home?" Rory said, nodding toward the Grant chieftain.

"He'll not leave until this matter with his grandson is settled," she said. "Unless ye want these Grants as permanent guests, I suggest ye come to an agreement with him about the lad."

"I'll not let him force my hand." This was not a conversation he wanted to have with her, but at least she was speaking to him.

She turned and fixed angry violet eyes on him. "Can ye afford to make the Grants your enemies now?"

"Ye know I can't."

"Then meet the man halfway," she said. "Grant told me that if ye let Kenneth remain here, that would show you're considering claiming him and would satisfy him for now."

"But I'm not considering it. I don't believe the lad is mine," Rory said for what felt like the hundredth time. "I'd do anything else ye asked."

"Then let the lad stay here."

A short time later, they were saying their farewells to the Grants. Rory's jaw hurt from gritting his teeth. Though he did not like it, he could not think of a better compromise. And what harm could it do to let the lad stay for a time?

"If I am any judge of women, your bride is none too pleased with ye," Grant said, and elbowed Rory in the ribs. "Mind your step, MacKenzie, or I'll steal her away."

By the saints, Sybil had even won over crusty old Grant. The man tried Rory's patience to the breaking point when he took his leave of Sybil.

"An older man has the wisdom to recognize a woman of value when he sees one," Grant said, and kissed her hand. "And he knows how to treat a wife."

CHAPTER 38

Hector had made certain the Grant chieftain learned of Rory's marriage, and he was looking forward to hearing how the old goat received the news. As he waited for Duncan, he rubbed the talisman of his dead brother's ear and imagined Grant's humiliation.

Grant needed to pay for raising a slut of a daughter. God how Hector had wanted that lass. More than any other, except for Agnes, of course. He gritted his teeth as he recalled how he'd burned with desire when she sent a message through her maidservant that she wished to speak with him in the castle courtyard. He thought she chose a place where they would be in view of others because she was an innocent lass who protected her reputation.

He remembered her smile as she told him she had given her virginity to Rory. I confess I can't control myself around your handsome nephew, *she'd said, all wide-eyed with feigned innocence. He would have knocked her to the ground and had his way with her until he wiped that mocking smile off her face, but there were too many witnesses.*

Aye, the Grants needed to pay for his humiliation, and it was only fitting that the slut's son play a part in Rory's destruction.

When Big Duncan came in, Hector poured them two whiskies and sat down to enjoy the tale.

"Old Grant got on his horse and rode straight to Castle Leod with his grandson to confront your nephew."

"Ha! I suppose it's too much to hope that they came to blows in front of both clans?"

"They might have, if Rory's new wife had not smoothed everything over, as if she was churning butter."

Hector slammed his fist on the table. His fury grew as Duncan related how the damned woman had welcomed the lad and won over the Grants, including Rory's castoff bride.

"No one knows how she persuaded him, but Rory allowed the lad to stay," Duncan said. "They say the lad sticks to her like a burr."

"The sly bitch." Hector drummed his fingers on the table. *"She must realize Rory can't afford a clan war with the Grants now. And she can always rid herself of the lad later."*

"What do ye want me to do?" Duncan asked. *"Have her killed?"*

"Not her. At least not yet." Hector went to the window and stared out over the fields in the direction of his enemy. *"The Grant lad can still serve his purpose."*

The boy was just one piece of his plan.

"Time to sharpen our swords." He was a fighting man and tired of sitting in Fairburn Tower. He was looking forward to the battles ahead.

"When do I get that lass ye promised me?" Duncan asked.

"You'll have her after her grandmother plays her part," Hector said. *"Then ye can do with her as ye please."*

Hector almost felt sorry for the lass. He had seen what Duncan did to the last one when they disposed of the body.

CHAPTER 39

Rory was training the younger men in one of the fields outside the castle when he saw Malcolm and Alex riding toward them. He signaled to the others to continue their practice, sheathed his sword, and went to greet them.

"'Tis good to have ye back," Rory said as he clasped arms with Malcolm in a warriors' greeting. He squeezed his brother's shoulders and asked, "How is your wife faring?"

"Grizel predicts another easy birth."

"I hear ye had a visit from the Grants," Malcolm said when they were out of earshot of the other men.

"Aye." At least Rory could rely on Malcolm and his brother to take his side regarding Grant's grandson.

"A bairn by another woman is not the sort of news a wife ever takes well," Alex said. "But for Sybil to hear it from a stranger and in front of the entire household, ach, that could not be good."

It was not. And the longer Grant's grandson remained under Rory's roof, the worse the tension between them became.

"Take advice from a man who's been wed a long time," Malcolm said, resting a hand on Rory's shoulder. "Don't let this trouble between the two of ye fester."

"Did Grizel send ye out here to tell me that?"

"Aye," Malcolm said with a smile twitching at his lips. "When we heard what happened and didn't see Sybil in the castle, Grizel feared she'd left ye."

Not yet. "She's gone off for a picnic by the river with the Grant lad."

"*The Grant lad*, is that what ye call him?" Alex said. "Folk are saying he's your son."

"Saying he is doesn't make him so."

"Hmmph." Malcolm and Alex both gave noncommittal grunts.

"This isn't just a brotherly visit," Alex said. "My bishop sent me."

"What could the bishop want with me?"

"He's concerned that the dispute between you and Hector will end in violence and sweep in other clans as well," Alex said. "He says it is his duty to act as an intermediary to reconcile the two of you before the whole region is awash in blood."

Unfortunately, the bishop was right about the risk of bloodshed. "Tell your bishop that Hector can end this anytime he wants by coming to Castle Leod and pledging loyalty to his chieftain."

"Perhaps God will surprise us with that miracle," Alex said. "The bishop, however, invites you and Hector to meet at Fortrose Cathedral tomorrow, with each of ye guaranteeing safe passage to the other. Hector has already agreed."

"I'd wager Hector is the one who asked for this meeting," Malcolm said. "He's up to something."

"The bishop is not fond of either Rory or me," Alex said, "but he'll not allow bloodshed in his cathedral."

"It could be useful to find out what Hector wants." And if there was any chance of resolving this without MacKenzie bloodshed, Rory had to take it. "Tell the bishop I'll come."

"He's waiting, so I'd best take my leave," Alex said. "I'll see ye at the cathedral."

"Let's ride out and join that picnic," Malcolm said after Alex left. "I want to have a look at this Grant lad—and you need to make peace with your wife."

Rory was about to say he had no time for a frivolous outing but thought better of it. Getting to know the lad would do no harm, and it would please Sybil. If it could help mend the breach between them, he was willing to do it. Nothing else had worked.

They had just mounted when Rory saw a line of horses galloping toward the castle. The first horse was several yards ahead of the others and had a small rider bouncing on his back.

"The lad's horse has bolted," Rory said, and spurred Curan.

Even from this distance he could see that the second rider was Sybil. Her hair streamed out behind her as she rode at a reckless pace. Sybil was rapidly closing the distance to the runaway horse while Rory and Malcolm raced toward it from the side. Rory cursed as Sybil caught up to the bolting horse, rode dangerously close side-by-side to it, and reached for its bridle.

Suddenly, the boy's horse stumbled and went down, flinging the boy over its head. Sybil pulled her horse up hard and jumped down. Her anguished wails filled the air as she leaned over the lad on the ground.

Rory reached them a moment later, leaped off his horse, and knelt on the lad's other side. When the boy opened his eyes, relief washed over him.

"I'm all right," the lad said, and started to sit up.

"Wait." Rory held him down while he ran his hands over the boy searching for broken bones or other injuries, then he signaled to Malcolm. "I don't see anything serious, but take him back to the castle and have Grizel take a look at him just to be sure."

Sybil appeared to have taken the fall much harder than the boy. She was shaking and pale as death.

"You're riding with me." He took her arm and helped her to her feet. "I'm sure the lad will be fine."

An hour after he left her with Grizel and the boy in one of the upstairs chambers, he returned to find the two women alone.

"Where's the lad?" he asked.

"He was only bruised, so I let him go," Grizel said. "Lucky for him, he's blessed with a hard head, like his father."

Rory let that pass. "He's all right, then?"

"Oh, aye," she said. "If he's anything like you were, he'll get himself into more trouble in no time."

Why did everyone assume the lad was his?

"How many times did I bind your wounds?" Grizel shook her head and started for the door. "I'd best refresh my supplies now that he's living here."

Sybil still looked shaken.

"Grizel is a good healer," Rory said, resting his hands on her shoulders. "If she says the lad is all right, he is."

"That's not what concerns me," Sybil said. "What about the next time?"

"I'll make certain he has a gentler pony until he learns to ride better."

"Kenneth is a good rider," Sybil said, "and there's nothing wrong with that pony."

"Nothing wrong with it? The men guarding you told me it reared and spun, trying to toss the lad off before it bolted."

"I know horses," she said. "That pony is sweet-tempered. Something made him go mad."

"Anything could have spooked him." Rory shrugged. "Perhaps a hare jumped in front of him."

"A hare would not make the pony behave like that," she said.

"Speak plainly." There was something more to this, something she was not saying. "What do ye believe it was?"

"What I don't believe is that it was an accident," she said. "Someone wanted to harm Kenneth."

"I selected the men who were guarding the two of ye myself," Rory said. "If ye accuse them, ye accuse me."

"Of course I don't believe ye would hurt a child," she said. "At least not on purpose."

"Hmmph." She seemed determined to insult him.

"You've made it clear to your men that ye never intend to claim Kenneth and that ye don't want him here," she said. "Perhaps one of them hoped to gain your favor by solving the problem for ye."

"They would never do that."

"I'm not saying it was one of them, but don't underestimate the power ye wield as chieftain," she said, clenching her fists. "For young Kenneth's safety, show your men that you accept him as your son. At the very least, behave as if ye might do it."

"I am chief of the great Clan MacKenzie," he said. "I'll not allow the Grants to coerce me into claiming that lad as my son and heir."

"For God's sake, forget your damned pride," she said. "The lad needs you. Ye must protect him."

"He fell off his horse," Rory said, throwing his hands up. "Every lad does that."

"I'm telling ye," she said, "Kenneth is your son, and he's in danger."

"He is my guest," Rory said, getting a wee bit angry himself. "And I will ensure his safety, as I would for any guest."

She stamped her foot. "There's too much at stake for ye to be so damned stubborn!"

"Aye, there is a great deal at stake." He took her hand. "Our son should be my heir and the next chieftain of Clan MacKenzie. Don't ye want that too?"

"Nay, I don't," she said, and jerked her hand away. "I wouldn't have my son be a thief and take it from the rightful heir. He'd be no better than Hector."

Rory tried to hold on to his temper and failed. "Do not compare any son of mine to that man."

"You've let your pride blind ye to the truth," she said with fire snapping in her eyes.

"And what truth is that?" he bit out.

"Kenneth is the very image of you," she said. "Your blood runs through that lad's veins. As I see it, ye have a duty to him, and 'tis high time ye accepted it."

"So the lad has red hair," Rory said, spreading his arms out. "Half the men in Scotland could be his father."

"One of the reasons I loved you—or thought I did—was that ye always chose to do the right thing, no matter the consequences," she said. "But you're not the man I thought ye were."

Though she was being wholly unjust, her words were like a blade she thrust straight into his heart.

"Power has made ye like every other man I've known," she said. "I liked ye better, Rory MacKenzie, when ye were just a warrior."

Having delivered her final stab to his heart and twisted the knife, she spun on her heel and left him without a backward glance.

CHAPTER 40

Sybil's opinion of him now was lower than dog shite. How would he ever win her back? He could not accept the Grant lad as his just to please her. If he somehow managed to hold on to the chieftainship, claiming the lad would make him the next chief. If the lad did not have MacKenzie blood, that would be wrong. A false chief inevitably brought bad luck to the clan.

The boy's mother had not named Rory as the father for eight years—if then. He had only Grant's word for her supposed deathbed confession.

And yet it was *possible* the lad was his.

He knew of no way to resolve that question, but there was another he could lay to rest. Sybil's accusation that someone purposely tried to harm the lad would nag at him until he proved it false.

After supper, he headed to the stables to examine the pony himself. When he asked where it was, the taciturn stable master pointed to the far corner of the stable. Rory paused when he saw a head of bright red hair pop up on the far side of the horse. His own hair had turned to auburn as he grew older, but when he was a bairn it was that same blinding shade.

The boy kept up a steady, soothing murmur as he brushed the pony.

"You're not afraid of him after he bucked and bolted on ye?" Rory asked.

The lad looked at him over the horse's back with wide eyes. He was clearly more frightened of Rory than of the horse that had nearly broken his neck.

"It wasn't his fault." The lad stroked the pony's neck as he spoke, a gesture that Rory suspected soothed him as much as the animal. "He's the best horse ever. I'll not let ye take him away from me."

"I won't." Rory patted the pony's rump. "I can see he's a fine animal and good friend to ye. A lad needs a horse like that."

"Thank you, Laird MacKenzie." The tension in the boy's body visibly eased.

He must have been worried sick he would lose his horse. For the first time, Rory began to see the situation from the lad's side. He was only eight, and his family had left him among strangers and in the care of a hostile stranger. He carried no blame for his mother's deception or his grandfather's scheme to make him the future MacKenzie chief.

"How would ye like to go hunting?" Rory asked.

"With you?" The boy's face lit up like a torch. "When? Tomorrow?"

"I have business away from the castle tomorrow." Rory had asked before he'd thought it through. He had a dozen things he ought to do instead of hunting, but when he saw the look of disappointment on the lad's face, he said, "But I'll take ye the next day."

Before he left, he ran his hands over the pony to see if he could discover what made him bolt. His legs and hooves were fine, and he had no sores from the saddle rubbing. The pony did have a couple of raised bumps on his rump, but nothing unusual for a horse.

Anything could set off a horse—a bee sting, a sudden noise, a nip from another horse. Luckily, there was no harm done.

***

Rory and his men rode across the Black Isle to the great red sandstone cathedral that had stood for more than three hundred years on the MacKenzie side of Moray Firth. Several highborn MacKenzies were buried here, along with a few Frasers.

Alex was waiting outside for them.

"Hector and his men arrived first," Alex said. "They and the bishop are waiting for us inside."

"I'm surprised the bishop is allowing us to bring our men inside."

"They must disarm, of course, but they are invited to bear witness to the bishop's peaceful—nay, miraculous—resolution of this dispute." Alex rolled his eyes. "The bishop appears to relish his role and wants to be lauded for it."

Rory drew a deep breath and crossed himself as he stepped inside the cathedral's hallowed walls. Even in the dim light of the cathedral, the bishop was hard to miss standing in the middle of the nave with his arms outspread and wearing his red silk tunic, snowy white gloves and stockings, a large, bejeweled cross, and purple ropes of braided silk embroidered with gold thread hanging from his neck.

Hector's men stood to the bishop's left along the north aisle. Rory thought he had steeled himself to see his uncle, but a blinding rage took hold of him when he saw Hector.

The bishop cleared his throat. "Shall we begin?"

Rory walked past the bishop to stand toe to toe with his uncle.

"Are ye not afraid of being struck down in this holy place?" Rory said. "The blood of my brother is on your hands."

"If you're speaking of our sadly departed chieftain, I did my best to protect him," Hector said. "But where were you when your chieftain needed you? You abandoned him, that's what ye did."

Alex hauled Rory back and said in his ear, "Don't let him bait you."

"Shall we turn to the matter that brought us here?" the bishop said. "I understand that you, Hector of Gairloch, have an offer to make."

"We can end this conflict right here, right now, without bloodshed," Hector said. "They pay good money for fighting men in Ireland and France. With a good ship and thirty strong warriors, a man could make a new life for himself."

Rory was stunned by his uncle's proposal. Surely Hector would not agree to go so easily.

"I give ye three days to accept my offer and leave MacKenzie lands," Hector said. "If ye don't, the blood of MacKenzies will be on your head."

"I came here to discuss the terms under which my uncle will cease his rebellion," Rory said. "If it takes bloodshed to end it, then so be it."

Rory was furious that Hector and the bishop had brought him here for nothing.

"Wait," the bishop said when Rory started to leave. "I believe Hector of Gairloch has brought evidence bearing on the question of who is the rightful MacKenzie chieftain."

"I *am* the MacKenzie, the 9th of Kintail."

"By what right," Hector said in a voice that carried to every corner of the cathedral, "do ye claim that honor?"

"Ye know verra well by what right," Rory said. "I have been chosen by our clan, and I carry the blood of chieftains from my father and his father and his father for as long as there have been MacKenzies."

"Your mother was not wed to my brother when ye were conceived," Hector said.

"Their marriage may have been irregular, but my father claimed me, as you and everyone in the clan knows."

"My brother was so bedazzled by Agnes Fraser that he was blinded to the truth," Hector said. "She was with child by another man before she ever went to my brother's bed."

Rory's vision was tinged with red. "That is a lie!"

"Your mother was a whore," Hector said.

Rory lunged for him, but Alex and several other men rushed between him and Hector.

"This is hallowed ground!" the abbot shouted, holding his hands up. "Any man who sheds blood here commits a sin against God."

"Not here," Alex said as he held Rory's arm. "Not unless ye want yourself and the whole clan excommunicated."

The bishop appeared to motion to someone behind Rory. He turned to see the figure of a hunched woman emerge from one of the chapels built into the south aisle. He did not recognize the woman at first. But when she stood in the light of the candelabra next to the bishop, he knew who she was.

"Isn't that Mother's old servant?" Alex whispered.

"Aye. She's also a wise woman." Rory felt as if a hole was opening beneath his feet. "And a midwife."

Rory knew what was coming. He should leave now, but something compelled him to stay and watch the disaster unfold.

The bishop made the old woman hold the large, heavy cross he wore and swear by the blood of Jesus Christ that every word she spoke was true.

"My mistress," she began in a soft voice.

"Louder," the bishop told her.

"My mistress, Lady Agnes, was with child by one of the stable lads in her father's castle and was frantic not knowing what to do about it," the old woman said, glancing several times at Hector. "When the MacKenzie chieftain laid siege to the Fraser castle and demanded to wed her at once, Lady Agnes believed her prayers were answered, and readily agreed."

"How do you know this?" the bishop asked.

"I was her personal maid, and she confided in me," she said, with another furtive glance at Hector. "I'm a skilled midwife as well and helped her deliver the child. She confessed to me again then that the babe was her lover's babe, and I agreed to say he was born early."

Hector had coerced the poor woman to say these lies. Rory should have foreseen this. The damage was done now.

"And who was this child?" the bishop prodded her.

"It was him, Rory." The old woman looked at him for the first time, and there was sorrow in her eyes. "He was a fine, fine boy and always her favorite."

"I forgive you," Rory told her in a soft voice.

A tear trickled down the old woman's cheek.

"I am the MacKenzie," Rory said, locking gazes with Hector. "And one day ye will answer for this."

Then he turned and walked out of the church.

"You can never be the true chieftain when ye don't have chieftain's blood!" Hector shouted after him. "You'll bring bad luck to yourself and the clan."

Rory kept walking.

"You've no right! I warn ye, you'll lose everything and destroy the clan." Hector's voice rang out through the cathedral. "Everything ye touch will turn to ashes."

CHAPTER 41

The river was swollen from the winter rains, and the rushing water drowned out other sounds as Rory and the Grant lad walked the trail along its bank. He was glad to be away from the demands of the castle for a couple of hours. Between his troubles with Sybil and yesterday's meeting at the cathedral, he needed the chance to clear his head and think.

Kenneth picked up a rock and threw it into the water.

"Mind ye don't go near the edge," Rory said, pulling him back. "The ground is slick with mud and the current is fast. If ye slipped and fell in, you'd drown long before I could get ye out."

The lad nodded and looked up at him with his usual serious expression. "I won't fall in."

Farther up the trail, Rory caught sight of a flash of brown through the trees and signaled to Kenneth to keep quiet. Moving silently into the wood, he stalked the animal for several yards until the stag, sensing danger, paused and lifted its head, ready to bolt.

Holding his breath, Rory drew back his bow and took aim. Ach, this fellow was a beauty. Just as he was about to release the arrow, a child's scream rent the air and echoed off the hills.

Rory dropped his bow and ran through the woods toward the boy's shouts. He'd gone farther from the path than he realized, and it seemed as if he would never reach the river. When he did, he caught sight of the boy a hundred feet downstream, his head bobbing in and out of the water. *Jesu.*

"Kenneth!" Rory shouted. "I'm coming!"

His heart was in his throat as he raced down the path. The fast current was carrying the lad downstream toward the falls. *Just like my mother.*

This was not the same river, not the same falls, but Rory felt as if he was in the nightmare he'd had a thousand times, in which he watched her body being swept over the falls and battered by the rocks. He could not let that happen to the boy.

He flew over the ground until he was just past where the boy was in the river. In an instant, he jerked off his boots, stripped out of his heavy clothes, and dove in. The icy cold hit him like a wall of ice.

He looked around frantically. God have mercy, he could not see the lad anywhere.

"Kenneth! Kenneth!" He could hardly hear his own voice over the rushing water. "Kenneth!"

He feared the lad had been sucked under and drowned when Kenneth's head popped up some distance ahead. The current was pulling him downriver, ever closer to the falls.

He was only thirty feet away, but it seemed a mile. Rory closed the distance to twenty feet, then ten. Kenneth's head sank and popped up and then sank again. Rory swam as hard as he could toward where the boy had gone down. A heavy tree branch rammed into him, knocking him sideways, but he kept his eyes fixed on the spot where the boy should be.

The roar of the falls grew louder, pounding in his ears. In his mind's eye, he saw the boy's battered body at the base of the falls. He had to reach him *now*.

"Kenneth!"

The lad's head broke the surface just beyond his reach. Rory lunged and caught hold of his shirt. Wrapping one arm around the lad, he swam like hell for the shore. The fierce pull of the current was like a giant beast trying to drag them over the edge. He could see the drop of the falls on the edge of his vision.

With his free arm, he caught hold of a low-hanging branch. He pulled himself and the boy along the branch toward the riverbank until he gained purchase with his feet. The stones were slippery with algae, and he went down, banging his injured leg, but he managed to keep the lad's head above water and regain his footing.

Finally, he climbed out and crawled onto the bank.

He was on his hands and knees, gasping for air. Water streamed into his eyes as he looked down at Kenneth's still form. *Jesu,* he was not breathing. Quickly, Rory turned him on his side and slapped him between his shoulder blades.

Breathe, Kenneth! Breathe! Rory thumped his back again. *Breathe!*

The lad's small body convulsed, and he coughed and choked as water gushed out of his mouth. *God be praised.* Rory sat back on his heels and let out a shuddering breath.

The boy rolled onto his back and looked up at him with wild eyes.

"You're going to be all right," Rory said as he wiped Kenneth's face off with the edge of the lad's sopping shirt.

The lad's skin was blue, and he was shivering like a frozen leaf in a winter storm. Rory scooped him up against his chest, heaved himself to his feet, and started down the path.

"I left my plaid up the trail," he said, talking to reassure the boy. "We'll get it and dry ye off."

When Rory reached his pile of discarded clothes, he stripped the boy of his wet clothing and wrapped him in his plaid. Then he held him and rubbed his back and limbs until Kenneth finally stopped shaking.

The lad was bruised and bleeding, and his face was so pale that the sprinkling of freckles across his nose and cheeks stood out. He could have worse injuries Rory could not see. Rory had to get him back to the castle quickly. When he lifted him in his arms again, he seemed so small and fragile.

Sybil's words came to him. *The lad needs you. Ye must protect him.*

She was right. His life could be extinguished in a careless moment. And nearly was.

Rory had tried to ignore this child, to deny the blood tie that would take everything away from the son he hoped to have with the woman he loved, the son who should be his heir. Sybil had been wiser, and certainly more generous, and embraced the truth.

Holding this child in his arms now, he needed no proof. He felt their blood bond. He could no longer deny that this copper-headed lad was his. And he did not want to. He prayed it was not too late.

"Ye don't need to carry me," Kenneth said in a voice that was so weak it sent fear pulsing through Rory's veins. "I can walk."

"Water that cold takes a toll," Rory said, pretending calm as he raced down the path. "We can't have ye slip and fall into the river again, now can we?"

"I didn't fall," the lad murmured.

His head lolled against Rory's chest, and his breathing was dangerously shallow. Panic choked Rory as he ran faster and faster to save his son.

CHAPTER 42

Sybil left her drawings on her table and went to look out the window again. As long as Kenneth was with Rory, she knew he would be safe, but she was anxious to hear how their outing had gone. She should not have pushed Rory so hard to accept the boy. Left alone, he would come to it in his own time.

She regretted her harsh words even more. She had blurted out the hateful words because she had been so frightened after Kenneth was thrown from his horse. Perhaps she was wrong about that too, and it was only an accident.

The breath left her lungs when she saw Rory come through the gate at a dead run. He was stark naked, his hair was streaming wet, and his leg was covered in blood. A moment passed before she noticed he was holding something wrapped in his plaid.

Oh, Mary, Mother of God, it was Kenneth.

She ran down the stairs to the hall screaming for help. The next hour was a blur. Grizel took charge, ordering Rory to take Kenneth to an upstairs chamber, sending a servant to fetch her bag of medicinal herbs and ointments, and directing others to build up the fire and bring extra blankets. Then she shooed everyone but Sybil out of the room.

"Comfort him while I work," Grizel ordered.

Sybil held Kenneth's hand and spoke softly to him while the older woman mixed a salve and applied it with quick, practiced hands to the countless cuts and scratches covering the lad's body. She gave Sybil a worried look as she wrapped a strip of clean linen over the deep gash on Kenneth's forehead. The boy was pale and too quiet.

"There's nothing more we can do for him now," Grizel whispered after they got a tincture down his throat. "Go fetch your husband so I can see to him. That looked like a bad cut on his leg."

Sybil wiped her forehead and tried to calm herself before opening their chamber door. Rory was pacing when she entered but came to an abrupt halt. He had put on a léine, the knee-length shirt Highlanders wore, but his skin was still damp beneath it.

"How is Kenneth?" Rory asked.

"Grizel has done what she can and says he's in God's hands now." Sybil looked down at the long jagged cut on his leg that tore open the newly-healed arrow hole. "She wants to bind your wound."

"That can wait." He made an impatient wave of his hand. "She must give all her attention to the lad."

Something caught Sybil's eye, and she turned to see that Rory had found the sketches she left on her table and spread them out over the bed.

"You've a talent for drawing." He picked up a sheet on which she'd drawn several side-by-side images of Rory and Kenneth and shook his head. "I've been so blind."

"So ye see the likeness now?" Hope stirred inside her.

"I can see it now." He turned and met her gaze. "But I felt it in my heart first when I carried him in my arms."

Tears filled her eyes and spilled down her cheeks. "I'm so glad."

"You were right all along," he said. "I'm sorry I've been so blockheaded—and not just about the lad. Can ye forgive me?"

She stepped into his arms and rested her head against his chest. "If you can forgive me as well."

"I love ye so much," he said against her hair. "Promise ye won't leave me."

"I won't," she said. "Not ever."

Before they could say anything else, Grizel poked her head through the doorway. Sybil held her breath, fearing Kenneth had taken a turn for the worse.

"Perhaps the laird will let me take care of his wound now," Grizel said, a smile playing on her lips. "The lad's alert and hungry. God be praised!"

Sybil and Rory rushed past her and up the stairs to the chamber above. Though Kenneth had cuts and bruises on his face and arms, he was sitting up propped by pillows. Malcolm, who had come into the room since Sybil left, gave her his chair next to the bed.

Sybil smiled at Kenneth and squeezed his hand. "How are ye feeling?"

"I'm starving."

The adults laughed with relief. Hunger was a very good sign.

"Only broth for now." Grizel handed a bowl and spoon to Sybil. "Don't let him eat too fast."

While Sybil spooned the broth into Kenneth's mouth, Grizel tsked over the jagged cut on Rory's leg, slathered a smelly poultice on it, and bandaged it. He escaped her ministrations before she could start on his lesser injuries and came to stand beside Sybil next to the bed.

"That cut on your forehead will make a manly scar," Rory told Kenneth with a wink. "But a knock on the head can make ye feel a wee bit confused for a time. Do ye remember what happened?"

Kenneth gave him a solemn nod.

"You remember falling into the river?"

"I didn't fall," Kenneth said. "I did just as ye told me and stayed away from the edge."

"Then how did ye end up in the river?" Rory asked. "Ach, don't tell me ye jumped."

"Lads!" Grizel said behind them. "'Tis a wonder any of them live to be men."

"I didn't jump," Kenneth said.

"Hmmm," Rory said. "Then I suppose ye must have glided down to the river on a faery's back."

Rory and Grizel were taking the boy's denials with humor, but a cold chill of premonition went up Sybil's spine.

"There's no shame in admitting a mistake," Rory said, turning serious, "so long as ye learn from it."

"But I didn't fall or jump," Kenneth said in a stronger voice. "I was pushed."

***

"He was pushed!" Rory shouted, raising his hands in the air. "Who would do such a thing to a bairn? And on MacKenzie lands!"

Sybil watched Rory pace up and down their bedchamber, where they had retreated after Grizel told them Kenneth must rest.

"So ye do believe someone meant to harm Kenneth?" she asked.

"Harm him? Nay, they meant to kill the lad," he said, his eyes blazing. "And they had the bollocks to attempt it while he was with *me*," he said, ramming his thumb against his chest. "Right under my damned nose!"

"Now that ye know the threat exists, ye can protect the lad."

"I'll give whoever did it his just desserts and drown him in the river," Rory said, squeezing his hand as if he were holding someone by the neck. "I'll hold his head under and watch the life go out of him."

He looked so fierce that Sybil had to brace herself not to take a step back.

"Ye can't drown whoever is responsible until ye know who it is," she said. "Ask yourself who would gain by Kenneth's death—that is, besides you and me."

"Besides you and me?" Rory said, his tone full of outrage.

"People will assume I want my own son to be the heir," she said. "As for you, ye made it clear to the Grants that you didn't want to claim him and resented being pressured to keep him here."

"That doesn't mean I'd harm him." Rory scowled at her. "For God's sake, he's just a bairn."

"*I* know ye wouldn't." She rested her hand on his arm. "But if Kenneth died under suspicious circumstances while living under your care and protection, the Grants would be sure to cry foul and blame you."

"And who would benefit from that?" he said, echoing her question. "I see what you're saying—and who must be behind this."

Sybil nodded. "It's got to be Hector."

"He wouldn't risk doing it by his own hand, especially this close to the castle." Rory clenched the handle of the dirk at his belt and looked off into the distance with narrowed eyes.

Watching him, Sybil thought that whoever had done Hector's foul bidding and attempted to harm this child was a fool. Rory would find him and kill him.

And Hector should be worried, for his time would come too.

***

Rory sat with his claymore sword across his knees and watched his son's chest rise and fall with his steady breathing. Grizel had given him a sleeping draught so that the pain from his injuries would not interfere with his rest. When Rory sent her off to get some sleep herself, she reassured him again that the lad was out of danger. But Rory knew better.

As the door creaked open, he tightened his grip on the hilt of his sword. When he saw Sybil in the glow of the candlelight, he relaxed.

"You should get some sleep." Sybil smoothed his hair back with her fingers and kissed his forehead, a gesture he had missed without knowing he had.

"I can't leave the lad's side when I don't know who I can trust," he said. "Whoever did this is close by."

"Ye don't know that it was someone in the castle," she said as she settled onto the seat beside him. "Hector could have had one of his men watching the castle for an opportunity."

"Either way, I can't take the chance of leaving him unguarded," Rory said. "If you're right that someone made his pony bolt—and I think ye are—this is not the first attempt, and it's unlikely to be the last." He did not know how many were involved in the plot, but the bastards were bold and determined.

"Ye can't watch Kenneth every moment." She propped her elbow on her knee and rested her chin on her hand. "We'll have to find another solution."

"Malcolm is here, and I'll send for my brother in the morning," he said. "We can watch the lad in turns."

"Hmm."

Apparently she did not think much of that plan. He had to admit it was a short-term solution at best. "What are ye thinking?"

"That the best way to keep Kenneth safe is to let him die." When he raised his eyebrows, she said. "Not *truly* die."

"Create a deceit, then?"

"Everyone saw ye carry his limp body into the castle," she said. "In the morning, ye can announce the dreadful news that the poor lad didn't survive the night."

"Once he's recovered, it will be difficult to keep a rambunctious lad hidden from the household for long."

He loved how she bit her lip as she applied her quick mind to the problem. Working together felt like it used to be before their falling out. This was how it should be between them.

"Until we can eliminate the threat, the safest place for him is with the Grants," Sybil said. "I'm sure they'll agree to keep his presence there a secret until we can bring him home again."

Rory did not like the idea of having Kenneth out of his sight, but she was right. The danger to him was here, from within the MacKenzie clan. The Grants would guard him well, and having him in their protection would free Rory to deal with Hector and his accomplices.

"We'll either have to make a pretense of delivering his body to them in a funeral cart or secret him out some other way," Rory said. "There will be trouble, though, if word of his death reaches the Grants before we can get him to Urquhart Castle."

"We can't let that happen." Sybil's hand went to her throat. "That would cause them unnecessary sorrow."

"Not to mention a clan war, which is just what Hector wanted," Rory said. "I'll send a message ahead, but I doubt Grant will believe it. He doesn't trust me when it comes to the lad."

"Grant trusts me," she said. "I'll write the message and mention a private conversation we had so he knows it's from me."

Rory recalled that conversation all too well. "Tell him you're not exchanging your younger husband for an older one—and that we'll meet him just outside of Beauly, by the river."

He could hardly believe they were actually going to try this scheme, but *múineann gá seift, need teaches a plan*.

A smile played on Sybil's lips as she leaned back and folded her arms. "Hector will believe he has succeeded, and then we will have him right where we want him."

This was the Sybil he knew and loved. Her eyes were shining as she envisioned the defeat of his enemy. How had he ever doubted her loyalty? As Catriona said, the best luck of his life was when Sybil's brother deceived him in a game of cards.

He pulled her onto his lap and was about to kiss her for the first time in far too long when Grizel interrupted them—again. This time, Malcolm was with her.

"Lucky we came to relieve you," Grizel said, "or the lad might wake up to see something he shouldn't."

Rory shared the plan with the older couple while Sybil wrote out the message to Grant.

"I'll have my grandson Ewan leave at first light to deliver it," Malcolm said. "He's a fast rider and will have it to Urquhart Castle before the false news can reach the Grants."

When they started to debate how best to get Kenneth out of the castle without anyone guessing he was alive, Grizel interrupted them.

"You're going to wake the lad with all your jabbering. This can wait till morning," Grizel said. "Off to bed with the two of ye. Malcolm and I will stay with the lad the rest of the night."

Rory caught the look that passed between the older couple and realized they were trying to give him and Sybil time alone. He was sorely tempted, but he was uneasy about leaving his son.

"I'll bar the door and keep my sword at hand," Malcolm assured him, then he leaned closer and said, "Now go make up with your wife while ye have the chance."

Malcolm's words were a reminder that one could never know what tomorrow would bring. But tonight, he would have Sybil back in his arms again.

"You're a wise man," Rory said, squeezing Malcolm's shoulder. "No wonder my father made you his chief counselor."

Rory followed Sybil down the stairs with his heart in his throat, not certain if she had truly forgiven him. When they reached their bedchamber and closed the door, he stood still, aching to touch her, but not knowing if she would have him. He wanted her so much his hands shook.

***

Sybil watched Rory's chest rise and fall with his ragged breathing.

"I love ye so much," he said. "Do ye think it possible for ye to ever love me again?"

She felt too choked with emotion to speak at first. She rested her hand over his heart and felt it pounding beneath her palm.

"I'm willing to wait as long as it takes," he said.

"I never stopped loving you," she whispered, looking into his eyes. "I never will."

When she rose on her toes to meet his lips, his kiss was so full of longing it made her heart ache.

"Sybil, I'm so sor—"

"Shhh." She touched her finger to his lips. "We've both made mistakes and hurt each other, and we'll need to talk it all through. But the night is short, and I want to spend what's left of it in your arms."

She took his hand and led him to the bed.

They did not need words tonight. They showed each other their love and forgiveness with every touch, every kiss, every sigh.

Tears filled her eyes as she kissed Rory's battle scars and the new bruises from saving his son, marks of a man willing to risk his life for others.

Though Rory was bound to cause her anguish each time he put his life in danger, she knew how lucky she was to be loved by a man who was brave and honorable to his core.

They made love slowly savoring each moment, as if it might be their last time. As they melded together in a sensuous rhythm, Sybil felt as if their bodies and hearts were one.

Rory held her face between his hands as he moved inside her with excruciating slowness. When she saw the love in his eyes, she had no doubt that he was hers again.

And she was his. She had been from the start.

They lay wrapped in each other's arms until dawn, which came all too soon. Rory lifted her chin with his finger to look into her eyes.

"Neither of us has found trust easy, *a chuisle mo chroí*," *pulse of my heart*, he said. "But if we are to get through this, we must trust each other now."

"No matter what comes," Sybil said as she held his face between her hands. "Ye have my heart, always."

***

After making the grim announcement of Kenneth's death to the household, Rory rejoined the others upstairs in Kenneth's chamber.

"You're sure he's well enough to travel?" he asked Grizel.

"He's a strong lad," she said, mussing Kenneth's hair. "He'll do fine so long as he takes it easy."

Since they'd settled on a plan to take him in a cart covered in a shroud and blanket, that would not be a problem.

"It'll be fun playing dead," Kenneth said. "See if I don't fool them all."

Rory exchanged a worried look with Sybil. They were not entirely happy with their plan but had not come up with a better one. The cart would make the journey slow, and it would be unseemly to take the body of the Grant chieftain's grandson without a large escort, which meant Kenneth would have to lie still under the blanket for a long while.

"Your grandfather and Flora will be so happy to see you," Sybil said, "but we'll miss you."

Kenneth's smile faded. "Am I coming back?"

"Of course ye are," she said. "Isn't he, Rory?"

"Aye." He squeezed Kenneth's shoulder. "You belong here, son."

Rory was about to leave to gather the men who would ride with them when someone pounded on the door.

"Open the door!" Alex shouted from the other side. "Hurry!"

When Rory unbarred it, both his brother and sister hurried in, and he shut it behind them.

"I came as quickly as I heard," Alex said between gasps for breath.

"How did ye hear about Kenneth's accident so soon?" Rory asked.

"What? The lad's been hurt?" Alex's gaze shifted to where Kenneth lay on the bed.

"He's going to be fine." Rory gripped his brother's arm. "What did ye ride here to tell me?"

"I heard a confession this morning from a Gairloch man," Alex said. "Hector is laying an ambush near Loch Ussie for the Munro chieftain and his guard."

"Ye must stop them!" Catriona interjected.

"Hector plans to slaughter them," Alex said. "And ye know the blame will fall on you."

"Aye." As chieftain, the actions of his clan were his responsibility. The Munros would believe he either gave the order or should have been able to control his clansmen. Rory cursed his uncle for planning a senseless killing. And for what? To create more enemies for Rory to face.

"Ye can't let this happen," his sister said, clinging to his arm. "Ye must do something."

"I fear it may be too late already," Alex said.

"Pray it's not," Rory said, and grabbed his sword. "I'll take all the men I can spare from the castle and go at once."

"What about the Grants? They'll be on their way to Beauly by now," Sybil said. "If we fail to meet them with Kenneth, they're bound to think the worst."

"The Grants will have to wait," Rory said. "Malcolm, I leave my wife and son in your care."

Rory lifted Sybil off her feet and kissed her. And then he was gone.

***

A sense of premonition hung over Sybil like a dark cloud as she stood at the window watching Rory ride out with his men. Of course Rory had to try to prevent the massacre of innocent men. That left the Grants to her.

She drew Malcolm aside. "We need to take Kenneth to Beauly."

"Ach, lass," he said, "I was afraid you'd say that."

"We've no other choice," she said. "If we're not there, Grant will believe Kenneth is dead. Do ye want him to attack Castle Leod while Rory and half our men are gone?"

"We can't leave the castle undefended, and we don't have men to spare to escort a funeral cart."

"Aye, we need a different plan," she said. "Rory sneaked me out of my brother-in-law's castle rolled in a blanket. We can do the same with Kenneth."

"Rory would never allow you or Kenneth out of the castle without a guard."

"No one will know it's me and Kenneth," she said. "We'll say Alex was worried about his wife, who's ready to deliver her babe, and begged ye to take Grizel to her. I'll dress as a servant and cover my head in a hood."

"There's no need for you to go at all," Malcolm said.

"If his grandson arrives without Rory and with only one man for protection, Grant will be insulted. He'll believe Rory just wants to be rid of the lad," she said. "But if I come in disguise and with no guard, he'll believe our situation was desperate."

"I don't like it," Malcolm said. "It puts both you and the lad at risk."

"This is where he's not safe," she said. "Someone here wants to kill Kenneth."

"Don't think I didn't notice that ye waited to suggest this until Rory was gone."

Of course she had. Rory would not have let her take the risk, and she'd have no chance of convincing Malcolm to go against a direct command.

Sybil turned to find Grizel and Catriona behind her, listening in on their conversation.

"The lass is right. We need to get Kenneth away," Grizel said. "I'll gather my things and get him ready."

"What about me?" Catriona asked.

"Stay here and make certain no one comes into this chamber and finds there's no dead body," Malcolm said. "And if Rory returns before we do, ye can tell him where we've gone."

"Ach, he's going to be furious," Catriona said.

"Beauly is not far," Malcolm said. "With any luck, we'll return long before he does."

In the trunk in their bedchamber, Sybil found the tattered cloak she had worn on the long journey to the Highlands. Luckily, she had been unable to bring herself to throw it away. When she put it on, she was flooded with memories of their journey.

Since their wedding night, they had wasted precious time because they failed to trust each other. Last night had gone a long way toward healing their hearts, but she wished she could leave Rory a message to tell him how much she loved him and to ease his worry for her, in case he returned before she did. If only he could read. With a sigh, she started for the door, then stopped.

Rory knew the pendant from her mother was her most prized possession. She unfastened the clasp from her neck, kissed the stone, and left it on his pillow.

CHAPTER 43

He was too late.

Curan's sides heaved from the hard gallop to reach this valley to stop the ambush. Rory was filled with rage and sorrow as his gaze traveled over the hillside, which was strewn with the headless corpses of slain Munro warriors.

"Rory," Alex called up to him from the base of the hill, where there was a natural spring that was well known as a holy well. "Ye need to see this."

Rory dismounted when he reached Alex, and they walked through the tall grass to the spring. His stomach turned at the sight that greeted him. Heads of the dead Munros had rolled down the hill and filled the spring.

"God forgive us." He knelt with his brother and made the sign of the cross. "Hector and his men have shamed the MacKenzies this day."

"As long as there are Munros in Scotland," Alex said, "this holy well will be remembered for this terrible deed."

This was a disaster in every possible way. The Munros were favored by the crown, and their young chief was expected to replace his father as the crown's justiciar for the region. In addition to making the Munros bitter enemies, the unprovoked nature of the attack could bring the wrath of the crown down on them.

And yet the massacre would be hailed by Hector's followers as a cunning attack that would serve as a warning to the clan's enemies. Hector fabricated threats, whipped up fear, and presented himself as the great war leader who could protect them.

As Rory looked at the grisly sight in the spring, he felt weighed down by the part he had inadvertently played in this atrocity. Hector had done this not to protect the clan, but to serve his goal of taking the chieftainship from Rory. If he had let Hector have what he wanted, these men would be alive.

He and his men stopped for the night at a tavern in the nearby town of Dingwall. He asked the tavern keeper what he'd heard about the attack.

"One of the Munros fled the battle and made it here to our church seeking sanctuary," the man said. "Big Duncan of the Axe was chasing him, but he made it inside the church."

That was one survivor. Rory drank down his ale, intent on heading to the church to speak with him.

"When Big Duncan caught him by the arm inside the church door, the Munro warrior shouted, *Sanctuary saves me! Sanctuary saves me!*" the tavern keeper continued his tale. "But Big Duncan pulled him back out the door. *You're not in the church now,* he said, and killed him with one stroke of his axe."

Rory rubbed his forehead. This just got worse and worse. "Did ye hear if any of the Munros escaped?"

"If they did, they didn't pass through here."

Rory prayed the Munro chieftain had survived. He disliked the arrogant young man, but wished him no harm. And as bad as the situation already was, killing their chieftain would lead to all-out war with the Munros.

***

"Where's my grandfather?" Kenneth looked up at Sybil with Rory's green eyes, but she had no answer.

"We'll wait a little longer." She strained to see the trail into the village through the branches of the trees. Malcolm had insisted they wait in the thick foliage along the river where they would not be seen by a chance traveler.

Perhaps the Grant chieftain was away when the message arrived. She imagined it lying on his table unopened, awaiting his return.

Malcolm pulled her aside. "We've waited long enough. They're not coming."

"Then we'll have to take Kenneth to them," she said. "We're halfway to Urquhart Castle already."

"We shouldn't have come," Malcolm said. "It'll be dark soon, and I'll not take my laird's wife and son any farther without his approval."

"But—"

Malcolm held up his hand for quiet and drew his sword.

"What is it?" she whispered.

He tilted his head to the side, listening intently. "Someone is coming. A large party of riders."

Relief swept over her. The Grants had come at last. She could hear the horses now herself and stepped out onto the trail to greet them.

"Wait until we see who it is!" Malcolm hissed.

His warning came too late. Twenty mounted warriors rounded the hillside and entered the narrow valley some distance ahead. As soon as they saw her, they whipped their horses and charged toward her. In that instant she knew that these men had come expecting to find her here. And they were not the Grants.

Someone had betrayed them.

"Get off the goddamned trail," Malcolm called to her. "Those are Hector's men!"

There was no point in running. They had seen her and would chase her down before she could reach her horse. But they had not yet seen her companions. She could still save them.

"Take Kenneth and your wife away!" she called to them while keeping her gaze fixed on the warriors galloping toward them. "Go!"

Out of the corner of her eye she saw Malcolm signal to his wife, who was crouched in the brush with her hand over Kenneth's mouth. She prayed the three of them would escape.

Hector's men were almost upon her. The man in the lead wore a black helmet obscuring his face and rode his steed straight at her. She stood her ground. If he meant to trample her to death, she would not give him the satisfaction of cowering or shrieking in fright.

Suddenly, Malcolm was in front of her brandishing his sword. The horse's whinny filled her ears like a scream as it reared up, hooves shooting past her face in a blur. Time seemed to momentarily halt as the hooves of the great beast hovered above her head, then they came crashing down, barely missing her and Malcolm.

"Show your face, ye filthy bastard!" Malcolm shouted. "I know it's you, Hector!"

The rider took off his black helmet. He would have been a striking man with his rugged features and jet-black hair with streaks of gray, but for his eyes, which held a malevolence that turned Sybil's blood to ice.

"I might have known you'd be here, old man," Hector said.

She swallowed as twenty horses surrounded them. Their riders had blood splatters on their arms and faces.

Hector dismounted, drew his sword, and signaled to his men to move back.

"Please, Malcolm," Sybil whispered, "don't sacrifice yourself for me."

"I always hoped for a warrior's death," Malcolm said. "I'll take this traitor with me if I can."

"It will be a pleasure to run my blade through your heart, old man." *Whoosh whoosh.* Hector whipped his sword in the air. "I've been waiting to do it for years."

Malcolm fought well, swinging his claymore with remarkable power and precision. In his prime, he might have been better than Hector. But he was not now. Hector fought with a terrible ferocity, each strike harder than the one before and with such speed that his blade was a blur.

Sybil watched in horror as Hector's sword left a red streak of blood across Malcolm's thigh and then another across his right arm. Malcolm fought on valiantly with only his left arm. He managed to draw blood on Hector's cheek with the tip of his sword, but anyone could see how the fight would end.

"Nay! Nay!" she shrieked when Hector plunged his sword into Malcolm's belly and the older man fell in a heap.

She managed to sink her teeth hard into the hand of the man holding her and break free. She fell on top of Malcolm, covering his body with hers to protect him. When her captors hauled her away from him, she clawed and kicked and bit at them like a wildcat.

"Let me go!" she cried. "Let me help him!"

"He's dead," Hector said, and slapped her so hard her ears rang. "Now keep your mouth shut, or I'll let my friend here ruin your pretty face—and worse."

She sucked in her breath as an enormous man with a pockmarked face appeared in front of her. To confirm her fears, she slowly lowered her gaze from his hideous face until she saw the giant axe tucked in his belt. Its blade was covered with blood.

God have mercy on her. She was face to face with Big Duncan of the Axe.

CHAPTER 44

"Duncan, find any others who were traveling with them," Hector ordered. "When you've taken care of them, meet us back at Fairburn Tower."

Sybil was careful not to look toward the bushes where she had last seen Grizel and Kenneth hiding and prayed that they had managed to get far enough away during the fight that Duncan would not find them. One look at his massive frame of solid muscle told her the odds were against an old woman and a young boy.

Sybil rode with her hands bound and a rope tied loosely around her neck. Hector's men taunted her with obscene remarks, but they eventually lost interest when she failed to react. In truth, she was so numb with shock and grief that she barely heard them.

Her scheme to deliver Kenneth to the Grants had led to utter disaster. Malcolm was dead. Grizel and Kenneth were in grave danger, perhaps already killed at the hands of that monster Big Duncan. And it was all her fault.

Questions swirled around and around in her head. Why had Grant not come to meet them? Did he not receive her message, or did he believe Kenneth was dead and her message a ruse to buy time?

If these men killed her, would Rory ever know what happened to her? It pierced her heart to think he might believe she had left him. They had only reconciled last night, and she feared his trust in her was still fragile.

Dusk had fallen when her captors stopped at a tower house. Someone lifted her down, then Hector pulled her into the house by the rope around her neck as if she was a goat. She was past hope and past care. He could not do more damage than she had done herself.

"I've no time for ye now." Hector held her by her chin as he leaned so close to her that his foul breath filled her nose. "But I'm looking forward to getting to know my nephew's bride verra well."

She was taken down to the undercroft, where her guard unlocked a door, shoved her through it, and locked it behind her. The room she was in was pitch black. Feeling her way along the wall, she took a step. The ground disappeared beneath her, and she stumbled down several stone stairs and fell to her knees on a dirt floor.

Exhausted from grief and despair, she leaned against the cold stone wall in the eternal darkness of her prison.

***

With a heavy heart, Rory rode back to Castle Leod. The only thought that eased his burdens was knowing that Sybil was waiting there for him. He desperately needed to hold her in his arms. And perhaps she could help him to see that all was not lost.

Rory's own clansmen were trying to murder his son. Grant was likely preparing for war in the belief that they had succeeded. After the slaughter of the Munro chieftain's party, their former alliance seemed beyond repair. What had been strained relations with both clans during his brother's time as chieftain was on the verge of erupting into war across Eastern Ross.

The even greater danger to the clan was that the MacDonalds would learn of it and launch an attack from the west. Hector had brought too many warriors with him who should be defending their western shores.

When they finally reached Castle Leod, Rory took the steps to the keep three at a time, with Alex behind him. He scanned the hall for Sybil, but she was not there. Catriona saw him and rushed to his side. She caught his arm as he strode toward the stairs that led to the bedchambers above.

"What happened with the Munros?" she asked. "Did ye stop the attack?"

"We'll speak upstairs." He pulled her along with him to the laird's chamber.

It was empty. Sybil must be in Kenneth's chamber with Malcolm and Grizel. When he turned to go there, his sister stood in his way.

"Tell me what happened with the Munros," Catriona demanded.

"We were too late," Rory said.

"Nay!" Her hands flew to her face, and she went deathly pale. "Was the Munro chief slain?"

"We did not find his body among the dead." Alex spoke in a soft voice and put his arm around Catriona. "There is hope that he and others survived."

"I'm going upstairs to see Sybil and the others," Rory said.

"She's not there," Catriona said. "None of them are."

Rory felt as if his stomach had dropped to the floor.

"I've been waiting with no word from any of you." Catriona wrung her hands as she explained how Sybil and the others had gone to Beauly to meet the Grants. "They should have returned last night."

"I should have foreseen that Sybil would attempt some bold and risky plan, with no thought for her own safety." Rory ran his hands through his hair. "This is so like her!"

"She was trying to protect Kenneth and prevent trouble with the Grants," Alex said. "And it doesn't sound like a *bad* plan."

"Not a *bad* plan?" Rory said, raising his hands in the air. "They've disappeared, and I don't know where in the hell they are or what's happened to them."

"I found something when I was looking for a hair comb I lent Sybil," Catriona said. "It probably has nothing to do with this, but—"

"For God's sake, Catriona, what is it?"

"I found this at the back of the drawer in her table where she keeps her hair ribbons and drawings." She paused, testing his patience, then withdrew a folded parchment from her sleeve. "It has a fancy seal, so I thought it might be important."

He tore the parchment from her hands and thrust it at Alex. "Read it to me."

Alex scanned it first, then looked up. "Promise you'll remember that ye have no reason not to trust Sybil."

The warning caused the hair on the back of his neck to rise. "Just read it."

Rory gritted his teeth as Alex read the lines from her despicable brothers. When Alex read her uncle's message about a ship waiting for her at Inverness to take her to join her brothers in France, Rory sat down hard on the closest chair.

He remembered so clearly telling her that it was easy to take a boat from Beauly to Inverness. She had been adamant about going with him to Beauly to meet the Grants. And when he could not go, she went anyway.

Alex read a line scrawled in yet another hand noting the ship's name, *La Fleur*, and today's date with *at dawn* underlined twice. That explained why she could not wait another day and hope Rory could rearrange the rendezvous with Grant.

He had no doubt that she loved his son and would not have left until she delivered Kenneth safely to the Grants. But did she ever truly love him? Or did she just not love him enough to give up her chance at life in the French court for the dangerous and hostile world he had brought her to?

If she could persuade Malcolm to take her to Beauly, she could easily find an excuse to slip away from him long enough to find a fisherman who would take her to Inverness in exchange for a silver coin or a smile. Malcolm was probably still looking for her, afraid to face Rory until he found her.

But it was too late to catch her.

Sybil was gone.

CHAPTER 45

Sybil awoke hours later to what sounded like a moan.

"Is someone there?" she called out into the darkness.

When she heard another low moan, she crawled toward the sound, awkward on her forearms because her hands were still bound, until her fingers touched cloth. She reached out and felt a limb beneath the fabric. She had a fellow prisoner, and he appeared to be badly injured.

"Tell me where you're hurt and what I can do to help you," she said.

"My leg," he said in a hoarse whisper. "I'll die if we can't stop the bleeding."

"I'll cut a strip from my gown."

Hector's men had taken the dirk strapped to her thigh. While she had been lost in self-pity and despair, she'd forgotten that she wore the ragged cloak from her long journey north. Quickly, she felt along the bottom of it until she found the small, thin blade Rory had insisted she hide in the hem for added protection.

Removing the blade was fairly easy, but sawing through the rope binding her wrists was a struggle. The poor man moaned again. She was taking far too long.

"I'll help." The voice that came out of the darkness was young and female.

"Please!" Sybil did not have time to ask questions.

Cold fingers found her hands and took the blade from her. As soon as her hands were free, she took the knife back and cut a long strip of cloth from the shift under her gown. The injured man had gone quiet, and she feared he had died on her.

"I can't see." She shook his arm. "Ye must show me where I should tie this on your leg."

He guided her hand to the gaping wound on his thigh. She swallowed back her panic and sopped up the blood with the skirt of her gown as best she could.

"I'm Sybil, the MacKenzie's wife," she said to distract him from the pain as she and the girl worked together to bandage his wound. "Who are you?"

"Lùcas," he croaked.

"Malcolm's grandson?" Oh, God, he had not delivered the message. That meant the Grants had heard nothing except that Kenneth was dead. Tears filled her eyes as she remembered that the boy might truly be dead now.

"And you, lass?" she asked, trying to keep her voice steady. "Why does Hector have you here?"

"I'm Brighde, the wise woman's granddaughter," she said. "He's told my grandmother he'll give me to Big Duncan of the Axe unless she does what he says. But I believe he'll do it no matter what she does."

Nay, Sybil would not let this poor girl fall into Duncan's hands. Nor would she let Malcolm's grandson die here. It was time to stop wallowing in despair.

"The three of us are going to escape," she said. "We just need a plan."

***

"Quick, Brighde!" Sybil said when she heard the grate of the iron lock turning. "Help me retie my hands."

Her heart pounded in her ears as she fumbled in the dark to find the longest piece of the cut rope. A shaft of light appeared at the top of the stairs. Somehow, the two of them got it tied, but she hoped her captors would not notice that the rope was shorter than before.

In the light from the guard's torch as he came down the steps, Sybil saw the girl's face for the first time and her heart clenched. The girl was young, not more than fourteen, and fair and pretty.

"We will get out," Sybil whispered to give the girl hope just before the guard yanked her feet. Hope was a dangerous thing to lose.

A short time later, she stood alone in a room with Hector and Big Duncan. She squinted against the bright light of day as she took in the exquisite tapestries and French furniture.

Hector came toward her with his dirk pointed at her belly. She gasped as he flicked his wrist and the rope fell from her hands. After waving her into a chair, he handed her a cup of wine.

"Go ahead and drink," he said. "I'm not a subtle man. If I decide to kill ye, it won't be by poison."

"How reassuring," she said, and took a tiny sip.

"Tell me how it is that instead of Rory," Hector said, leaning back in his chair, "I find his lovely Douglas bride dressed in rags and protected by just that tired old warrior Rory was so fond of."

She swallowed at his mention of Malcolm, but she could not think about his death now. She needed to keep her wits sharp and decide how she would play this.

"Ye know I caught your messenger, so I know Rory planned to deliver Grant's grandson at Beauly," he said. "Why wasn't he there?"

"One way or another," Duncan said when she was slow to answer, "you're going to tell Hector what he wants to know."

"Sadly, the lad drowned in the river yesterday," she said. "Rory made me write that message saying he was still alive to buy time to prepare for an attack."

If Duncan had found Kenneth and Grizel, they would know she was lying. She held her breath for a moment, half expecting to be cut down on the spot, then took a sip of wine to cover her pause.

"Then this morning," she continued, "Rory rode off without a word to me."

"Ha, I knew he would charge off to try to save the Munros," Hector said. "I sent one of my men to make confession to Alex—when it was too late, of course."

"We were already chopping off heads by then," Duncan said, running his hand over his axe handle.

"On the chance I misjudged Rory, we rode to Beauly after our victory in hope of catching him off guard," Hector said. "Which brings us back to the mystery of why we found you there."

"There is really no mystery to it." She turned her head to the side and blinked back tears. "They say we women are fickle, but it's men who pledge their hearts and then cast us aside."

"I'm not fond of riddles," Hector said. "Speak plainly, lass."

"Rory wed me because he was desperate to have me in his bed," she said in a bitter tone. "Now that his lust has waned, he wants a marriage alliance with a powerful Highland clan more than he wants me. I know he intends to set me aside, so I've left him."

She hoped her performance was persuasive. When she mentioned Rory, the tear that slipped down her cheek was real enough.

"Most women are foolish, but I hear you're a clever one." Hector leaned forward, his cold eyes piercing her like shards of ice.

"I know you're lying because I know who ye are and that you've no place to go."

For the first time since the mysterious priest brought it to her, she remembered the message from her family and realized she could offer Hector proof for her false story.

"My family got word to me that they arranged passage for me on a ship bound for France, where my brothers are in exile," she said. "You can ask at Inverness if the French ship *La Fleur* anchored there. It would have set sail this morning for Calais."

She hoped that giving him details that he could easily check would convince him. Hector narrowed his eyes at her for a long moment, then finally nodded.

She shrieked in pain as Big Duncan lifted her out of her chair by her hair.

"Since Rory doesn't want her, are ye done with her?" he asked Hector.

"She's still a valuable asset," Hector said. "Returning a Douglas traitor for justice could make the crown more inclined to recognize me as chieftain. Or I can sell her to James Hamilton of Finnart, son of the Earl of Arran."

Finnart? How did Hector know about Finnart?

"I can see I surprised ye," Hector said with a satisfied smile. "Once I heard that Rory had wed Lady Sybil Douglas, I made it a point to find out all I could about ye. Turns out, you're a rather famous lass."

***

When the hall door opened, Rory looked up expecting to see Sybil. Despite the evidence to the contrary, his heart could not accept that she had left him.

Instead of his wife, one of Malcolm's sons came through the door.

"Has your father returned yet?" Rory asked.

"Nay," the man said. "Neither has my son Lùcas, the one ye sent to Urquhart Castle."

Rory wondered if the Grants were holding his messenger hostage until Kenneth was delivered. That would be a common precaution.

"I started to ride to Urquhart Castle to ask after my son," the man continued, "but I had to turn around to tell ye what I saw."

Rory could see from his face that it was more bad news.

"The Grants have set bonfires on their hilltops to call their men to battle," he said. "I'd wager we have two days at most before they're ready to attack."

Please, God, not this too. Rory's one comfort had been the knowledge that his son was safe with the Grants. The Grants' call to battle could only mean they believed Kenneth was dead.

If the Grants did not have Kenneth, where was he?

Could Sybil have taken his son with her? Could she be that cruel to leave him and also take his son?

He went up to their bedchamber. He hardly knew why. As soon as he opened the door, he was flooded with images of Sybil. He saw her brushing her midnight hair by the window, heard her irresistible laughter that always lightened his burdens, and imagined her eyes dancing with amusement as she teased him.

He could not avoid looking at the bed, though those memories gave him the most pain. Unable to help himself, he lifted the pillow and buried his face in it to breathe in her scent. What a sentimental fool he had become.

He pounded his fist against the bed. How could she leave him when he needed her so much? If she had left before when he refused to trust her, he would understand. But why leave now? She had seemed so sincere when she said she forgave him and loved him still. And when they made love, she made him believe it with every touch and sigh.

He still believed it. She had not deceived him, not this time. What had he missed? An uneasy feeling that Sybil was in trouble settled in the pit of his stomach.

He heard a faint *clink* as something fell off the bed and hit the floor. Without knowing why he bothered, he dropped to his knees to see what it was. Just under the edge of the bed, a glossy black stone caught the light.

Sybil's pendant.

In that moment he knew for certain that Sybil intended to return. She never would have left the pendant behind if she meant to leave for good.

He rubbed his thumb over the stone's smooth surface, as he had seen her do a hundred times. She had left it on the bed as a message for him. If she did not intend to disappear, where was she?

Gripping the stone, he pressed his fists against his forehead. Perhaps the stone did have magical protective powers, for she'd never been without it before, and she had survived so many dangers with him.

And he knew in the depths of his soul that his beloved was in danger now. *Damn him!* His mistrust of her feelings for him had prevented him from realizing it sooner. He could almost hear her calling to him.

If he was wrong about Sybil leaving on that ship for France, then he was wrong about Malcolm looking for her and everything else.

He broke out in a cold sweat as the certainty swept over him that all four of them—Sybil, Kenneth, Malcolm and Grizel—were in grave danger. As he ran from the room, he prayed to God and all that was holy that he was not too late to save them.

Rory rode hard for Beauly with a score of MacKenzie warriors. If Sybil and the others had been captured, he would find the trail at Beauly and follow it until he found them. If they were killed...he would not let himself think of that.

They were only a mile from Castle Leod and rounding a curve when Curan whinnied and danced sideways to slow his pace. Ahead of them, a small figure appeared in the middle of the path. Rory's heart slammed against his chest.

"Halt! Halt!" He held up his hand to signal the riders behind him and leaped off Curan's back.

He ran to his son and swept him up into his arms.

"Praise God," he said as he held him against his chest. Then he leaned back to examine him. Kenneth looked tired and dirty, but unharmed. "How did ye get here? It's ten miles from Beauly."

"I walked," Kenneth said. "Grizel sent me."

Rory's joy at finding his son was swept away in a wave of fear. "What's happened?"

"You've got to come," Kenneth said, fighting tears. "Malcolm is hurt bad."

"What about Sybil?" Rory could not breathe. "Is she hurt as well?"

"I don't know," Kenneth said. "Grizel and I had to hide in the reeds in the river for a long time, so I didn't see what happened to her. When we came back to help Malcolm, Sybil was gone. Grizel thinks they took her."

"Who took her?" Rory asked, gripping his son's shoulders. "Who?"

"Grizel said to tell you it was Hector and his men," Kenneth said. "And she says to hurry or Malcolm won't make it."

The ride to Beauly seemed to take an eternity. On the trail to the village, Rory drew Curan to a halt beside the dark patch of blood where Malcolm had fallen. Kenneth led him from there to the thicket where Grizel waited with Malcolm.

Rory's heart fell to his feet when he saw his old friend covered in blood and lying motionless with his head in his wife's lap. Rory had never seen Grizel shed a tear before, but her face was wet with them now.

Malcolm's eyes flickered open when Rory took his hand.

"Don't let me die here," Malcolm whispered.

"I won't," Rory promised. "I'll get ye back to Castle Leod."

***

Malcolm still clung to life by a thread when they reached the castle. Rory carried him upstairs to his own bedchamber and laid him gently on the bed. He left him and Kenneth in the care of Grizel and the other women, with instructions to call him if Malcolm woke again.

Then he set his sorrow aside. He had to protect his son and rescue his wife. He posted half a dozen men at the chamber door and ordered that no one be allowed to enter except at Grizel's request, then he went down to the hall.

Everyone except the men who had gone with him to Beauly was whispering about the dead boy come to life and making signs of the cross. Clearly, it was too late to maintain the pretense that the lad was dead.

"Kenneth is my son," he shouted over their voices, "and he was never dead."

When the room quieted, he explained the reason for the hoax.

"The person who attempted to harm him may be in this castle," he said. "Kenneth is my heir and your future chieftain, so I charge every one of you to protect him."

He could not risk Hector hearing from one of his spies that Kenneth was alive.

"No one leaves the castle until I return," he said. "If anyone attempts to, they will be executed at once."

There was a general intake of breath. He had no time to discuss it further. He called his senior men to his private room behind the hall.

"While ye were gone, we learned that the Munro chieftain survived the ambush," one of the men reported.

Here, at least, was one piece of good news. "How do we know?"

"He led raids on two MacKenzie villages along our shared border."

Rory rubbed his forehead. "Anything else?"

"The MacDonalds have burned MacKenzie boats in Gairloch Bay and attacked villages all along our seacoast in the west," another man reported.

"*A' phlàigh oirbh MacDonalds!*" *A plague on the MacDonalds*, several of the men said in unison.

And a plague on Hector for leaving their defenses so thin in the west. *Damn him!*

Everything Rory touched had turned to ashes, just as Hector predicted. For the first time, Rory considered that it might actually be true that he was not his father's son and that he had brought all this on his clan because he did not have chieftain's blood.

Regardless, he knew what he had to do.

He sent a man to ride ahead to alert his uncle, then he set out with his brother and thirty men for Fairburn Tower.

As he approached the fortified tower house, he counted the warriors in the clearing surrounding it.

"I see two hundred to our thirty," Alex said beside him. "And that's just outside the house."

"There are more men in the woods," Rory said. So far his uncle's men were letting them pass.

"I'm not sure this is wise," Alex said. "I hope ye know what you're doing."

Rory hoped he did too. But he could think of no other way out of this.

"Hector of Gairloch!" he shouted when they halted in front of the house. "I've come to discuss the terms under which I will leave MacKenzie lands."

CHAPTER 46

Rory laid out his conditions for leaving.

"You will cease provoking our neighboring clans and make peace with the Munros and the Grants," Rory said. "If ye lay the blame for your attacks and the death of Grant's grandson on me and say you've banished me, that will go a long way toward appeasing them."

Hector shrugged. "I've no need to fight them now."

"I have one last condition. Ye must return my wife to me," Rory said. "I know ye took her, and if you've harmed her, there will be no deal between us."

"Now that I know how much she means to ye, I wish I had kept her," Hector said. "She said that the trouble with the Grants led ye to set her aside in favor of Grant's daughter. I felt sorry for the lass, ye sending her off in rags with no protection, so I let her go."

"I did not set her aside," Rory said between his teeth.

"Then that lass is a damned good liar," Hector said. "She begged me to let her board a ship that was waiting to carry her to France."

Rory's heart lurched, but he kept his expression passive. He told himself that Hector could have invented the story, for it was common knowledge Sybil's brothers were living in exile in France.

"The ship had some frilly French name. Ach, what was it?" Hector said. "*La Fleur*, that was it, and it was sailing for Calais."

Hector could not know the name of the ship and where it was sailing without speaking to Sybil. "She's here," Rory said. "I know she is."

"Ach, ye hurt my feelings with your lack of trust." Hector spread his arm out to the side. "But you're welcome to search the house."

Rory knew exactly where to look. When he was a bairn, his uncle locked him in the dank dungeon beneath the tower and left him there until his mother found him hours later.

He charged down the stairs and through the undercroft, grabbed a torch from the wall sconce, and pushed open the door to the dungeon.

No one was in it. But on the stairs, he saw fresh drops of blood.

***

"Rory is not the man ye thought he was," Hector said with a satisfied smile. "He's given up on the chieftainship without spilling a drop of blood."

Hector had kept Sybil bound and gagged watching from an upstairs window in the tower long enough to see Rory ride up and to hear his declaration. It had broken her heart to hear it. As Rory and Alex entered the tower, Hector's men hustled her out a back door to her new prison, a small, windowless hut a few hundred yards from the tower house.

Now Hector had come to gloat.

"The man who deserves to lead is the one who can outwit his opponents," Hector said, tapping his finger against his temple. "Rory is no match for me."

"If Rory gave up the chieftainship, it was because he knew you'd destroy the clan if he didn't," she said. "He put the welfare of the clan before his own ambitions. That's what a great leader does."

"That's a surprise, coming from a Douglas," Hector said with a smirk, and sat down on the only chair in the hut.

She glanced at Brighde and Lùcas, who were bound together in the corner and had the sense to keep quiet. At least they were still alive.

"He was willing to give up on you as well," Hector said. "Once he's gone, I'll make certain he hears ye chose to be Finnart's mistress rather than live with him now that he's a lowly warrior who must earn his living with his sword."

"He won't believe that," she said. "Rory knows I love him and that I'd never go to Finnart. And I won't!"

"I suppose ye can jump overboard and drown instead," he said. "But ye strike me as a survivor, so I'd wager ye won't."

She would get away somehow and find Rory no matter where he was.

"Which would ye say pains a man more," Hector asked, "losing the woman he loves to death or to another man?"

Surely death would be harder if he truly loved the woman. She shook her head, unwilling to seal her fate. So long as she lived, there was a chance of escape.

"I can tell ye which is worse." Hector swirled the whisky in the cup he brought with him and stared into the amber liquid. "If she's with another man, he has hope that she'll leave him. Hope is a wound that festers every day, driving him mad."

"What would you know of love?" she said.

He looked up, as if he suddenly remembered she was there and realized he had spoken his thoughts aloud.

"I want her son to suffer as I did," he said. "That is the only reason I'm letting ye live."

CHAPTER 47

"Duncan will come for me now," Brighde said, in a high voice. "Hector doesn't need my grandmother now that the laird has given up."

"When he comes, that will give us our opportunity to escape." Sybil put her arm around the girl and nodded at Lùcas, who was more alert now, but still very weak.

They would have one chance, and that was all. Sybil had her blade, and they had searched the hut's dirt floor until they found two small shards from a broken pot. They each had a weapon now, and they had surprise on their side.

She tensed as she heard someone sliding the wooden bar on the outside of the door.

"Just like we practiced," she whispered to the others.

But when Big Duncan filled the open doorway, she knew they could never be ready. He was too big, too powerful, too skilled a warrior. Their weapons were pathetically tiny, Lùcas could barely stand, and Brighde was little more than a child. But they had to try.

They remained in their places on the floor, holding their hands behind their backs as if bound, waiting for Duncan to make the first move. Their plan was to wait until the last possible moment to launch their attack.

Duncan did not even look at Sybil and Lùcas. Without a moment's pause, he pounced on Brighde like a starving wolf attacking a helpless lamb. Brighde screamed.

Fury surged through Sybil, obliterating all fear and any thought of their plan. She flew across the hut and landed on his back like a wild cat, driven by rage and the instinct to protect her own. Before he knew what hit him, she plunged her blade into the side of his neck.

Duncan bellowed and arched back. She clung to him with her legs and one arm around his enormous neck as she stabbed him again, this time in his back. All her efforts seemed to do was enrage him.

He spun, knocking her against the wall as he tried to shake her off. *Oof!* The breath went out of her as she hit the wall again, but she managed to hold on. But then he caught hold of the back of her gown and flipped her over his head, slamming her onto the floor on her back. She lay stunned, her vision sparked with stars.

Just before the beast of a man fell on top of her, she managed to roll to the side far enough to avoid his full weight. But she was trapped under his leg and arm.

"Run! Run!" she shouted to the others. The door was open. "Get help!"

She bit Duncan's arm and wriggled out from under him while he cursed her. She stumbled to her feet and ran out the door after Brighde and Lùcas.

Duncan caught her around her knees and she fell in the tall grass. Duncan turned her over and leaned down, his hideous face distorted by rage. "You're going to pay for this!"

She struggled against the enormous brute, but he had her pinned, and he was so heavy she could not move at all.

"Rory!" she screamed as Duncan started pulling up her skirts. "Rory!"

***

Rory lay flat on his belly watching the hut. He suspected Hector had moved Sybil out of the Fairburn Tower so he could make that show of letting Rory search the house. That must have amused the bastard. After riding away, Rory sneaked back and watched the tower house until he saw Duncan leave.

It was always Duncan who did Hector's dirty work, so Rory followed him. He could not risk giving away his presence until he was sure this hut was where Sybil was being kept. He wouldn't have a second chance, so he held his breath and waited while Duncan went inside the hut.

Rory heard a scream and took off running across the field toward the hut. A young man leaning on the shoulders of a lass scurried out of the hut. As Rory raced across the field, the pair saw him and waved frantically.

A moment later, Sybil ran out of the hut with Duncan right behind her. Duncan dropped her, and cold fury shot through Rory's veins. As Sybil screamed his name, he barreled into Duncan.

As they rolled on the ground, Duncan slammed a heavy fist into Rory's bruised side, where he'd cracked a rib in the river. The blinding pain just made Rory more furious. He rammed the heel of his hand up against Duncan's nose and heard the satisfying snap of it breaking.

Rory sprang to his feet with his dirk in his hand. Duncan was quick for such a big man. He was standing almost as soon as Rory, with his infamous axe in his hand.

They circled each other. Big Duncan's blood was up and he was accustomed to overpowering his opponents with little trouble.

"How's your nose?" Rory taunted him. "Gives ye the devil of a headache, doesn't it?"

When Duncan roared and swung his axe, Rory danced out of his reach, then swooped in and struck Duncan's thigh with his blade. Duncan's next swing was low, and Rory had to jump to avoid losing a leg. The next, Rory felt the wind in his hair as he ducked below the axe. In between Duncan's swings, Rory cut the big man's shoulder, his side, and his other leg.

Duncan was a mountain of a man, and none of the injuries Rory inflicted seemed to slow him down. Rory needed to end this before any of Hector's other men came this way.

Before Duncan could recover from the next swing to bring his axe back again, Rory stepped in close and rammed his blade to the hilt up under Duncan's breastbone.

Big Duncan of the Axe fell like a stone. Blood seeped from his mouth as he stared up in shocked surprise.

Sybil ran into Rory's arms. He held her close and buried his face in her hair. He had come so close to losing her.

"I tried to be brave," Sybil said against his chest, "but I was so afraid I'd never see you again."

"You're the bravest lass in all of Scotland." He brushed her hair back and looked into his beloved's violet eyes. "I'll never let ye go."

When the pair who had run out of the hut joined them, Rory was relieved to see that the young man was Malcolm's missing grandson, Lùcas. He was injured, but they did not have far to go. Though he did not know her name, he recognized the girl as the wise woman's granddaughter. He knew now why the woman had lied about his birth.

The girl went to stand over Duncan.

"Burn in hell," she said, and spit in his eye.

A fitting end to an evil life.

"We'd better hurry now," Rory said. "I have a boat to catch."

"I'd go anywhere with you," Sybil said, "but I hate to see you give up the chieftainship to Hector. Your clan needs ye here."

"I've no intention of giving it up," he said, and gave her a wink. "I told Hector I would leave. I never said I wouldn't come back."

CHAPTER 48

Rory and his thirty chosen men boarded the birlinn, a Highland longboat that was fast and sleek, on the MacKenzie side of Beauly Firth and under the watchful eyes of Hector and a hundred of his men.

Hector would have men farther up the shore watching to make sure their boat passed by, but it would soon be too dark for anyone watching from the shore to see their sail. Rory had asked for a few hours to allow his men to bid goodbye to their loved ones and prepare for the journey, which ensured their departure would be near dusk.

They sailed through the night for an hour. When they were near Avoch, Alex's parish, Rory ordered the sail dropped. The men rowed toward the shore, the birlinn cutting silently through the water like a hot knife through butter.

A night fog had rolled in, hiding the shore. Rory tensed, ready to give the order to reverse oars if they were met by Hector's men.

But all was quiet. Without a word, he and his men slipped over the sides of the boat and hauled it onto the shore. He did not relax until Alex emerged from the fog.

"I'm glad to see you, Brother," Alex said, putting an arm around Rory's shoulders. "The horses are tied just behind that rise."

Rory was not pleased when he saw Sybil. "You were supposed to stay at Alex's house."

"I'm going with you." She rose on her toes and kissed him on the cheek. "I want to be there to see it finished."

"I want ye in a safe place," he said. "Whether I succeed or no, this will not be a pleasant sight."

"I *need* to be there, and I've earned the right," she said with that stubborn look. "Years from now, I want to tell our children and grandchildren that I saw it with my own eyes."

Rory heaved a sigh. He suspected he'd have to tie her down to keep her from following. "All right, so long as ye promise to stay well back."

It felt good to have Sybil riding behind him on Curan across the fields. He and most of the thirty men had grown up in this part of MacKenzie lands and knew the trails well enough to ride them at night.

Rory's plan depended on his uncle's confidence in his victory. He was counting on his uncle relaxing his guard while he celebrated—and on Hector not discovering Duncan's body. If they arrived to find a hundred sober men posted around the tower house, this would not go well.

They dismounted and left their horses a quarter mile from Fairburn Tower. While the others waited, Rory and a couple of his men sneaked through the wood to the edge of the clearing around the tower house. Boisterous laughter and drunken songs drifted from inside. A few men, who should have been watching the parameter, stood outside the door passing a jug and talking in loud voices.

His plan just might work. By the time Rory rejoined his men, they had a small fire going.

"Remember," he cautioned them, "silent as the dead."

At his signal, each man picked up a burning stick from the fire or one of the iron pots of oily tar they had brought with them.

"You can come to the edge of the wood with us, but no farther," Rory said, holding Sybil by the shoulders. "At the first sign of trouble, you run back to the horses and ride as fast as ye can to Avoch."

"Aye," she said, though not as convincingly as he would have liked.

He kissed her hard. "Do as I said."

Rory stood before his men, raised his sword high, and gave the MacKenzie battle cry in a loud whisper. *"Tùlach Àrd!"*

"Tùlach Àrd!" the others said in unison, and they started through the wood.

When they reached the edge of the clearing, Rory made the sound of the morning dove, *whoo-whoo whoo-whoo*, and the men dipped their arrows in the tar mixture.

Whoo-whoo whoo-whoo, he signaled a second time, and they lit the ends of their arrows. All along the edge of the clearing he saw the small bursts of flame.

Whoo-whoo. He gave the final signal, took aim, and thirty flaming arrows shot through the night sky. A handful of his men ran to the door to hold it shut, while others subdued the drunken guards, and the rest of them continued shooting flaming arrows.

As he watched the roof catch fire and burn bright against the night sky, Rory was taken back to the night Killin burned. He could feel Sybil's limp body in his arms, the floor burning his feet, and the smoke choking his lungs as he kicked at the shutters that were nailed shut.

He had vowed revenge for that night, and he would have it now.

The first shouts and cries of alarm reached him through the crackle of the fire. Men inside began pounding on the door to get out. Rory was unmoved. He remembered the heads of the Munro dead in the holy well. Hector and his men deserved their fate. When a woman's scream pierced the night, however, he realized there were innocents inside as well.

"Send out your women and children!" he shouted up at the windows. "They will not be harmed!"

His men opened the door and stood guard on either side of the doorway with their swords drawn, ready to cut down any man who attempted to escape with the handful of terrified women who ran out, some of them holding children. When the last one escaped the fire, he signaled for the door to be closed again.

Hector's men called out from the windows, begging for mercy. In the light of the flames, Rory could see the growing unease of the faces of his men. He reminded himself that Hector's men had refused to pledge their loyalty to their rightful chieftain, and they were responsible for many misdeeds that endangered the clan.

"These are our clansmen," Alex said beside him.

"They don't deserve mercy," Rory said.

"Mercy is for the undeserving," Alex said.

"Our father and grandfather were great chieftains, and ye know damned well neither of them would have spared men who rebelled against them."

He glanced at Sybil, who had come out from the woods to comfort the women and children. She wanted to tell their own children and grandchildren the story of how he had outwitted his uncle, but this was not the story she would be proud to tell them.

And in his heart, he knew she and Alex were right.

"Any man willing to swear his loyalty shall be spared!" he shouted. "Drop your weapons as you come out!"

One after another the warriors streamed out, their faces marked with soot. They dropped their weapons in the growing pile and then dropped to their knees wherever they could find a place. There were so many surrendering that they filled the clearing.

"There must be three hundred of them to our thirty," Alex said. "You've humiliated Hector with such a crushing defeat. Every MacKenzie who has not yet pledged his loyalty will be as anxious to do so."

Rory had done what he set out to do.

Sybil came to his side and hugged his arm as she looked up him. "I knew ye would succeed!"

The flow of men fleeing the house had finally stopped. He stood with Sybil on his right and his brother on his left, ready to accept the oaths from Hector's men.

"Where is Hector?" Sybil asked in a low voice.

"He's chosen to die in the flames rather than face execution for his treachery." Rory's pardon did not apply to their leader.

Rory watched the door as a last man stumbled out and fell to his knees.

"Mercy!" he croaked. "By the blood we share, mercy!"

Hector. Rory drew his sword and walked toward his uncle. The heat from the fire was so intense this close to the house that it burned his skin, but it was nothing compared to the fire exploding inside him.

"I pledge my loyalty to you, the one true chieftain of the MacKenzies," Hector cried out in a voice loud enough for those in the clearing to hear. "And I beg for mercy."

"I know ye told Buchanan where he could find Brian," Rory said, leaning close to look his uncle in the eye. "When my brother ran out of that house, did Buchanan show him mercy?"

"I had nothing to do with that," Hector said, a lie that only fueled Rory's anger.

"Did ye show Malcolm mercy? Or the Munros?" Rory said. "After all you've done to try to destroy me and our clan, how dare ye ask me for mercy."

"After I've sworn my oath to you in front of my men, they'll never follow me in rebellion again." Sweat from the searing heat left sooty streaks down Hector's face. "And ye need me in the west to fight the MacDonalds."

"You kidnapped my wife and tried to murder my son!" Rory lifted his sword to cut his uncle's head off.

But Sybil was suddenly beside him and lunged for his arm. He checked his swing and reluctantly let her draw him a few steps away.

"Ye can't do this." Her hair swirled around her face from the wind created by the fire. "I know ye want to kill Hector, and he deserves to die. But not now, not like this."

"Why not?" Rage pulsed through his veins.

"Because you're not like Hector," she said. "Because if ye kill him when he's surrendered and on his knees, it's murder."

Rory wanted to see the blood of his uncle on his blade and watch him die. "Then I'll give him back his sword and let him fight."

"If ye force him to fight after he's submitted to your authority, you'll lose the hearts of the men you've just won to your side," she said. "And what about the MacDonalds? You've told me ye need Hector in the west to defend against their attacks."

Rory clenched his fists in frustration. "I want vengeance!"

"Sometimes a leader must compromise." She leaned closer to make sure they weren't overheard. "And sometimes he must bide his time before he reaps vengeance."

Rory turned back to Hector, who was still on his knees.

"I will let you live, uncle, for now," he said. "But if you ever disobey me, or give me cause to *suspect* ye have, I'll have your head on a spike and feed your body to the pigs."

Rory laid out his terms for Hector's surrender in a loud voice for all the men to hear. They included immediately relinquishing possession of Eilean Donan Castle, returning what he had stolen from the clan, and never setting foot in Eastern Ross.

"I accept your terms," Hector said.

"You were right about one thing," Sybil said as she leaned over Hector. "The man who can outwit his opponents is the one who ought to be chieftain."

CHAPTER 49

"I saw Malcolm helping Kenneth with his sword practice today and thought how lucky we are to have them both," Sybil said as she washed her husband's back.

"Aye," Rory said. "It was a miracle Malcolm survived."

"When Kenneth returned from visiting the Grants last week, he said his grandfather and Flora are fighting because she refuses to wed any man he suggests," Sybil said. "Perhaps we should help find a good husband for her."

Rory leaned back and smiled at her. "I'll leave it to you, *mo rùin.*"

"I don't think we've had a quiet afternoon like this since you became chieftain," Sybil said as she ran the sponge down Rory's arm.

"It's been too quiet," Rory said. "Hector is planning something."

Rory's mistrust of his uncle festered like a wound that would not heal. Sybil kneaded Rory's shoulders, trying to work out the tension in them.

"In the three months since he gave his oath, he's done everything ye asked of him," she said. "The MacDonalds have ceased their attacks."

"Leaving Hector alive is like inviting a poisonous snake to slither into this tub with me."

"What about me?" Sybil slid her soapy hand down his stomach to divert him. "Would ye let me slither into the tub with ye?"

She shrieked when he pulled her in, clothes and all, then laughed. They both had been so busy since Rory became chieftain that they'd had too few lighthearted moments like this.

"This is a new gown that ye got all wet," she said.

"Now that's a problem I can fix," he said, and reached for the laces.

An hour later, she sighed with contentment as she lay on the bed with her head on his chest. There were a couple of topics she had been waiting to raise with her husband, and this seemed like the right moment.

"I'm so proud of all that you've accomplished," she said. "You've made allies of all our neighboring clans."

"Except the Munros," he said.

"Aye, except the Munros." She ran her fingers over his chest. "'Tis time ye made peace with them, *mo rùin*."

"I've tried," Rory said. "The Munro chieftain knows I did not order that ambush and that I've killed Duncan and banished Hector, who were responsible. I don't know what else I can do to appease the man."

"Well," Sybil ventured, "ye might consider the most common means of forging an alliance…"

When Rory gave her a blank look, she stifled a sigh. Men could be obtuse when they really did not want to hear something.

"You could suggest a marriage to bind the two clans," she said.

Rory pressed his lips together and glared at the ceiling.

"The Munro chieftain is not married," she said. "And neither is Catriona."

His eyelid twitched. "Ye can't mean for me to give my sister to that arrogant, pigheaded Munro."

"Munro has many fine qualities that will make him a strong chieftain and a good husband." She refrained from mentioning his fine looks.

"It would be an insult to my sister if I made the offer and he refused."

"He won't," Sybil said. "He has an eye for her."

That did not seem to please him at all.

"I agree that the match would have advantages for the clan, but I won't force my sister to wed a man she doesn't want." Rory cupped her cheek and looked into her eyes. "I want her to have a chance for the kind of happiness we have."

"Ask her if she's willing." Sybil could not hold back a smile. "You should do it quickly."

Rory narrowed his eyes at her. "What do ye know that you're not telling me?"

"If you don't arrange the marriage, they'll go through with their scheme."

"What scheme would that be?" Rory asked.

"Munro doesn't believe you'll agree to give him your sister," she said, "so he means to steal his bride."

"What?" Rory sat up in bed. "I'll—"

"And your sister means to let him steal her," Sybil said. "After all, it is her plan."

Rory flopped back down on the bed.

Sybil suspected that the reason Catriona visited Alex's family so often was because it was easier to sneak away from their house than from the castle to meet her Munro chieftain.

"If that's what Catriona wants, I'll agree to the marriage," Rory said. "But they'll have to wait a few years, until she's older."

"Catriona is old enough." Sybil rested her hand on his chest. "She loves him, and making her wait won't change that."

Rory heaved a sigh.

"The house at Killin is almost finished, and Catriona won't want it now that she's marrying the Munro," Sybil said. "After the wedding, let's go there. Just you and me, like your parents used to do."

"That sounds perfect, *mo chroí*," Rory said, and kissed her softly on the lips.

* * *

Sybil hummed to herself as she arranged the flowers she had picked earlier. She wanted everything perfect when Rory arrived for their first night at Killin since it was rebuilt.

She had left Castle Leod first thing this morning with servants, rugs, dishes, and bedding to finish setting up the house. She surveyed the main room, pleased with all they had accomplished. All was ready, including wine and a simple supper waiting on the table, so she sent the servants off to the new servants' cottage behind the house, telling them they could have the evening off. She could not help grinning when she told them she could make a passable porridge, so they could sleep in as well.

For the tenth time in an hour, Sybil looked out the window hoping to see Rory. He promised to be here before supper, and she hoped he would beat the storm. Though it was midafternoon, storm clouds darkened the sky to the west, and the wind was picking up.

She closed the shutters on all the windows, lit the candles on the table, and then went into the bedroom to fluff the pillows again in anticipation of the night ahead. She was looking forward to having her husband all to herself.

But she was not good at sitting and waiting. She drummed her fingers, then sprang to her feet when she remembered something she had been meaning to do for a long time. Catriona said she hid the Eilean Donan ledgers in her mother's secret hiding place, a wooden box buried in the barn. Sybil wondered if there was anything else in that box.

Sybil smiled at the two guards posted outside the door to the house—she knew better than to try to dismiss them—and breezed by them on her way to the barn.

It did not take long to find the wooden square flush with the dirt floor where Catriona had swept aside the straw. Excitement stirred in Sybil's belly as she knelt and tugged the top off. She saw nothing, which was disappointing, but it was too dark inside the box to see all the way to the bottom. She reached inside, hoping she would not find a rat.

"Aha!" There was a cloth bag down there. The box was so deep she had to stick her head inside as she strained to grasp it and pull it up. The bag was light and felt as though it contained papers.

The wind whistled outside the barn, reminding her of the coming storm, so she decided to take the lost treasure back to the house. Back in the bedchamber, she sat on the floor to examine her find. Dirt spilled onto her skirts as she unfolded the bag and pulled out the contents.

There were two parchments. The first one appeared to be a letter to Rory. She set that one aside—and gasped when she saw what the other one was. She had never seen a papal bull before, but the heavy lead seal with the heads of Saint Peter and Saint Paul on one side and the pope's name in Latin, *Iulius II*, on the other told her this had to be it.

Her heart raced as she read that his holiness the pope declared the marriage of Rory's parents valid and the three named children by that marriage legitimate in the eyes of God and the church.

She could not wait to show it to Rory. This would lay to rest any whispers about Rory's birth and right to the chieftainship. Heart singing with joy, she picked up the other parchment again. Should she read it? She was burning with curiosity, and Rory would ask her to read it to him anyway, so she gave in.

Oh my God. Once she read it, she was sorely tempted to hide the letter and never tell Rory about it. She had promised never to deceive him again, but she was afraid of what he would do.

She was so absorbed in what Agnes Fraser MacKenzie had written to her son that she almost failed to hear Rory open the front door. She quickly placed the two documents back inside the bag, slid it under the bed, and ran down the stairs to greet him.

He must have gone to look for her at the back of the house, but he'd left the door open, and the cold wind blew through the house, threatening to blow out the candles. He must be anxious to see her. Smiling, she shut the door and spun around to find him.

The scream caught in her throat. Hector's eyes were wild, and he held a dirk dripping with blood.

"You're not supposed to be here," she said, inching her way back to the door. "Rory ordered ye never to set foot in Eastern Ross. He's on his way. Ye ought to leave before he gets here."

"Ye made a mistake coming to Agnes's house," Hector said, stepping toward her. "I knew this is where I'd find ye."

***

The first drops of rain pelted Rory's face as he galloped through the fields.

He opened the door to the house and shook the rain off. Sybil must be upstairs. He barely noticed the supper on the table. He was hungry, but not for food. He took the stairs two at a time, hoping to catch Sybil in the bedroom before she came down.

Candles and fresh flowers were on the small table by the bed, and the pleasant smell of fresh-cut wood from the new bedframe filled the room.

"Sybil!" he called as he went back downstairs. She could not be far. She would not have left candles burning with no one here, at least not for long.

As he paused to examine the room more closely, his heart thudded in his chest. A chair had been pushed over. Her cloak was on the back of the door and her boots beside it. He opened the door and saw what looked very much like the scratch marks on the new doorframe.

In his mind's eye, he saw Sybil clawing at it as she was pulled from the house. His heart pounded in his ears. Where were the guards? He had been so anxious to see his wife that he hadn't even noticed they weren't there.

After he found their bodies on the side of the house, he ran to the servants' cottage. The servants said they saw Sybil come in from the barn a quarter of an hour ago. He had just missed them!

He had to find her. He found tracks in front of the house. Whoever took her had made no attempt to cover them, which meant either her abductor was unskilled…or he wanted to be followed. Given his boldness in riding up to the house to take her and his success in doing so, Rory assumed it was the latter.

He mounted Curan and followed the trail as fast as he could without losing it.

Who would use Sybil to lure him? This was not another clan dispute over territory. Nay, threatening a man's wife was a vengeful act by someone who knew him well. Someone who wanted to rip out his heart.

All reports told him Hector remained in Gairloch. But the cold fear in his gut told him Hector was here.

And he had Sybil.

Rory spurred Curan into a gallop. He did not need to follow the trail anymore. He knew where it led. Hector had taken Sybil to the waterfall where Rory's mother died.

When he heard the roar of the falls over the wind and rain, he prayed hard that Hector wanted a confrontation and that he had not led Rory here just to find Sybil's broken body on the rocks at the bottom of the falls.

He left Curan out of sight and sprinted the last few yards through the brush on foot. His breath caught when he saw his beloved standing with her back to the falls. The rock ledge beneath her feet was slippery with rain.

Sybil glanced to the side to where he was hidden in the brush and seemed to look right at him through the hair whipping around her face. It was only for an instant, then she turned her gaze away.

"How long are ye going to keep me standing here, Hector?" she shouted over the noise of the storm and the falls.

His clever wife had seen him and was letting him know his uncle was here. She was also prodding Hector to speak and reveal where he was hiding.

"My legs are tired," she said. "I'm sitting!"

"You'll stand if ye don't want to be pushed off." Hector's voice came from about five yards to Rory's right.

Sybil ignored the command and lowered herself to the rock. That was a wise move, as she was less likely to slip or to be knocked over the edge in a scuffle, but Rory intended to keep the fight as far from her as possible.

"I said stand up!" Hector shouted.

Sybil used a Gaelic phrase advising him he could have sexual relations with himself. "If ye want to push me off, what are ye waiting for?"

Ach, his wife was bold and full of courage. While she drew Hector's attention, Rory pulled the dirk from his boot and skirted through the brush toward his uncle. As soon as he caught sight of Hector's plaid, he launched himself at his uncle. But Hector had not survived so many battles without having sharp instincts. At the last moment, he leaped to the side, and Rory's dirk sliced Hector's arm instead of his heart.

Rory rolled as he hit the ground and sprang to his feet, ready to fight. But the sight before him made him break out in a cold sweat. Hector held Sybil at the edge of the ledge with a dirk at her throat.

"It seems fitting for ye to lose the woman ye love the way I lost your mother," Hector said.

"Did ye murder my mother?" Rory asked as he inched closer. "Did ye push her over these falls?"

"I didn't kill her," Hector said. "I loved that woman."

"Loved her?" Sybil shouted. "Agnes left a letter. I know what ye did to her. I know!"

Sybil was trying to give Rory his chance.

"Agnes wouldn't have ye, would she?" Sybil said. "So ye raped her!"

Rory controlled his rage with an effort and crept closer.

"She should have given herself to me," Hector said. "She was supposed to be mine. Even after she chose my brother over me, I wanted her. I waited for her for years!"

"Ye drove her to her death," Sybil said. "Dying was the only way she had of getting away from you and protecting her son."

"I tried to save her," Hector said.

"She warned ye what she'd do if ye came back, but ye didn't believe her," she said. "Ye couldn't believe she hated ye that much."

Sybil shot a glance at Rory, but they were so close to the edge that Rory was afraid that if he threw the blade now, Hector would take her over the edge with him.

"When I came to the house, she rode off in that terrible storm," he said. "She was standing here when I caught up with her."

"Ye wouldn't leave, ye selfish bastard," Sybil said. "Ye gave her no choice."

"I begged her not to step back, not to go over the edge," Hector said.

"Rory was only fifteen," Sybil said. "Agnes knew he would try to kill you if he learned what you'd done to her, and Rory was bound to find out if it happened again and again, as it would have."

"It was his fault." Hector pointed at Rory. "Her precious boy. She would have come away with me if it weren't for him!"

While Hector held her with only one arm, Rory had to take his chance. He would dive for Sybil's legs as he threw his blade into the middle of Hector's forehead. Though Sybil was several inches shorter than Hector, it would be close.

"If ye throw that blade," Hector shouted, "I swear I'll take her over the falls."

To prove his intention, Hector started to take a step backward. Rory threw his blade just as Hector stepped down and his feet went out from under him on the slippery rock. Sybil's scream filled Rory's ears as he dove to catch her.

He caught her by the legs, but all three of them spun and slid sideways in a tangle across the flat, slippery rock. Rory kicked Hector off him and tried desperately to gain traction with his boots as Sybil slid dangerously close to the edge of the rock ledge.

Sybil went over the edge, pulling him with her. Rory let go of her with one arm to grasp a tree branch that hung over the top of the falls. With all his might, he swung his legs up and locked them around the thick branch. Sybil was hanging upside down and sliding through his arm.

His heart beat frantically as he worked his way along the branch as fast as he could with his legs and one hand toward the tree's trunk on the riverbank. As they neared it, Sybil flailed her arms, trying to catch hold of a tree or shrub. The movement caused her to suddenly slip through his arm.

His heart stopped in his chest as he caught her ankle and swung her hard toward the safety of the bank before she slipped through his wet hand. She landed in the thick brush along the falls several feet below him and the ledge. *Praise God.*

He was climbing down from the tree limb when she shouted. "Watch out! He's coming!"

Rory landed on his feet and reached for the dirk at his belt. But it was gone, lost in the river, like the blade from his boot. Through the pouring rain, he saw Hector coming slowly toward him across the rock ledge with his dirk in his hand and murder in his eyes.

"Ye can't protect her now," Hector taunted him over the wind and rain. "I want ye to know as I drive my blade into your heart that I'll have your wife begging for death before I finish with her."

Rory did not wait for his enemy to strike first. He grabbed a heavy stick from the ground and ran straight at Hector. As he crashed into him, Rory blocked Hector's blade with the stick. They fell to the ground and rolled across the flat rock. Hector tried to stab Rory in the throat, but Rory caught Hector's wrist and fought to take the blade from him.

From the corner of his eye, Rory saw Sybil crawling toward them. Her face was bloody with scratches, but she had a blade in her hand and that determined look in her eyes. *Jesu*, she was going to get herself killed trying to save him if he didn't kill Hector first.

Rory was distracted for barely a moment. It would not have been enough time for any other warrior to gain an advantage on him, but it was long enough for Hector. Rory was slammed onto his back. At the last second, he caught Hector's arm with the dirk just inches above his chest.

"I should have been chieftain! I should have had Agnes! I should have had that Grant lass!" Hector said, putting his weight behind the blade as he tried to drive it into Rory's heart. "First your father took everything I wanted, and then you did."

Rory's arms shook with the effort of keeping the blade from piercing his chest. He could not hold Hector off him much longer. But this was a fight he could not lose. His clan needed him.

Sybil needed him.

As he and Hector struggled against each other, Rory felt the edge of the rock ledge beneath his shoulder.

"You've been a curse on this clan since the day ye were born," Rory said through clenched teeth. "Today it ends."

Rory gritted his teeth and with one final surge of strength, he turned and pushed, sending Hector over the falls.

Hector's scream was swallowed by the wind.

When Sybil collapsed beside him, Rory rolled away from the edge and enfolded his beloved in his arms. They lay together, not caring that the rain was beating down on them.

"When I realized Hector had taken you," he said cupping her lovely, dirt-smudged face with his hand, "I was so afraid I'd lost you."

"I knew you'd come. Ye always do," she said. "And it would take more than Hector MacKenzie to pry me away from you."

Rory smiled at his brave and clever wife. With Sybil at his side, he knew he could protect his people and become the chieftain his clan needed him to be. They were both free of the past now.

And he held his future in his arms.

EPILOGUE

November 1524

Eilean Donan was stunning with snow dusting the mountaintops and a rare winter sun shimmering on the lochs surrounding the castle. When the gates were opened wide to admit the MacKenzie chieftain and his family, Sybil exchanged a smile with Rory. How things had changed since the first time he brought her here.

The Macrae guard who had warned Rory to escape that day stood at the front of the household gathered in the courtyard to welcome them. He now served as constable of the castle for Rory.

Kenneth hopped down from his horse and held out his arms for his baby sister. "Let me take wee Agnes while Da helps you down."

Kenneth was more like his father every day. Sybil wondered if her daughter would ever know how lucky she was to have an older brother who would always look out for her.

They planned to stay through Yuletide and expected a large gathering. Malcolm, Grizel and their enormous extended family would join them, as well as Catriona and her husband. Once Rory saw how happy his sister was and that Munro was utterly devoted to her, the two men had formed a close friendship. In fact, they had been appointed as the crown's joint lieutenants of Western Ross responsible for containing the threat from the MacDonalds. Though the MacDonalds were relatively quiet at the moment, Rory and the Munro were here to ensure that they remained that way.

Before going up to their chamber, she and Rory stopped in the castle's small chapel to say a prayer at Brian's tomb. Rory had finally made peace with his brother's death after Lovat used his connections to have Brian's head returned from Edinburgh. In the end, Rory and his sister and brother decided to bury Brian here in the beauty of Eilean Donan, where he had spent much of his life.

A short time later, Sybil and Rory were settling into the laird's chamber when a maidservant appeared at the door.

"A priest left this for Lady Sybil a few days ago," the woman said and handed a letter to Rory, as Sybil was holding the baby.

Alex was able on occasion to have letters from her Douglas family in the Lowlands carried in secret by priests, but this was the first one she had received in months. Sybil kissed Agnes, who had fallen asleep, and laid her in the cradle beside the bed.

"It's from your sister Alison," Rory said and held it out to her.

Though Rory could read fairly well now—he'd asked her to teach him—he knew Sybil would want to hold her sister's letter in her hands and read the familiar script herself. She tore it open and began reading.

"She and David have yet another babe!" she said.

Alison's letter was filled with amusing stories about the children and fairly glowed each time she mentioned her husband David. The feared Beast of Wedderburn was a doting husband and father. Sybil read the next part aloud.

Our brothers and uncle have returned. Archie has the backing of his brother-in-law, the English king, and his titles and properties have been restored. Archie, of course, assumed his wife would follow his and her brother's command to welcome him back, but when he approached Stirling Castle, the queen had the cannons fired on him. That was amusing, but I fear he has learned nothing from his last fall.

"She closes by asking for our prayers for Margaret."

Sybil wiped away a tear. When the men of their family fled, Sybil thought she was the one in greatest danger. As things turned out, she found love and happiness beyond her hopes, and it was dear Margaret who had suffered most.

"With your brother on the rise again," Rory said, "it may soon be safe for ye to visit your family."

"My family is here," she said, resting her palm against his check. "I hope one day my sisters and cousin Lizzie can visit us, but I'll not travel to the Lowlands and risk my brother dragging us into his conflicts."

"This time, Archie may very well end up ruling Scotland in his stepson's name," Rory said. "Ye don't mind missing all that?"

"The only good the men of my family ever did for me was gamble me away to a wild Highland warrior."

Rory laughed and pulled her into his arms. "The luckiest day of my life was when I claimed a bride that wasn't mine."

Sybil looked up at the man she loved and trusted with all her heart. She knew that no matter what lay ahead, Rory would always be at her side.

"Close the door," she whispered, "and claim me again, Highlander."

THE END

HISTORICAL NOTE

Archibald Douglas, who first appeared in my earlier series, THE RETURN OF THE HIGHLANDERS, is a real historical figure. His marriage to Margaret Tudor soon after the death of her husband, James IV of Scotland, made the handsome young Douglas chieftain stepfather to Scotland's two-year-old king. This put him in a position to vie for control of the crown, which everyone except the queen realized was his goal in marrying her. For many years, Archibald alternately rose and fell from power, and the Douglas family fortunes rose and fell with him.

Archie, his brother and his uncle were forced to flee Scotland more than once, but in my research I found no mention of their sisters, wives or mothers escaping with them. Information on the Douglas women is sparse, but I did learn that Archie's sisters were called in for questioning during one of his exiles, and his stepson, James V, eventually burned one of the Douglas sisters at the stake, though there was no evidence she was complicit in Archie's schemes.

After I discovered how the men of their family had put them in danger and left, I decided to write this series and give the Douglas lasses happy endings with loyal men.

Sybil Douglas is a wholly fictional character, but her sisters Alison (Captured by a Laird), Margaret (Kidnapped by a Rogue) and Janet, as well as her brother George and her uncles mentioned in this book were real. As a fiction writer, I adjusted facts and filled in the personalities of these and other historical characters to suit the needs of my story.

Turning to the MacKenzie side, I should note first that clan history of five hundred years ago is based on oral tradition and mixed with legend. That said, I changed my hero's first name to Rory, but he is based on John of Killin, one of the great chieftains of Clan MacKenzie. John (Rory) was a cunning and capable leader who significantly expanded the MacKenzie's territory and influence. In real life, he married the daughter of the Grant chieftain, and their son Kenneth became the next chieftain. I, however, had to get rid of his Grant wife to make room for Sybil.

The conflict between John of Killin and his uncle Hector Roy of Gairloch probably took place ten to twenty years earlier than in this book. By some accounts, John's older half-brother was murdered by Buchanan. John of Killin was still a minor when that happened, and his uncle Hector served as his tutor (guardian) and usurped his estates, claiming John was illegitimate.

In the traditional account of the fire at Fairburn, John of Killin sailed from Gairloch and pretended to leave for Ireland before sneaking back with his thirty trusted men to burn his uncle's house. At some point, the king's council took John of Killin's side in the dispute and ordered Hector to relinquish the rents and possession of Eilean Donan Castle to his nephew.

John of Killin lived to be an old man and ruled his clan for half a century. His siblings included the Priest of Avoch, who was married, and a sister who was the wife of the Munro chieftain of Foulis.

I drew the story of the marriage between John of Killin's father and his mother, Agnes Fraser, from traditional accounts. Their "irregular" marriage was supposedly validated and their children legitimized by the pope. The Well of the Heads incident is based on a tale of an ambush of Munros by MacKenzies that was even deadlier than the one I wrote here.

I found Rogi Falls on a map of the area and just used the name for the falls in my book, but most of the other places in this book are real. I was lucky to travel across the traditional MacKenzie lands and visit many of the places where I set scenes, including Eilean Donan Castle, Beauly Priory, Castle Leod, and Fortrose Cathedral. The area is stunningly beautiful, and the medieval buildings, many of which are in ruins, are amazing.

Big Duncan of the Axe was at least a legend, and James Hamilton of Finnart was a power-player in his time who had perhaps ten illegitimate children. Margaret Douglas's husband was James William Douglas, the 7th Baron of Drumlanrig. You can find out what he did to Margaret to save himself in my next book.

Excerpt from *CAPTURED BY A LAIRD (The Douglas Legacy #1)*

Scotland
1517

Burning her husband's bed was a mistake. Alison could see that now.

Yet each time she passed the rectangle of charred earth as she paced the castle courtyard, she felt a wave of satisfaction. She had waited to commit her act of rebellion until her daughters were asleep. But that night, after her husband's body was taken to the priory for burial, she ordered the servants to carry the bed out of the keep. She set fire to it herself. The castle household, accustomed to the meek mistress her husband had required her to be, was thoroughly shocked.

"Do ye see them yet?" Alison called up to one of the guards on the wall.

When the guard shook his head, she resumed her pacing. Where were her brothers? They had sent word this morning that they were on their way.

As she passed the scorched patch again, she recalled how the flames shot up into the night sky. She had stood watching the fire until dawn, imagining the ugliness of the past years turning to black ashes like the bed. The memories did not burn away, but she did feel cleaner.

Destroying such an expensive piece of furniture was self-indulgent, but that was not why she counted burning it a mistake. While she could not tolerate having that bed in her home, it would have been wiser to give it away or sell it. And yet she simply could not in good conscience pass it on to someone else. Not when she felt as if the bed itself carried an evil.

Instinctively, she touched the black quartz pendant at her throat that her mother had given her to ward off ill luck. It had been missing since Blackadder broke the chain on their wedding night. After the fire, she found it wedged in a crack in the floor where the bed had been.

"Lady Alison!" a guard shouted down from the wall. "They're here!"

The heavy wooden gates swung open, and her two brothers galloped over the drawbridge followed by scores of Douglas warriors. *Praise God.* As the castle filled with her clansmen, Alison immediately felt safer.

One look at Archie's thunderous expression, however, told her that his meeting with the queen had not gone well. Without a word, her brothers climbed the steps of the keep, crossed the hall where platters of food were being set out on the long trestle tables for the Douglas warriors, and continued up the stairs to the private chambers. They never discussed family business in front of others.

"She is my wife!" Archie said as soon as they were behind closed doors. "How dare she think she can dismiss me as if I were one of her servants?"

Alison tapped her foot, trying to be patient, while her brother, the 6th Earl of Angus and chieftain of the Douglas clan, stormed up and down the length of the room. When Archie's back was to her, she exchanged a look with George, her more clever brother, and rolled her eyes. This was all so predictable.

"I warned ye not to be so blatant about your affair with Lady Jane," George said in a mild tone.

"My affairs are none of my wife's concern," Archie snapped.

"A queen is not an ordinary wife," George said as he poured himself and Archie cups of wine from the side table.

Alison found it ironic that the Douglas clan owed the greatest rise in their fortunes to Archie's liaison with the widowed queen. Usually, it was the ladies of the family who were tasked with securing royal favor via the bedchamber.

Archie, always overconfident, had gone too far. While the Council had been willing to tolerate the queen's foolishness in taking the young Douglas chieftain as her lover, they were livid when the pair wed in secret, making Archie the infant king's stepfather. The Council responded by removing the queen as regent. She fled to England amidst accusations that she had tried to abscond with the royal heir.

"How was I to know my wife would return to Scotland?" Archie said, raising his arms. "Besides, I'm a young man. She couldn't expect me to live like a monk while she was gone."

Doubtless, the queen, who was pregnant with Archie's child when she fled, expected her husband to join her. But while the queen paid a lengthy visit on her brother Henry VIII, the Douglas men retreated behind the high walls of Tantallon Castle and waited for the cries of treason to subside.

That was two years ago. And now, Albany, the man who replaced the queen as regent, was on a ship back to France, and the queen was returning. Archie had gone to meet her at Berwick Castle, just across the border.

"Is there no hope of reconciling with her?" Alison ventured to ask.

"I bedded that revolting woman four times in two days—and for naught!" Archie thrust his hand out. "I had her in my palm again, I swear it. But then some villain sent her a message informing her about Jane."

"Must have been the Hamiltons," George said, referring to their greatest rivals.

"Despite that setback, I managed to persuade the queen—through great effort, I might add—that we should enter Edinburgh together as man and wife for all the members of the damned Council to see," Archie said, his blue eyes flashing. "But then she discovered I'd been collecting the rents on her dower lands and flew into a rage."

No wonder the queen was angry. After abandoning her, Archie had lived openly with his lover and their newborn daughter in one of the queen's dower castles—and on the queen's money.

"You're her husband," George said, leaning back in his chair. "Ye had every right to collect her rents. Still do."

Alison did not want to hear about husbands and their rights. She folded her arms and tamped down her impatience while she waited for the right moment to ask.

"Enough talk. We must join the men." Archie threw back his cup of wine. "We'll ride for Edinburgh as soon as they've eaten their fill."

George was already on his feet. She could wait no longer.

"Ye must leave some of our Douglas warriors here to protect this castle," she blurted out. "The Blackadder men are deserting me."

She hoped her brothers would not ask why. She did not want to explain that burning her husband's bed had insulted the Blackadder men and spurred many of them to leave. They disliked having a woman in command of the castle, and she had unwittingly given them the excuse they needed.

"I can't spare any men now," Archie said, slapping his gloves against his hand. "I must gather all my forces in a show of strength to convince my pigheaded wife that she needs my help to regain the Regency."

"The Hamiltons will attempt to do the same," George added.

"But what about me and my daughters?" Alison demanded. "What about the Blackadder lands Grandfather thought were so important that I was forced to wed that man? I was a child of thirteen!"

"For God's sake, Alison, we're in a fight for control of the crown," Archie said. "That will not be decided at Blackadder Castle."

"Please, I need your help." She clutched Archie's arm as he started toward the door. "Ye promised to protect us."

Archie came to an abrupt halt, and the shared memory hung between them like a dead rat.

"Mother did not need to remind me of my duty to my family," he said between clenched teeth. "And neither do you."

Unlike the Douglas men, who lauded Archie's seduction of the queen as a boon for the family, their mother begged him to end the affair. A generation ago, one of her sisters had been the king's mistress. After it was rumored that the king had fallen so in love that he wished to marry her, all three of their mother's sisters died mysteriously.

When Archie wed the queen in secret, knowing full well that every other powerful family in Scotland would oppose the marriage, their mother made one demand of her sons. Archie and George promised her, on their father's grave, that they would protect their four sisters.

"I'll find ye a new husband as soon as these other matters are settled," Archie said. "You'll be safe here until then."

Another husband was not what Alison asked for and was the last thing she wanted. "What I need are warriors—"

"Who would dare attack you?" Archie said. "Now that we are rid of Albany, I am the man most likely to rule Scotland."

Before she could argue, Archie pushed past her and disappeared down the circular stone stairwell.

"Don't fret, Allie," George said, and gave her a kiss on her cheek. "Your most dangerous neighbors were the Hume lairds, and they're both dead."

***

David Hume left his horse and warriors a safe distance outside the city walls and proceeded on foot. If the guards were watching for him, they would not expect him to come alone, or so he hoped. Keeping his hood low over his face and his hand on his dirk, he mingled with the men herding cattle through the Cowgate Port to sell in the city's market.

A month ago, David would have been amused to find himself entering the great city of Edinburgh between two cows. But his humor had been wrung from him. As he walked up West Bow toward the center of the city, the rage that was always with him now swelled until his skin felt too tight.

He paused before entering the High Street and scraped the dung off his boots while he scanned the bustling street for anyone who might attempt to thwart him. Then, keeping watch on the armed men amidst the merchants, well-dressed ladies, beggars, and thieves, he started down the hill in the direction of Holyrood Palace. He spared a glance over his shoulder at Edinburgh Castle, the massive fortress that sat atop the black rock behind him. If he were caught, he would likely grow old in its bleak dungeon. He'd prefer a quick death.

David had walked this very street with his father and uncle. With each step, he tried to imagine how that day might have ended differently. Could he have stopped it? Perhaps, perhaps not. Regardless, he should have tried. From the moment they entered Holyrood Palace, he had sensed the danger. It pricked at the back of his neck and made his hands itch to pull his blade.

The Hume lairds had been guaranteed safe conduct. Relying on that pledge of honor made in the king's name, David did not follow his instincts, did not shout to their men to fight their way out. Instead, he watched his father and uncle relinquish their weapons at the palace door, and he did the same.

Never again.

When he saw the stone arches of St. Giles jutting into the High Street, David's heart beat so hard it hurt. The church was next to the Tolbooth, the prison where the royal guards brought his father and uncle after dragging them from the palace. David's ears rang again with the shouts and jeers of the crowd that echoed off the buildings that day. As he crossed the square, he did not permit himself to look at the Tolbooth for fear that his rage would spill over and give him away.

He turned into one of the narrow, sloping passageways that cut through the tall buildings on either side of the High Street and found a dark doorway with a direct view of the Tolbooth. Only then did he lift his gaze.

Though he had known what to expect, his stomach churned violently at the sight of the two grisly heads on their pikes. His body shook with a poisonous mix of rage and grief as he stared at what was left of his father. They had made a mockery of the man David had admired all his life. His father's sternly handsome features were distorted in a grimace that looked like a gruesome grin, his dark gold hair was matted, and flies ate at his bulging eyes.

David's chest constricted until his breath came in wheezes. He wanted to fight his way into the palace, wielding his sword and ax until he killed every man in sight. But Regent Albany, the man who ordered the execution, was no longer in the palace, or even in Scotland.

In any case, David had too many responsibilities to give in to thoughtless acts that would surely result in his death. He was the new Laird of Wedderburn, and the protection of the entire Hume clan fell to him. When he thought of his younger brothers and how much they needed him, he finally loosened his grip on his dirk, which he'd been holding so tightly that his hand was stiff.

The execution of the two Hume lairds and this humiliating display of their heads made their clan appear weak and vulnerable. That perception put their clan in even greater danger, and so David must change it. This first step toward that end required stealth, not his sword.

He would have his bloody vengeance, but not today.

While he waited for nightfall, he pondered how Regent Albany had managed to prevail over men who were better than him in every way that should matter. The first time Albany captured David's father and uncle, they persuaded their jailor, a Hamilton, to free them and join the queen's side. A furious Albany responded by having their wives taken hostage.

David wondered if Albany understood at the time just how clever that move was, or if he had merely taken the women out of spite. In any event, the trap was set.

By then, Albany was planning to return to France, which was more home to him than Scotland. David's uncle was inclined to wait and seek the women's release from Albany's replacement. But David's father and stepmother had a rare love, and he was tortured by the thought of her suffering in captivity. Because of his weakness for her, he persuaded his brother to accept the regent's invitation and guarantee of their safety.

"Free my wife! Avenge us!" his father had shouted to David as the guards dragged him away.

His father's final words were burned into his soul. While he kept his vigil in the doorway, they spun through his head again and again. He wanted to smash his fist into the wall at the thought of his stepmother living amongst strangers when she learned of her husband's death. Nothing could save the man who held her hostage now. Vengeance was both a debt of honor David owed his father and necessary to restore respect for his clan.

When darkness finally fell on the city, David gave coins to the prostitutes who had gathered nearby and asked them to cause a disturbance. They proved better at keeping their word than the regent. While the women created an impressive commotion, screaming that they had been robbed, David scaled the wall of the Tolbooth.

Gritting his teeth, he jerked his father's head off the pike and placed it gently in the cloth bag slung over his shoulder. He swallowed against the bile that rose in his throat and forced himself to move quickly. As soon as he had collected his uncle's head, he dropped to the ground and left the square at a fast pace. He could still hear the prostitutes shouting when he was halfway to the gate.

A short time later, he reached the tavern outside the city walls where his men waited for him. His half-brothers must have been watching the door, for they ran to greet him as soon as he opened it. Will threw his arms around David's waist, while Robbie, who was four years older, stood by looking embarrassed but relieved. David should admonish Will for his display in front of the men, but he did not have the heart. The lad, who was only ten, had lost his father and missed his mother a great deal.

"I told ye I'd return safe," David said. "I'll not let any harm come to ye, and I will bring your mother home."

Their mother was being held at Dunbar, an impregnable castle protected by a royal garrison. While David did not yet know when or how he would obtain her release, he would do it.

He planned his next moves on the long ride back to Hume territory. In the violent and volatile Border region, you were either feared or preyed upon. David intended to make damned sure he was so feared that no one would ever dare harm his family again.

He would take control of the Hume lands and castles, which had been laid waste and forfeited to the Crown. And then he would take his vengeance on the Blackadders, the scheming liars. While pretending to be allies, the Blackadders had secretly assisted in his stepmother's capture and then urged Albany to execute his father and uncle. It was a damned shame that the Laird of Blackadder Castle was beyond David's reach in a new grave, but his rich lands and widow were ripe for the taking.

And the widow was a Douglas, sister to the Earl of Angus himself. For a man intent on establishing a fearsome reputation, that made her an even greater prize.

ABOUT THE AUTHOR

Margaret Mallory is a *USA Today* bestselling author and recovering lawyer who is thrilled to be writing romantic tales with sword-wielding heroes rather than briefs and memos. Her Scottish and medieval romances have won numerous honors and awards, including National Readers' Choice Awards, *RT Book Reviews*' Best Scotland-Set Historical Romance, and a RITA© nomination.

Margaret lives with her husband in the beautiful Pacific Northwest. Now that her children are off on their own adventures, she spends most of her time with her handsome Highlanders, but she also likes to hike and travel.

For information about Margaret's other books, as well as photos of Scotland, historical tidbits, and links to Margaret on Facebook and Twitter, please visit her website, www.MargaretMallory.com.